THE OBSCENE BIRD
OF NIGHT

THE
OBSCENE BIRD
OF NIGHT

by José Donoso

translated from the Spanish by
Hardie St. Martin & Leonard Mades

NONPAREIL BOOKS
David R. Godine, Publisher · BOSTON

This is a NONPAREIL BOOK published in 1979 by
David R. Godine, Publisher, Inc.
Horticultural Hall, 300 Massachusetts Avenue
Boston, Massachusetts 02115

First American edition published in 1973 by
Alfred A. Knopf, Inc.

First published in Spanish as *El Obsceno Pájaro de la Noche*
by Editorial Seix Barral, S.A., Barcelona.

Library of Congress Cataloging in Publication Data

Donoso, José, 1924-
    The obscene bird of night.

    Translation of *El obsceno pájaro de la noche*.
    Reprint of the 1973 ed. published by Knopf and
distributed by Random House, New York.
    I.   Title.
[PZ4.D68490b   1979]   [PQ8097.D617]   863   79-88419
ISBN 0-87923-191-2

Second printing, August 1988

Author's Note

Since this novel first appeared in Spanish, I have made
certain cuts and changes which are incorporated into the
English-language edition, and which will be used in any
future editions of the book.
                     –José Donoso, 1973

The Spanish edition of this book was written with the help
of a Guggenheim Foundation fellowship.

Assistance for the translation of this book was given by
the Center for Inter-American Relations.

MANUFACTURED IN THE UNITED STATES OF AMERICA

For my parents

Every man who has reached even his intellectual teens begins to suspect that life is no farce; that it is not genteel comedy even; that it flowers and fructifies on the contrary out of the profoundest tragic depths of the essential dearth in which its subject's roots are plunged. The natural inheritance of everyone who is capable of spiritual life is an unsubdued forest where the wolf howls and the obscene bird of night chatters.

Henry James Sr., writing to his
sons Henry and William

One

1

MISIÁ RAQUEL RUIZ (*Mistress* Raquel Ruiz, that is) shed many tears when Mother Benita called up to tell her that Brígida had died in her sleep. Then she calmed down a little and asked for more details.

"Amalia, the little one-eyed woman who was a sort of servant to her, I don't know if you remember her . . ."

"Why, yes, Amalia . . ."

"Well, as I was saying, Amalia brewed Brígida her cup of tea, very strong, the way she liked it at night, and Amalia says that Brígida went right off to sleep, as peacefully as ever. It seems that before she went to bed she'd been darning a lovely nightgown, cream satin . . ."

"Oh, my God! It's a good thing you mentioned it, Mother! I've been so upset, it slipped my mind. Have them wrap it for me and tell Rita to hold it in the vestibule. It's my granddaughter Malú's bridal nightgown, she just got married, you remember how I was telling you all about it. The nightgown got caught in the zipper of her suitcase during the honeymoon. I used to like to take Brígida a little needlework, to give her something to do and make her still feel like part of the family. There was no one like Brígida for delicate work like that. How good she was at it! . . ."

Misiá Raquel took over the funeral arrangements. A wake in the chapel of the Casa de Ejercicios Espirituales de la Encarnación, the retreat house at La Chimba where Brígida spent the last fifteen years of her life, with High Mass for its forty women inmates, three nuns, and five young orphans, as well as Misiá

Raquel's own children, daughters-in-law and granddaughters who attended the service. Since it was to be the last Mass celebrated in the chapel before it was deconsecrated by the Archbishop and the Casa was torn down, it was sung by Father Azócar. Then, burial in the Ruiz family's mausoleum, as she'd always promised her. Unfortunately, the mausoleum was very crowded. But, with a few phone calls, Misiá Raquel arranged things so that, by hook or by crook, they'd make room for Brígida. The blind faith the poor old woman had had in Misiá Raquel's promise to let her too rest under that marble enabled her to live out her last years in peace: in Mother Benita's archaic but still touching rhetoric, her death became *a little flame that flickered out.* One of these days, of course, they'd have to see to the weeding out of some of the remains interred in the mausoleum—all those babies from a time when they hadn't even found a cure for diphtheria, some French governess who died far from her own country, old bachelor uncles whose identities were fading—in order to store that miscellany of bones in a small box that would take up only a little space.

Everything went according to Misiá Raquel's plans. The inmates spent the entire afternoon helping me put up the black hangings in the chapel. Other old women, close friends of the deceased, washed the corpse, combed her hair, inserted her dentures, got her up in her finest underclothes and, lamenting and whimpering as they tried to decide the best way to dress her for the last time, finally chose her Oxford gray jersey dress and her pink shawl, the one Brígida kept folded in tissue paper and wore only on Sundays. We arranged the wreaths, sent by the Ruiz family, around the bier. We lit the candles . . . It's really worthwhile being a servant like that, with an employer like Misiá Raquel. Such a good lady! But how many of us women have Brígida's luck? None. Look at Mercedes Barroso, only last week. A public welfare truck came to carry off poor Menche, and we ourselves, yes, it's hard to believe that we ourselves had to pick a few red geraniums from the vestibule court to dress up her coffin, and her former employers, who, over the phone, kept promising poor Menche the sun, the moon and the stars . . . wait, woman, wait, have patience, better wait till summer, no, better still when we get back from the summer holidays since you don't like the beach, remember how the sea air always gives you a windburn, when we come back that's when, you'll see, you'll love the new chalet with its garden, it has a room over the garage that's ideal for you . . . and, you see, Menche's employers didn't even show up at the Casa when she died. Poor Menche! What hard luck! And she was so good at telling dirty jokes, and she knew so many of them. Who knows where she used to dig them up. But Brígida's funeral was something else again: she had real wreaths, with white flowers and all, the way funeral flowers ought to be, and with calling cards too. The first thing Rita did when they brought the coffin was to run her hand under it to check if that part of the box was well polished like first-class coffins in the old days. I watched her purse her lips and nod approval. Such a fine job was done on Brígida's coffin! Misiá Raquel even kept her word about that. Nothing disappointed us. Neither the hearse drawn by four black horses bedecked with caparison and tufts of feathers nor the Ruiz family's gleaming cars lined up along the sidewalk, waiting for the funeral procession to start.

But it can't start yet. Misiá Raquel remembers, at the very last minute, that she has a bicycle that's a bit damaged but, with a little fixing here and there, will make a perfect gift for her gardener on the feast day of St. Peter and Paul . . . go Mudito (I was *Mudito* to everyone because I was mute), take your cart and fetch it for me, my chauffeur can put it in the back of the station wagon and save an extra trip.

"Aren't you coming back to see us any more, Misiá Raquel?"

"I'll have to come when Inés gets back from Rome."

"Have you had any news from Misiá Inés?"

"Not a word. She hates writing letters. And now that the famous business of the beatification fell through and Jerónimo signed the chaplaincy of the Azcoitías over to the Archbishopric, she must be hiding her head and she's not even going to send postcards. If she stays in Rome much longer, it'll be a miracle if she finds the Casa still standing."

"Father Azócar's been showing me the plans for his Children's Village. They're lovely! You should see all the glass windows! The drawings made me feel a little better about . . . this being the last Mass in the chapel."

"One of Father Azócar's tall stories, Mother Benita. Don't be so naïve! He's the worst kind of scheming priest. This property Jerónimo signed over to the Archbishop is very, yes, very very valuable. Children's Village! I'll bet anything they divide all this into lots after they tear the Casa down and sell it, and the money will evaporate in smoke. Mudito's taking long, Mother, and with Brígida waiting for us to bury her! What can be holding him up? Of course the Casa's so big it takes all day to make your way through all the passageways and corridors that lead to the cell where I keep my stuff, and Mudito's so thin and sickly. But I'm tired, I want to go bury Brígida, I want to get away, this whole business is too much for me, I'm burying a whole life, poor Brígida, only a couple of years older than I, my God, and, to keep my word, I gave up my vault in the mausoleum for her to start rotting in my place, keeping it warm for me with her remains so that when they take them out mine won't get numb, won't be afraid, giving up my vault to her for the time being was the only way to keep my word, now that even relatives I haven't so much as said hello to in years come around claiming—I don't know what makes them think they have a leg to stand on—that they must be buried in the mausoleum, but I'm not afraid that they'll steal my place now, she'll be there, holding it for me, heating it with her body like in the days when she used to turn down the covers and slip a good hot water bottle under them, for me to go to bed early when I came in exhausted from running around on business errands in winter. But when I die she'll have to move out of my vault. What can I do? Yes, Brígida, yes, I'm going to hire lawyers to strip those relatives of their rights, but I doubt that we'll win the lawsuits . . . you'll have to get out. It won't be my fault. I won't have to answer for it anymore, Brígida, no one knows what they'll do after I'm gone. You can't say I haven't been good to you, I've done everything you told me, but I'm afraid because when they take you out I don't know what they're going to do with your bones, nobody will give a rap . . . who knows how many years from now I'll die, fortunately I'm in very good health, imagine, I haven't spent a single day in bed this winter, not even a chill, Mother Benita, not a thing, half of my grandchildren down with the flu and my daughters calling me up to please go over and help them because even their servants are sick . . ."

"How lucky! Almost all the orphans here came down with it. But then, the Casa's so cold, and coal is so expensive . . ."

"Imagine! It's the last straw! All this talk about a Children's Village, and look at the miserable conditions they keep them in. I'm going to send you a little contribution next time I go out to the farm. I have no idea what's left over from this year's crops, but I'll send you something so that you'll all remember poor Brígida. Were you able to get the bicycle in, Jenaro?"

The chauffeur sits next to Misiá Raquel. They can get under way now. The coachman climbs into the driver's seat of the hearse, Misiá Raquel's daughter-in-law puts on her perforated driving gloves, the black horses stamp, tears fill the eyes of the old women who go out on the sidewalk muffled up, shivering, coughing, to see the procession off. Before Misiá Raquel gives the order to get under way, I go over to her window and hand her the package.

"What's this?"

I wait.

"Malú's nightgown! My God! If this poor little man hadn't thought of it, I'd have forgotten, and he'd have had to pull the cart back here again for me . . . Thanks, Mudito . . . no, no, wait . . . have him wait, Mother . . . here, Mudito, for cigarettes, for your little vices, go on, take it . . . Blow the horn, Jenaro, get the procession started . . . Well, goodbye, Mother Benita . . ."

"Goodbye, Misiá Raquel . . ."

"Goodbye, Brígida . . ."

"Goodbye . . ."

When the last car disappears around the corner, we go in—Mother Benita, I, the old women who mumble as they slowly scatter to their courts. I bolt and lock the outside door. Rita closes the inner one with its rattly glass panes. Straggling behind, one of the old women picks up a white rose from the tile floor of the vestibule and, yawning and tuckered out from all the excitement, pins it on her bun before disappearing into the passageways to look for her friends, her bowl of watery soup, her shawl, her bed.

IN A NOOK in one of the corridors, they stopped before the door I sealed off with two boards nailed crosswise. I'd loosened the nails, to make it easy for them to pry off the boards and go up to the next floor. The orphans pulled out the nails, took the boards off and helped Iris Mateluna go up . . . Get a move on, chubby, I'm scared, these stairs don't have a railing, some of the steps are gone . . . hey, fatso's so heavy everything's creaking under her . . . They take their time going up, studying where to take each step so the whole works won't collapse, looking for solid places so as to get Iris to the next floor. Ten years ago Mother Benita had me board up those doors so as to forget about that section of the Casa once and for all and not have to think about cleaning and keeping it neat, because we just don't have the strength to do it anymore . . . Mudito, better let it go to pot and not lose any sleep over it . . . Until the five little girls, bored with wandering about the Casa with nothing to do, discovered that they could open this door and go up to the cloistered galleries on the next floor that surround the courts . . . let's go up, kids, don't be scared . . . scared of what, when it's still light out, let's go see what's there . . . like what, nothing, filth, same as all over the Casa, but at least it's fun because no one's allowed to roam there because they say it might cave in . . . Eliana warns them to watch their step and make sure nobody sees them from downstairs but it's not too risky today because they're at the doorkeeper's, seeing Brígida off. Still, they'd better not take chances, Mother Benita's in a nasty mood . . . make yourselves useful, you little pests, pick that up, help with this pile of spoons and plates, they have to be left clean, now that they're going to hold an auction, fold the napkins, count them, sweep, get some washing done, wash your own things at least, you've been going around filthy as pigs, don't spend all

your time playing . . . shshshshshsh, kids, shshshshshsh . . .
careful, or we'll get punished . . .

They round one court and then another, until they come to
a door Eliana pushes open. A room with twenty rusty iron bedsteads, disassembled, others crippled—missing rollers, patched-up
springs—but set up in two rows against the walls, like beds in a
boarding school. Twin windows: high, narrow, deeply recessed,
their glass painted a chocolate brown up to a person's height so
that no one can see anything outside except the dark clouds
veiled by chicken wire and iron bars. I also loosened the nails
with which I myself sealed the two windows. The orphans already know how to open them and they did it in time to wave
goodbye to Brígida's hearse led by the four plumed horses followed by nine automobiles. Eliana counts eight, Mirella nine
. . . no, eight . . . no, nine . . . and when the procession disappears the little neighborhood children take over the middle of
the street again, scrambling after the soccer ball . . . Good pass,
Ricardo! Kick, Mito! Quick, after it, Lucho, pass it, now, kick,
there, goal, gooooal . . . a shrill scream from Mirella, who
cheers her friends' gooooooooooal and applauds and waves to
them.

Iris has stayed behind, at the back of the dormitory, sitting
sleepily on an innerspring. She yawns. She leafs through a magazine. The orphans make faces at people going by, talk in shouts
to their friends, sit in the window recess, laugh at a woman passing by, yawn. When it begins to get dark Iris calls Eliana.

"What do you want?"

"You promised to read me this one with Pluto the dog and
Popeye the sailor man."

"No. You owe me for two readings."

"I'm going to get together with the Giant this evening and
play yumyum. I'll pay you tomorrow."

"Then I'll read for you tomorrow."

Eliana presses up against the window bars again. The street
lamps begin to go on. A woman in the house across the street
opens her balcony window. As she combs her long jet-black hair,
looking into the street, she turns on a radio . . . ta-ra-tat-tat-

tatatat-tat-tatat . . . syncopated piercing sounds from electric guitars and twanging voices pour into the dormitory, the orphans rouse Iris from the bedsprings and get her to stand up in the aisle between the two rows of beds when they hear *babalú, babalú ayé* . . . hey, do a little dance for us, Gina, they urge her, come on, do your stuff . . . tossing her neck back like a mare, she twirls her long wavy hair, swaggering down the aisle, a look of ecstasy in her eyes half-closed like those of actresses in cheap illustrated love stories . . . I don't feel lazy anymore, I'm not yawning, I want to get out and dance like Gina, the actress who lived in a convent run by bad nuns in the love story Eliana read to me . . . Iris stops. She digs in her pockets. She smears her lips with a purplish lipstick, the horrible dark color turns to unbaked dough . . . Come on, Gina, do your stuff, dance down the aisle for us, shake it, that's it, that's it, more, more . . . At the window, Eliana's lighting two candles she stole from the chapel where Brígida lay in state; all she can do is set the stage, she's too young, the youngsters in the street don't call up to her, they want Iris, Eliana doesn't have breasts to show off or thighs to put on display. She shoos the other orphans over to the farther window and helps Iris climb up on the window recess.

"Look, Gina, the Giant's here."

"Yell down to him that I'll go out as soon as the old ladies are in bed."

"The guys want you to dance for them."

She's the only one left at the lighted window. She grinds her hips. Sticking out her breasts, she smooths her sweater with a long caress that runs the whole length of her body and ends with her hiking her skirt to show her heavy thighs that are a quivering mass, while her other hand piles up her hair and she puckers her lips as if she were about to give someone a madly passionate kiss. The group gathering under the streetlight cheers her on. The woman combing her hair in the window across the way turns up the music, resting her elbows on the railing to get a good look. Iris begins to move very slowly, only rubbing her thighs together at first, then shaking her whole body to the wild beat of *babalú*, whirling, hair flying, arms outstretched, hands open as if searching for something or someone, whirling again,

again, bending, stretching; she tosses back her head and lets all her hair spill forward, her gyrating body moving to the rhythm of rock, the frug, anything, as long as she can rotate and show her thighs and her filthy panties and her bouncing breasts, her tongue hot and searching like her hands, as she dances at the window so that the people in the street will applaud and egg her on and yell up to her . . . come on, give, Gina baby, give it all you've got, good-lookin', shake those tits, shake your ass off, burn down the Casa, burn us all . . . And the Giant, with his enormous papier-mâché head, steps into the middle of the street and dances as if he were dancing with Iris, Iris sways, grinds her hips, gyrates, shakes and screams from her candlelit cage that seems to hang from the side of the Casa as she dances like a Virgin Mary gone berserk in her niche. The Giant stands on the sidewalk in front and calls to her: "Gina, Gina, come on down so we can play yumyum, hey kid, yell up at her, she can't hear me because I'm shut up inside this stinking head."

"He says for you to come down, Gina!"

"Hey, Eliana, ask him what kind of present he's brought me today. Otherwise I won't go down."

"Not money, he says, but he's got five love story magazines for you and a lipstick that's not new but's real good and comes in a gold case."

"It must be gold-plated, gold ones are very expensive."

"Don't accept any of his crappy stuff, Iris, don't be stupid. You gotta get money out of him so you can pay me for the readings."

"If you don't read to me Mirella will, so who cares."

"But you like how I read because I explain the story, otherwise you don't understand a thing. I've got you where I want you, Iris Mateluna, right where I want you, because if I don't read and explain the love stories and Donald Duck you get bored to death here in this shithouse . . ."

Iris hangs on to the bars to get a look at him . . . it's him with his eyes that are as big and round as saucers and his laugh that's always the same because he never gets mad, he's good, we play yumyum real nice and when he calls me Gina he raises his eyebrow and the wrinkles on his forehead hold up his silly little hat . . . it's him, he wants to marry me because he likes the way I play yumyum, he's going to take me to see movies that show real live actresses so that pain-in-the-ass Eliana won't have to read anything to me, the Giant's going to take me to one of those tall buildings downtown so I can dance in a contest and win the prize, a makeup kit they say they give to the girl who dances best, and afterwards her picture comes out in the love story magazines and that moron Eliana and Miss Rita and Mudito and Mother Benita and the girls and all the old bags will see my picture in the magazines.

"What are you gonna pay me with if the Giant doesn't give you money today?"

Iris shrugs.

"Because you've got to pay me before you get married, you hear, or else I'll get the cops after you, the same ones who carried off your old man, to make you pay up, and if you don't pay they'll drag you off to jail too. I'll settle for the lipstick and two of the magazines the Giant's going to give you today."

"Do you think I'm stupid? One magazine and you can use the lipstick twice, and that's it . . ."

"It's a deal. But you'll have to give me the lipstick case when it's all used up."

"It's a deal."

MOTHER BENITA remains very still for a second in the vestibule, her hands together and her eyes closed. Rita and I wait for her to move, to open her eyes, and she opens them and motions me to follow her. I know very well that, stooped and rickety or not, I have to pull my little cart as if I were her idiot son pulling a toy. I know why she wants me to follow her. We've done it so many times: to clean up what the dead woman left behind. Misiá Raquel told her to divide Brígida's things among her friends. No, among her *mates* is what she said, as if this were a finishing school. I don't want to look at Brígida's room, Mother, for God's sake, I don't want to, I don't want to go over anything or look at anything, no, there can't be anything of value so I don't want to look at anything, I tell you, you can do what you like with her things, Mother Benita, give them away, these old women are so poor they'll be happy with anything they can remember Brígida by, she was so well liked here at the Casa.

I follow her down the corridors, pulling the platform on four wheels. I put brooms, buckets, rags, feather dusters on. In the court where the kitchen is, a group of old women forming a circle around Mother Anselma peel potatoes into a huge pot . . . what a lovely funeral Brígida had! . . . Misiá Raquel's princesse overcoat, they say they're coming back . . . the coachman had a mustache, I'm not sure it's right to let coachmen who drive first-class hearses wear a mustache, it's a sort of lack of respect . . . the funeral would keep tongues wagging for months . . . another group of old women farther over have already forgotten about it, they've forgotten Brígida, they're playing cards on a sugar bin . . . Watch out for that step, Mother, it's a step, not a shadow, and we come out into still another court that's not the one where Brígida lived, so we have to go down other passageways . . . One, then a second empty room, rows of vacant rooms, more doors, some open, some closed, because it's all the same if they're open or closed, more rooms to cross, shattered windowpanes coated with dust, the semidarkness sticking to the dried-up walls where a hen pecks at the centuries-old adobe, hunting for specks of grain. Another court. The laundry court where no laundry's done anymore because only three of them are left now, the court with the palm tree, the one with the linden, this court without a name, Ernestina Gómez's court, the refectory court no one uses because the old women prefer to eat in the kitchen, endless courts and cloisters connected by corridors that never end, rooms we'll never try to clean again even if up until a short time ago you used to say, yes, Mudito, one of these days, the first chance we have, we're going to clean everything out with brooms and dusters and rags and pails and soap powder because it's such a filthy mess . . . Watch out, Mother, I'll give you a hand, let's step around this rubble, better walk down this corridor that leads into still another court that's on a different level because of the now-forgotten purposes it once served, and opens onto rooms where sounds are softened by cobwebs and onto galleries where the echoes of forgotten comings and goings linger, or perhaps it's mice and cats and chickens and pigeons chasing one another among the ruins of this wall no one ever finished tearing down.

I walk ahead of Mother Benita. I stop next to a cluster of shacks made of tin, boards, cardboards, branches—shacks as flimsy and gray as though they were built with the well-worn cards the old women use for playing their age-old games . . . You've tried so many times to convince them to sleep in the rooms. There are hundreds and hundreds of them, good, spacious, all vacant . . . pick the ones you like in whatever court you like, Mudito and I will make them comfortable for you . . . no, Mother, we're afraid they're much too big and the ceilings are too high and the walls too thick and someone may have died or spent her life praying in those rooms and that's enough to scare anybody, they're damp, bad for rheumatism, they're enormous and gloomy, all that space when we're not used to living in rooms with so much space because we're servants used to living in cubbyholes crammed with all kinds of things, in the back part of our employers' houses, no, no, Mother Benita, thanks just the same, we prefer these rickety shacks that are sheltered by the long balconies, because we want to be as close to one another as possible so as to hear someone else breathing in the shack next door and smell stale tea leaves and listen to another sleepless body like our own tossing and turning on the other side of the thin wall, and the coughing and farts and intestinal rumblings and nightmares; who cares about the cold coming in through the cracks in the badly fitted boards as long as we're all together, in spite of the envy and greed or the terror that shrivels our toothless mouths and makes our gummy eyes squint, we're together and toward evening can go to the chapel in groups, because it's terrifying to go all by yourself, we can cling to one another's rags, through the cloisters, down passageways like tunnels that never end, through unlit galleries where a moth may brush against my face and make me scream because I get frightened if anyone touches me in the dark when I don't know who it is, we're together and can drive off any shadows that drop from the beams and stretch out toward us when it begins to get dark . . . Here comes the crotchety old woman who lines her eyebrows with black crayon. And here's Amalia . . . good afternoon Amalia, cheer up, wait for me here, I want to talk to you when I've tidied up Brígida's cell . . . no, no thanks, Mudito will help me as usual, look he's opening the padlock on Brígida's door . . . And Rosa Pérez, who can stir up a courtyard full of women with her gossip . . . Good afternoon, Carmela . . . yes, yes, they'll come for you, wait, woman . . . but you've been waiting for ten years and nobody comes . . . they say Rafaelito rented a house with an extra room . . . this little lock of hair I keep here, look, Mother Benita, it's one of his as a little boy when I was bringing him up, blond as a corn tassel and none of that drugstore-blond stuff like other kids, that's what his hair used to be like before it started turning darker, what a pity he's bald now, so they say, I called him on the phone the other day but that new wife of his said to me, call him some other time . . . wait Carmela . . . but Carmela is waiting for what all of them are waiting for with their hands crossed in their laps, staring through the secretions that have collected in their eyes, to see if they can make out what's creeping up on them and growing and beginning to cover up the light, a little at first, not quite all the light, and then all of it, all, all, all, all, all, total darkness suddenly in which you can't cry out because in the dark you can't find your voice to call for help, and one fine night you sink and you're lost in the sudden darkness like Brígida night before last. And, while they wait, the old women sweep a little as they've done all their lives or darn or do their laundry or peel potatoes or whatever there is to peel or wash, as long as it doesn't require much strength because there's no strength left, one day exactly like the next, one morning repeating the one before, one afternoon the same as all the others, sunning themselves as they sit by the cloister's drainage ditch and drive away the flies that feast on their slobber or their sores, their elbows digging into their knees and their faces buried in their hands, tired of waiting for the moment none of them believes she's waiting for, waiting as they've always waited, in other courtyards, beside other pilasters, behind other windowpanes, or else whiling away their time picking red geraniums with which to decorate the wooden box in which they carted off

Mercedes Barroso, so that poor Menche wouldn't leave this earth without so much as a single flower even if they could provide only those dusty geraniums . . . she was a scream when she did the dances Iris Mateluna taught her, the frug, rock, with the rest of the orphans and even we keeping time by clapping so they could dance together, Iris and Menche . . . poor Menche . . . Mercedes Barroso must of died of sheer fatness on a night exactly like this one that's beginning to fall.

I step back a little so you can go in. The dresser with its mirror and the brass bed barely fit in here. The sheets are rumpled so little that no one would guess a woman passed away between them forty-eight hours ago. Brígida's still alive here. This place is still here, it keeps another Brígida alive while the body of the dead one is beginning to feed the worms: this peculiar arrangement, these objects she gradually wore out with her attachment to them and with her pursuits, this attempt at elegance . . . look, Mother Benita, at the way she attached the Easter palms to a corner of the print showing the Annunciation, how she used Christmas wrapping paper to cover the Coca-Cola bottle she turned into a vase. Photographs of the Ruiz family. Holy pictures. She was so painstaking at her needlework that she was able to restore the embroidery on some chasubles Father Azócar took away because, he said, they were eighteenth-century ones and were too precious to let go to ruin here at the Casa. They were the only things of any value here, Mother Benita, everything else is trash, it's hard to believe that this country's ruling families haven't been able to collect anything but filthy junk in this place. And, without disturbing anything on the dresser, you run your fingertips over the perfect row formed by the thimble, pincushion, nail file, small scissors, tweezers, buffer—everything neatly arranged on the fresh, starched white runner. Mother Benita, you and I have come here to carve up this Brígida who's still alive, to divide her up, to burn her, to throw her out, to eradicate the Brígida who hoped to live on in the orderliness of her possessions. To wipe out all traces of her so that tomorrow or the next day they can send us another old woman who can start leaving the particular imprint of her dying hour on this place, an imprint that's not much different but is unmistakably her own.

She'll replace Brígida as Brígida replaced . . . I can't think of the name of the quiet old woman with hands disfigured by warts who lived in this shack before Brígida came here.

The news that Mother Benita's started cleaning out Brígida's hovel travels through the Casa. Old women come from other courts to snoop. Mother Benita never favors any of the beggars and that's why, at first, none of them comes too close, they maraud silently or muttering under their breaths, they go past the door for a second: she smiles at you sweetly, she winks at me, and I wink my Mudito's eye back at her. They go past the door, slowing down more gradually until they barely stir, darkening the doorway like flies glued to a drop of syrup, whispering, shuffling, shouting, till you finally beg me to chase them off . . . get them out of here, Mudito . . . get out, for God's sake, let us get our work done in peace, we'll call you later. Once more they fall back a little. They sit down on the side of the corridor, at the foot of the pilasters, their hands fidgeting in their laps . . . look at Brígida's blue satin quilt, I hear it's all down, I wonder who they're going to give it to, I think the one who'll get the good things like that is Misiá Raquel, she'll take them for her house . . . look at the radio, Zunilda, I'll bet they're going to send it to some auction, radios are expensive, I'd love to own a radio like Brígida did, because she used to stay in bed on Sunday and listen to the Mass sung in the cathedral, and I'd love to hear Mass in bed some Sunday when it's cold. And that black shawl, take a look, Clemencia, I tell you it's the black shawl I was telling you about the other day, see, the one Miss Malú gave her on her birthday and she never wore because, you see, Brígida didn't care for black . . . it must be like new . . .

You roll up her sheets along with the stains and odors of her final moment, a moment no one was there to witness . . . straight to the wash! I take up the two layers of the mattress to air them out in the passageway. You strip off the ticking that protects the mattress from the rust on the spring—a wire cage that's a den where flat, long, soft, square, shapeless creatures crouch: dozens, hundreds, of packages, cartons tied with strips of cloth, balls of string or wool, a broken soap dish, an odd shoe, a bottle, a dented lampshade, a raspberry-colored bathing cap.

All of them are velvety to the touch, homogeneous, motionless under the soft dust that covers everything with the silky, delicate fuzz that the slightest movement, like the flicker of an eye or someone's breathing, could scatter through the room, choking and blinding us and causing all those creatures that are resting quietly in the momentarily gentle shapes of small bundles of rags, sheaves of old magazines, umbrella ribs, boxes, box tops, pieces of box tops, to spring to life and pounce on us. More and more packages under the bed, and . . . look, Mother Benita, under the dresser too, between it and the wall and behind the curtain in the corner . . . and everything hidden just below or beyond eye level.

Don't stand there dangling your arms. Don't you know this Brígida who tamed the dust and tamed uselessness itself? Does this Brígida disturb you? Ah, Mother, you don't know it but that old woman had more secret recesses in her than the Casa. The pincushion, the scissors, the buffer, the white thread—yes, to the eye, everything was in order on the runner. Very touching. But now, suddenly, you have to face this other unofficial Brígida, the one who didn't leave herself open to view on the starched runner, the one who was queen of the inmates, who had a queen's funeral, who, from the pulchritude of her embroidered sheets, with her perfect hands and pleasant look, passed judgment by simply dropping a hint, gave orders with a moan or a sigh, changed the course of other people's lives with the flick of a finger . . . no, you didn't know her and you could never have known her, Mother Benita's eyes don't reach under the beds or into the hiding places, it's preferable to feel sorry for people, to serve them, to stick to this, even if it means working yourself to the bone as you've done for years among these decrepit old ladies in this condemned place, surrounded by imbeciles, by the sick, by the wretched, by the abandoned, by executioner and victim you can't tell apart—all of them complaining and suffering from the cold and hunger you try desperately to relieve; they drive you crazy with the anarchy of old age, which has first call on everything . . . poor old things, something must be done for them, yes, you've worked yourself to death in order to ignore Brígida's other side.

She sighs as she bends over to fish out a square package, done up in manila paper and string, from under the bedspring. I dust it with my rag and we have to wrinkle our noses because the tiny room fills up with fuzz. You begin undoing the package; it contains one of those cardboard mats on which they used to mount studio photographs with raised garlands and the photographer's signature embossed in gold in one corner, but there's no photograph. I take the paper and the cardboard out to the middle of the court and start the pile of trash that will turn into a pyre. The old women move in to rummage and grab anything they can find, but there's little, very little. Nothing. Anyhow, this is only the beginning. And it's going to be something! Because Brígida was rich. A millionaire, they say. All they have to do is wait a bit longer. The old women who've stationed themselves in the corridor or mill around never take their eyes off us.

Everything you find is tied, packaged, wrapped in something, inside something else—tattered clothing wrapped in itself, broken objects that crumble as you unwrap them, the porcelain handle of a demitasse, ribbons from a First Communion sash, things saved for the sake of saving, packing, tying, preserving this static, reiterative community that never lets you in on its secret, Mother Benita, because it's too cruel for you to bear the notion that you and I and the old women who are still alive and those who are dead, and all of us, are tied up in these packages you want to force a meaning from because you respect human beings, and if poor Brígida made up all these little packages, Mother Benita muses, carried away by her feelings, it was in order to raise a banner reading, "I want to protect, I want to rescue, I want to preserve, I want to survive." But I can assure you, Mother, that Brígida had more complex methods to make sure of her survival . . . little packages, oh yes, all old women make little packages and stow them away under their beds.

Let's open the packages, Mudito, there may be something important here, something that . . . you can't finish what you started to say because you're afraid to tie it to an incoherent idea, and instead you begin to play the game of supposing that by undoing knots, unwrapping rags, opening envelopes and cartons, you're going to discover something worth saving. No, everything into the trash pile! Rags and more rags. Papers. Cotton brown with blood from some past wound. Bundle after bundle. Don't you see, Mother Benita, that the act of wrapping, and not what's inside the wrappings, is the important thing? I go on heaping up trash in the court. A steady hum swells from the hive of old women who, as they rummage, fight over a cork, a brass knob, buttons kept inside a tea tin, an insole, the top of a pen. Sometimes, when we clean out the hovel of an inmate who just died, some familiar object turns up among her things; this black wooden curtain ring, for instance, is the very one we threw in the trash last week when Mercedes Barroso died, and she, in turn, had salvaged it, for no particular reason, from another dead woman's belongings and that one from still another's, and another's . . .

The toothless crone who winked at me tries on the raspberry-colored bathing cap and struts to the applause of the others. Dora unravels the remains of a moth-eaten cardigan, rolling the curly wool into a ball and piecing it together so that she can wash and then knit it into a little sweater for the baby that's going to be born. This package: this one. You're becoming tense, impatient, it has to be the package with the key to what Brígida was trying to say. This one. Do you want to open it? All right. Yes, Mudito, open it with respect, because Brígida wrapped it so that I would understand . . . no, Mother Benita, no, don't be fooled, Brígida made this package and the others because she was afraid. She was queen, scourge, dictator, judge, but she tied things and saved them the same as the rest of the old women. I know you're praying for this package to have something other than junk in it. You strip off the brown paper and throw it out. There's more paper, finer stuff, all wrinkled up, you tear it and drop it on the floor. Why go on opening and tearing wrappings —this apple-green taffeta one with a piece of newspaper underneath showing Roosevelt and Fala and Stalin's smile on board a ship—if you surely know you won't find a thing? This gray cotton shoulder pad is what made the parcel soft and bulky. You search, your anxious fingernails pull the shoulder pad apart and let the padding fall to the floor. There's still another hard little package you hold between your forefinger and your thumb.

You peel off the layer of rusty homespun and press gently . . . yes, yes, dear God, there's something inside, something solid, with a definite shape—this object I finger anxiously. Your fingers get all tangled up undoing the homespun, only to discover a ball of silver foil. You rip it to shreds that remain in the open palm of your trembling hand. I'm about to blow on those shreds and scatter them but you snap your fist shut just in time, grabbing it away from my breath, and your fingers reconstruct the silver ball in a second. You look at it and glance toward me, inviting me to accept the wholeness of this thing you've restored. You move to the door. The old women stop, quiet down, their eyes trace the swoop of your arm and then the arc of the shining little sphere as it falls. They run toward the trash pile and pounce on the silvery thing that streaked through the air. Don't worry, we'll find it again among some other dead old woman's things.

Why do you cover your face with your hands, Mother? You rush down the passages, the galleries, across the courts, the cloisters, with the old women tagging after you with their gnarled faces and pleading gummy eyes as they ask for things—one of the women in a voice that's muffled because of the shawl she wears to protect her mouth from some imaginary chill or some imaginary contagion, another in a voice that's harsh from smoking too much and drinking too much scalding-hot tea to warm her body that's stiff from the cold. They reach out to touch your habit, to hold you fast, to hang on to your denim apron, to your sleeve . . . don't go away, Mother, I want the brass bedstead . . . and me the glasses she sometimes let me wear because I don't have any and I like to read the papers even if they're old . . . a blanket for me because I can't stand the cold at night even in the summer, I was her friend, she liked me better, I was her neighbor to the right . . . I was to her left, I used to trim her nails, even her toenails and her corns too because I used to be a manicurist when I was young, she liked me much better than Amalia, who used to charge her too much to wash her clothes . . . hands like tongs with wooden claws grab me by the arms, wrinkled mouths claim things I don't know anything about . . . I'm a widow, the little scissors were mine . . .

look at Rafaelito's lock of hair, Mother Benita, what a pity the boy's bald now, and they even say he's gotten fat . . . a needle I lent her just the other day, and me a piece of crochet work . . . and me some buttons . . . These withered hands are stronger than mine, their fingers shoot out like branches to hold me back, their pleas and litanies bind me . . . for me, for me, Mother Benita . . . I want, I need . . . why don't you give me the tea Brígida left, you know how poor I am . . . no, not to her, me, give it to me, everybody knows she's a thief, keep an eye on the things because she's liable to steal them . . . give it to me, to me . . . old women in a corner, whose voices are as soft as balls of fluff, are stirred up by want or greed, chipped fingernails, filthy rags that fall apart on their bodies, bodies with the stench of old age that back me against this vestibule door with broken panes. The key! I open, I slip out and shut the door. I turn the key from the outside. I take it out and put it in my apron pocket. At last, dear God! They remain on the other side of the door like prisoners, collecting dust. Their arms, their faces twisted by grimaces, stick out through the broken panes . . . the wail of their pleading voices dies out.

2

THE OLD WOMEN leave the kitchen in pairs or in groups as if they were going, not to bed, but to melt back into the darkness. Inside the kitchen cluttered with benches, with marble tables greasy with leftovers, with pots stacked in the stopped-up sinks like monuments made of soot and grease, the women's voices slowly die out, like the embers, with the passing of the hours and the minutes that never seem to pass.

The last ones to leave were always the six women sitting at the table nearest the stove's heat, around Brígida, a group of intimates I always saw fluttering around Iris Mateluna, plying her with candy and magazines, enjoying themselves by giving her the most incredible hairdos, as if they were playing with a doll. I used to sit farther down at the same table. Listening to the eternal hum of their voices gradually made me so sleepy that after my last sip of tea my head slumped down on my arms, which were crossed on the table. I could hear their running commentary: one of them had hurt her foot on a pebble, Brígida announced the news that Misiá Raquel had received a postcard from Misiá Inés in Rome, some riddle repeated a hundred times over, or a story to amuse Iris as she sat on Rita's lap, muffled up in one end of the woman's shawl.

That night one of the women, I can't remember who, was telling a story that went more or less like this:

Once upon a time, years and years ago, there was a landowner, very rich but kindhearted too, who owned vast tracts of land in every part of the country—mountainous land in the north, forests in the south, sandy farms on the coast and especially irrigated lands in the district that runs north to the Maule

River, near the towns of San Javier, Cauquenes and Villa Alegre, where everyone acknowledged him as their leader, their cacique. And so, when bad times hit—years of skimpy harvests, of heat and drought, of poisoned animals and children born dead or with six fingers on one hand—the peasants looked to the land-owner for some explanation of all their misfortune.

This man had nine sons, who helped him look after his lands, and a daughter, the youngest child, the apple of his eye and a joy to his heart. The girl was blond and as sunny as rip-ened wheat, and she was so industrious that her talent for run-ning a house was well known throughout the entire region. She sewed and embroidered beautifully. She made candles from the tallow produced on their farms, and blankets from the wool. And in summer, when the yellowjackets droned greedily over the well-ripened fruit, the air among the trees turned blue and pun-gent from the fire lit by her servants under the copper pots in which she stirred the blackberries, watermelons, quinces and plums with which she made sweets that tickled the palates of the men of the house. She learned these timeless feminine arts from an old woman whose hands were deformed by warts who took charge of looking after her when her mother died in childbirth. When the last meal of the day was over, after overseeing things at the table where her father and her brothers sat down with their dusty boots, exhausted, she kissed each of them affection-ately before going down the hall, which was lighted only by the candle her nursemaid carried, to sleep in the room the two of them shared.

Whether it was because of the privileges her closeness with the girl accorded the nursemaid or because the blame had to fall on someone, since nothing seemed to explain so much misfor-tune, and bad times breed bad ideas, the rumor began circulat-ing. The stableman must have told it to the cheesemaker or the cheesemaker to the stableman or the vegetable man or the black-smith's wife or niece. At night, groups of farmhands would gossip as they squatted around the fires burning behind the pigsties, and if anyone came by they immediately stopped talking. The rumor spread slowly but spread it did, until the hired hands and the shepherds in the remotest hills of the estate learned about it:

it was said, it was said that it was said or that someone had heard it said, no one knew just where, that on moonlit nights a horrible head would fly through the air, trailing a long mane of wheat-colored hair, and that its face was the lovely face of the landowner's daughter . . . it sang the spine-chilling choo-ay, choo-ay, choo-ay of the ugly chonchón of ill omen. It was witch-craft, black magic, and that's why the peasants were being crushed under the weight of endless misfortunes. Over the bone-dry plains, where the animals swollen with thirst were dying off, the head of the landowner's daughter, flapping huge sinewy ears that were like bat wings, would fly after the yellow bitch dog—it was warty and scrawny like the girl's nursemaid—that guided the chonchón to a place indicated by the rays of their accom-plice, the moon, on the other side of the hills. It was they who were to blame for everything, for the girl was a witch and so was the nursemaid, who taught her these arts too, as feminine and timeless as the more innocent ones of preparing sweets and running the house. They say that it was their own tenant farm-ers who started the rumors and that then the tenants of neigh-boring estates spread them to the migrant workers who, when they went their separate ways after the crops had been gathered or the grain threshed, spread the rumors to every corner of the district, until no one doubted that the landlord's daughter and her nursemaid had the whole region under a spell.

One night, in a hut, the oldest of the brothers got up sooner than usual from the bed in which he was sleeping with the woman he had at the time in order to get back to his father's house at a decent hour. She shouted at him from the tangled bed-covers that were still warm from his body:

"I'll bet your sister hasn't gotten home yet. Witches come back at cockcrow, when it starts to get light . . ."

He thrashed her to within an inch of her life, until her mouth bled, and he made her confess everything. And after he got it out of her he hit her some more. He rushed to the main compound to tell his second brother and each of the others in turn, and neither in secret council nor individually would they let themselves admit that the rumor was anything but a dirty lie that amounted to a slur on them all. The terror of it all made its way from the unsheltered world of the poor laborers into the protected atmosphere of the house run by the sister no one could regard as anything but a young girl with a simple, happy nature. There was no need to believe the rumor. All they had to do was not take it to be true. They stopped talking about it. And yet, after a day's work they came back with their heads bowed and without having made any sales of livestock at the fair or remembered to get in the rest of the harvest before the storm. They no longer drank freely and gaily as they used to, because they were afraid the wine would loosen their tongues in front of their father, who was not to know a thing.

But sometimes, either all together or, after they told themselves it was a lie, each one on his own, as though keeping out of the others' sight so it wouldn't cross their minds that there might be a grain of truth to the rumors, the brothers used to listen at the door to the girl's room at night. They always heard the same thing. Inside, their sister and the old woman would laugh together and propose riddles or sing a few songs, and afterwards the brothers would hear them say a Hail Mary or a paternoster before putting out the candles and falling off to sleep. They never heard anything else, it was always a repetition of the same thing. Nothing to be concerned about. Just a woman's island in a house of men, inaccessible to them but not dangerous. When did they go on the forays they were accused of, then? After watching them like this for a while, and convinced that the rumors were groundless, they went to tell their father so that he could deal with those who spread such terrible gossip. Wild with rage and anguish, the cacique questioned his daughter but, when the girl denied the accusations she was too innocent to understand, her eyes remained so innocent-looking that her father felt reassured and, seating his darling on his knees, asked her to sing him something. All smiles now, the youngest son picked up a guitar from a corner of the drawing room and accompanied her:

> To fetch a rose, I'd leap into the sea,
> But that its dangerous waters frighten me.
> So let the churchbells ring, and cattle bells
> To let you know this love that in me wells.

In the next room, the brothers decided it would be wise to wait a few days but there was no doubt they'd have to get rid of the nursemaid, because, if anyone was guilty, she was, for having compromised an innocent girl by her suspicious presence. What did sacrificing a nameless old woman matter, anyway, as long as it cleared the air once and for all? After so many sleepless nights, they all went to bed with easy minds. At one in the morning, a farmhand banged on the cacique's door:

"Master, master, the yellow bitch and the chonchón are roaming around out there . . ."

And he got out of sight before the cacique, brandishing his whip and dressed in his nightshirt and his poncho, could come to the door and shout at his sons, at everybody, to get to and get dressed, to get a move on, to saddle the horses and be off . . . the ten men left a swirl of dust behind them in the dark as they galloped across the fields, asking questions, looking everywhere, listening, trying not to lose the chonchón and the bitch dog and this unique chance to uncover the truth. A howl in the distance made the posse twist its course toward the woods. A caw, and then a rock rolling down a slope, made them go up the mountainside and search any caves that might be the entrance to the witch's grotto. They went down to the river because the barking of a dog, maybe the yellow bitch, led them there, but it wasn't, they never found the yellow bitch, and the cock crowed and day broke and the witching hour was over and the ten men had to return to the compound, heavy with defeat. When they arrived, they heard the leaves rustle in the vineyard.

"Grab her, don't let her go, it's the yellow bitch trying to get into the house, the chonchón can't be too far away . . ."

And the ten men rushed to surround her like in a roundup and cut off her escape and catch her and whip her to death on the spot. The horses reared, whips cracked, the bitch was lost in the cloud of dust raised by the hooves that couldn't stop her from slipping past and disappearing in the uncertain light of dawn. The farmhands were ordered to look for her. They were to find her, whatever the cost, because the bitch was the nursemaid and the nursemaid was the witch. They were not to dare to come back without her. They were to kill her and bring her hide.

With his sons behind him, the landowner forced open the door to the girl's room. He let out a scream as he went in, and he threw out his arms so that his huge poncho instantly hid from the others what only his own eyes saw. He locked his daughter in the next room. Only then did he allow the others to come in. The old woman was lying motionless on her bed, her body smeared with magic ointments, her eyes half-closed, breathing as if she were asleep or her soul had taken leave of her body. Outside, the bitch started to bay and scratch at the window.

"Here she is, kill her or I'll kill all of you . . ."

The bitch stopped baying. The girl was crying in the room where her father had locked her up.

"Nana, dear Nana! . . . Papa, don't let them kill her, don't let them kill her, tell them to let her back into her body. If you promise to let her live, I'll confess everything, I swear . . ."

"Hold your tongue. You have nothing to confess!"

Everybody went out into the yard to take a look at the bloodstained hide. It hadn't been hard to catch her, she seemed all in, trembling, as she crouched under the girl's window: that's what the farmhands kept saying, while the ten men examined the yellow bitch's hide. All they had to do now was dispose of the witch's body. She was neither alive nor dead. She might go on being dangerous; burying a witch's body poisons good croplands for miles and miles around, so it has to be gotten rid of some other way, the landowner said. He ordered them to lash the body to a tree and whip it until the woman woke up and they could all hear her admit to her crimes. The lacerated body bled, but the witch didn't open her eyes or her mouth, although her breathing didn't stop, and she remained in a state that was neither life nor death. Then, since there was nothing else to do, they chopped the tree down with axes. And the nine brothers with their share-croppers and the sharecroppers of the nearby estates hauled the witch's body to the Maule River and threw it into the water, lashed to the tree trunk to keep it afloat.

The landowner stayed in the compound. One hour after the uproar died down he left for the capital with his daughter. He shut her up in a convent where some cloistered nuns could look *after her, and she was never seen again, not even by her nine brothers who loved her so much.*

In the meantime, the band of horsemen strung out along the Maule, following the body as it floated downstream. If they saw it drifting in toward the shore they pushed it away with long prods. When the current seemed to carry it too far to the middle they hauled it back with drag hooks. At night, they used the same hooks to moor the witch's body to the shore, while they unsaddled their horses, lit fires, had a bite to eat and then, stretched out on their fur cloaks and their ponchos, traded stories of witches and apparitions and other monsters fear takes the shape of during bad times. They told all they knew about witches, what had been told in whispers for generations—someone had once told one of their ancestors that anybody who wanted to take part in witches' orgies had to kiss a young goat's sex organ—and they talked about fear, about past fear and present, about fear at whatever time, and silence fell over them, and to drive off the shapes about to take form in the night they congratulated themselves on their good luck because this time the witches hadn't been able to steal the landowner's lovely daughter, which is what the witches were after, to steal her and sew up the nine orifices of her body and turn her into an imbunche, *because that's the reason witches steal poor innocent children, to turn them into* imbunches *and keep them in their underground grottoes, with their eyes sewed up, their sex organs sewed up, their anuses sewed up, their mouths, nostrils, ears, everything sewed up, letting their hair and their fingernails and their toenails grow long, turning them into idiots, making the poor things worse off than animals, filthy, ridden with lice, able only to hop around when the goat and the drunken witches command them to dance . . . one time, someone's father had talked to someone who said he saw an* imbunche *once and the fear he was seized with paralyzed one whole side of his body . . . A dog bayed. The frightened voices fell silent again. The eyes of the half-asleep laborers shone as the flames from the bonfire dispelled the shadows cast by the brims of their straw hats.*

They saddled their horses early the next morning. They cut

the ropes tied to the trunk of the tree and all day, under the
scorching sun and over the bald hills of the coast, they followed
the witch's body downstream. The news that they were getting
rid of the witch at last, that the region would be free of her
black magic, that women would now give birth to normal babies
and there'd be an end to floods, spread from village to village
and, as the band of horsemen advanced, all kinds of settlers and
tenant farmers joined it. Before sundown, they knew they'd al-
most reached the sea. The river widened, the current became
gentler. An islet came into view. Sandbanks softened the river's
shores. The water was ashen instead of green, until they finally
sighted some black rocks and the white stripe left by the waves
on the sandbar.

The nine brothers went out in a skiff and, using hooks and
ropes, dragged the witch to the sandbar. The currents were grad-
ually undressing her and had tangled her tatters and her hair.
The fish that had gnawed at her flesh were floating around the
skiff, dead. The crowd of sharecroppers on foot and on horse-
back, settlers, children with their dogs, neighboring people and
curiosity seekers clambered up the hill overlooking the sea. A lot
later, the wind blowing against their ponchos carried the yell of
triumph the nine brothers let out: they'd finally gotten the body
to penetrate the green mountain of churning waves and be swal-
lowed up by the sea. All that was left was a mere dot dissolving
on the golden sea to the west. The horsemen gradually separated
on the way back. Each one headed back to his own town or his
farm, his mind at ease and his fear gone, now that bad times in
the district were finally coming to an end.

I was telling how in the kitchen that night the old women
were telling this story, *more or less.* I can't recall which of the
women it was, because I've heard it so many times and in such
contradictory versions that it becomes confused in my mind, but
it's all the same. According to some accounts, there weren't nine
brothers, but seven or even three. Mercedes Barroso used to tell
one version in which, terrified by the landowner's rage, the farmhands must have slaughtered an ordinary bitch to show him its
hide, in which case the real yellow bitch would have remained
alive. Only the essential facts always stay the same: the father's

huge poncho blocks a doorway and, under its discreet cover, he makes the noble daughter vanish, thus removing her from the center of the story in order to shift the attention and vengeance of the farmhands to the old woman. A person of no importance, like all other old women, somewhat of a witch, bawd, midwife, wailer, healer, servant, who seems to lack an individual psychology and characteristics of her own, she takes over the girl's leading part in the story and she alone expiates the heavy guilt that comes from contact with forbidden powers. This story, popular throughout the entire country, originated in the region south of the Maule, where the Azcoitías have been feudal lords since colonial times. Inés too, since she has Azcoitía blood on her grandmother's side, knows a version of this story, of course. Her nurse, Peta Ponce, must have told it to her when Inés was a little girl. In her frightened mind she separated, and surely forgot, the story of the girl-witch from the other face put on the same legend: the proud family tradition the Azcoitías preserve of a girl-saint who died in the Casa in the odor of sanctity at the beginning of the last century and whose beatification has been a failure so bruited about that even the radio commentators and newspaper columnists have had their fun with it. But the story is kept alive by the voices of old peasant grannies who repeat it winter after winter, changing it a little each time, so that their grandchildren, huddled around the fire, can start learning what fear is.

It's been told so many times, right here in the kitchen, that Iris fell asleep in Rita's lap while listening to it as she sucked her thumb . . . She's really kind of big for this, Rita, you have to make her stop that ugly habit, they say you can make them stop by rubbing chili pepper on their thumb, or doodoo, dog doodoo . . . no, no, leave the poor thing alone, she'll stop it soon enough, don't you know the first months of pregnancy are the worst, they walk around tired, sleepy, with their tummies full of gas, their legs swell up and turn red, and they even get varicose veins, look at Iris's legs, they've always been fat but now it looks like the elastic on her socks is going to slice through her ankles.

I wasn't sleeping. But when I heard Iris was going to have a baby, I didn't raise my head from my crossed arms on the table, because I wouldn't have raised it even if they'd repeated that potato plasters are better than plasters made of cigarette butts, or that "if Clemencia weren't so selfish she'd lend me her flowered washbasin." These grumblings are only the thread their voices are rolling into a ball that never grows, because it's only another version of silence . . . no: someone retching, Iris vomiting, the old women holding her forehead to let her throw up without pain, Iris whimpering . . . Mudito, come clean up the vomit, hurry before Mother Benita pops in and starts asking questions.

I refused to do it.

I looked straight at the six old women. Then I made a gesture to indicate I'd found out that Iris was pregnant . . . yes, yes, don't try to put one over on me, that's why the bunch of you have been so close together and so quiet around that stupid Iris, spoiling her and letting her have her way all the time, that's why her breasts are so big, yes, I was beginning to smell a rat, I'm going to call Mother Benita, she'll decide what's to be done about something like this, I don't want to get into a jam, you may even try to make me take the blame afterwards . . .

"You, Mudito?"

"Why, you're only *part* of a man."

"Who's going to make *you* take the rap? . . ."

They laughed so hard they almost cried, in spite of Mudito's continuing to make his threat, which they disarmed with the laughter that brought tears to their eyes and with the insulting way they pointed their twisted forefingers at him, until finally they crushed it out of existence . . . no, Mudito, my handsome one, don't snitch on us, don't be naughty, can't you see we're all crazy about you, you're such a doll, stay here with us, it suits you, we're going to give you a lot of nice loving up that you're going to like because you're such a he-man, especially when it comes to sex, that you don't even dare go out in the street; if you don't keep your trap shut, you lousy little mute, we'll throw you out and steal your keys and not let you back in the Casa ever again, and you'll get lost in those streets that are like long back tunnels where Don Jerónimo de Azcoitía and the doctors and the police hunt people down with their dogs. Yes. They've already gone for them. Don't you know they starve them for days to make them ravenous and bloodthirsty? . . . Zoom! One snap of the policeman's fingers and the barking dogs tear off into the night. They howl as they come after me through the streets and the rain, across the part swarming with beasts that howl at me, down unbearable avenues, across the bridge from whose ironwork I let myself drop down into the river. They come howling after me over the slippery rocks, over these mounds of rotting garbage, I trip over a stick, I fall and cut myself on a sharp tin can that may poison me, septicemia, tetanus, look at my hands getting all red with blood, I struggle to my feet by using my bloodied hands and knees, I flee under the bridges, among the puny bushes of this rocky gorge where the wind swallows up my voice and leaves me dumb . . . I'm done for, help me, please help me, I swear I won't tell on you . . . we don't believe you, squealer, faggot, lousy mute, you're a piece of shit, you're dirt, dirt . . . I run and run to keep them from catching me, because I hear the beasts racing after me with their fetid breath and seething snouts, and then their claws pull me down. I try to get up but can't because their fangs pin me to the edge of the water that carries away the city's waste . . . with their phosphorescent snouts, the animals are tearing me to pieces, they're destroying me with their fangs, their steaming tongues, their eyes that drill holes into the night as the snarling beasts rip me apart, snatching hot chunks of my viscera, splashing about in the pool of my blood, fighting over my guts and cartilage, ears and glands, hair, nails, kneecaps—each organ of mine that's no longer mine because I'm no longer me but these bloody scraps of flesh.

"What happened?"

I take my hands off my face. I look, and I recognize them: Dora, Brígida, María Benítez, Amalia, Rosa Pérez—all except Rita, who went to put Iris to bed.

"Are you going to squeal on us?"

I promise them I won't. I get down on all fours and start cleaning up the vomit of that daughter of a jailbird who slashed his wife's windpipe in bed one morning, and left Iris to wake and find herself swimming in her mother's blood . . . watch me wipe up Iris's vomit . . . But why are you all going? Haven't I groveled enough to please you? Don't go away like that, don't leave me, listen to me, I can help you, yes, yes I can, I have the keys to all the doors of the Casa in my keeping, if you ever happen to need them, and you may need them some time, don't say no, don't look down on this little bit of power I'm offering you . . . don't you know that you're only six old women and you have to be seven, seven is a magic number, not six, let me be the seventh witch, don't go, I want to help you and I can . . .

They didn't leave. They accepted my help and I was grateful. It was Brígida who said:

"He knows the Casa inside out. Let him find us a room, a hidden loft, someplace no one knows about, where we can bring up the miraculous baby that will be born of Iris's womb . . . Mudito, find us a place, understand, where . . . no one is to know . . . no one is to hear . . . no one is to see . . ."

Only when I told them I'd found just the right place, a cellar, was I accepted and allowed to be the seventh witch.

3

THE CHAPLAINCY FOUNDED by the father of the lay sister whose beatification Inés tried to promote in Rome has kept the Casa in the Azcoitía family for a century and a half. In the beginning, it was a modest retreat house for cloistered nuns, having been built by the landowner on his valuable properties in La Chimba, north of the capital, to provide a shelter for his daughter during her lifetime. After her death, the Archbishop could decide what the house would be used for. But legally, if not in practice, the founder's oldest descendant, who passes on the family name, retains the right to sell, transfer, divide, donate, or pull the place down, as he sees fit. No Azcoitía has ever exercised these rights, thus reaffirming from generation to generation the family's loyalty to the Church as well as a certain indifference toward something as unproductive as a chaplaincy dating from the end of the eighteenth century. And yet, in drawing up his will, or on his deathbed, no Azcoitía ever fails to make it clear that the Casa, along with his other numerous holdings, is to go to his heir, thus keeping in mind something that, in the final analysis, was really never forgotten: this chaplaincy that was buried away in archives and was the concern only of devout aunts and needy female cousins has linked and related the Azcoitías to God for a very long time, and they *cede* the Casa to him, in return for his preserving their privileges. In any case, lest they be pestered by what nobody can fathom, don't let them bother us with talk of nuns and refuges and meddling priests and indigent spinsters and chaplaincies that are outdated in the contemporary world. Let the Monsignor do as he pleases with that nuisance of a retreat house. Fortunately we're a long way from needing the money the sale of the property would bring in. The political plots and the deals, the heroic efforts and sacrifices involved in the politics of the country we're trying to build here are what absorb us, we can't waste time on matters that lead nowhere. So the Monsignor says that the daughter of the chaplaincy's founder performed miracles and deserves beatification? Well, let *him* worry about it, if he's interested; mysticism, spiritual things, are his business. Ours is the rough and tumble of politics, down-to-earth things. Let's not be bothered by the Archbishop with unnecessary consultations about the Casa! The Monsignor knows perfectly well that he's free to add all the new patios he wants, build all the wings he needs, raise another story, enlarge cloisters and extend galleries and knock down walls if he wants to, as long as he doesn't expect us to foot the bills.

Left to the random demands and needs of different times, this structure has grown so much and so erratically that no one remembers now, and perhaps only poor Inés is interested in finding out, which section went up first, which the original courts destined to confine the founder's daughter. The city expanded beyond the river to the north and this bank was settled. Miserable alleys took shape that pushed the little farms, whose peaches and melons fed the city, farther and farther out, the expanding side streets of La Chimba turned into avenues named after the defenders of workers' rights, and as they surrounded and extended beyond the Casa de Ejercicios Espirituales de la Encarnación at La Chimba, they closed it in like a cyst, mute and blind, in a very central section of the city.

When the chaplaincy was founded, no one dreamed a day would come when there wouldn't be a male to inherit the family name and pass his rights on, for according to the contemporary records that I was careful to include in the dossier Inés took to Rome, the founder had nine sons who could marry and, like everyone else, have many sons and grandsons and great-grandsons. But, from way back, the Azcoitías were always riding horses and getting into fights and so, as soon as the wars of independence broke out, they organized mounted revolutionary troops that were so fierce that the Spanish enemy found the country south of the Maule impassable. The Azcoitías were covered with glory. They were on every patriot's tongue. But their number was cut down considerably.

Besides, in the century following Independence, the Azcoitía family, as if under a curse, produced mostly females who were beautiful and rich and virtuous, who married young and well, connecting the Azcoitías to all the high society of the time by way of *the bottom sheet*, wielding the power that stems from gathering around the brazier, pulling the slender wires that snare men with their whispering and gossip, with the bedtime kiss that presides over their children's dreams, with the farewell smile that makes or breaks reputations and traditions. They were women who remained in the background, discreet and silent in their world of sewing and servants and illnesses and visits and novenas, women who kept their eyes lowered over the multi-colored silk threads in the embroidery frame while rough male voices grew heated as the menfolk argued over things that we women neither can nor should understand because we understand only unimportant things like the openwork adorning the border of a low neckline, or whether it's worthwhile ordering kid gloves from France, or whether the priest at the church at Santo Domingo is a good or a bad preacher. And while the family's power kept spreading, hidden beneath generations of women with the family blood but incapable of passing on the family name or preserving the family identity, the Azcoitía male line gradually weakened: each generation produced many females, but only one male, except in the case of the clergyman Don Clemente de Azcoitía, the brother of Don Jerónimo's father. The family name was in danger of dying out and, with it, prebends, rights, properties, power, sinecures, honors, that, split up among cousins with other surnames, would break down the power of that one Azcoitía that was needed in each generation.

The Archbishop was waiting for the Casa, the project for the Children's Village being ready. Jerónimo could sign it over whenever he felt like it, but he still kept alive the insane hope that his wife's useless womb would procreate, and he could never bring himself to part with anything, not even the most useless things. That's why no one could believe it when he suddenly, in his own lifetime, signed the batch of papers turning title to the

Casa over to the Archbishop, with Inés still in Rome. Not even Mother Benita believes it, in spite of her enthusiasm over the project. Neither do I, in spite of my fear. But Father Azócar warned us to start thinking of putting the Casa in readiness for an auction of what he called *all this mess*, before the demolition gets under way once the place is vacated.

This block of walls, scarred where chunks of plaster have been breaking off, has the neutral color of adobe. From the outside, rarely can a glimmer of light be seen in its hundreds of windows covered with dust, or covered because I sealed them with boards nailed over and over again (others are covered even more, because I walled them up on account of their being dangerous). As night approaches in this noisy neighborhood of modest houses that surround us, houses also built of adobe and tiles but painted pink or pale blue or lilac or cream, the lights go on, the barbershop and bakery radios, the television sets in crowded bars, deafen you, while in those places and in the motorcycle repair shop and in the shop where novels and second-hand magazines are bought and sold, and in the corner grocery, the life of the neighborhood, from which we're excluded, continues its course.

Not only have I been boarding up all the outside windows. I've also been closing off unsafe sections of the Casa like the upstairs floor, for instance, ever since Asunción Morales leaned on the banister and everything collapsed—banister, honeysuckle vine, and Asunción. There's no need for much space now, that's why we have to cut down. It's not like before, when the Archbishop subsidized the Casa handsomely and selected it year after year for his retreat, accompanied by uppity clerics, canons, secretaries, deacons and subdeacons, friends, relatives, and sometimes even a very very pious minister of state. Groups of very prominent gentlemen, religious congregations, schools for lily-white girls, the most distinguished organizations in the country, made reservations months in advance to come and shut themselves off from the world and get close to the Lord again. From the pulpit and the confessional, silver-tongued friars who called for penance and sacrifice, magnanimity and repentance, awakening vocations whose light, sometimes, brightened the pages of

History. At times, after dark, crying and moaning could be heard far into the night behind the doors of the hundred cells that form a U around the court with the orange trees: the pain of those who rid themselves of their guilt with nocturnal flagellations, ending up with a lacerated body but a pristine soul, only to surrender it the following morning, after a fervent Communion, to peaceful monastic dreams in the lushest corner of the garden, slumbers that usually culminated in a splendid donation.

Nowadays, of course, no one thinks of coming to the Casa de la Encarnación at La Chimba for his spiritual exercises. They have institutions that are flooded with light, heated or cooled, depending on the season, and have picture windows opening on the matchless panorama of the snowy mountain range, that are ready to receive penitents. Why take the chance, then, of being kept awake not by an examination of conscience but the gurgling of broken pipes and the enormous rats scurrying through the lofts? Up until a short time ago, not anymore, girls from some obscure school or members of some second-rate institution would retire to the Casa to have little chats with the Lord and listen to lukewarm sermons inspired by well-known social injustices rather than by the Magnificence and the Wrath and the Love of God, as in the good old days.

But what can you do? They say nothing's what it used to be in the good old days. And yet, this place remains the same, and all the uselessness persists. There are only three nuns left now, whereas at one time an entire congregation saw to the comfort of the penitents so that their souls would soar, without material obstacles, to the purest regions of ecstasy. Only three nuns and, of course, the old women who eventually die off and are replaced by other identical old women who also die when the time comes to make room that other old women come to claim because they need it. And the orphan girls who, almost a year ago, were sent here one day, for a couple of weeks . . . Mother Benita, you have more than enough room to lodge them for a couple of weeks while the finishing touches are put on the new wing at the orphanage, you know how long these finishing touches take and how workers nowadays get drunk and don't show up for work, the five little orphans are so forlorn in this labyrinth, so hungry and bored, with no one to put some kind of order in their lives because Father Azócar keeps promising . . . in another week, Mother Benita, a few more weeks . . . and no one gives them a thought . . . I have the keys and I lock the doors. Ladies recommended by the Archbishop or Inés rent cells from us to store their junk, it's not worth anything but it's little things you hate to part with and there's no space for them in the small houses we have to live in these days. The ladies turn up from time to time, looking for some item or to pay the back rent, yes, we need the money, we've come to this, we have to rent cells to pay our most pressing debts because the Archbishop sends very little money. What he sends are truckloads of rubbish more than anything else: broken statues of saints that can't be thrown out because they're religious objects and must be treated with respect; mountains of magazines and old newspapers that clutter room after room with dead news items that have turned into food for mice; additions to my library of incomplete encyclo-pedias, of bound collections of *Zig-Zag, Life, La Esfera,* of books by authors no one reads anymore, such as Gyp, Concha Espina, Hoyos y Vinent, Carrere, Villaespesa; truckloads of assorted objects such as clocks, burlap sacks for wrapping heaven knows what; pieces of worn-out rugs and hangings; armchairs without a bottom—all the things that fill the endless cells and yet seem to always leave room for more.

Jerónimo has never in his life been inside the Casa. On the other hand, Inés used to visit very often before leaving for Rome —twice, sometimes three times, a week—to ransack her suitcases and junk in the four large cells she took over, as *owner* of the Casa. The authority with which she rings the bell, not releasing her finger from the button until poor Rita with her incurable bunions runs to open the door for her, bespeaks her privileged position. Sometimes Misiá Raquel came along with her and listened to her patiently without trying to dissuade her as she watched her rummage in the overstuffed drawers, taking out papers and photographs and charts and relics she might be able to use, motioning to me to take down the round basket on top of the wardrobe, to move the roll of hallway carpeting out of the way and reach up for a leather hatbox in which there might be a package with an envelope in it in which, ages ago, she might have put away an important certificate or a photograph, and I'd take down the basket and hand her the hatbox although I knew the certificate wasn't there, because I know better than she herself what's in every drawer, basket, suitcase, trunk, wardrobe in her cells . . . And yet, putting together everything she could, looking very elegant, in severe black, Inés left for Rome, with the papers I myself packed into an ordinary plastic bag, and presented her petition to the solemn cardinals, magnificent in their purple robes, who shook their heads, giving her to understand that nothing she had with her would help and that she ought to stay put in her country and make a donation worthy of her rank.

The Azcoitías' total lack of interest in the Casa goes way back. It's as if they had a fear of it they didn't admit even to themselves and preferred to have nothing to do with it, aside from preserving their rights to it as proprietors. They've exercised these prerogatives, as far as I know, only when they sent Don Clemente here to die. On that occasion too they said there was so much excess space in the Casa, yet they added more; after all, he was an Azcoitía and had every right to move in.

When they brought him here, he was a very quiet, sad little old man. Mother Benita used to spoon-feed him like a baby and, between us, we'd undress him and put him to bed. I used to help him with his body functions because he gave no warning, and we had to see that he didn't mess his clothes several times a day. Don Clemente would sit by the window in an easy chair, leaning on his stick, smiling sadly, without saying a word, until little by little, as though a curtain were being drawn very slowly, his smile gradually disappeared, leaving only a set look of sorrow carved on his Azcoitía face. Then we began to notice that this sadness in his blue eyes welled up in tears that one fine day started rolling down his cheeks as if his eyes no longer had the strength to hold them back. He spent weeks at a time sitting in his velvet easy chair, staring quietly at the orange trees in the court, without asking for food or to be cleaned, silent, with the tears running down his face and drenching his cassock the way a baby's drool soaks his bib. And then he began to whimper like an animal, softly at first, as if something hurt him, that's all, like a dog you pat when it whimpers and ask, "What's the matter old man, what's the matter?" even though you realize the poor brute can't answer and whimpers over something you can't understand, and you feel helpless about it because you can't do anything to ease his suffering so as to quiet his maddening groans. After a time, Don Clemente went from whimpering to moaning, he didn't sit still anymore in his easy chair and look at the orange trees in the court. He began to get excited in his cell, banging on the door and the windowpanes, until his moans turned into howls and he smashed the glass and almost knocked down the door with his banging, and we had to lock it; or else we stumbled into him when he'd get lost in the corridors, and it wasn't easy to drag him back to his cell, because of his kicking and scream- ing with what little voice he seemed to recover, pronouncing syllables that had the sound of fear and night and prison and darkness and deceit—the things, or snatches of things, he screamed when we left him to fall asleep at night and he latched on to our clothes to stop us from leaving. He'd sit up, want to follow us, wouldn't let us put his nightshirt on him and help him into bed, would fight us off to keep us from undressing him or putting covers on him, not that he wanted his clothes on either; he'd rip his cassocks and the old women would mend them, only to have him tear them again and not let us put them on him. He walked around half nude in his cell and, after we locked the door, stark naked. He'd come to the window naked, begging for help, for someone to come and stay with him, to rescue him from this terrible hospital where they mistreated him. Neither Mother Benita nor the old women entered the naked Don Clemente's room; I alone did, and he used to chase me out . . . you filthy beggar, get out of here, don't touch me, if you lay a finger on me I'll cane you to death . . . and he'd go back to the window with the broken panes, stark naked. The old women and the nuns didn't dare cross the court with the orange trees anymore. We decided that the best thing was to board up the shutters of his cell. But he always managed to break them down. Until one night, as Don Clemente slept, I walled up his window with bricks and cement, the first window I walled up in the Casa. Then, and this was my idea, I painted it over on the outside, the same color as the wall. And now you can't tell where the window used to be.

Then, one afternoon, Don Clemente broke down the door to his cell. He came out to roam the hallways, nude, leaning on his stick, and during the rosary, with all the women of the Casa present, he appeared in the presbytery as naked as God cast him into the world, and, with his stick, began smashing everything he could find, as the old women wailed and screamed and fled, scandalized by the naked Don Clemente who desecrated the chapel and their eyes purified by old age, misery, and suffering. Finally, as he lashed out with his stick, the old man stumbled and struck his head. I rushed over to cover him with an alb and I took him to his cell, where, speechless once more, weeping broken-heartedly, he passed away two days later.

There are old women left who boast that they've been in the Casa such a long time that they remember the terrible afternoon when Don Clemente de Azcoitía went into the chapel stark naked. I don't believe them. Perhaps they say it because they know how it is to confuse one old woman with another. In any case, one of the main reasons for their terror, what stops them from going around alone in the corridors when dusk comes, is that Don Clemente, they say, appears completely naked and chases them, and they're much too old to run. They tell how sometimes he has his hat and his garters on. Or shoes and socks. Or an undershirt that doesn't reach his belly button. He never wears anything else. Whenever word gets around that Don Clemente's apparition's been seen, a pious shudder runs through the Casa, and the old women shut themselves up in their shacks and recite rosary after rosary, Hail Marys and Our Fathers and Hail Holy Queens; I've heard them droning on, scared out of their wits, raving, obsessed, saying more and more rosaries because they're sure that the prayers will succeed in putting clothes on the ghost of poor Don Clemente, whom God's condemned to wander naked through the Casa to punish him for scandalizing them with the exhibition of his privates and that God will forgive the old cleric only when so many of the women have said so many rosaries that He, in his mercy, will consent to give him back his clothing one piece at a time so that he may enter the

Kingdom of Heaven with his clothes on. In the meantime, he has to go on wandering through the Casa to remind the old women to pray for him and make God give him back his shoes, cassock, shorts—yes, his underpants are the most urgent. They say Don Clemente hasn't appeared without socks and undershirt for some time now. That's something, at least. It stands to reason, then, that his underpants are the next thing God will give back. Let them be long underwear, the old women pray. And made of flannel, for winter. The hum of their rosaries at dusk fills the Casa like the buzzing of insects busy spinning cloth for those underpants, when Don Clemente, naked, pounces on some old woman at dusk while she's thinking his thoughts are elsewhere.

4

RITA NEVER SAW blood on Iris's panties. She herself used to wash them for her. Poor motherless child. With the cold weather, her hands swelled up with chilblains. But not a sign of blood.

Rita locked herself in a room with her and questioned her. . . . Haven't you ever had any bleeding? . . . Bah, you all think I'm just a little kid, and I'm not, I'm a woman, I have my period every month and I bleed a lot, I'm the only one of the orphans who has a period, and the others sure are little kids and that's why I get sick of them, but when I'm bleeding I wash my own panties so's not to bother you, Miss Rita, you're so good to me.

Rita didn't believe a word. She knew her too well: Iris was neither clean nor considerate with others. The old woman tried to hint at what went on between a man and a woman. But how? After all, she herself was a virgin. She wasn't sure about any of it. She didn't know what to think. No men ever came into the Casa. Iris had never been near the street since she was brought here. But the poor girl knew so little about what happens with men that she yawned, bored stiff with the conversation, unable to keep her mind on what Rita, who was a model of discretion with her questions, was asking her in a roundabout way so as not to open her eyes and destroy her innocence. Iris just kept sucking her thumb and curling her hair with her finger . . . hey, cut that out, stop sticking your finger up your nose and eating your snot, you little pig . . . yes, she was innocent. Still, Rita couldn't believe she washed her own panties when she had her period. She kept an eye on her: sure enough, nothing this month, nor the next, it wasn't true that she washed anything.

And, worst of all, she kept putting on more and more weight, getting lazier and drowsier.

Rita went to Brígida with her secret worry. She, who knew everything, must also know about things such as these; she'd had two babies, stillborn, of course, God knows why, his will be done. And, not long after that, her husband passed away. Brígida listened from her bed, absorbed in what Rita was telling her and, after thinking it over half a minute, said that it was, of course, a miracle. When babies are born without a man doing the filthy thing to a woman, it's a miracle . . . an angel comes down from heaven and there you are. Miracle. Naturally the first thing to be done was examine Iris to make sure she was pregnant . . . María Benítez is a medicine woman. But how can we tell her about the miracle, Brígida, the whole Casa will hear about it by prayer time and they'll take Iris and the baby away from us or take her away and punish her, because people are big heretics these days and don't believe in miracles, they say there are people now who don't even believe in the Virgin . . . But Brígida insisted that the medicine woman be called in; she was to examine her very carefully, without sticking anything up her, because Iris was a virgin and was not to find out what was happening to her. María Benítez said, yes, she's expecting, I'm telling you, these kids nowadays just sniff a pair of trousers and they get knocked up.

To shut her up and stop her from talking any more sacrilegious filth, they let her know they were dealing with a miracle. She was crushed. No one else must get wind of it. The old women were an envious bunch and would try to rob them of the baby, while, this way, they could take care of it just between the three of them, secretly, and the three had tea in Brígida's tiny quarters and, since Amalia was serving them, they told her too about the miracle . . . there are four of us—no, Rita confessed that she had confided her first suspicions to Dora, who knew how to write too and filled in for her in the doorkeeper's office, jotting down telephone messages left by Father Azócar and the relatives and former employers of the inmates . . . They were five, then. And, when they noticed Rosa Pérez starting to hang around them, itching to know what they were always up to with Iris, Brígida, who had a head on her shoulders, thought they'd better tell the blabbermouth about the miracle, to be on the safe side, or else, with all that poking around, she'd find them out and then, good Lord, the whole Casa would come down on them, she might even take it into her head to call up the Archbishop and report them; yes, better tell her the whole thing. That way she'd be even more anxious than any of them to keep it quiet. Because no one, absolutely no one besides the six of them, was to share the privilege of knowing that Iris was expecting a little baby. Then Brígida started talking to them:

"Amalia, pass around the cookies, they're in that tin. Mother Benita's walking around in a fog, with the rumor that they're going to tear down the Casa and build the Children's Village and make her chief administrator, they say Father Azócar promised her that. She can't keep her mind on anything, not even on the little girls, although in the beginning she talked about setting up classes for them and all. Just look at the rags she has them wearing now! When the baby begins to show on Iris, I'm going to let her have a brown overcoat I've got stored away. It'll be too big for her. But if Mother Benita asks any questions, I'll answer her: But Mother, the poor angel was going around shivering with cold, that's why I gave her this coat, it's a little big on her but as soon as I have a little free time I'm going to take it in so it'll fit her right. And later on, with nobody but the six of us knowing about it, the baby will be born. We have to look for a room in the back of the Casa where we can keep it hidden, nobody must know the child was born, and it'll grow up beautiful and holy, without ever in its whole life leaving the room where we'll have hidden it from the evils of the world. And we'll take wonderful care of the little thing. It's so lovely, taking care of a baby . . . bundling it up in shawls so it won't feel cold . . . feeding . . . washing . . . diapering it carefully . . . dressing it up. And as he grows up the most important thing of all is for us not to teach him how to do anything for himself, not even talk, or walk, then he'll always need us to do every single thing. God grant he can't see or hear! We'll be his devoted mothers and we'll be the only ones who'll understand all the signs he makes, and he'll have to depend on us for everything.

It's the only way to bring up a baby to be a saint, you have to bring him up so that he'll never, not even when he grows up to be a man, leave his room, and nobody will even know he exists, with us looking after him always and being his very hands and feet. Naturally we'll gradually pass on. But it doesn't matter. There will always be old women around. And, in spite of all the talk, there will always be a Casa, Misiá Raquel was telling me that this demolition business was all Father Azócar's idea, to get money out of the Azcoitía family, out of Misiá Inés's husband, Inés being such a good person. Whenever one of us passes on, another one must be elected so the child can go from one old woman to the next, from hand to hand, until he expresses his will and decides some day that there's been enough dying and takes us to heaven with him."

The *imbunche*. All sewed up—eyes, mouth, anus, sex organ, nostrils, ears, hands, legs. From deep within her country roots in some region and some other century, when some half-Indian ancestor threatened, in order to make her behave, to change her into an *imbunche*, the scared little girl that she must have been then and the temptation she probably felt to become one or create one remained buried in Brígida's mind and was now emerging in the form of an explanation of the future of Iris's child. All sewed up. Once all his body's orifices were closed up and his arms and legs trapped in the strait jacket of not knowing how to use them, yes, the old women would graft themselves onto the child in place of his limbs and organs and faculties, ripping out his eyes and his voice and robbing him of his hands, rejuvenating their own weary organs in the process and living a life other than the one they'd already lived, ripping out everything in order to renew themselves by means of the theft. And they'll do it. I'm sure of it. The old women have a lot of power. It's not true that they're sent to the Casa to end their days peacefully, as they'd have us believe. This is a prison, full of cells, with windows with iron bars, with an implacable jailer in charge of the keys. Their employers have them locked up here when they realize how much they owe these old women and are terrified because, one fine day, these miserable creatures may show their power and destroy them. Servants accumulate the privileges of misery. The demonstrations of pity, the ridicule, the handouts, the token help, the humiliations they put up with make them powerful. They save up the instruments of vengeance because their coarse warty hands collect, bit by bit, that other side of their employers—the useless, discarded side, the filth and the sordidness that, trusting and sentimental, they've been putting into their servants' hands with the insult of each shabby skirt they give them, each nightgown scorched by the iron. Why shouldn't they have their employers at their mercy, when they've washed their clothes, and when all the involvements and dirt they wanted to eliminate from their lives passed through their hands? Who else but they swept the fallen crumbs from their dining rooms and washed the plates and the dishes and the silver and ate the scraps from their tables? They dusted their living rooms, they picked up the snips of thread left by their sewing, the crumpled paper from their desks and offices. They restored order to the beds where they made licit or illicit love, satisfactory or frustrated love, without being repelled by the odors and stains of others. They mended the rips in their clothes, blew their noses when they were little, put them to bed when they got home drunk, cleaned off their vomit and their urine, darned their socks and polished their shoes, trimmed their nails and their corns, scrubbed their backs in the bathtub, groomed their hair, gave them enemas and laxatives and all sorts of infusions for fatigue, colic, or sadness. By performing these tasks, by taking their places in doing things their masters refused to do, the old women slowly robbed them of an essential part of themselves . . . and their avidity grows as they get their hands on more things, and they covet more humiliations and more old socks as a reward for their service, they want to get their hands on everything. That's why Brígida cooked up this scheme to rob the child Iris carries of its eyes and hands and legs; they want to hoard it all in a great common pool of power they'll use someday, who knows when or for what purpose. Sometimes I get the feeling that, instead of sleeping as they should, the old women are very busy pulling things out of drawers from under their beds and out of little bundles—things they've been hoarding, such as their employers' fingernails, snot, rags, vomit, and bloodstained sanitary napkins—and reconstructing with all that filth a sort of photographic negative not only of the employers they robbed it all from, but of the whole world. I feel the weakness of these old women, their misery, their state of abandonment, as they gather and concentrate in these passageways and empty rooms, because the Casa's where they come to store all their talismans, to pool their weaknesses in order to form something I recognize as the reverse of power: no one's going to come and snatch it from them here. And because Jerónimo de Azcoitía, who's always been afraid, although his arrogance won't let him confess being afraid of anything—yes, afraid of ugly and unworthy things—has never in his life dared set foot here, although the Casa was his until he got rid of it. He shouldn't have done it. It was a mistake. One should hang on to things, there's always some hope left. This will have to be set to rights somehow because, even if you don't know it, your line will continue, and your son must go on being the owner of this place; the old women—the seven of us, now that they've stripped me of my sex and taken me into their number—are looking after *his* son in Iris's womb. I'll turn him over to Don Jerónimo so that he'll inherit the Casa, in spite of the papers that have been signed; it will never be destroyed and I'll be able to remain safe here where Don Jerónimo will never come looking for me, because he's terrified of the corns the old women pared and stored away, the hairs that clogged the washstand—the things they still keep bundled in rags and little scraps of paper. Yes, Don Jerónimo, don't look down on them, they're not as stupid as they look, or rather their stupidity's a kind of wisdom. That's why they hold on to those amulets, to hold you in check. Don't come sticking your nose in here! I was once your loyal servant, Don Jerónimo. I still can't quit, even if I try. You branded me on the ear like a sheep. I go on serving you. And by serving these parasites, by being the servant of servants, by laying myself wide open to their mockery and obeying their orders, I'm becoming more powerful than they because I'm accumulating the waste products of the waste products, humiliations by the humiliated, mockery by the mocked. I'm the seventh old woman. I'll take it upon myself to watch over the Azcoitía about to be born. Iris's vomit, which I washed from the kitchen tiles, anointed me. I keep it wrapped in a floor rag, with my books and my manuscripts, under the bed, where all old women keep their things.

THE FIRST THING I had to do was win them over. If I didn't find a way to dazzle them, I'd be accepted by them in name only, even though I'd groveled for them. I let a few days go by while I laid my plans, letting them go on barely talking to me and watching me on the sly. Until I finally told them one afternoon that I thought I'd found the ideal spot for Iris to give birth without being found out, and where the seven of us in on the secret could bring up the boy without interference from anyone.

I led them to the court way inside the Casa where I live, which also serves as a graveyard for statues of saints. The crones crossed themselves as they passed the chapel, we traversed the court with the orange trees and disappeared into the inner recesses of the back part of the Casa, that jumble of courts and less important ways only I know about, finally reaching my court.

The moment I threw open the door and heard their cries, I knew I'd won them over, simply by opening the door for them to the graveyard of broken plaster saints. They moved forward, with shouts of joy, among headless St. Francises; St. Gabriels Archangel minus their pointing finger; maimed and crippled St. Anthonys of Padua; Virgins of Mount Carmel, of Perpetual Help, or of Lourdes, with their robes faded and their distinguishing features blurred; Holy Infants of Prague with neither crown nor hand holding up the globe, the feigned elegance of their ermines and the pretense of their painted plaster jewelry faded by sun and rain; saints with faces all gone; a monster with his arms girdling the world under a pair of feet that Brígida said she'd keep because they were part of a Virgin . . . hold her for me someplace, Mudito, we'll see if we can't find the rest of her and put her back together . . . angels without wings; unidentifiable saints, in pieces, without limbs, of all sizes—fragments the years and the climate have been wearing down, the pigeons have been dirtying on and the mice nibble at, figures whose eyes and belly buttons the birds peck at . . . yes, of course, you just can't throw out fragments of objects that have been sacred, they must be treated with respect, they can't be thrown into the garbage, along with scraps of food or the sweepings of the house, no, they must be brought to the Casa de Ejercicios Espirituales de la Encarnación at La Chimba, where there's room for everything. . . . Mother Benita asks me to fetch my little cart, I load the fragments on it and pull them to my court for time and the rains to finish off, while new and almost identical statues ordered from the manufacturer take their places at the same altars; maybe this version of Bernadette won't be as cross-eyed, maybe the ringlets on the Infant Jesus will be a different yellow, maybe St. Sebastian's stance will be less suggestive. Mother Benita isn't familiar with my court. She's made it strictly off limits to everyone. It's Mudito's court. He picked it out. It's his business if he feels at home there. Let him have at least that much for his very own to do with as he pleases, a speck of privacy, we must respect the poor man's right to it, he's been sacrificing himself for us here for so many years.

The old women spread themselves about my court, crying out, going down on their haunches and standing up again, waving chunks of plaster—hands, torsos, crowns and draped clothing—poking about, exhuming obscure saints only they can recognize: St. Agatha and St. Christopher and St. Raymond Unborn . . . no, Dora, dear, that habit belongs to St. Francis, not St. Dominic de Sales, don't you see the brown cowl . . . I must say the St. Sebastians are very hard to find . . . hey Amalia, find me the other piece of the Virgin . . . it's going to be difficult, but here's a head with stars, maybe it belongs, I'm not sure, and I'm going to look for the raised finger of this St. Gabriel to complete him and get hold of some Virgin—who's going to notice?—and I'm going to fix up an Annunciation on top of my bureau.

"The Incarnation is on March twenty-fifth . . ."

"What a shame we don't celebrate it here at the Casa."

"But the birth of the Christ child, nine months after Saint Gabriel Archangel appeared, we do celebrate that . . ."

"But the Incarnation isn't the same as the Annunciation . . ."

"I don't know, let's go ask Mother Benita."

"Let me see if I can find the archangel's finger."

I had to clap my hands like at recess in a girls' school to draw their attention and jolt them back to reality and all we still had to do . . . this way, don't trip, I live here, this is my room and this is my bed, there's nothing else here except this back door leading to a cellar, the cellar I have ready for you, I'll always be here, watching the entrance . . . Not only had I sanded and waxed the dried-up wooden floor and papered the walls with old newspapers but, since I know what each lady keeps stored in each suitcase and each crate in each one of the cells and what cells belong to the ladies who never come near the Casa, I sacked several wardrobes that hadn't been opened in years, dragging out rugs and pictures, beds with blankets and bedspreads, night tables, a brass crib with knobs and a canopy—everything a bit damaged but, after all, there was nothing you could do about it, and in the dimness of the cellar everything took on luster in the eyes of the old women.

I also would have liked to bring out those baby things of Boy's that Inés keeps in a special trunk in her second cell, the one she visits most. I couldn't get up the courage, because Inés knows exactly what she has and where it's stored. She's very particular, neat, meticulous. It's been years since we last opened the trunk with all Boy's baby clothes, that brass-riveted black trunk filled with marvels intended for the Azcoitía her obstinate womb wouldn't produce. As I went around looking for things for the Boy another will produce, I couldn't help opening the trunk to see the marvels again and I had to struggle against the temptation to steal at least some little thing, a bib embroidered by her nurse, Peta Ponce, or a pair of pale-blue woolen booties. I didn't. Maybe when Inés returns from Rome in defeat, after making a fool of herself with the beatification, and she has nothing to keep her busy or help her kill time, she'll come to the Casa more often than ever, to live in her limbo of junk, which she'll arrange and clean and rearrange. If she asks who tampered with anything in her cell while she was away, I'll tell her it was me, that I gave the place a general cleaning and, to be on the safe side, put mothballs in the clothes. Then she'll give me a tip, which I'll accept as one more insult to add to all those I've been collecting.

For two months now, we seven old women have centered our lives on getting ready to receive the child. We're sewing clothes for him, fine diapers from a linen sheet contributed by Brígida . . . we must take apart this shawl and wash the wool thoroughly, it's first rate, not like the wool nowadays that has electricity, and we must knit the shawl again; let Dora do it, there's nobody can touch her when it comes to knitting. And we'll decorate the brass crib with this tulle, it's a bit patched up but what can you do, we're poor, but the child's going to have a crib that, in this dim light, will look fit for a king. What a shame Brígida passed away and won't get to know him! She was the most enthusiastic of all of us. Of course the child will fetch her from her grave and take her to heaven with the rest of us. Oh well. That's life. The months ahead will be the hardest because Iris isn't feeling too strong, she's always got a headache and she's swelling up too much . . . María, you're a medicine woman, you should know what's ailing the girl.

We have to make her lie down . . . Are you feeling bad again? This is your bed and this is the crib for us to play mamma with you, let's make believe you're lying in bed and you're the mamma . . . But if we're going to play mamma, Miss Rita, then why don't you bring me a doll, even if it's only something put together with rags like when I used to play with dolls when I was little, the game's no good without a doll, you all told me you were going to give me a big doll that opens and closes its eyes and says mamma, as big as a real baby, but it's not true . . . Wait, Iris, get some rest, we'll give it to you soon . . . there, be a good little girl, go to sleep, you don't have to know you're expecting, you'd be scared to be expecting a miraculous baby and you might tell on us, and they'd steal our baby.

The cellar's warm from the brazier we keep burning day

and night so that the paste Mudito used to paper the wall will dry. Amalia irons diapers. María Benítez wants to have everything ready well before the birth of the child; she stirs sweet-smelling mixtures over the fire, waits for them to come to a boil, throws in other herbs that change the fragrance in the room, a little more water; she strains the concoction, lets it cool, pours colored liquids into bottles . . . This is good for stopping the bleeding, you never know with the firstborn. And this is a disinfectant. And this is for applying compresses if her headaches continue. Don't talk so loud, let her get her sleep . . . Look how she sleeps! Come look, isn't she pretty? Look at her face, like a saint, just like the full-color picture Mother Benita has of the Virgin in her office. So young! What a lovely complexion! Isn't it a fact that the complexion becomes lovely during pregnancy? . . . Not always, sometimes it ruins their faces something awful, but not hers . . . Damiana, the new woman, brushes Iris's cheek ever so lightly with the back of her hand. Smooth as silk . . . She's going to look so beautiful with her baby, breast-feeding it here in this warm hidden room with its nice smell . . . We all walk around on tiptoe, so as not to wake up the future mother, in awe of the mystery enclosed in her womb and protected by the successive layers of intestines, flesh and skin that are designed for that purpose.

Iris lies asleep on the bed with her thumb in her mouth, sucking, while we go about the timeless female chores of preparing the room where the child will be born, luxuriating in the ceremonies that rouse our instincts that lay asleep on the brink of the pit into which Brígida fell such a short time ago. On that also solemn occasion, our instincts were revived in a similar way by the splendor of the rites of death, and we cried and lamented because old women have wept from the beginning of time, and it's good to weep and lament at funerals, as it's good to rejoice at the birth of a child. Our voices, the endless ball of yarn that is our talk, crack with age . . . shshshshsh, not so loud, don't wake her . . . the sound's embellished now by a new warmth, a shyness, as if our voices had come to life again with the prenatal ritual, a liturgy in which no man can take part.

Yes. Iris's pregnancy's a miracle, the old women say. Once

that fact was established, no one questioned it; it was simple for us to accept the absence of a man in the phenomenon of pregnancy. How happily we forget the act that produced the child and replace it with the miracle of a mysterious incarnation, in a virgin's womb, that banishes man! We need to reject the idea of a man's participation in it. We have to cast off the fear that a father may come to claim his son. Why should we share a son with a man when the woman does all the suffering? He doesn't know how to bring it up; she's the one who makes the sacrifices, the man has only the pleasure of begetting it—a dirty, ephemeral pleasure that, if we ever feel it, is long forgotten and replaced by the pleasure of being a mother, speaking for those of us who've had that happiness . . . Iris is chaste. No man has any claim to what she carries in her womb. No one must find out. No one must see her. Here in the cellar Mudito prepared for us—he's such a good person, what would we have done without him?—we're reaching total fulfillment as we iron and fold diapers for the child, knit shawls—lots of shawls so that the infant won't have to be wrapped in just any old rag when the weather's cold, it's dangerous for babies to catch cold, although I hear that there are suppositories now that stop a runny nose in a couple of days, we must buy some—and attach yellow lace with silk ribbons to the hangings suspended from the brass-knobbed canopy . . . here's the rubber sheet to keep the mattress from rotting with the child's urine, rotted mattresses stink something awful and hardly any air at all gets into this cellar, we'll have to make bibs with this silk, it's so pretty, so fine, blue silk because it's going to be a boy . . . no, silk bibs are no good because you can't hand-launder them, don't you see, we're not going to be sending them to the cleaner's each time the baby messes, and babies mess a lot of bibs, several a day . . . but really, Amalia, silk's washable, how can you be so stupid as not to even know that? Natural silk, the kind that's really fine, has to be soaked well and aired out a little and then, afterwards, with an iron that's not too hot . . .

5

IT'S NOT BECAUSE I heard footsteps or voices or felt someone keeping an eye on me in the passageways that I got up and
searched through this unfathomable place. But it slowly occurred to me, and later I confirmed it, that someone had started
to wander through the courts, empty rooms and passageways,
just like me. It wasn't the old women, who take to their lairs
early, and it wasn't the nuns, who drop exhausted into their
beds as soon as the inmates shut themselves in their courts.

It was you, Iris. I guessed it from the beginning. I couldn't
see or hear you, but I was suddenly dead certain that you, your
obscene and unwashed childish body, were sharing the same
space that enclosed me. Why? You should have been in bed like
the other orphans at this time of night, not awake and wandering around, perhaps, or standing still, not very far sometimes
from where I was walking. Why did you roam the passageways
at night? So, you were only pretending, then, to be as scared as
the old women of the dark, cobwebs, ghosts, *imbunches*, cave-
ins, attackers, Don Clemente, savage dogs, holes you might fall
into, gypsies who steal children, black shapes? Spook, spook!
. . . Why were you following me? Or were you after me? No,
you weren't after me. It was just that someone, and the someone
had to be you, was upsetting the balance of the emptiness of my
nights, in which nothing could touch me—not even memories,
not even desire—in which there was no other presence to
threaten my vulnerability. You must have sneaked out of bed to
find out if I stay up very late every night, sometimes all night,
roaming through the Casa, because I never sleep, and you
crossed my path, at first without showing yourself, only forcing

me to feel your presence occupy the space of the night, my territory, and demanding that I follow you without seeing you, like a dog tracking down a scent.

In the daytime, I'd be crossing a court in order to go and plug up a broken pipe that threatened to flood a cloister, and I'd see you, playing hopscotch with the others, near the linden tree . . . before going on my way, I'd watch you from the shadows of the cloister, to see if you let on or gave me a sign. I don't even know if you saw me. But perhaps you did see me, because you can see without looking and know without realizing that you know. I'm not in love with you. You don't even arouse one of those aberrant urges men my age feel around someone young; you're an inferior being, Iris Mateluna, a blob of primary existence wrapped around a fertile womb that's so much the center of your being that everything else in you is superfluous. But your presence in the Casa commanded my attention so utterly that I had to stop waiting for chance meetings during the day and I began to invent ways of running into you, and I'd wait for a signal. You never looked at me. You didn't see me. I'm used to eyes sliding over me without finding anything to fix on. Why did you follow me, then, if you didn't mean to acknowledge my existence by so much as a glance?

You dragged me from one side of the Casa to the other, every night, to look at the street lamps reflected on the roof tiles, to listen to the automobile horns, to hear the children on stifling summer nights as they played on the sidewalks at *make a wish your lordship, man-dee-run dee-run dee-run, I wish I had a son, man-dee-run dee-run dee-run, and what name shall we give him, man-dee-run dee-run dee-run* . . . and I'd follow you everywhere, lest you get lost and be trapped forever in some secret room; you might disappear, and I might be left without the solution to the puzzle of the nightly walks we take together without seeing each other . . . you wanted to open the sealed doors that lead to the floor above, to pull the nails out of those crossed boards, force the doors open, but they didn't give when you pulled . . . open this door, open it for me, don't be mean, it's easy for you to open one door so I can go up and see what's up there, what can be seen from the next floor, I've never seen it . . . Finally, one night, after several nights of going to that door and standing in front of it and then going away, you tried to open it once more and found the nails loose, and the boards gave because I'd understood your orders, I'd carried them out; I opened the sealed door so you could go up and roam through the galleries on the next floor, I opened the dormitory with the twenty bedsteads for you and I unnailed the windows so you could see the city. My surrender appeased you.

You went up to look at the street from the window every night. You made friends with the neighborhood children. You talked to one another by shouting, you danced in the window recess for a group that gathered round to cheer you on, with new children joining it all the time. You stopped wandering aimlessly through the Casa. With you up there, leaning out the window with your back to me, the peace of the corridors and the galleries was again my refuge.

I know that when a person gives in to a demand he humiliates himself, and appeasement's therefore only temporary; the greedy monster will bare its claws again to demand more and more and more. I know you'll soon stop going to the window and, not satisfied, will exact something else, or the same thing only more and more of it, taking up the chase again through the galleries at night, hunting me down to make me give you what you demand, and I don't want to obey you, Iris Mateluna, you're nothing but a blob of animated meat, you've already forgotten your father, who slit your mother's throat in the bed where the three of you slept, as you're now forgetting everything by substituting one elemental desire for another—the light at the top of a wall, then a street window, now . . . I couldn't give it to you and, to keep you from demanding it, I fled until I was swallowed by the depths of the Casa. But I could never hide, you always found me and made me follow you, getting me all confused in passageways I thought were a labyrinth for everyone but me, making me lose my bearings in the Casa, *my* Casa, that I know like the palm of my hand, so that when I believed I'd led you to a nook where I was going to lock you up forever, I suddenly found myself in the vestibule court. How?

I hid in the geranium bushes that adorn the imitation rocks

of the Shrine of Lourdes. I watched you remove the crossbar from the street door. Then I heard you jiggle the latch, without forcing it, only to check what you already knew, that it was locked, like every night . . . click, click, click . . . but, more than anything, to let me know your command. No, Iris. That's going too far. My hand tightened around the keys in the pocket of my dustcoat. I didn't have to obey you. After all, you'd never seen me follow you. You simply took it for granted, and if your vengeance for my not obeying you became public, all I had to do was play dumb. You remained waiting there, pretending to play with a stone, like in hopscotch, giving me time to open the door. I wouldn't do it. I didn't obey you. And you disappeared through the cloister, hopping on one foot, kicking the small stone. You'd left the crossbar off. As soon as I saw you'd gone, I ran over to put it back, it's my job, I've been doing it every night for years and years. I don't like the street door to be left without the crossbar at night.

You did the same thing several nights. You lifted the bar off, jiggled the latch back and forth when you knew very well you'd find it locked—click, click, the message was the thing— and then you went off to your court. You must have hidden for a moment in order to fool me, and three minutes later, as soon as I put the bar back and hid, you returned to the door and found the bar back in place. You didn't even bother to jiggle the lock. Why? After all, you'd found me out, hadn't you?

"Mudito."

"Iris," I answered. You didn't hear me, because no one can hear my voice. I didn't come out of the shrine. But you'd tricked me into complicity. The following night, as soon as the Casa was asleep, you went to the door. You found the bar off. Unlocked. I fixed my eye on you; you didn't act strange or surprised. You opened the door and went out into the street.

I waited for you among the faded cement rocks. I could close it. Lock it and put back the crossbar. Make up a fast story to account for your disappearance: you were stolen by gypsies, the bogeyman ate you, you ran off with your father the murderer, you were swallowed up by the darkness of the Casa, you fell into a draw well, you got lost in the lofts, you must have got trapped inside some trunk you were poking around in; they'd believe anything, and only I'd know that I left you out there in the clutches of the police.

But, before I could act and leave you to your persecutors, the door opened and you came in after less than ten minutes outside, humming out loud, much too loud, as if you couldn't care less about keeping things secret anymore because I, your accomplice, had the mission of covering up for you. As you passed in front of Our Lady of Lourdes, you crossed yourself without interrupting your song, *negra, negra consentida, mueve tu cintura, muévete para acá,* or the rhythm of your steps. You didn't even wear a guilty smile. Nothing. You were singing away. Yawning. And you slipped out of sight.

I went over to bar and lock the door. You hadn't even bothered to pull it shut after you; I found it standing wide open, and the terrifying night reigning peacefully outside.

From time to time I'd leave the street door open for her to go out. I'd remain waiting for her to come back, sometimes for hours on end, until daybreak, concealed by the stonework of the grotto. But I no longer remained in the Casa. Iris was out there making her way through the tangle of places she wandered around in—places with insatiable dogs, very tall houses and buildings from which she was being spied on, bridges, avenues, cars, noise—dragging me around until I was ready to give myself up to Don Jerónimo.

Because she dragged me. Like a dog. On a chain, so that I'd have to follow and obey her blindly, my will broken, chained to stop me from going into the road and being run over by a car, chained to a collar with teeth in it, the kind used for training dogs; there's nothing to do but obey because it cuts when we resist and the barbs cover the collar with blood when our owners decide to tug and we hold back, even if only a little, until at last our neck is so raw that we can't resist anymore and obey because it hurts too much when we don't obey and try to assert ourselves and have our way, until finally, to stop the pain and the bleeding when she pulls on the chain and the teeth stab, I reach the point where I can't even remember that perhaps, some time far far back in the past, I had a will of my own or tried to disobey even after I knew what it meant to disobey. I don't disobey here. Iris is cruel and sometimes she makes the barbed collar pierce my neck just to watch me suffer as I follow her at a distance without losing sight of her but without letting her see me, leaving her free to talk to her friends . . . someone buys her a Coke . . . she goes into the place where the neighborhood boys get together to play the soccer pinball machines and sell or exchange secondhand magazines . . . they teach her new dances and the latest hits . . . they play ninepins and marbles and read comic-strip romances to her . . . She follows the Giant around, helping him distribute multicolored handbills: *Martín Pescador's. Easy payments. Mattresses. Beds. Blankets. Household items. Prices are so low you have to bend over to see them.* In the neighborhood they call her Gina, the Giant's girlfriend. All so innocent, so childlike.

What if Don Jerónimo ever finds out that Iris is dragging me all over the streets? He probably wouldn't recognize me, changed as I am into Iris's dog, stripped of everything of the Humberto I used to be, except the still-active principle of my eyes. I'm just another old woman, Don Jerónimo, I'm Iris's dog, let me rest, don't harass me, I've already served you, being a witness is the same as being a servant, you know that servants appropriate a part of their employers, you do know it, how can you help knowing it when I confiscated the most important part of you when you had me on your payroll to witness your happiness.

The happy couple's perfect bliss seemed as far away as a scene with beautiful mountains that I couldn't touch but that held my eyes in thrall with the wonder and desire Jerónimo and Inés recognized and needed in me and they couldn't live without my eyes there to create their happiness for them; the pain in my eyes, fixed on them, was the source of the happiness they consumed. It wasn't me—I could be discarded anytime—it was my envy Don Jerónimo had on salary all those years. But I kept my eyes, laden with power; that's mine, I won't give him my eyes,

I'm not going to let anyone take them, that's why I keep them hidden here in the Casa, so that you won't take them away, Don Jerónimo, so that you'll never come close to happiness again, that's why I'll never go out into the streets with Iris again, not even disguised as her dog, even if she kicks and beats me to make me obey, I won't go out, I'll stay where I am, as still as a plaster saint here among these artificial eyes.

THE GIANT AND IRIS made a happy couple. My eyes feasted on them, imagining the details of a relationship that excluded all others because Iris adored her Giant . . . he's going to marry me, she told the orphans, look at his picture here in this Mickey Mouse book, see, here's Pluto following him, it's him, the Giant, who comes to the neighborhood several afternoons every week and I wait for him on the balcony upstairs to make a date with him, I yell down, later, Giant, later, when the old ladies have gone to bed, wait awhile, I'll be coming down to meet you with that unusual face of yours that's bigger than any you see in the streets.

They used to sit on the curb and talk. I don't know about what. I can't imagine what anybody can talk about with someone like Iris Mateluna, the only thing she knows anything about is her own body, because the rest—her home town, her dead mother, her jailbird father—were left behind in another incarnation that has nothing to do with this one, the one that's the Giant's girlfriend and whose name isn't even Iris, but Gina, it's more modern . . . Gina, Gina, do a little dance for us, Gina, swing those tits, right here on the corner; come on, Gina, come on, shake it, shake it . . .

I must be truthful: at first Romualdo, the Giant, who's not really bad, was affectionate to Iris, like an older brother, as if he was sorry for her. He used to tell her things . . . the Turks who were the owners of Martín Pescador's were good-hearted; whenever somebody came in to buy something and said that the Giant had handed him one of their multicolored handbills, the Turks give me a tip, they let me sleep in the store, they put down a mattress for me near the entrance and let me have the keys, they trust me a lot, I'm the watchman and the Giant too, and some days I come to this neighborhood and other days to a different one, but I like to come around here better, I'd like to live in this neighborhood, when I start making more money I'm going to find myself a room around here but who knows when that'll be, and sometimes I hide in a place farther down the street and take a siesta, nobody bothers me there, there's a junky car, just the chassis, without any wheels or motor, and I get into the car and take a nap.

I followed him to the vacant lot. The huge painted papier-mâché head had taken over the driver's seat. Romualdo, curled up in a fetal position, was asleep in the back seat. I stuck my hand through the glassless window. I touched the Giant's painted eyes gently. Romualdo woke up yelling at me:

"Let me alone . . ."

I let him alone.

"Whadya want?"

"Nothing."

"Then beat it."

Frightened to death, covering my mouth with one hand and holding my throat with the other, I ran down the streets that my voice had turned into an abyss filled with the faces of people who all resembled Don Jerónimo, Emperatriz, Peta—cruel people who were going to report me to Mother Benita, who'd tell Father Azócar that my whole life was just a story . . . Mudito can talk, he has desires, his eyes have extraordinary power, he knows things, he can hear, he's a scoundrel, a dangerous person . . . and then they'd take away my keys, the ones I use to lock myself in here so that no one will catch or find me out, yes, they'd call up the Archbishop and he'd get in touch with Don Jerónimo to come and get me, because now I wasn't going out on Iris's leash anymore, but alone, on my own, as if I'd forgotten that Dr. Azula's going to gouge out my eyes and keep them alive and seeing, in a special jar, to be turned over to Don Jerónimo and then, only then, will Don Jerónimo forget about me and let me return to the trash heap where I belong, because my eyes are the only thing he's interested in, he always ignored everything else I had, but not my pained, longing, envious eyes, the rest of me was nothing to him, nothing, nothing. The accusing word had escaped from me and now it was burning my throat.

Locked up in my room and in bed, I'd never be found by them. Fever, shaking. The old women bundled me up like a baby. The swelling in my throat would have kept me from speaking even if I'd wanted to. Swallowing was impossible with this pain. My tongue all red, my palate bleeding, my throat rasping . . . no, no, cover me up, old women, bundle me up good so I won't shiver with fever, so I won't be able to move my arms, hands, legs, or feet, hurry, sew me all up, not only my parched mouth, but also my eyes, *especially* my eyes, so their power will be buried deep under my eyelids, so they won't see, so never will *he* see them again, let my eyes burn up their own power in the darkness, in the void, yes, sew them up, old women, in that way I'll make Don Jerónimo impotent forever.

THE OLD WOMEN gave me very effective liquids to make me well again. María Benítez swabbed my throat with methylene blue. My mouth was a cavern I didn't dare show because even the old women laughed at my purple lips and my gray tongue . . . another swabbing, María, even if I don't need it, because, with my mouth blue like that, I won't dare go out into the street, because people would think I was crazy and would have me put in the insane asylum . . . we can't go on swabbing you forever, Mudito, your fever's gone, you can get up if you want, you're better now, and look, look at the sun, see how wonderful the autumn sunshine is . . .

I knew the Giant's habits. He was lazy. In spite of all his talk about fantastic tips, he was unhappy with his job and the miserable pay. It was exhausting, and humiliating besides, to walk the streets with the great big silly head on, passing out handbills nobody was interested in but the children who folded them over and over again into little boats they floated on the thin streams of water that ran down the drainage ditches in winter. He worked as little as possible. In summer the heat inside the head was stifling. When it was cold out, he shivered in his cotton print suit. He improvised himself a kind of home in the abandoned Ford on the lot: blackened tin cans for making tea, faded magazines, cards to play solitaire with, on the windshield he pasted the picture of a long-haired musical group, the Giant's head separated from his body and resting on the front seat. I used to hang around and look at it. I watched Romualdo sleep. But I didn't want him to sleep and I touched his eyes once again.

"Again? What the shit d'ya want?"

The Giant's head. That's what I want. To rent it from you, Romualdo, and put it on so I can be part of the happy couple. You were going to ask me what I wanted it for, but you broke off in the middle of your sentence and asked, instead, how much? A thousand. A slow smile under your black mustache exposed your teeth, white and wet . . . okay, but no, I can't, the Giant's my job, the Turks own the head, it's real fine quality, take a look, papier-mâché, real light, with a shiny Duco finish, see, the Turks keep an eye on me to make sure I cover my territory right and give out the handbills, see, this is advertising . . . the Giant's head is theirs, not mine, if it was mine, shit, I'd gladly lend it to you, but it ain't mine . . .

"Fifteen hundred."

"For how long?"

"I don't know, an hour, maybe a couple of hours . . ."

"It's a deal."

The question "What for?" made your tongue burn . . . but what the hell, why should I stick my nose in other people's business, this guy's quite a weirdy, that's some voice he's got and a purple mouth like the polar bear in the zoo . . . and fifteen hundred never hurt anybody. Who's gonna notice I'm not the Giant if people don't even look at the Giant in the street anymore when he goes by, and besides he's promised to pass out the handbills just like it was me.

"It's a deal."

You take the monstrous head from the front seat, the ungainly, red, freckled mask of a clown, puppet, demon, doll, with a fixed smile that reveals a couple of rabbit teeth.

"Okay. I'm gonna dress you up, then."

"Okay."

"Fork over the fifteen hundred."

I hand them to him. Romualdo gives me a pair of flowered cotton trousers. I pull them on.

"Does the jacket come next?"

"No, first the head, then the jacket, to cover up the strings I'm gonna tie the head on with real good."

You put it over me, as if going through a ritual, like a mitered bishop crowning the king, eradicating with this investiture each of my previous existences, every one of them: Mudito; Don Jerónimo's secretary; Iris's dog; Humberto Peñaloza, the sensitive prose writer who offers us, in these simple pages, such a deeply felt and artistic vision of the vanished world of yesterday, when the springtime of innocence blossomed in the wisteria gardens; the seventh witch. All of us dissolved in the darkness inside the mask. I can't see. Now, besides lacking a voice, I'm sightless, but no, there's a slot here in the Giant's neck to see through. No one will think of looking for my eyes in this papier-mâché puppet's throat.

"No, it's not comfortable, I'm not gonna tell you different, and you're such a weakling. But see how it's not as heavy as it looks at first? That's because it's real fine, the papier-mâché's real thin, top quality. You gotta get used to lookin' through the hole, that's the main thing. And don't go crashing into anything and smashing up the head, look, the boss is mean as they come and this head's very expensive. Okay, the jacket now."

The officiant of this ritual withdraws, bowing, respectful. The jacket's also flowered, but of a different shade, as if they'd made my ceremonial finery with remnants of washed-out cotton. I take one, two ritualistic steps, holding on to the crown, but I quickly realize that it's not hard to keep in place up there because it's my own head, yes, I feel the breeze caressing it and my hand touching my cheek . . . goodbye, Romualdo . . . I speak loud and clear, I see the city enfold me as benignly as the Casa, because no one can find me out under this costume. I see everything from my heroic height, greater than Don Jerónimo's, with my magnificent papier-mâché eyes up there reviewing the glass towers of my realm. I turn down the first street I come to. I don't bother to look at the name because I'm so sure I'll get back without losing my way, I know I'm not going to get lost because the Giant doesn't lose his way in his own realm.

It's the dimmest time of day. If something doesn't happen to save things, everything can vanish before my extraordinary height. The long block of houses is a single wall with doors at regular intervals, mauvelilacroselemon, patches of different colors around each door identify the different houses, plants, a bench, the dripping faucet, the trough, the whisk broom, the lady who bought a liquefied-gas stove, the begonia in the dented kettle; each door opens into a different world, and the row of bare walnut trees along the sidewalk Gina and the Giant come walking down together, laughing and she asking him for a Coke, which he buys her, and tossing up handbills whose colors can't be distinguished in the tricky light at this hour, whirling about in the shower of them as they fall, catching the paper slips she's tossed into the air for the pleasure of spinning around among them. A little woman takes a brazier out to the sidewalk. The water running down the gutter reflects the blue flame that will flash from the charcoal and transform it into glowing embers. Gina gives her a handbill.

"Is it a circus, miss?"

"No, it's a movie."

"Who are you?"

"I'm Gina, the Panther Woman of Broadway."

Muffled-up figures whispering on street corners, lowered voices and deadened sounds wait for the spell to be broken in order for them to open up and become real. Iris doesn't lead me, I lead her, because I'm familiar with all this, despite the dim light of the open streets. Farther on, an old woman squats, hunched up like a gargoyle as she blows on the coals of another brazier . . . the trail of sparks invades the street, it's the crackling breath that comes out of this benign witch's mouth to ignite the street lamps that light our way. The gaudy magic of the electric lights suddenly alters the character of things, pale blue turns to violet, pink to purple, lemon to orange, and the figures stationed on street corners like conspirators . . . I recognize them, the light gives them away, but not me, I go on being the Giant who knows everybody in the neighborhood. The Four Aces smoking on a corner aren't plotting against anyone, they're Aniceto, Anselmo, Andrés, Antonio . . . now come on, Rosie, let go your boyfriend, don't be so brazen, can't you see the lights have gone on? . . . and we walk on down the sidewalk where more women come out to light their braziers, they blow on the coals and gossip . . . look at her, the kid from the Casa, the one that dances, Gina they say her name is . . . that's not right, her name's Iris, she's the Giant's girl . . . let's go across the way . . . and we hold hands and, for an instant, the headlights of a car that comes to a halt transfigure us into spotlighted, theatrical figures that are bigger and more beautiful than the everyday things the hours slowly deteriorate, as the lights, for the moment during which the car stops, isolate and stop time for us, and we don't hear the angry shouts of the driver, who moves on and disappears into reality, around other corners. I take Iris to the vacant lot. We hide behind the Ford.

"Let's play yumyum."

Nothing in me hesitates. Neither my burning hands nor my eager sex organ, as she caresses my papier-mâché cheek, nor my weight, which crushes her and makes her writhe and close her eyes . . . you're my love, I want to marry you 'cause you're so beautiful, 'cause the yumyum you're playing with me's so delicious, don't leave me . . . more yumyum, more . . . and I give her more and more love because I can give her love till she's had her fill . . . till it's time to separate . . . I have to go, Giant, I promise to spend a whole night with you so we can go have fun and dance together . . . yes, Gina, and I'm going to buy you pretty things . . . when, Giant, tell me when . . . I don't know, I can't promise you anything because I don't know when I'll be able to come back to this neighborhood again, because if the Turks catch me they'll give me the boot, don't you see I've got to do all the neighborhoods around Martín Pescador's, I don't get anywhere covering the same section all the time when I'm supposed to be advertising and that's what they

pay me for . . . when, then, Giant . . . I don't know, I don't
. . . well, I'll wait for you every evening in the upstairs window,
I'll be keeping an eye out to see if you come and then I'll come
out and meet you, give me a signal and I'll come down . . .
goodbye Giant, the yumyum was so nice . . . goodbye, Gina
. . . and I wait for you, hidden among the grotto's rocks.

6

I'M THE FATHER of Iris's son.

It's not a miracle. I have something Don Jerónimo, with all his power, has never had: this simple, animal capacity to produce a son.

I used to watch secretly for Romualdo's arrival. I'd fix it so that Iris could go out; I'd go out a little later and replace my head with the Giant's, and we'd play yumyum. Romualdo'd begun by buying a gold watch on the installment plan, paying for it with the money I gave him every week to lend me the Giant's head. After María Benítez examined Iris and said, yes, of course she's expecting, I'm telling you, all it takes for these kids to get pregnant nowadays is just a whiff of a pair of trousers . . . that same afternoon, I told Romualdo I wouldn't be needing the Giant's head anymore.

"What about my watch?"

I shrugged.

"How'm I gonna finish payin' for it?"

I didn't answer. I wanted him to find a solution for himself, so that he couldn't blame me for anything.

"I'm gonna have to rent the head to other kids."

Exactly. Right. Good for you, Romualdo, you're the perfect middleman. Iris already had my son inside. The rest of her, what surrounded the womb occupied by my son, was useless and had to be destroyed. I glanced at Romualdo. Hadn't he been too quick to find the right solution? I suggested that he himself use the Giant's head to make love to Gina.

"I don't need no mask to fuck that nutty kid."

I asked him if he'd already done it.

"No."

I didn't believe him. I had to be absolutely certain that Iris's child was mine. I made him a bet. If he could seduce Gina without the Giant's head I'd give him money to pay the balance on his watch.

"It's a bet."

I watched the whole thing through the Ford's rear window. When Romualdo started taking off the head, Iris howled, "*Chonchón, chonchón!* Don't let him fly off! Witch, evil one!" . . . the head toppled to the ground. Romualdo tried to pin her against the car's trunk but she scratched his face, screaming and crying and crossing her legs and biting his hands, with which Romualdo, excited and infuriated at the same time by the blood and the struggle, was trying to grab her breasts. I put on the head while they battled. I pulled on my cotton clothes and went and rescued her from the hands of her depraved attacker, leading her down the street with my arm around her, consoling her . . . yes, he's a bad man, it's a sin to get mixed up with anybody besides the Giant, I'm the only one that's good, Gina . . . here, take the handbills and start giving them out . . . here, I brought you these magazines as a present . . . look, do you want me to read you this love story? . . . here, take this blue velvet ribbon for your hair . . . and a pair of stockings . . . a Coke . . . some triple-flavored ice cream.

Romualdo said okay, I'd won the bet. He admitted he wasn't too worried about the watch anymore because he had two customers for the head, two young kids who, of course, weren't going to give him fifteen hundred, but, a thousand, yes . . . who knows what they wanted the Giant's head for, but how people got their kicks wasn't his affair.

As I let her go out a lot, Iris soon built up a fabulous clientele in the neighborhood. I used to hide in the Ford and watch her make love with the Giant's head that was me, screaming with pleasure, rolling her eyes, giggling, stroking my cheek, wallowing in my stare. Before long, her reputation spread through the city like wildfire. They came from faraway sections of town to make love with her. Schoolboys and skilled workers were the first, then flashy types in cars. Later on, I saw gentlemen in automobiles driven by uniformed chauffeurs; diplomats in cutaways; generals with glittering epaulets; distinguished academicians with their chests covered with medals and gold braid; potbellied priests as bald as kneaded greaseballs; landowners; lawyers; senators who, while they made love with her, made speeches about the terrible state of the nation; movie actors made up like whores; radio commentators who knew the absolute truth. They switched their finery for my costume, their faces for mine, which revitalized them, and they rubbed up against Iris, burying their hands in the soft flesh that was in love with me and which, from the Ford's rear window, I could see as it yielded to my pressure and my caresses. On one occasion, I saw Don Jerónimo de Azcoitía step out of his Mercedes Benz, talk to Romualdo, pay him, and put on my head. I wasn't afraid; Iris's womb already belonged to my son. On the contrary, I felt sorry for Don Jerónimo because, ever since I left him so many years ago, he tries everything, anything, even the wildest things, to recover his potency, which I keep under guard in my eyes. He's not so young anymore. His lackeys find him abnormal opportunities and experiences, to which he subjects himself out of desperation. But it's no use. You know it's useless, Don Jerónimo, without my consent. And the poor devil remains locked up in his own shell, unable to break out, his sex organ as limp as an empty sleeve.

When I saw him and didn't feel afraid, I knew immediately that I had to run a risk, but a worthwhile one: to let him disguise himself as me and make love with Iris Mateluna. All I had to do was watch him make love, to play, for a few moments, my old role as witness to his happiness and his triumphs.

My head swallowed him up. And, when Iris arrived, he leaned her against the wall and they threshed about, but to no avail . . . what's wrong, darling, that you don't make love to me without a stop anymore, you love somebody else . . . no, no, wait, I'm tired, wait a minute . . . the anguish of his urgent need, his desperate appeal for my help, his invocation of my name, his yearning for my gaze, reached me through the cotton of the too-tight costume. When I felt his anguish ready to explode, I peered through the Ford's rear window to let him see me, Humberto Peñaloza, the one who'd gone along with him to whorehouses when Inés was pregnant and he was afraid to touch her and destroy the perfection of the child that was to be born . . . come on, Humberto, come with me . . . and he'd keep me there, watching him enjoy himself with some whore or other . . . see what a man I am, Humberto, watch me satisfy her, I'll bet you couldn't satisfy her like me with my unusual virility and the strength of my arms and the skill of my legs and my hands and my tongue and my lips, look, Humberto, watch her, listen to her scream, now you know what a poor fish you are because you can't arouse her like me, anguish lashes and tortures you, let your envy crush whatever's left of you, eat your heart out because you can't do what I can . . . that used to be, Don Jerónimo. Not anymore. Today you can, because I allow you to see my face framed in the window of the car, to see the torture in my eyes as I watch you, the torture that still inhabits the pupils of my eyes; that's why you were able to make Iris Mateluna scream with pleasure.

I'm not too callous to imagine the torment that made Don Jerónimo waver when he saw me: whether to leave Iris right there, interrupting his only display of virility in many years, in order to come after me and take possession of me at last, or stay with Iris and, in enjoying her, lose me and lose himself forever. He caught only a glimpse of me and knew it was I, not a hallucination. I fled and hid in the Casa. I'm never going out again. What for? Everything's ready, my plan laid out; I won't have trouble persuading Don Jerónimo that my son who'll be born of Iris Mateluna's womb, is his, the last Azcoitía, yearned for, waited for, and sought for in Inés's womb. Don Jerónimo will acknowledge him. He'll give him his name and his lands. He'll become the owner of the Casa. He'll keep it from being destroyed and it will go on as now, a labyrinth of solitary, decaying walls within which I'll be able to remain forever.

What would my father, my poor father, a grade-school teacher, say now if he knew that a grandson of his, my son, the great-grandson of the railroad engineer on a train whose soot linked together two or three towns in the South, will bear the Azcoitía family name? No, no, Humberto, we must show respect for the order of things, one can't deceive or steal, to be a gentleman one must begin by being honest. We can't be Azcoitías. We can't even touch them. Our name's Peñaloza, a surname that's common and ugly, a name used in cheap jokes in skits, a symbol of the irremediable ordinariness that clings to the ridiculous stage character and seals him up forever in the prison of the plebeian appellation I inherited from my father. Because I did have a father, Don Jerónimo, yes, even if you don't believe it, even if you never bothered to find out or ask me about that undeniable fact, I had a father, and I had a mother, and I had a poor sister who was the first to disappear, swallowed up by a humiliating but necessary marriage to the owner of the corner stationery store where I bought my first notebooks to scribble poems in, and she postcards with pictures of Cleo de Merode, Pastora Imperio and La Bertini, she's lost now and perhaps already dead in the rainiest town in the southern provinces. The only forebear my father could recall was his own father, the railroad engineer, beyond that there was only the obscurity of people like ourselves, people without an individual family history, people who belonged to the masses, among whom identities and deeds are blotted out and give birth to popular legends and traditions. He couldn't remember our history, he was only a Peñaloza, a teacher of spoiled little brats who frayed his nerves. I can hear my father's voice as he sat by our lamp that reeked of kerosene. At night, after eating a stew that contained more of my mother's imagination than of substance, my father would lay plans for me so that somehow I would fit into something other than the emptiness of our sorry family that was without a history or traditions or rituals or memories, and the wistful evening would unfold to the accompaniment of the hopeful voice in which my father expressed his longing to make something of me, and the insistent leak in the ceiling that stubbornly contradicted him as the drops of water plopped into the chamber pot. My father used to explain everything to me. With the vehemence of his tender but bashful hand that wanted to touch mine, without daring to, across the tablecloth embroidered by my sister, who succeeded in disguising the ordinariness of our table but not its disequilibrium, he'd demand, without demanding, that I amount to something . . . Yes, Dad, of course

I can, why not, I promise, I swear I'll be somebody; instead of this sorry Peñaloza face without features, I'll acquire a magnificent mask, a great big, bright, smiling face with well-defined features, a face no one can fail to admire . . . And, pitying me and my futile undertaking, my mother would lift her eyes for a second look at me, and then she'd fix them again on the skirt she was mending for some wealthy matron in the neighborhood. Someone. To be someone. From the very first, my mother knew I'd never be anyone. Perhaps that's why I've forgotten her so completely, in spite of her sacrifices to help us with dreams she didn't believe in. I never felt close to her, she remained on the periphery, looking after us, but she was never immersed in what impelled my father, my sister and me. To be someone. Yes, Humberto, my father used to say, to be a gentleman. He had the heartrending certainty that he'd never be one. That he wouldn't be anyone. Not have a face. Not even be able to create a mask for himself to hide the avidity in the face he didn't have because he was born without one, without the right to be called a gentleman, and that was the only way he could have had one. All he had was the ridiculously careful diction of an insignificant schoolteacher and his tormenting anxiety about paying his debts on time, things I found out later aren't essential attributes of gentlemen. He used to repeat to me, there in the lamplight, in the chill that smelled of stew and things that have gradually been turning soft with humidity, that he wasn't, of course, naïve or given to fantasy, that he knew I'd never get to be a real gentleman like so-and-so, for instance, who appeared in the morning paper on the occasion of his signing a treaty establishing a boundary line with a neighboring country, or like the big shots who promoted censorship or industrial development or agricultural laws, or like those others who had a hand in mining and land transactions and ran this tiny country where *everyone knows everyone else* and where, nevertheless, no one, absolutely no one except other sorry little teachers, no one except the butcher on the next block and the woman farther down the street who had the vegetable stand, no one who was *someone,* knew us Peñalozas . . . no, he wasn't a fool or a dreamer who aspired to my being a gentleman like them, because he took it for granted that it was impossible; one is born a gentleman, he's such by the grace of God and, after all, I'd always, come what may, be a Peñaloza and he was nothing but a grade-school teacher in a suit covered with chalk from the blackboard and my grandfather had been nothing but an engineer on a locomotive that spewed out a lot of smoke but swallowed up few miles. No. Not that. He didn't have his sights set that high. But, who knows, with sacrifice and hard work I might get to be something at least bearing some resemblance to those men of importance my father was in awe of, a facsimile that would build a bridge—any kind, provided it was honorable— that would enable me to brush up against them. Why not? Wasn't there a good deal of talk about the rise of the Middle Class in our country? Who knows whether, belonging to the Middle Class—he mentioned this class with a reverence exceeded only by the reverence with which he pronounced the word *gentleman*—I mightn't become something similar? An attorney, for example, a notary public or something of the sort, or a judge. And go on to politics. It was well known that many young men like myself, without pull, money, family connections or fine presence, young men as obscure as myself and bearing family names very nearly as ridiculous as mine, had secured a foothold in politics and crossed the barrier, becoming *someone,* escaping from the limbo inhabited by the faceless. My father was unable to escape. He never tried. For him the world of the others, of those who were *someone* in their own right, *known people,* was of magical proportions and fabulous consequence. How was it possible that my poor father's imagination, so feeble and limited in other respects, was so overflowing in this regard? How dinner was served to them. What their houses were like. What they talked about, the words they used and how they pronounced them. Where they went on a Sunday, or any other, afternoon. The money my mother earned by taking in a little sewing, he spent on all the magazines and newspapers, and he'd suddenly be tempted by something very expensive, like an issue of *La Esfera.* While we waited for supper under the lampshade with its torn fringes—my lazy fat sister would sigh as she looked at elegant drawings by Bartolozzi and read Villaespesa's poems and García Sanchiz's descriptions of enviable part-naïve, part-depraved women who received their female friends in mysterious places called *boudoirs* to talk about lovers—my father turned the pages of the newspapers as he read, absorbed and inspired, and speculated out loud about those beings whose faces couldn't be denied because he, who didn't know them personally, could recognize them. He wanted us to hear what he was telling us about them, feel the poison of the monotonous sadness his dream was injecting into us. I remember his small myopic eyes behind his glasses as he read the news, those eyes whose color I can't remember because he sank out of existence, still dreaming.

Much later, when he no longer existed, if he really ever existed and all this isn't an invention of mine, I was able to prove for myself that his obsessions were pure fantasy, because people who are *someone*, people with faces, were almost like us: they too ate onions, the chairs they sat in weren't far behind ours in ugliness, the refinement that so dazzled him was nonexistent save in a handful of families who'd done some traveling. The majority of *known people* turned out to be ignorant, avaricious peasants who used dirty language, had noisy parties in whorehouses, beat their wives, cheated on them. They were, in fact, very much like us and the other teachers and the butcher and the grocer. But if anyone had suggested this in front of my father at the time, he wouldn't have believed it. He knew otherwise. He read all the papers. He was very familiar with the great things they were capable of, things from which he as well as we were excluded. How could he help being affected by this exclusion, how could *I* help being affected when I saw how much it affected him? Because my father wasn't an upstart . . . Don Jerónimo, I won't allow you to believe this, not for a second . . . I can't even say he was an ambitious man who coveted material things; for instance, the thought of encouraging me to make a fortune as a stepping stone to becoming *someone* never crossed his mind. No, my father was something else, a dreamer, an obsessed man, a creature desperate because he was excluded from his own dreams . . . He lived with an eye forever on the impassable barrier that separated us from the possibility of becoming *someone*. Yes, don't think it was something else; my father was an outsider, a man gnawed from within by his yearning, a sad, heartsick man. And, on the corner where we used to stand watching them, in the afternoon as their carriages headed toward the park, he'd point out the fortunate beings, one by one, who didn't have to kill themselves, as I would, to have faces of their own. He taught me to recognize those mustachioed gentlemen reclining alongside fabulous ladies who, to my childish eyes, were fleeting blurs beneath pink or lemon parasols.

One morning my father was leading me by the hand downtown because, with the little nest egg accumulated by my skeptical mother who nevertheless sewed on and on, he was going to buy me my first dark suit so that, from childhood on, I'd feel the need to dress like a gentleman. And a white shirt, a black tie with ready-made knot, and a pair of patent leather shoes—the time-honored outfit destined to become shiny at the seat and elbows. Imbued with his passionate yearning, which would perhaps be appeased for a few moments while he bought me my gentleman's disguise, I was happy as I accompanied him, as if the new suit would throw open a window on an unsuspected landscape where everything was possible . . . yes, why not, Papa, I'm going to be somebody, a famous lawyer, a famous politician, look at the excellent grades I get in school, listen to what my professors say about my progress in history, in English and French and Latin, yes, I'm going to study hard, I'll do everything you tell me, I promise, I'll make your dream come true and you won't suffer anymore, I can't bear to feel the sadness you feel . . . The suit we were going to buy had to be good, wear well, be roomy enough so that I wouldn't outgrow it too fast, not too lively, so that people wouldn't notice it was my only suit, and as cheap as possible. We stopped to window-shop at all the elegant men's stores downtown, although we knew it wouldn't be there but on credit, at some second-rate shop in our neighborhood, where his signature wouldn't be questioned, that I'd acquire my first disguise. But it was spring. Women were dressed in light clothing. There was no charge for looking in store windows filled with magnificent things.

Suddenly my father gave my hand a jerk. My eyes followed his stare and joined it. Coming down the sidewalk in that morning's bustling crowd was a big but graceful man, with very pale hair, with lively eyes filled with what I interpreted as elegant disdain, dressed as I'd never dreamed of seeing a man dress: all in such light shades of gray as pearl, dove, smoke: pointed shoes, suede spats, and gloves that were neither gray nor eggshell nor yellow nor white and were made of very soft pure leather that was almost alive. He wore binoculars that were slung across his chest, and he wore one glove and held the other in his hand . . . As you passed me in the morning crowd, the glove you held in your hand brushed against me here, on the arm, right on this spot. I feel it right now, after all these years, still burning me under these rags that also cover up a bullet wound.

Then, as I watched you, Don Jerónimo, a gap of hunger opened in me and I wanted to escape through it from my own puny body and merge with the body of that man who was passing by, to become part of him, even if I were only his shadow, to merge with him or tear him apart completely, to dismember him and appropriate everything of his—his bearing, his coloring, the self-assurance with which he looked at everything without fear because he needed nothing, because not only did he have everything but he was everything. I, on the other hand, was nothing, nobody; that was something my father's stubborn longing had taught me. He was pronouncing the syllables of your name—Jerónimo de Azcoitía—which I managed to make out from his stammering. I kept staring at you, both of us hungry, as you paused on the steps of the bank and spoke with a group of friends or lifted your gray silk hat to greet some acquaintance going by.

We went on our way only because we couldn't stand there all day with me staring at him forever, which is what he and I both wanted. My father sighed. The man had come so close to us! And we didn't know him so we couldn't greet him, and we didn't even know anyone who knew somebody who knew him and could at least mention our name in his presence. Not only because that might be enough to assure me of a career, if Don Jerónimo deigned to fit me like a tiny cog into the many wheels he manipulated, now that he'd finally returned from Europe and, it was rumored, was going to get married. That wasn't the only reason my father sighed that morning, Don Jerónimo. He also sighed because of the other thing, because of the incurable longing that showed in his pained look and was beginning to be my own as well. My father sighed because of the pain of the unattainable, of a fantastic idea, of the sorrow caused by what's beyond one's reach and by the humiliation that comes with the knowledge that one's incapable of attaining it. It was that pain that caused my father to sigh that morning, Don Jerónimo.

7

WHAT'S UP, TITO? How'd it go?"

"Lousy."

"How come?"

"She wouldn't let me. She laughed the whole time because a dog got into the Ford and watched us from the window and then got out and licked her leg and started tugging at my pants. Look, it ripped them right here. And Gina laughed so hard she wore herself out, the dumb dame. Then, when I thought I had her pinned good, with her panties down and her legs open, because we thought the dog had gone away, it showed up again, looking at us from the window, like it was laughing, licking its chops and wagging its head like it was so good, see, and it made me laugh so hard my prick got soft, and I couldn't do a thing, and Gina started laughing too and pulled her panties back on and there I was with hot nuts . . ."

"Shit, what a stupid business! Tough luck, kid, there'll be another time. I'm gonna get you a real hot piece. But it's Gina's fault. That yellow bitch dog's always trailing her around and I hear it loused it up for other guys too. That's not fair. I'm gonna talk to Romualdo. He's gotta give you back your money."

"Yeah. I didn't even get to kiss her tits."

Gabriel's Tito's older brother and owns the store that sells secondhand magazines and comic books. He's managed to buy two pinball machines the neighborhood kids are playing soccer on now. Romualdo scratches his mustache as he prepares to make a terrific play. As he argues, yells, kibitzes, he displaces more air with his gestures than all the other boys. He's older than they. He's thinking of buying himself a motorbike. Some of the kids get fed up playing with him, because he thinks he's stronger than others, they remark . . . I don't know what's got into him but he's changed a lot since he bought his watch . . . might as well go over to the racks, where we pick up magazines, leaf through them, put them back in the racks, take out another one, show it to someone leaning on the counter or sitting next to Gina on the bench. After school we spend the afternoon in Gabriel's store, especially afternoons when it gets dark early, pretending we may buy a comic book but have to go through it first to make sure we want it. Gina lets the guy reading to her feel up her legs . . . Tito hid my head and my costume behind the counter . . . his face is narrow like a bird's, blotchy with acne.

"Hey, Romualdo, you've got to give my brother his money back. Gina didn't let him do nothing to her."

"Look, kid, I don't know what kinda things Tito tried to do with her, I hardly know her. I rent out the Giant's head to anybody who wants it, but I don't know why they rent it, that's each guy's business, so don't come cryin' to me."

"Don't come around here and try to play dumb, see."

"If your brother was a real man, a real stud, he'da screwed her good."

"My brother's just a small kid, so don't come around saying nothin' bad about him to me . . . better watch it."

The Four Aces come over to listen.

"Yeah, kid. It's not my fault about that there bitch dog. Tito rented the Giant's head from me, I gave him a good deal because he's your brother, but I don't have to know what he rented it for. I ain't interested."

We've moved away from the magazines because there's going to be a fight here, and we forget about the soccer machines. The Four Aces like Tito a lot. They're not going to stand by and let somebody like Romualdo gyp him, Tito's just a young kid and he wanted to find out what it's like . . . you've got to start somewhere . . . Aniceto is the angriest of the bunch.

"You lousy pimp."

Romualdo lets him have it in the eye. The other three Aces jump him but Romualdo breaks free . . . don't give me any shit, Gina's a whore and her name isn't even Gina, what's she to me, cut the crap, you asshole kids, this is what I get for goin' around with babies like you, I've had enough, I'm leavin', where's my head, I'm takin' my head with me and I'm never comin' back to this neighborhood. Andrés has ducked behind the counter and reappears wearing my head, holding it in place with his hands, dancing.

"Take off my head, you lousy kid!"

"*HIS* head, *his* head, Mr. Big's head, just take a look at him . . . Don Romualdo's head . . ."

Gabriel squares up to him. We all get into the argument, this isn't going to stop here, things are beginning to warm up . . . Don't be a lousy bastard, Romualdo, all of us around this neighborhood know what you do with Gina and with the Giant's head, using the kid because she's not all there . . . Romualdo better get out of here, we say, he's not needed here, since he bought the watch with the phony gold chain he thinks he's Mr. Big, shit, nobody's swallowing all that crap about the motorbike, Romualdo better get out of here, he's a fuckin' pimp. But he'd better give Tito back his money first.

"I'm not givin' it back."

Andrés takes off my head.

"I'm tellin' you to hand over my head. Hell, I'm leavin' this neighborhood for good and that's all there is to it . . . what a crummy neighborhood . . ."

"Oh yeah? Crummy, huh? Look, Don Romualdo wants *his* head, we'd better not disobey him, now that he's so important and is going to buy himself a motorbike."

"Don't they say he's shoppin' around for one of those great big black automobiles, with chauffeur and all?"

"Seems to me I heard he preferred one of those white soft-top jobs . . ."

"Or red."

No one pays any attention to Iris, who's whining because she sees Andrés throw my head on the floor. The clitter-clatter of the machines has stopped. Now, Gina, cut it out, stop being a crud, somebody hold her . . . looks like she's blown her lid, and she's not gonna let us talk with *Don* Romualdo.

"Hey, Anselmo, I want you to know that *Don* Romualdo, because we've got to call him-*Don* with all due respect, now that he owns the Giant's head and is buyin' himself an automobile, Don Romualdo says would you people be good enough to let him have *his* Giant's head, because it might get dirty."

"That's very strange. I didn't know it was his. I thought this Don Romualdo was a poor slob, a fuckin' pimp who didn't have the price of a park bench to drop dead on."

"Hey, how could you think anything like that!"

"Watch out, Antonio, don't you go hurtin' *Don* Romualdo's head, it's the finest."

"Let me have it, shit . . ."

Gabriel steps up to him.

"Don't come yellin' around here, Romualdo. And you too, Gina, shut your face, don't be a shit. The cops might come and close down my place, can't you see it's not licensed, I don't have a permit. Come off it, Gina, shut up, you shit, hold her good, you guys, we can't even hear ourselves talk."

Iris throws herself on the floor and puts her arms around me. The dust on the floor makes my eyes itch. Andrés grabs me, starts beating me as if I were a drum, while the other three Aces and Tito improvise a dance . . . tum-tum-tum-tum . . . as if their pummeling palms didn't hurt me . . . tum-tum-tum . . . they pick Iris up off the floor . . . tum-tum . . . come on, Gina, shake it, more, more, once more around . . . and Romualdo breaks up our group, charging at Andrés, who drops me. Iris whimpers, defending me from the others who want to pick me up, all of us want to get hold of the Giant's head because the little game's getting to be real fun, and between us we all bring down Romualdo. The Four Aces pin his back to the floor, he kicks, spits, but soon quits kicking and spitting. We don't even have to pin him down now. He puts his hand on my hooked nose. He's surrounded by our amused, menacing boyish faces hovering over him and Iris, who's blear-eyed with tears. Gabriel says to Romualdo:

"You degenerate."

Romualdo opens his eyes, which are despoiled of their black precision. Slowly, he tries to struggle up, leaning on one elbow. The Four Aces stop him by stepping on him. He sprawls again, without touching me now, his eyes shut, his muscles limp, his mop of hair all mussed up, his clothes in tatters. Only his lips move:

"Another guy's the one who's to blame, not me . . ."

He wants to squeal on Mudito. He wants to explain who he is. But he doesn't know who I am. No one around here knows me, because I never go out. They don't know I'm protected by the papier-mâché walls of the Giant's head, taking it all in.

"What other guy?"

He can't explain. He says:

"Gina's a whore."

"Hey, Gina, Don Romualdo's saying nasty things about you . . ."

"Who? It's the *chonchón* . . . bah, he's mad because I wouldn't let him play yumyum with me. He's a pain in the neck, it's a good thing the Giant stuck up for me . . ."

"Isn't it true that he's a poor slob?"

"He never gives me any presents."

"Scare him, Gina . . ."

Iris snarls, makes scary faces, curling her lips, clenching her teeth and mussing her hair.

"Grrrrr, I'm the Panther Woman of Broadway, grrrrr, and I'm going to eat you alive grrrrr . . ."

"Eat him up, Gina."

"Kick him."

"Grrrrr, I'm the Panther . . ."

The knot we form to take in the show has closed in so tight around Romualdo and Iris that our legs hide me . . . you haven't looked at me in the past five minutes, Iris, and you've already put me out of your mind; you're the Panther Woman of Broadway, who dances on street corners and in the window at the Casa, carried away now by this new game that blots out and replaces previous games, doing a savage dance around the prostrate body of your victim. From the floor, through the tangle of legs, I watch you kick off your shoes, raise your skirt to show your thighs, wiggle your behind, and we applaud enthusiastically, we always applaud you, you stamp on Romualdo and the rest of us also place one foot on his chest when he tries to get up. Andrés looks for me.

"Look, Romualdo, look at this beautiful little thing I found. You want it? Take it, play ball, Aniceto . . ."

My head flies through the air, Aniceto catches it, he tosses me and Antonio catches me, he too throws me, I fly, fly, my sinewy ears beating the air above the kids, who play with me like a huge ball . . . Tito . . . Gabriel . . . Iris screams in terror: the *chonchón*, it's the *chonchón*, Romualdo's a witch and he turned my Giant into a *chonchón* . . . I fly from hand to hand until someone drops me. The blow bruises one of my ears. I don't have any hands to feel the piece of gray papier-mâché that hurts where the paint scraped off.

"Be careful with my head I'm tellin' you, you sons of bitches."

"Precious darling's head . . ."

"Don't get it dirty, you bums . . ."

"Look, Romualdo. See? It's peeling here on the ear. We'd better pull out that whole little chunk."

Gabriel wrenches off a piece of my ear with one pull and holds it up like a trophy, while we yell and cheer. Iris snatches it away from him. She whimpers and drops on her knees next to me, crying because she knows what's going to happen, what, fired up by all the fun, we're going to do to me, and I have no hands to defend myself, no legs to run, only eyes to see with and this delicate skin of paint to protect me from the blows.

"Look, look at what you guys did, its ear, you'll have to pay to get it fixed."

"Nobody's goin' to fix it, Romualdo. You're all through."

They pass me from hand to hand, they drop me on the floor, they toss me through the air, Iris runs after me to save me, they let her take me and then they snatch me from her hands . . . no, no, don't kill the Giant, he's good . . . they send me flying again, bruised, aching, scraped, the gray papier-mâché showing through the coloring on my skin, they drop me, my hat snaps off but at least that doesn't hurt. Romualdo drags himself over to where I've been left, at the feet of one of us, Anselmo's. Just as Romualdo's about to cover me with his body to protect me, Anselmo pushes me away with his foot and sends me rolling to the feet of Aniceto, who asks:

"How about it, you gonna give Tito's money back?"

"No."

In answer, Aniceto kicks me right in the face, his foot sticks in my torn flesh, which clings to the foot that's destroying me, now, once again, I have no face, my features have started to vanish. I can hardly see out of my crumbling eyes, I'm going to lose my sight and yet I won't be sightless because none of me will be left, Anselmo begins to walk around with his foot jammed in my face, he tramples my insides, he drags his foot, the rest of us split our sides laughing . . . hey, wow, that's a hot one, this son-of-a-gun Aniceto's funny as hell and that moron Romualdo chasin' him on all fours all over the floor to catch the head . . . as if it weren't just a pile of papier-mâché strips now, as if he could still save it, dented and scraped as it was, its paint peeled off, and silly Iris chasing after Romualdo, chasing the head and Aniceto, what can she want it for, now that it's only good for the trash heap; in trying to get it away from Aniceto she cracks it open even more and screams with terror . . . look . . . she was left with the hat in her hand . . . put it on, Gina, it's too big for you . . . dance with the Giant's hat on, Gina, dance, like that, that's the way I like it, baby . . . give me the hat so I can put it on . . . me . . . no, me, I want it . . . let's split it up, an ear for me . . . no, no, please, what are the Turks gonna say to me, how'm I gonna pay for the Giant's head when I'm so poor and they're gonna kick me out of my job on account of you kids, you'll have to pay for the head, look, a piece of eye, you lousy kids, I'm gonna call the cops so they can throw all of you in jail, beginning with you, Gabriel, your business is illegal so you'd better watch your step . . . just go ahead, Romualdo, you bastard, if the cops come we're gonna tell them you're makin' money off Gina, the poor nut, and she's a minor, in fact all of us are minors except you, you're twenty-one and you're a draft dodger . . . look at the way the poor kid's cryin' like an idiot, with the Giant's nose in her hand, she must think it's a prick, an enormous, limp red prick . . . must be the Giant's prick, then, since it's so big . . . dance with the prick, Gina, dance, stop cryin', cut it out, don't be a fool, dance, I tell you . . . Throw me another chunk of head, Gabriel . . . me, Antonio . . . me, Tito . . . I want the other ear . . . let's split these rabbit teeth—one for you and one for me . . . when the cops get here and we tell them you're makin' money off Gina, who thinks she's a dancer because the poor kid doesn't even know she's a whore, the cops won't like what we tell 'em, not one bit, so you're the one who's gonna lose out . . . come on, somebody go call the cops, nothin's gonna happen to us, but it will to you, for bein' a pimp, a degenerate . . . No, Gina, don't go, because you gotta be a witness when the cops get here . . . look at how Andrés is dancing with the nose put on like a cock . . . it's all that's left, I'm down to that, my enormous nose, changed into a phallus, nothing but a drooping hollow phallus made of papier-mâché, all limp, without blood or nerves . . . someone grabs me . . . awright, let go my cock, you faggot . . . let me take it away from you, the Giant's cock's for me, I want the Giant's cock . . . where can the stupid fool Iris have gone off to, she's missing the best part . . . she ran out because she's scared of the cops . . . come on, Anselmo, kiss my prick if you want me to give it to you, shove it up that one's ass . . . come on, let go, you're cracking it . . . why are you ripping it when they've already torn all the rest to bits, look at the pieces on the floor, all the gray chunks of the Giant's head, and it was so pretty, no don't destroy that, it's all that's left of me, leave me that . . . they grab the phallus away from one another, they tear me apart, fighting over my magnificent phallus, now in two, in three, pieces . . . nothin's left now and that silly Gina went off, she'd have loved to have us stick this great big cock into her, they say she wriggles like mad when she's gettin' screwed, she shuts her eyes and opens her mouth and sighs like a movie actress when she kisses and says yumyum is so nice, baby, more yumyum, where could Gina have gone off to in this rain. Too bad, now that there's no more Giant she's not gonna come to the upstairs balcony anymore to dance for us . . . that silly Gina was a good dancer, yeah . . . she may be silly but, when it comes to dancin', the kid's real sexy . . . Romualdo crawls as far as the door.

Nobody gives him a thought now. He gets up, breathing heavily. Only then does Gabriel notice him.

"Don't you leave."

"Give back the money, Romualdo."

"Thief."

"Degenerate."

"Corruptor of minors."

Before the kids even have a chance to dry their eyes full of tears from laughing so much, Romualdo escapes down the darkened street. They bunch up in the door and yell: degenerate, miserable dog, deadbeat, pimp, thief, as they wave pieces of the Giant like handkerchiefs in farewell. None of them tries to follow him because the rain's coming down harder and, in no time at all, Romualdo disappears down an unlighted street.

"Great."

"The party was great."

"It was worth the money he screwed you out of . . ."

"Yeah, sure, you had fun and I paid."

Gabriel tells his brother not to worry, he'll give him back the thousand pesos. The Four Aces slap him on the back . . . take it easy, man, what's a thousand pesos, we're gonna get you a real broad, a real broad you'll be able to get into bed with naked, none of that shit of gettin' into a papier-mâché head to fuck a chick standin' against a wall, that's okay for feelin' a dame up, yeah, but for fuckin' there's nothin' like a bed with a hot little broad in it, the whole night . . . I can't stay out the whole night, my parents would raise hell because I'm kinda young . . . I'll cover up for you, Tito, I'll get around Mom so that you can go out and spend a whole night with a hot broad in a bed like you should, otherwise it's no good, and I'm gonna give you the thousand pesos so you'll forget everything and start puttin' enough money together to pay for a real good broad.

Some of them have been going off one by one in the rain. Andrés suddenly says it's late and leaves the store. Gabriel asks the rest who are still there to help him straighten up the place a little, because his mother told him: okay, I'll let you have the only room on the side street of the house for your secondhand magazines and comic-book business, but I'm old now, I've got a lot of chores and I'm not about to kill myself sweeping your shop or giving you a hand . . . So now you guys'll have to help me clean up all this mess you made.

Gabriel picks up the magazines scattered all over the place. He arranges them in racks. Someone fools around with a pinball machine, then leaves it and pushes together pieces of Giant, halfheartedly, with his foot. Aniceto and Anselmo drift over to the pinball machines but don't even touch the mechanical players, they're only dismal substitutes for the heroes of real prowess. They yawn, leave the shop and dash out into the rain without saying goodbye, each going off in his own direction. Only Aniceto lags behind, helping the brothers collect the litter in pails. If they find a piece that's too big for the pail, they break it to make it fit in. There's another section of eye here, white, with black points shaped like a star, and this must be the lobe, I say, of a red ear. When it's all cleaned up, Gabriel discovers the Giant's suit, limp and faded, behind the counter.

"Hell, we forgot all about this."

"What are we gonna do with it?"

"It's no good for anything."

"Let's give it to Gina."

They laugh.

"The dope was like she'd lost her mind."

"Do you think she really believed . . . ?"

"She's a whore. She puts us on with this thing about the Giant."

Aniceto stays in the doorway watching the rain, waiting for it to let up before going out. He remarks:

"I don't think so. She's kinda strange. They say she's like only playing a game when she screws, not serious like other chicks who're less ignorant, and she says yumyum, yumyum, like baby talk. Listen, sometimes I feel like goin' and tellin' the nuns about it, something bad could happen to this kid and, besides, they say she's an orphan."

"Don't get involved, Aniceto."

"Yeah, don't butt in."

"Right, I'd better not get mixed up in it."

"Okay, go on, Aniceto, I wanna lock up."

"She must get bored in the Casa."

"And Romualdo, he was really upset."

"We're never gonna see hide nor hair of that guy around this neighborhood again. And what are the famous Turkish gentlemen gonna say to him, eh?"

"Okay, Aniceto . . ."

"Don't hang around talkin'."

It's letting up.

"I'm goin'. How much did you pull in today?"

"I don't know. Not much, I don't think, I'll check the cash box tomorrow. I never pull in much when it rains. And what really bugs me is that some wise guys took advantage of the racket you guys started, and stole some comic books like brand new that somebody'd promised to buy."

"I'm leavin'."

The brothers don't answer. The houses across the way have turned purplish. The branches of the walnut trees aren't smudges now, they're scrawlings on the light from the street lamps.

"What time are you gonna open tomorrow?"

"Depends."

"Maybe I'll drop by. So long, Gabriel."

"So long."

"So long, Tito . . ."

"Bye."

8

THE CELLAR'S warm and fragrant, lit up by the candle burning in its small candlestick. We seven old women stretch Iris out on the bed . . . This poor child's not well at all. Rita and Dora undress her quickly and start drying her hair, which isn't an easy job, because it's wavy . . . Iris has so much hair, my God, it's simply never going to dry and she can catch pneumonia with all that wet hair . . . they put warm clothes on her: flannel nightgown, socks, sweater, a shawl . . . what else, yes, a hot water bottle at her feet but if the water's boiling we have to get a straw from the broom and put it in the bottle to keep the boiling water from breaking it . . . María Benítez brings over the brazier. They cover Iris well with shawls . . . for goodness' sake, what's happened to this child, we found her soaked through to the skin, sprawled in a puddle in the vestibule court, she didn't even have any shoes on, God knows where she left them . . . They feel her forehead, María Benítez tells us that she's not running a temperature . . . nothing serious, keep her warm, hot lime tea with lemon, make sure she doesn't take it into her head to slip out of bed again, the obstinate child, it's windy and cold and raining. Have the lime tea ready for her when she wakes up, Amalia can start preparing it. She ought to get some rest. Let her sleep.

"We mustn't make any noise."

Damiana's sweeping. Dora's knitting. Rosa Pérez, who's not much good at anything, starts to make compresses, just in case, to stop the bleeding, you can never tell with firstborns, you have to be very careful with them; afterwards, with the second baby or the third, it's easy, one of my aunts had eighteen children.

Our puttering about produces only soft sounds, cottony sounds, with no edge to penetrate sleep. Iris begins to toss.

"Miss Rita . . ."

Rita comes over. We all move in closer. Rita sits on the edge of the bed, she strokes her forehead, Iris feels around for her hand and squeezes it. Forever on the verge of tears, our eyes moisten as we watch this touching gesture.

"How do you feel, dear?"

Iris looks at us in surprise, suddenly peering into a horrifying new world, her lips quivering, fear coming over her tightened features. She hides her hand. She cries a little, and then more and more . . . why it looks as if the poor thing's heart were about to break, what can be ailing her, but it's as though nothing ailed her, as though it were something else, I wonder if somebody told her they condemned her father to death for premeditated murder, yes, I heard Mother Benita and Father Azócar say he was going to be shot.

"Besides, it came out in the papers."

We all turn to Damiana.

"And how do you know?"

"I read it . . . in the paper about two months ago, of course, when his picture was even printed, not bad-looking at all . . . he must be dead by now . . ."

"I'll bet you told her and that's why she's like this."

"Me? Why would I be telling her that?"

We've elected Damiana to take the seventh place, Brígida's, in order to complete the number of seven old women who officiate at the rites of birth and death. Damiana's small, almost a dwarf, with stumpy arms and legs, her enormous mouth as toothless as a nursing baby's, her face a tangle of wrinkles intertwined around a pair of tiny bright eyes. She goes on sweeping. She has no reason to come as close to Iris as we do. She's still too new, the last one of all. But there's no denying that she's very willing, she's happy that we chose her instead of Zunilda Toro, even if they say she was thrown out of all the houses she served in because she was always out in the street. She tries to please, as if she were our servant.

"Damiana, thread this needle for me, I can't see a thing."

"Damiana, the kettle's boiling . . ."

"Damiana, let's see, I guess you know how to make a hole in the nipples for the baby bottle, look, you heat a needle in the fire and wipe it clean and then . . ."

"Iris, take this hot lime tea with lemon, it'll do you good, and don't cry anymore."

Iris doesn't fall asleep. She keeps staring at the ceiling and we try to talk about something else, about dress yokes and sour milk and gas, but we can't help noticing that Iris's eyes are welling up with tears that stain her face. The eyes are sharply defined now in the face from which, suddenly, the baby fat is all gone. We don't recognize her. We don't know what to do. She's starting to whimper now. Damiana, as tiny as a mouse, slips into our circle, looks around, goes over to the night table where the baby's bibs are, takes one and puts it on, crawls into the brass crib decorated with pale-blue hangings, babbling goo, goo, as she looks up with her enormous innocent eyes and, with her tiny hands uplifted, asks to be cuddled.

"Goo . . ."

"Now, Damiana, stop . . ."

"You're going to dirty the crib with your filthy hooves."

Iris looks at the monstrously old baby offering her its tiny arms and saying mamma, mamma as it smiles at her with its innocent eyes and begs her to take it in her arms and pet it—because babies love their mammas to take them in their arms and pet them, and mammas love to take their daughters in their arms and pet them—as it thrashes about with its varicose legs up in the air, with its feet knotted with corns and bunions, with its lined blotchy face, and demands to be petted while slobbering the exquisite bib with its ancient slobber. Rita dries the tears in Iris's eyes, Iris sits up a little and takes a white baby cap with a pompon from the night table. She bends over Damiana and puts it on her. The old woman blubbers and cries while Iris ties the ribbons under her hairy chin. When the bow's been tied, the baby makes a face. All of us, including Iris, go into peals of laughter.

"Take off that cap, Iris."

"Damiana has lice."

"The cap's for your doll."

"Damiana's my doll."

"Your doll has such an ugly puss."

"That's a lie, she's pretty and she says *mamma* . . ."

"Me cold, mamma . . ."

"Hand me the shawl so I can cover her."

We hand it to her. Iris gets off her bed and wraps the crone's hips and legs in the shawl . . . Upsy-daisy . . . upsy . . . we help Iris take Damiana, all dressed up in the cap with the pompon, the embroidered bib, and the shawl, in her arms. The baby starts whimpering.

"You have to walk babies to keep them quiet."

Iris walks back and forth . . . shshshshsh . . . shshshsh, little one, shshshsh . . . until Damiana's crying lets up.

"She's fallen asleep."

"She's going to wake up hungry."

Damiana opens her eyes.

"Me want titty, mamma . . ."

Iris sits on a stool next to the brazier, thoughtful, uncommunicative. She unbuttons her blouse. She takes out one of her heavy breasts.

"Titty, mamma . . ."

"Suck, my little baby."

"Come now, Damiana, take your titty, don't make her beg you, better take it while the taking's good . . ."

Damiana's toothless mouth grabs hold of Iris's nipple and we hold our sides with laughter . . . this Damiana's turned out to be funnier than Menche, she looks like a circus baby . . . what an ugly baby, look at the funny thing you had for a baby, Iris, aren't you ashamed, hide her, better hide her someplace so people can't see her, else she might frighten them or they might laugh at you . . . such a hairy baby, just take a look, I never saw the likes of it . . . and Iris says: no, my talking teeny-weeny doll's so cute, and it feels so good the way she sucks my nipples . . . Damiana, go on, baby doll . . . suck, my little one, and afterwards I'm going to rock you and play yumyum with you and ask the old women to let you sleep in the same bed as me so you can keep me warm, I need to keep warm now, because

I always feel cold even if I'm fat . . . now now, Damiana, you've sucked enough, don't be greedy, taking advantage like that, enough now . . . Iris withdraws her breasts. She paces the basement again with the baby in her arms, patting her on the back to make her burp . . . Iris, slap that dirty old thing on her back real hard, look, if she doesn't burp she'll swell up later and cry and she won't let anybody in the whole Casa get any sleep because, once Damiana gets going, she really bawls, remember how she bawled when Brígida passed away, why they must have heard her all the way downtown . . . slap her some more, Iris, more . . . Finally, Damiana lets out a belch that rocks the basement, and we roar with laughter.

"They must have heard that way over at the Plaza de Armas."

"Mamma, mamma, me make weewee . . ."

"Why, the pig, she'd better not."

"She's capable of it."

"Let's hope she doesn't stain the shawl, it's brand new."

"She has to be changed right away or she'll get chafed."

"Yes. You've got to change your baby, Iris . . ."

Iris lays Damiana down on a towel so that she won't stain the sheet. Rita hands her a brand-new diaper, Amalia brings her the talcum, Rosa Pérez a sponge, María Benítez some salve, Dora rings a bell to amuse the baby so it won't go into a tantrum while it's being changed; babies often do, you know. The mother lifts up Damiana's skirt and stinking petticoat, pulls down her woolen stockings and her wet drawers . . . I need warm water . . . no, not hot, I don't want to scald the child . . . but where in heaven's name did this kid learn so much about babies, why she handles herself like she's never done anything else in her life but take care of babies, look at her, she's got over her grieving, because it was grief she was suffering from, Iris is laughing now, happy, look at the way she laughs at the sight of that useless, lifeless, black vagina that's more wrinkled than a dried fig . . . Almost blind with laughter at the faces Damiana's making, Iris washes the old woman's vagina with great care. It mustn't hurt my precious, she has such a young little pussy, so delicate . . . open it up, Iris, let's see how old and smelly it is—like an asshole, but open it up real wide, don't you know, Iris, that with baby girls you've got to open it up wide in order to wash it inside because otherwise with so much powder and ointment, it gets mucky and an infection can set in . . . like this, inside, gently, but wipe it well so there won't be any filth left . . . gently, like that, like that . . . ah, mamma, mamma darling, I want more, it's so delicious, mamma darling, don't wash me with that rough sponge, do it like this with your fingers, mamma, there, right there, right there . . . my baby girl's darling vagina has to be handled gently, it belongs to my talking doll, and I never had anything but a stick done up in rags when I was little, and she's more fun than the doll they'd promised me, because this is a live doll . . . she's fondling your pussy with the sponge so you'll quiet down, and talk, and say *goo, mamma, mamma* . . . your rough hands, my baby's hands, touching my cheeks . . . I give you two little slaps on your soft buttocks, yes, your buttocks are soft, Damiana, even if the other crones gag laughing because you rock and roll your hips while I keep washing you, washing your vagina with my fingers, with warm water, your hands holding down my arms, my fingers, my fingers, my soft fingertips, in your vagina, I wash and wash it until you sink your nails into my arms and let out that little scream, and you keep very still now, you're not moving your hips anymore, your eyes close. I plant a kiss on your wrinkled belly.

"My baby girl has such a cute little tummy."

Damiana seems to have fallen asleep. Iris hums as she dusts talcum on the black bush. The rest of us want to teach her how to put on the diapers . . . that's not the way to do it Iris, like this, this is how, it's better this way . . . no, like this, Dora, the diaper fits too tight now and then the baby will cry because it hurts and she can get chafed . . . the worst part is when babies get chafed . . . just wait and see, Damiana, you pig, how it's going to hurt when your ass gets chafed because you're such a pisspot . . . I tell you it's better this way, it's how I used to diaper Misiá Gertrudis's babies, and they never got chafed on me.

Each of us goes off to our respective chores. Iris wraps Damiana in the shawl and sits in a corner, lulling her to sleep, rocking her gently in her arms, her cheek against the old woman's scaly cheek, as she croons softly:

The Virgin did the wash, did she,
Saint Joseph spread it out to dry.
It was so cold, yes, verily,
It made the infant Jesus cry.

When the baby starts whimpering again, asking for her breast again . . . mamma, me want more titty . . . Iris takes out her breast and the baby sucks on it once more . . . This baby needs to get some sleep, she just won't go to sleep, better sing her something else, something that'll frighten her and make her fall asleep, otherwise we'll never get through and we won't be able to sleep either.

O sleep, my little darling, sleep,
Or else the bogeyman will steal
Your little bottom for to keep;
You've messed, that's how your diapers feel.

FROM NOW ON, the baby and Damiana are inseparable. We've all forgotten that the old woman's name is Damiana. We call her Iris's baby. The minute we're sure there are no outsiders around, snoopy old busybodies like Carmela with her everlasting complaints or Zunilda Toro, fluttering around us like a vulture, waiting for one of us to die so we can elect her, even if she doesn't know what she'd be elected to, Iris opens her arms, the ugly baby springs into her lap to sit there or snuggle in her arms, and mamma plays yumyum with her . . . yumyum, my good little girl who doesn't make doodoo in her panties 'cause the bogeyman will find it . . . and baby's nose runs and her mamma wipes the hairy nose, and she pees and Iris changes her diapers and, when she asks for titty, takes out her white, heavy breast again and the baby sucks, lets out her little belch and falls asleep. She's generally wet when she wakes up, it's a habit the old women haven't been able to cure her of, despite their protests . . . this baby's wet again, my God, when's she going to learn to warn us so we won't have to slave all the time washing diapers, with all the work we have to do . . . yes, she has to be changed right away, otherwise she'll be chafed, and we all know how awful that is.

Iris spreads Damiana's legs. I'm not revolted by the ugliness of her uncovered privates. On the contrary. The fact that we old women, who are so modest and chaste, are not ashamed to let Mudito see the most jealously guarded part of the body means that belonging to the circle of the seven has removed all traces of my sex. I'm shrinking little by little. I can conceal my sex. Just as I've concealed my voice. And my name, repeated nine thousand three hundred times in the hundred copies of my book that Don Jerónimo keeps sealed up in his library among the bibliographical curiosities no one ever consults, on the shelves to the right as you enter the room with the wood paneling which has been steadily drained of its color, and the furniture covered with the quietest velvet. Without knowing it, he preserves me, watches over me, cooperates with me, helps me, I use him to protect my name, to hide its syllables and see to it that no one remembers them anymore except him; I don't have to worry about myself, because I sometimes forget them, I don't exist, I have no voice, I have no sex, I'm the seventh old woman. I destroyed my intelligence a long time ago by helping Mother Benita clean and sweep and fight what defies fighting . . . What's to be done about Carmen Mora's bunions that are making her walk with a limp? . . . Only chickpeas are left and the women prefer beans and since there's no more coal to keep us warm, Mudito, we'd better start pulling out the floorboards in the rooms at the back of the Casa, and the window frames, and the beams, what does it matter when they're going to tear the Casa down anyhow . . . sweeping, cleaning, sometimes lighting the candles at the altar and beating my breast and tinkling the little sacring bells, helping at a Mass for a God whose inefficacy I know well. I can't hear, I can't speak, what more do you want from me, my sexuality was the hardest of all, but I'm the seventh old woman, my member's a rag of meat and useless skin that's been shriveling up, that's hardly distinguishable from Damiana's vulva. When the sun comes out or the wind blows, we hang out Iris's baby's diapers in the court with the broken saints to dry and air out, Iris's little baby mustn't be without clean clothes. We call Amalia, who's off somewhere in other courts, looking for some statue's missing finger, to come and take in the diapers.

Damiana has shrunk a lot. She's rounder and lighter. She's lost her power of speech, like me; all she says is: me seepy, titty mammy, more titty, goo, goo, me wanna made doodoo, and, very gently, she amuses herself with Iris's nipples, she holds them in her rough fingers, plays with them, munches on them with her rubbery gums, drools on them and laughs, because she's centered the whole universe on those two tips of pleasure that imprison Iris in the dream we've built around her to reap what we want: her son, our miraculous son who'll take us all to heaven without going through death, which it's better to avoid, my son, Don Jerónimo de Azcoitía's son who'll continue our line. We become rapt in conversations about menstrual flows, in the knowledge handed down for generations about baby food and certain ointments, about satin ribbons and rubber sheets. Iris has also changed, replacing one incarnation with another without remembering the one before, as if her memory consisted of matter so slippery that nothing adheres to it. She's no longer Gina, the Panther Woman of Broadway, the Giant's girl. She doesn't remember the Giant. Now she's wholly and completely Damiana's mother. Not a particle of Iris remains outside this new game that's replaced the one before.

But what am I to do with Iris's shell, the useless container that encloses her womb, once she's carried out her specific function of giving birth? I can't permit successive incarnations to go on obliterating previous ones until Iris disintegrates, shredded and divided, bits of her found in dead old women's bundles, or in the bundles we store under our beds—I too like to store away useless objects under my bed, manuscripts I'll never publish and notes and notebooks filled with what we used to call *pensées* in my time, and clippings of reviews that mention my name; I also have my name stored away with the old junk I keep collecting under my bed, I like to hang on to things, I don't want the others to steal pieces of Iris's discarded shell from me, I want her all for myself.

I MEANT TO go down to the basement, because I thought you were alone at the time. I didn't go down. I hung back in the shadows, listening to the two of you, watching you and your horrid baby, who's not your baby because she doesn't say *seepy, weewee, doodoo;* she says Americans Bomb Vicinity of Hanoi, Onassis Speaks, Panagra the Modern Man's Airline, Allende for President, Miniskirts Barred by Archdiocese Cathedral, Fidel Castro Declares Intellectuals Must Take Part in Sugar Harvest This Year, Fi-del Cas-tro, Castro, now, Iris, you have to learn the alphabet correctly: C-A-S-T-R-O, tell me where the A in Castro is in this word, Nikita . . . right, that's the A, you see how you're not stupid and it's not hard, but why do you want to know why they kicked out the man called Nikita if you can't read well yet, better wait before you start asking why things happen . . . but I do know how to read, Damiana, not fast, but I almost never make mistakes, see, here: the entire production of ten thousand mimosa trees sold out, my God, what can they do with the flowers of ten thousand mimosa trees when they last such a short time, Families Spending Season at Panimávida Hot Springs: The Cristi Ramoses—Palma Cristi, Cristi Cristi, Pieyre de Baudoin Cristi . . . what a drag, all those cousins . . . parasites from La Belle Époque . . . I don't know what that means, Damiana, it's in another language I don't understand . . . now look at this, Iris, this is really pretty, the picture of the little dog Laika, the one they sent up to the moon . . . let's see, where's the A . . . right, that's the one, you got it even though it was capitalized, now, you see how this is more fun than all that nonsense about Donald Duck or those love stories in picture magazines, and, besides, it's all made up, Iris, don't you go believing a word of all that pap, it's more fun reading this stuff because they're real things that happen to real people, not to people who look like painted monkeys, you have to read the papers, everything comes out in the papers, that's how I found out about your father . . . yes, yes, have a good cry, you see, now you've started to care about them shooting your dad, at the last moment, that's when, what can you do, my dear, it was fate . . . see how you have to learn to read so you can read the papers and not go on being a stupid ignoramus and let all these old hags use you and make you believe I'm your baby, I'm not, I'm Damiana, and they mean to put the idea in your head that the baby you're going to have is a miracle, that you're a virgin, how can you be a virgin if you got pregnant by sleeping with Romualdo, the boy who owns the Giant's head, who's your baby's father, we have to look for him so he can come for you and marry you and you can have a man to work for you and support you, and you'll take care of the baby, not these old hags, you've got to learn to look after yourself, that's why you have to learn to read, let's see now, what does it say here . . . stop crying . . . what does it say here on this line, Hippie Revolution, I wonder what hippies are, I don't know things anymore, I'm getting on in years, but you might know what hippies are, see, there's a picture, they look like fairies with all that long hair, but they go around with their arms around women so they can't be fairies, and it says here . . . a gigantic Damiana bathed in light by the open glare from the window of newspapers I papered the walls with, her eyes with their sharp pupils peering through that window and she ready to jump through it with Iris, all that light in their faces awestruck by reality, all that precision in the letters, the syllables, the exactitude of Damiana's forefinger as. it picks out the letters and the sentences and the headlines by the light of the candle the old woman, standing beside Iris on top of the bed, uses to pore over that literature, from which all urgency has passed away, by moving the candle back and forth, up and down, all the way up to the ceiling, in search of more news, more sentences, as the pair, appearing enormous, gaze through the window.

I can never leave them alone again. I have to keep an eye on them constantly because Damiana's been deceiving us in order to steal the baby from us and disappear with him into some smelly sty where no one will ever discover Don Jerónimo de Azcoitía's son under her beggar's rags. Every second those two spend together is dangerous. I have to work out some way to get rid of Damiana, but I can't keep an eye on them all the time, they sleep together and I can't sleep with them. When the old women meet in the cellar, Iris picks up Damiana in her arms and, cheek to cheek, as if crooning, they talk, I know they talk, they're planning to break out and go look for Romualdo, the father who's not the father but nevertheless should be the father, I must warn Don Jerónimo this very day to come and rescue his son from the mire Damiana wants to sink him in, they're planning a getaway, they're not crooning, they're not saying baby things to each other, they're scheming, plotting, while Dora knits, María Benítez stirs her mixtures over the fire, Rosa Pérez irons, Rita ties a satin bow, Amalia rinses out her blind eye in a blue eyecup, and Damiana, tiny once more, nods sleepily in Iris's lap, waiting for God knows what moment, what opportunity, and Iris, bloated, sticks her finger up her nose and yawns.

"When do you think he'll be born?"

"That's something nobody can predict about miraculous births."

"What a pity we can't ask her when it happened."

"When what happened?"

"Well, when we should start counting the nine months from . . ."

"Amalia, the nine months don't mean a thing when it's a miracle, I'm telling you, don't be pigheaded, the baby will be born when it has to be born and that's all there is to it . . . we have to wait . . ."

"And how about the Virgin?"

"What?"

"Sure, the Feast of the Incarnation, when the Archangel Saint Gabriel appeared to the Virgin Mary with his finger sticking out, and she said His will be done, it's March twenty-fifth, nine months before to the day."

"But Iris isn't the Virgin Mary, it's an ordinary miraculous birth, there are lots of miraculous births, so quit asking questions, Amalia, it's bad."

"I don't know. And when the baby's born, will Iris go on being a virgin? Babies come out through the same . . ."

"God, I don't know, we'll have to see . . ."

"Is Iris a virgin, then?"

"Why shouldn't she be one, Amalia? Brígida said so and María Benítez examined her . . . Isn't that right, María?"

María doesn't answer.

"Isn't that right, María?"

María stops stirring her sweet-smelling mixtures.

"I don't know . . . I wanted to tell you . . . but I hadn't had a chance . . ."

"What?"

"Well, the other day when we found her lying sick in the court, as though she'd had some kind of strange fit, I'd like to ask whether someone couldn't have sneaked into the Casa."

"How?"

"I don't know, men are such pigs and she's so pretty. I'm afraid . . . they say when a woman has something to do with a man, once she's expecting, the baby's born a freak of nature. Brígida, may she rest in peace, told me that that's why she never let her husband touch her, once she was in the family way. Of course all her babies were born dead, that's life, it was God's will. They say when a man has something to do with a pregnant woman the child's born a freak of nature, a monster with a great big head, with short arms like penguin flippers, a toad's mouth, a body covered with hair or scales, they can even be born without eyelids and that's why monster babies can't sleep and they cry all night long from sheer heartbreak over being monsters and also because they don't have eyelids to close so they can fall asleep, it must be terrible not to be able to sleep at night, they say . . ."

They say . . . they say . . . they say: omnipotent words in the ragged mouths of the old women, syllables that store all the knowledge accumulated by the miserable creatures . . . they say . . . they say that Brígida was a millionairess, they say that silk has to be ironed with a warm iron, after it's sprinkled a little bit . . . they say they're never going to tear down the Casa . . . they say if you put a straw in a bottle of boiling water the glass won't break . . . *they say* . . . *they say,* following the repetition of these words down the meandering years, or perhaps centuries, that *they say,* who knows who or to whom or when or how, but say they do, and now they repeat, with the certainty *they say* affords them, that when a man has something to do with a pregnant woman the child's born a monster. In the dim light of the cellar occupied by old women who are like heaps of rags that barely move, María Benítez stirs the contents of the pot over the glowing coals, and the fragrant vapor of this infusion of saltwort *they say* is so good for the stomach is thickening little by little in order to give form to that unquestionable truth: the monstrous son of Don Jerónimo and Iris whom someone else engendered, and when Inés finally became pregnant . . . I don't want to touch her, because I'm afraid of disfiguring my son who has to be perfect, and *they say* that if you make love with . . . who knows where or when Don Jerónimo heard this *they say* that's defining this son of his that's been deformed by all the neighborhood boys, by all the downtown dudes, that have been tossing with Iris, by all the generals and academicians hidden in the Giant's head, yes, Don Jerónimo, your son's going to be a sensational monster worthy of an Azcoitía . . . go on, María, you're a medicine woman and you know what they say, go on stirring the pot that gives off the vapor that's the deformed face, its outlines the misshapen body that will tear Don Jerónimo away from the placidity of his easy chair at the Club where he reads the newspaper and dozes, forgetting all lofty enterprise, renouncing the cares of state, all bygone struggles, because he'd rather cultivate the flabby double chin with which he betrays the pain of my father who deserves respect, you have no right to disappoint him, Don Jerónimo, all for naught—for no blessed thing, as María Benítez, who keeps stirring the pot that's assembling the savior monster, would say . . . and you, Amalia, go ahead and tell them that you've heard the same thing too . . . don't interrupt her, Dora, nor you, Rita, by insisting that it has nothing to do with Iris, because the poor thing's never had anything to do with anyone, not before and not afterwards, men don't exist . . . Brígida invented the miraculous birth,

Brígida conceived Iris's son, Brígida's the monster's mother, Brígida knew everything . . . María goes on stirring the pot over the coals, and that twisted and maimed Azcoitía smiles at me from the steam, I want to rock him in my arms while the old women talk and make comments and say things and whisper and listen to María Benítez, who's a medicine woman and, they say, knows many things—not to the same degree as Brígida, but, when it comes to knowing, María Benítez knows plenty:

". . . It merely occurred to me—don't be offended, Rita— that the night we found her . . . well, somebody may have broken in to molest the poor innocent thing, they say there are degenerates who look for little girls like Iris and do filthy things to them and, of course, then, with the fright, all the body's humors are poisoned . . . and, if it's like I say, if the baby isn't dead yet, I'm positive it will turn out to be a monster."

"He's not dead."

"I put my hand on her tummy yesterday, and he was moving."

"Could be indigestion, she ate bananas very late . . ."

"No, they say bananas are bad with beer at night, they're heavy on the stomach, but Iris didn't drink any beer, where would she get her hands on beer?"

"Then it means that it's going to be a monster."

We all exchanged glances without knowing what to say, till Damiana said, from the sleeping Iris's lap:

"And what's the difference if the baby turns out to be a monster?"

We didn't know what to answer. Go on, Damiana, go on:

"It might even be better. If he turns out to be a monster, nobody's going to want him and they're not about to come barging into the Casa to claim the baby. People are afraid of monsters. Of course, they say the doctors sometimes come for the babies who are born monsters and take them away to examine them in the hospitals and experiment on them. The poor things suffer a lot. Monsters are pretty valuable, they're hard to find, there are almost none around. I had a friend who had a baby who was a freak. The doctors stole it on her, and they say they stuck it inside a glass jar filled with red water and used to feed it through tubes, and my friend never saw her son again, and they didn't even pay her a nickel for him."

I know why you're encouraging them to believe that Iris's son will be born a monster: in order to calm their fears, while you and Iris work out your escape to what you believe is reality. You're sure, you poor thing, that the Giant's the father. That Romualdo was the only one who got into the Giant's head. In your conventional mind there's a father who must be found and saddled with Iris's baby. You don't know the other side of things, the dozens of fathers the Giant's mask covered up, what I schemed before you hatched your poor realistic story: family, mother, father, son, home, support, food, suffering . . . go on believing in those things, Damiana, plan your little story of ordinary happiness, of everyday sadness, while with the vapor that's thickening and solidifying I plan something born of the anarchic freedom with which the minds of old women, of whom I'm one, operate.

"Yes, but we're not that stupid. We don't mean to hand him over to doctors or anybody else, not even to Mother Benita or Father Azócar. Now that we know he's going to be a monster, we have to look after him much more carefully, to keep someone from finding out that he exists. And keep him locked up in here till he's ready to go to His Heavenly Glory with all of us, in a beautiful hearse like the one that Brígida was taken away in, only all white and with white horses instead of black ones and it'll have to be with wings so it can fly up to heaven in a hail of flowers and with celestial music all around us . . ."

"If only poor Brígida were living!"

"I hope we don't die too!"

"Such a lovely funeral, Brígida's."

"Lovely."

"The loveliest we ever saw at the Casa."

It was necessary to keep an eye on Damiana and Iris all day long, until it was finally time to eat and go to bed. When sleep blotted us out in the depths of our hovels, Iris and Damiana waited until everything was totally silent before slipping out of bed. To keep an eye on them. To follow them. Why should I be afraid, when I always have all the keys on me? But Damiana's a hairy, screaming menace who wormed her way into the Casa, then into our circle, to destroy everything. She goes up to the floor above with Iris at night, stealthily, and they stay up there watching the city's splendor, the blinking scarlet lights of the airport, the searchlights of the transmission towers, the neon scrawls on the glass buildings downtown, the searchlights swinging in the darkness as they search them out . . . catch that beam, Iris, catch it, it's headed this way now, wait till the next time around and catch it then and climb onto it . . . and Iris raises her arm and her hand catches hold of the beam but it slips away to light up other corners of the city, which sprawls out as far as the mountains. From the window I opened for them, Damiana's showing Iris the entire layout of the city: the river, the squares, the downtown area, the avenues . . . don't you get lost . . . tracing routes they'll follow down streets Damiana knows inside out because when she was a servant she was famous for liking the streets, pronouncing each syllable of the names precisely, so that they'll penetrate Iris's thick skull and stick, so that she won't get lost as I would if I went out of the Casa into the streets Damiana knows and I don't.

I thought they were up to something more there at the window, I imagined they'd file the iron bars and let themselves down with sheets and escape. But they soon shut the window. They came downstairs. They said good night with a friendly kiss on the cheek. Each went to bed in her own room. I hung around, roaming through the cloisters, gripping the keys in my dustcoat pocket. I'm not going to sleep, not tonight or ever, they'll get into my room some night and take the keys from under my pillow before I know it, even if I stick them under my bed together with my manuscripts, they'll carry off everything with them when they run away from the Casa, because they're going to run away, tomorrow or the day after, that's why I have to let Don Jerónimo know immediately that he's about to lose his son to anonymity and misery, I'm going out this very night to warn him because I know what they're hatching in order to take away the only chance he has left of being great and noble again, by meeting the challenge of being father to a monster son, yes, I can't lose time, I have to tie my keys and my manuscripts in a bundle of rags, but what if they make off with the whole bundle, escape with it, scattering through the streets strings, rags, my manuscripts covered with my handwriting and my name, handing them over to strangers, perhaps to Peta Ponce, who'll know where to find me, to faceless people like my father, papers, papers that neither they nor those they turn them over to will ever read, because they're worthless, they'll dump them in the street and automobile wheels will soil them, children will make toy boats or peaked hats with them as if they were multicolored handbills, until one of the handbills falls into Peta Ponce's hands and she rushes here to force me to make love to her again, the filthy old hag, the lecherous, insatiable old hag, I don't want to go out, I'm not going out . . .

Mudito. Mudito. Her voice urging me to come out of the shadows where she knows I hide, even though I know how to walk without making a sound, racing down the passageways when she sets a faster pace in the dark . . . another night, Mudito, Mudito . . . watch out, Iris, there's a step, don't trip, you might kill your son, maybe that's what you're after, that's your revenge, to kill that vaporous shape that slowly issued forth from María Benítez's pot, the concoction of that witch who's not a witch but a healer and a medicine woman, because none of us are witches, only old women, nothing more, old women with old women's privileges . . . Mudo, Mudito . . . yes, Damiana ran off, you don't know that Damiana ran off and you couldn't stop her, Damiana knows how to sneak out, she doesn't need your keys, there are holes in the Casa you don't know about, people you don't notice come in and go out through them . . . Damiana disappeared, we're only six old women now . . . give me the keys, Mudito, I want to go and join Damiana . . . wait, wait until she calls me, because she's going to call me as soon as she finds Romualdo, who used to disguise himself as the Giant and is my son's father . . . run, run down the passageways without making a sound, Mudito . . . but, I beg of you, Iris, don't repeat the word *Mudito, Mudito, Mudito* so loud, someone might hear you, you're almost shouting, as if you couldn't go on another second without me, hush, hush, they're going to hear us. Mudito . . . Mudito . . . the giant rats and the mice scamper out of our way, we slash through the structures spiders throw across corridors, I discover you among the orange trees laden with golden fruit, hiding to watch me pass, I have to hurry to the vestibule to make sure the door's double-locked. This isn't a deep passage; someone, perhaps I, painted an infinite perspective over a walled-up window, maybe Damiana got lost in those simulated depths . . . look for her there . . . but you're not fooled, you realize it's only some lines over a false wall and you stop and turn down another corridor to look for me. Panting from pursuing you, I dodge into a corner to catch my breath; you're young and I'm decrepit. I don't hear your footsteps now and I rest a little in the vestibule before going out to tell Don Jerónimo to come and fetch the vaporous monster son now in your womb, before another carries you off as I'm pursued down the galleries, your breath seething down the back of my neck like the breath of the fierce animals before they tore me to pieces; if I could only rest, breathe in peace, sunk here in this corner no light reaches down into.

You touch me.

"Mudito."

You talk in a very quiet, calm voice that's new to me.

"I want to go out."

I know it, Iris.

I smell your odor of grime, of old clothes, of the ointments we smear on you . . . this salve's good for the bronchial tubes, Amalia, you're stronger than me, give the child's back a proper rubdown, and this liquid that looks like water is just the thing to massage that swelling ankle of hers . . . I shake my head no. You grab hold of my wrist. I let go the keys in my dustcoat pocket. You take my hand and place it on those breasts of yours, that will suckle a monster, not Romualdo's son, even if you and Damiana think so, and it's not my son because I'm the seventh old woman and I'm sexless . . . Peta: I swear I'm sexless, so don't come sneaking into the Casa. It's the son that Don Jerónimo de Azcoitía, animated by my envious eyes, engendered in a criminal's daughter.

"Feel."

I feel.

"Yummy?"

I don't answer.

"Squeeze, silly. Think I don't know you want to play yum-yum with me? Here, feel it all you want and then let me go out. Come on, I tell you, open up the door for me."

I can't hear. I'm deaf and dumb; you know it, Iris, I don't know why you keep chattering away when you know I can't hear. I don't understand a thing you're telling me, and so even if I could or wanted to do your bidding I wouldn't obey you.

"Liar. Faker. You're not dumb. I caught on from the beginning that you're not dumb, and you're only making like you're dumb. That's why I went down the corridors and called you, so you'd hear me and let me go out. You're not dumb and not deaf. When you jingle the keys in your pocket you keep time to We Love God in Our Laws in Our Schools and in The Home, We looooooove God . . . and real dumb people can't keep time to anything 'cause they can't hear, so don't try to put one over on me. Before she skipped out of the Casa, Damiana said she was going to report you to the Archbishop so, you'd better watch your step, you're going to get it one of these days. Let me out, if you don't want me to report you to Mother Benita."

That's a perfect deduction, Iris, congratulations, your deduction drives me into a corner and strips me bare, leaving me wide open because I'll have to drag everything out from under my bed—my voice, my hearing, my long-forgotten name, my lifeless sex organ, my unfinished manuscripts—I'll have to undo everything and use it. What will I do with my humility? . . . Yes, ma'am, my head bows and nods, my little cart is at your service . . . I'm not an old woman, I'm Humberto Peñaloza, the father of your son, miraculous pregnancies are stories told by old women, whose circle you won't let me belong to because you're tearing me away from this sweet refuge to get me to let you open the door and disappear into the fate Damiana's convinced you is your true fate, but don't you believe her, Iris, people have many fates, any one of which can swallow them up, and the one Damiana offers you is literal, poor, dull, miserable.

"I want to go out."

"Alone?"

"Sure."

"To go and join Damiana?"

"Filthy old hag."

"Why?"

You wait a moment.

"I'm pregnant. Damiana took off with the story that she's going to look for Romualdo, but it's not true, she's not going to look for him, because she wants me for herself. I'm not about to go off and live with that dyke Damiana at the home of some lady that she knows who could put me up till we find Romualdo, and where there's other kids, but I don't want to. I want to go find the guy who left me pregnant, I want to go live with him."

"It wasn't Romualdo."

"Who was it, then?"

"I know who it was."

"Sure, the Giant."

"No, the guy who was inside the Giant."

"Sure, Romualdo . . ."

"No, another man, a gentleman . . ."

"Don't hand me that, let me out."

Your realistic dream's hard to destroy, an incarnation you don't want to give up, it suits you to a T, it's almost not a dream, you're just the right mate for Romualdo and you know this and don't want me to destroy that dream and start you off on another. The dream about Romualdo's entirely clear to you, but not the one I'm offering you, no, it's too big for you, but I can cut it down to your size, I can fit you into it little by little. You're anointed, you can't stand it anymore, all you want now is to get out, and get out now, you can't put off your desire to get out.

"It'll be your ruination."

"I don't care."

"You won't have any place to sleep or eat."

You give a shrug, in a gesture of contempt for my terror of the outdoors, a terror I don't want you to have contempt for because I need to have you make it yours too, at least for now, tonight. I talk to you, you hear me out, I explain that the whole thing about the Giant was a farce because the real father used to hide inside Romualdo, who was nothing but another mask like the Giant's, which she watched them destroy, and now we have to destroy Romualdo's papier-mâché mask to find the other one inside, your son's real father, he lives in his palace of iron and glass and lights, you can see it from your window, one of the palaces that shoot out those beams of light you try to catch in your hands and climb up on, you won't have to climb up on a beam of light, Iris, I'm going to destroy Romualdo's mask and bring the real father to you, wait for me here, the streets are terrifying, the darkness out there isn't like the darkness in the Casa, Iris, it's the darkness of people who don't even have where to drop dead, as the saying goes, and they don't have where to drop dead because that darkness is the void that swallows you up and, as you drop into it, you scream and never stop dropping and dropping and screaming and screaming, because there's no bottom, until finally your voice fades out as you go on dropping and dropping into that infinity of vertiginous streets with names you don't know, streets jammed with the faces of people who'll laugh at you, who live in houses they won't let you into and who do things you don't understand . . . don't come any closer, Iris, don't touch me like that, don't rub up against my body . . . you place your hand on my organ . . . no, Humberto, don't let Iris go on touching you, because she'll break down your disguises, if you don't escape you'll have to be a self again, whose identity you no longer remember and that exists you don't know where . . . you draw your fleshy lips to my mouth and your thighs dig into my poor trembling scrawny legs, your hand looks for my organ, unbuttoning my fly . . . don't let her turn you back into Humberto Peñaloza with his burden of unbearable yearning, escape so that your organ won't be aroused by the pressure of those fleshy palms and won't respond to her tongue as it explores your mouth and your tongue; remain stock still in the corner where her breasts and her hips are pressing up against you . . . Humberto doesn't exist, Humberto doesn't exist, only the seventh old woman exists. Your hand finds nothing between my legs.

"Iris . . ."

"What?"

"I'm going out to look for the father."

"Where?"

"I know where he lives."

"Where?"

"In a yellow house across from the park, it's many stories tall."

"Let's go."

"No, wait . . ."

"What for?"

"I don't know if he's in."

"I don't care if he's not in."

"But he's got four savage black dogs, and when he's not there they eat up people who go in, and since they don't know you . . ."

"What about you?"

"They know me."

"They're not going to eat you?"

"They won't do anything to me."

You're thinking.

"Is the house pretty?"

I answer, yes, Don Jerónimo de Azcoitía is an exceptionally sexy guy.

"I don't know . . . those dogs . . ."

That's why I'm going to fetch him, so he'll come and get you in his car with a chauffeur and all . . . no, I don't want one with a chauffeur, I want a red convertible . . . okay, Iris, anything you want, I'll tell him to come and get you in a red convertible and take you away from the Casa and Mother Benita and Damiana and me, because I don't want to see you any more.

"Wait for me here, Iris."

"Okay, But you'd better hurry if you don't want me to tell on you and have you arrested, because if you don't hurry I'm going to wake up Mother Benita and tell her all about it."

"All about what?"

She didn't answer.

"That I'm the father?"

"Yes."

"You believe it?"

She laughed, saying of course not.

"Switch off the light, Iris."

"Okay. I'll wait for you here in the vestibule."

"I'll be right back."

I remove the crossbar. I open the door and go out. But, inside, they immediately put the crossbar back into place . . . knock on the door, knock so they'll open for me . . . I'm sick, it's raining, I'm soaked to the bone, I have a fever . . . Mother Benita, please open up, forgive me for going out of the Casa, open, open up, I don't know who could have locked the door . . . I can't see, I can't cry out anymore, I have a fever, no one recognized me, they only humiliated me and threw me out into the park where it kept pouring and I kept running, and I scream and knock and I have no strength left to scream and knock . . . Mother Benita, save me, at least don't let Peta Ponce find me, let me in . . . I've got no fists left, no voice, I'm nothing but this limp sleeve at a convent door on a rainy night, and they won't open up . . .

9

WATER. MORE WATER . . . a cold cloth on my forehead,
but don't take away your hand, Mother Benita, please let me go
on like this with my hand in yours until they leave, because
they'll leave when they see that you're protecting me now, as
you've always protected me, with your silence, tell them to go
away, throw them out, people say they're fiends, that the police
torture us to make us confess stealing a scarf or a loaf of bread,
they whip us, they do humiliating things to us, they send electric
charges through us, they force us to wallow in our own excre-
ment and eat it. But what do they want me to confess, when I
didn't steal anything? That policeman's clenching his fists. Look,
his knuckles are white with rage, he's going to hit me, Mother
Benita, get between us, squeeze my hand so the blow won't hurt
too much, that's how they start off, by ramming their fists into
our faces, blow after blow, and, if you don't confess, they go on
to tortures that are really terrible . . . that's why, when the
cops are after us, we run and run and run and, before they can
nab us, we slit our bellies here, Mother Benita, look at my
wounds, we slit our bellies with a very fine knife again and
again, but only superficially, so that the cops will find us and
laugh away as we lie in our own blood . . . they'll take me to
the hospital, a good hospital where Dr. Azula, who's grasping
and cynical, won't be waiting to steal even a little patch of my
skin, or part of a gland, I'll be taken to a hospital he doesn't
know of, because no one, not even they, dares torture a
wounded person, the wounded are sacred. Wounded like this,
I'm safe, because now they're the ones who are afraid of me, not
I of them, I don't have to confess anything to them, I'll only tell

the truth to you, Mother Benita, yes, I stole something from Don Jerónimo's house, look, this small volume with a greenish spine, only one volume, although I wish I could have brought the hundred copies with me, but I couldn't, paralyzed as I was in his library, with the everlasting gray velvet armchairs around me, the dim lighting, the logs sputtering in the fireplace, as I stood on a rug of such deep tones that I was paralyzed by the terror of drowning in them and being swallowed up by their elegance . . . the thing to do is save what can be saved, I'll reach out for my books, in the place where those hundred copies have always been, intact as a joke among his collection of curiosities, those hundred copies for which he generously subscribed in order to help a struggling student publish the little book that repeats his name, and Inés's name, over and over again, on every page . . . Inés looked at him tenderly through the blue flowers she was arranging in a Lalique vase, Jerónimo de Azcoitía came down the stairs dressed in his traveling clothes to leave for La Rinconada, Inés and Peta were whispering next to the potted palm in the gallery, where they spent hours knitting Boy's baby clothes . . . and my name up there, over the text on all the left-hand pages: Humberto Peñaloza, Humberto Peñaloza, that reiteration of my name destined to conjure its shame away, to console my father, to mock my mother, to convince me that, after all, with my name in print so many times, no one could question my existence. Repeated how many times? Let's see, help me count, Mother Benita, this fever loosens my tongue but I can't concentrate enough to do simple arithmetic, each copy has one hundred and eighty pages, that makes ninety Humberto Peñalozas per copy, plus one each half-title page and once on each spine . . . let's figure it out: my name repeated nine thousand three hundred times in Don Jerónimo de Azcoitía's library. How could I help fearing that the rug resonant with symbols would suck me under: No, my name only nine thousand two hundred and seven times, because I stole *one* copy before I escaped. When I'm well again and my hands stop shaking with fever and my eyes don't blur, maybe, for you, for you because you're you and because you're holding my hand and listening to me, I'll read a passage here and there of the flashy prose, of the naïve fancies, of that consummate writer with the ultra-artistic style, with such choice sensibility, that budding poet of lyrics redolent of spring, that talented man just emerging from his chrysalis to breathe in the fragrant air of a rosy future that will add honor to the literature of his country, and, after reading you one of those portraits of women I used to write then, because I didn't know any and could only imagine them sheathed in a wave of Oriental perfumes, because perfumes were always Oriental in those days, and tunics always sumptuously embroidered, and poses languid, and those cruel but smiling flirts always broke men's hearts, and there was always a full moon, a world lost beyond other lost worlds beyond other lost worlds, one perfection supplanting the other, superannuated, perfection, monstrous papier-mâché head inside monstrous papier-mâché head . . . yes, Mother Benita, although you hold my hand in yours and your kind words comfort me, I am no more. When I'm well, perhaps the best thing I can do is get into the bundle of rags under my bed where I keep the Swiss chalet and my manuscripts, then they won't beat me up with their angry fists even though they want to force me to talk. I can't. I don't want to confess why I ran out of Don Jerónimo de Azcoitía's house.

The kick aimed at me by the cop misses its mark and I plunge into the stream of cars that are huddled under the rainstorm, jamming the street . . . stop, thief, thief . . . whistles calling more reinforcements, and, in the cars, they're returning from the latest Jeanne Moreau film and are going to eat steak with mashed potatoes; they see me through the transparent fan of their windshield wipers, apply the brakes . . . damn, I almost ran into someone, you can't see a thing in this rain . . . you lousy bum . . . God, the rain's really been coming down this year . . . they see me a yard away; in the spotlight scratched by the rain, I'm dissolved in rain, but the windshield wiper waves me back and back and back into the solid form I don't have and makes them see me, a blind-looking runt with bedraggled hair who's soaked to the skin, in the second during which the brakes are applied, as I flee in the dark amid the press of cars that squeeze me in, and the furious cops, their authority frustrated, blowing their whistles on the sidewalk, the pursued marionette dancing like a hallucination in the red lights that snap at his calves as he runs among the skidding Citroëns, the Fords that bump and honk . . . goddamn bum . . . and when's this downpour going to let up . . . throw on the brakes, be careful, Hernán, you're going to kill him . . . what the hell do I care, he almost made me smash up my brand-new Renault . . . but he's almost disappeared behind the Morris back there into the rain in the park and is going to hide down by the river . . . but I'm not a thief, Mother Benita, I swear it, you don't steal your own name, because it's yours to do with as you please . . . if I could only use one of those winter days, when it gets dark early, to burn all my papers, all my identical and reiterated names, without leaving any traces, I'll throw them from this black steel bridge to the rocky riverbed and, after letting myself down here, I'll light a sheet of paper, two, maybe a notebook, to warm my hands a little because it will be cold. That small lick of warmth won't be enough. I need more heat to fight off the terrifying bad weather. Other papers: *pensées,* vignettes, a week's diary I never finished, books lifted from public libraries where no one had ever borrowed them, notebooks filled with jottings in my shaky but vehement hand . . . Look, Mother Benita, the reddish circle's growing at my feet, listen to them, it's them, the ones who have no faces, joining my blaze one by one. Something stirs in those bushes: a dog comes and lies down near my fire. A shape's outlined against the water line, where mice fattened on garbage scurry off, and takes solid form, starts moving this way. A chunk of granite wall trembles and falls . . . no, don't be frightened, Mother, it's only a small boy who jumped from the mouth of a sewer . . . More books, more papers into the fire, and the books and papers in which my name burns increase the generous circle that they, those who've already undergone the surgery that erases their faces, are entering to warm themselves; no, that's not the only reason, to acknowledge and accept me as one of them, once I've completely eliminated my name. The tide of shadows slowly retreats, leaves them uncovered like rocks disguised in tattered algae, but I recognize them behind their disguises: the Oriental prince with turban, black beard, cloak, long nails, voluptuously stretches out his body next to my bonfire, on the golden burlap of the sack in which he must be carrying . . . nothing, things, rags, cardboard, nothing. The knot of children and flea-bitten dogs on the ground forms a single monstrous animal that's barefoot, covered with mud, motionless, and has burning eyes, spotted pelts, sores, tails, curled-up flews, translucent ears, dripping noses; and more and more wearers of ephemeral disguises show up (if we don't wear some kind of disguise we're nothing): monks with haggard faces that are almost hidden by the shadow of their cowls that flickers in my flame, the old woman who draws her hand, gnarled by warts, into the light, her hand so transparent that you and I can see the delicate bones covered by the flesh that crumbles beneath her rags as they disintegrate in the heat of my fire. Don't you smell the odor of overheated drenched rags, of scraps of stale bread set next to the fire of my papers to soften them up a little, of cigarette butts being lit at my fire? Boy will return all my books, the ninety-nine copies he still has left, so they can feed this immense flame they're all joining . . . look at them, Mother Benita, where can they be coming from, with the ocher of their misery, the pallor of their filth, the grays of their sumptuous tatters, more faces and figures and hands, and eyes revealed by a flash, and imperial folds, slashes that enable you to see the shininess of the coat of mail that's a vest that's disintegrating, fringes that are tatters, doublets that are old pajamas, emblems that are patches, crests that are mops of hair . . . finally I drop from exhaustion as I reach my last paper and the last copy of my book, and the fire smolders because I have nothing left to feed it . . . Wait, Mother Benita, don't leave, your duties can't be so pressing that you won't hear me out and watch the slow retreat of the princes with their courts of dwarfs and blackamoors, slaves and minions, courtesans and procuresses, confessors and children and mangy she-dogs, halberdiers, pages. You think they're only disguised as what they appear to be. Take off their disguises and they're reduced to people like me, without faces or features, who have to go rummaging in trash cans and forgotten attic trunks and picking up the castoffs of others in the streets in order to put together one disguise one day, another disguise the next, in order to give themselves an identity, if only for a few moments. They don't even have masks. There's a shortage of them, that's why I'm sorry the Giant's head's been destroyed. There are so many of us who go around collecting, here and there, whatever castoff enables us to disguise ourselves and feel we're somebody, *be* somebody—a well-known person, a picture in the papers with your name underneath; we all know one another here, in fact we're almost all blood relations . . . to be someone, Humberto, that's the important thing, and the lamplight flickers and the table wobbles under my sister's elbows as she holds her face in her hands like in La Bertini's latest postcard photograph . . . my sister's too is a mask, La Bertini's mask, because her own face wasn't enough; as one goes along he learns the advantages of the disguises being improvised, their mobility, how the last one covered the one before it. All that's needed is a checked kerchief tied around your head, a potato plaster on the temples, your mustache shaved off, going unwashed for a month so as to take on a new skin coloring, knowing how to change disguises and melt into their fluid existence that bestows the freedom of never being the same, because rags are never permanent, everything being improvised, everything fluctuating; today I'm myself and tomorrow no one can find me, not even I myself, because you're what you are only for as long as the disguise lasts. Sometimes I feel sorry for persons like you, Mother Benita, who are enslaved to one face and one name and one function and one station in life, to the clinging mask you'll never be able to shed, to the oneness that holds you prisoner in a single identity. Those who came to warm themselves at my fire, on the other hand, fluctuate like its flames and its shadows, they take me into their number benevolently, now that I've burned my name forever, lost my voice a long time ago, no longer have a sex because I can be just another old woman among all those in the Casa. I'm burning my papers that are incoherent with scribbling intended to plead for a definite and permanent mask for me, but not all of them, not all; there are so many volumes left there in the library with its gray armchairs. But they don't know it, they believe I'm like them because I've learned, as time's gone by, to disguise myself with the castoffs I find thrown into corners or into the street . . . someday I'll manage to become one of them

. . . to depart without leaving a trace . . . without leaving tracks on the ground . . . without casting a shadow like a paper cutout . . . that's the only way I'll be able to free myself from Don Jerónimo, who's looking for me because he needs me and needs things I preserve and can't relinquish yet, and from Peta Ponce, who never dies and reaches me like an echo that started with the original nightmare; I can't fool her with my successive disguises, if I could only lose myself among them, among the shadows, the backs weighed down with sacks, the beards, the toothless gums, the cigarette butt dangling from the corner of a mouth, I wish I could join their slowly disappearing retinue . . . they're going away . . . let's leave here, Mother Benita, let's follow them, it's cold here in this rocky riverbed, and up there the police are still lying in wait, to catch me because I stole my own book, but no, even the police are going off because it's late now. Don't disappear, Mother Benita, and don't leave me here to shake with fever and chills, alone, without your hand in mine, without your protection from these brutes who manhandle me . . . thief, thief . . . okay, let's go, to headquarters . . . I kick and scream as they drag me, and you don't come, Mother Benita, you're leaving me all alone, you let go my hand . . . don't leave me, don't leave me . . . don't hit me, I haven't done anything . . .

YOU'RE THERE, sitting across from me. I hear the rain coming down outside, the familiar leak, its unrelenting drip into the basin placed under the skylight's broken glass. Your face has been so badly patched up! How useless were Dr. Azula's efforts to create that parody of normal eyelids, that forehead without precise contours, to graft on ears where they should be, to shape the jawbone nature didn't give you. You're much more monstrous than the figure María Benítez threatens us with if Iris ever gets mixed up with a man, but she doesn't know that your mother had something to do with all the neighborhood kids, all the dudes and the city authorities, which is why you were born this way. A Chesterfield with its leather worn and stained, a desk with several drawers, a cracked mirror in which I see what might be my pitiful face, is all there is in this small room to which the police have brought me to wait for you. They've switched on a dim gooseneck lamp that throws light on each detail of the artificial features Dr. Azula put together for you, because you were born without a face in spite of being an Azcoitía, because of the unbelievable calamity of your twisted body the rubdowns and exercises thought up by Basilio couldn't correct. Don't think I'm surprised to see you. I've seen you so often since Don Jerónimo's death, I've followed you so doggedly, I've waited for hours at a time at the door of the tailor shop where they make the clothes that hardly dissemble your body's deformity. One day I intentionally bumped into you in a street-corner crowd, and I felt you in my arms, just as, when you were a baby, Miss Dolly used to hand me the bundle you were then, for me to rock you for a few minutes. You didn't even throw me a glance. You continued on your way. Had you looked at me and seen me, you wouldn't have known who I am. Were you very much surprised that the officer on duty in this police station told you respectfully, knowing you're the senator's son and deserve respect even if you're a monster, that a beggar broke into your house tonight to steal a small hundred-and-eighty-page book? It's the book you're now thumbing through. You know it well. After all, you owned a hundred copies. Hidden on a bench behind the acanthus hedge in the park, I've watched you reading by the window that's kept open in the summer, or else I've gone up to the blurry windowpanes in winter and have been able to see you climb the ladder to poke about, as though in search of something, going through your father's books without moving them out of place, as if you wanted to preserve some of the harmony that Don Jerónimo represented but that you contradict with your existence. You have a slouching gait, you're all hands and feet and you knock things over, your breathing is raspy, you're all twisted and bandy-legged. You belong to a gloomy, labyrinthine La Rinconada, an existence of passageways of forgotten nooks, where your being is shaped by the ulcerations of time in the plaster on a wall. You turn the pages of my book casually, halfheartedly, you have to go, to return to your yellow house opposite the park. Besides, I arouse no interest in you. In fact, you're a bit put out because they called you to headquarters at this hour for something so trivial. You're ready to go. You grant me no importance. You're going to leave my book behind and go away forever without knowing who I am or to whom you owe everything you are and are not, don't go, Boy, don't go, acknowledge me at least for one instant, at least repay me for your existence by giving me back the ninety-nine copies of my book you still have and aren't interested in, so that I may burn them and enter, once and for all, the world of those who've forgotten their names and their faces, don't abandon me like this, this is my last chance . . . and, fearing that you'll disappear forever, I prick your curiosity by tracing these words on a sheet of paper: *I wrote this book you're leafing through.* You obey me, you sit down again. Now you leaf through the book more attentively . . . You? Why did you break into my house to make off with it? Why did you use my name and my father's and my mother's as if they were only names made up for your book? How does a person like you happen to know us? I don't believe someone like you could have written this book . . . I can't hear you. You know it. They told you in the duty room that when they started to torture me into confessing my name, as if owning it were a shameful crime, I pointed to my mouth and my ears, no, I don't understand, I can't hear, I'm a deaf-mute, and I defeated them with my weakness, these brutes' fists didn't rain blows on me, because being a deaf-mute is the same as slashing your belly; the menacing hand of the cop who was about to slap me fell back powerless. They didn't beat me up . . . All right, what's the use, take him to the little waiting room to wait for the owner of the house to come and testify whether there was a theft or not, I don't believe so, this poor devil must have entered the house to get in out of the rain, that was some rain this evening, yes, he's deaf and dumb . . . I'm deaf and dumb. The officer so advised you.

With a pride that reminds me of your father's, you ask me: What connection is there . . . what contact *could* there have been . . . ? I can't hear you. I make you repeat your questions. You do so by pronouncing each syllable carefully so that I may read what you're expressing with the imprecision of your fish lips. Aren't you aware that your mouth is so malformed that it's impossible to read your lips? . . . How can you prove to me that it's true that you're the author of this book which speaks about me, about my father, about my mother. You go on turning pages. Suddenly you lift your gargoyle head and under those mere semblances of human eyelids, I see the electric-arc blue of your father's eyes, the blue that demands proof, because a man with Basque blood in his veins must never believe in things for which there's no proof. I feel cold. My hands are shaking with the same fever that makes them tremble, now that I'm handing you the book with the greenish spine, Mother Benita, so that you too may begin checking the truth of what I'm telling you. My clothes stick to my body because they're still heavy from being drenched. I write the answer on the sheet of paper: *To show you that I'm telling the truth, I can write down, from memory, any chapter of the book.*

You accept. You yourself place the paper on the desk, providing the light and handing me your gold Parker, because I've won, your curiosity's greater than your desire to return home, what's happening in this little room at headquarters isn't insignificant, coming out this rainy night was worthwhile . . . I'm going to write down the prologue . . . Open the book, Mother Benita, it's still a bit damp from the rain because I couldn't protect it while I hid from the police who cut me off at the river, but start reading so that you too will believe me . . . You sit right in front of me, under the wall mirror. I'm not looking at you. But you don't take your eyes off me for one second.

Humberto's Book

WHEN JERÓNIMO *de Azcoitía finally parted the crib's curtains to look at his long-awaited offspring, he wanted to kill him then and there; the loathsome, gnarled body writhing on its hump, its mouth a gaping bestial hole in which palate and nose bared obscene bones and tissues in an incoherent cluster of reddish traits, was chaos, disorder, a different but worse form of death. Until then, the noble family tree of the Azcoitías, whose name he was the last to bear, had produced only select, flawless fruit:*

forthright politicians, bishops and archbishops and a saintly girl of noteworthy piety, plenipotentiaries abroad, women of dazzling beauty, soldiers who'd been generous with their blood, and even a historian renowned throughout the continent. It was fair to expect that Jerónimo wouldn't be the last Azcoitía, that the luster of the name would continue in the seed of sons and grandsons so that the stock would go on producing more and more perfect fruit until the end of time.

But Jerónimo didn't kill his son. The horror of seeing himself the father of this version of chaos interposed a few seconds of paralyzing shock between his first impulse and its execution, and Jerónimo de Azcoitía didn't kill. It would have meant accepting defeat, letting himself be swept along by chaos, becoming its victim. And, locked up for weeks in the newborn baby's room, living with him and feeding him with his own hands, talking it over with his trusted secretary, who was the only person allowed in to see him, he arrived at a decision: well and good, this brutal mockery was a sign, then, that he was being forsaken by the traditional powers from whom he and his forebears had received so many blessings in return for maintaining His order in the things of this earth. He also saw himself forsaken by the dark powers he'd resorted to, convinced by Inés, who'd gone mad because of the desire to give him an heir. Now the powers of light and darkness were equally his enemies. He was on his own . . . But he doesn't need them. He's strong and will prove it, he'll prove that there's another dimension, other precepts, other ways of appraising good and evil, pleasure and pain, ugliness and beauty. The monstrous baby, thrashing around in his crib because he was hungry, was an abortion that would not only provide him with the means to prevail, but also to prove that he, Jerónimo de Azcoitía, was the greatest and most daring Azcoitía of all times, as he never wearied of telling his secretary.

Jerónimo didn't kill. He went on living almost—almost—as before. He was one of the most envied men in the country. Envied because, at the end of the mourning period for his wife, very few people recalled the existence of Boy, who lived at La Rinconada, a remote estate Jerónimo never visited, although he made sure that Boy was surrounded by all the comforts a son of

his could, and should, need. There's nothing strange about peo-
ple forgetting Boy. Time was an important factor, of course, but
neither the only nor the decisive one. People put Boy out of their
minds because it was so much more convenient. To remember
him would have meant admitting that a man as harmoniously
endowed as Jerónimo, who represented with such distinction the
best in all of them, could carry in him the seed of monsters, and
then living on friendly terms with the senator would turn out to
be not only disquieting but terrible. After all, no one except the
secretary had seen Boy. Who had any proofs of his existence? It
was easier to believe it impossible for this paradigm among
gentlemen to engender a deformed son, and from there go on to
say without the shadow of a doubt that naturally Boy was one
of those black legends with which envy surrounds illustrious
persons.

And perhaps people were right, since Jerónimo's silence
helped wipe out every trace of what must have been a tragedy
for him. Only by shunning all commiseration could he fully act
out his role of powerful landowner, of the senator who defends
the rights of his class against the claims of upstarts, of the figure
who drew all eyes to him in drawing rooms, at the races, on the
rostrum, at the club, in the streets. Simulating a deep interest in
politics, women attended sessions of parliament to hear the
widower speak and to drink in, from the gallery, the sight of his
classic neck and his heroic mien; the names of the ladies who
hoped to fill the void they glimpsed behind that magnificent
façade of words and noble bearing were no secret. But no one
ever penetrated the façade. His enemies branded him as ar-
rogant, even conceited. No doubt he was well aware of his im-
posing figure, but only in the same way that he was aware of all
refinement in himself and in others. Perhaps they were simply
annoyed by a certain mannered quality in the way he dressed, a
certain outdated affectation, doubtless a carryover from his ex-
tended stay in Europe where, rumor had it, he'd sowed his wild
oats with the leading dandies. The fact is that Jerónimo's figure
was a study in harmony, the despair of others because it was un-
matched in these barbarous latitudes. Even when he spoke in the
senate for the last time, before retiring to his lands to confine

himself to his private life, he adopted his usual statuesque poses, which were a bit spent by now, it's true, but always manly and convincing.

A deafening round of applause greeted the senator's farewell speech. His words were so brilliant that, on the following day, Don Jerónimo de Azcoitía's name was splashed all over the front pages of the newspapers, as a possible candidate for the presidency of the Republic. But he warned those party members who came to congratulate him not to count on him, that he was going to take a long vacation and do some traveling, or not do any traveling, but that in any case he looked forward to an indefinite period of rest.

Then Jerónimo disappeared from the capital without explaining anything to anyone, brusquely cutting off friendships and commitments, delegating duties and transactions to trusted administrators. Well, people said, after a few months, he must know what he's doing. As a matter of fact, his age was beginning to tell, and new voices that signaled new directions were arising in the traditional party. Moreover, they recalled briefly, before forgetting him, wasn't he a bit strange lately, now that one had the right perspective to judge him, hadn't he always been different, odd? Wasn't it true that his arrogance, which even those closest to him couldn't ignore, had finally imprisoned him behind a wall in a place where he reigned alone, lord and master of some evidently absolute truth whose secret he'd never disclosed to anyone?

And yet, the news of his death some years later caused real consternation. The entire country remembered, then, the eminent public man's services, and he was paid the country's highest honors; his remains were taken to the cemetery on a gun carriage shrouded in the nation's tricolor. Many considered this improper, for Jerónimo de Azcoitía's role had been political rather than historic, and his name would endure only in specialized texts. Despite the reservations about the honors granted him, or perhaps precisely because of them, everyone attended his funeral. At the family mausoleum, where his body occupied a vault with his name and the dates of his birth and death, which placed him on equal terms with the Azcoitías who preceded him, speak-

ers brought to mind his achievements, the lesson of his exemplary life that signaled the end of a race. The changes in the contemporary world notwithstanding, the country acknowledged itself his debtor. A heavy iron chain sealed the grille of the mausoleum where, within a few hours, the flowers would begin to rot. The gentlemen in black turned their backs on him and slowly disappeared between the cypresses, lamenting the end of such a noble line.

Do you see? Word for word. I didn't look at you even once while I wrote the prologue . . . But you never took your eyes off me. All the while, I felt the electric arc of your gaze as you scrutinized me . . . We've been enveloped in a great silence for more than two hours. I put in the final period. But I don't raise my eyes from the pages of my prologue, I insert a comma here, an accent there, I indicate a new paragraph with two small parallel lines, anything at all, because I can't tear myself away from what I've just written, although I hear you get up from the armchair under the mirror. When I finally lift my eyes, I see you framed in the blurry glass, my anguished face deformed in the cloudy water in which my mask is drowning, the reflection that will never let me escape, the monster looking me over and laughing with my face, because you've left, Boy, you don't even read the prologue I've written in which I announce your birth so that you'll know who you are, and they come back, without their ravenous dogs this time, to tell me: all right, you can go now, off with you, beat it, you've already given us enough work, and let's not see hide nor hair of you around here, you're lucky we're letting you go, the big shot couldn't come, he called up that he's very sorry but it's such a trifle, so unimportant, it's not worth the trouble walking the two blocks from his house to headquarters, especially in the middle of this storm that shows no signs of letting up, I've never seen it pour like this, it's raining pitchforks, here, what are those papers, take them, they're yours, put them in your pocket if you want, we don't want any dirty things left around here, take them with you, come on, I said get going, what do we care if a beggar like you gets drenched, you must be used to it, you'll take cover under an arbor in some park, under the bronze belly of an equestrian statue in some square until the rain stops, who the hell knows, or else you'll go back to the river, guys like you get together under the bridge, come on, beat it, and be careful not to enter gentlemen's houses, even if you don't steal anything, look, next time you won't get off as easy as you did today . . . and I scurry off, Mother Benita, through the park and the rain, without dogs at my heels, I scurry, lost in the streets, smothered by the void I find myself in, with nowhere to turn, because the rain's erased everything . . . the Casa, where's the Casa, how can I get to the Casa, this driving rain can dissolve its mud walls, the ancient adobe has to give way, the flooded labyrinths have to collapse, but no, they won't come down, because all the old women, protective and kind, and Mother Benita too, are waiting to open the door, to let me in and lock up after me and protect me, how can they help protecting and taking care of me, having found me lying unconscious next to the door that has to open up and let me in.

TWO

10

THE DOOR OPENED. She welcomed him with a warm smile and led him across the court, between the indifferent pigeons pecking at the tiles, to the other side of the corridor. He sat down and leaned back in the armchair. Its creaking wicker sounded friendly in the shade of the honeysuckle that preyed upon the pilasters. The servant told him that his uncle hadn't arrived yet but wouldn't be long. Jerónimo took a sip of brandy and thanked her. He snapped his fingers to interrupt the pigeons, but they went on, absorbed in their monotonous colloquy under the noonday sun, and even the retreating steps of the servant didn't interrupt them as she went by.

The only thing in his country that hadn't let him down when he returned from Europe was the fragrant conger eels served on Fridays at the table of his uncle, the Reverend Father Clemente de Azcoitía. The congers and, of course, what went with them: the sluggish silence of the patios whose crude adobe architecture suggested something that approached a frontiersman's life by comparison with the one he knew, and his uncle's conversation, more political than ecclesiastical, more worldly than mystical, spiced with juicy family gossip, gossip about the family to which they all belonged. Jerónimo had set out on the return trip to see if he might become part of that *family* at some level and thus belong at last. Now, at the end of two months and in spite of his uncle and the savory eels and the honeysuckle, he was toying with the thought of returning to the place where he'd started, even if only to commit the folly of throwing himself into the flames that enveloped Europe. He leaned over to set the glass on the table. This time, his slight movement was enough to make the inconsequential pigeons fly up to the tile roof and continue their chatter there.

It was not like Don Clemente to be late. He always sat waiting in that section of the corridor for his Friday luncheon companions, his paper read from cover to cover and his analysis of the party's latest action ready to be sprung on his guests, even before they had a chance to settle into their seats. The Archbishop had relieved him of his priestly duties so that he could retire, bedecked with honors, in order to finish out the rest of his life as a Creole gentleman and die in the house where he, as well as Jerónimo, had been born. But neither the years nor his failing health diminished the cleric's sociability. Every Friday, in his dining room, around a table heaped with seafood, he assembled a distinguished company of men who were expert at relating the ups and downs of the stock market to shakeups in the cabinet, a group versed in family bloodlines, well informed on the going prices of cattle and real estate, members of committees to receive foreign dignitaries who were bearers of sage advice, generous with appointments for those who, although not in their class, tried to imitate them. Rumor had it in the city that the country's political affairs were determined by a certain María Benítez, Don Clemente's lifelong cook, who was frequently caricatured in an insolent political lampoon as the embodiment of the oligarchy, a lady using a huge spoon to stir a cauldron labeled with the country's name. Don Clemente remarked between guffaws: "Why, they're only family luncheons!"

And it was true, for the blood relationships and the connections of the Azcoitías took in all branches of power. At the first of these luncheons Jerónimo attended, in the midst of the superb cigars proffered by Don Clemente, the men, with this or that vest button undone, greeted him warmly, recalling his father and grandfather, and pleased that, after being away for five years, he was finally back among them. One minister with an impressive paunch and whose forehead, tanned below and pale near the hairline, bespoke his customary use of the wide-brimmed hat of a landowner, said:

"Your place is here, son. Why do you want to go living in

Europe among unbelievers and degenerates, when here you're somebody? Sure, the women over there . . ."

With roars of laughter, his table companions cheered this proof of the minister's well-known insatiable appetites. Basking in their admiration, he drank another glass of red wine to the last drop and, after the first puff on his cigar, figured out Jerónimo's age:

"Let's see. Your parents were married at the end of the war in which we recovered the northern provinces. I remember it very well because I had to stay on at the border after the peace treaty, and so couldn't get to the wedding. And your poor father died a hero in the revolution. I was a minister by then and spoke at the funeral. I can see you now: very serious, with straw-colored hair like all the Azcoitías, as you led the procession. You must have been about eight years old. We all commented on your manliness. No one doubted that you'd fulfill the promising career your father's premature death had cut short. How can I help remembering that you were, let's see . . . almost twenty-six when you left for Europe, since I myself, to try to keep you here, offered you a job as my secretary at the time of the border question? You must be around thirty."

"Thirty-one . . ."

To shift a conversation that linked his personal history so uncomfortably close to his country's, Jerónimo explained that he'd come back because of the war more than anything else. The men forgot their glasses and drew their chairs around him to ask about Verdun . . . But interest in these things soon flagged, the talk gradually shifted to the recently imported vinestalks, to the possibility that a French disaster would open a wine export market for them and thus buttress the party for the coming elections. That was the important problem. In a certain key province there was need of a candidate who could draw the masses, a man with a fortune who'd be prepared to buy what couldn't be obtained otherwise and who had a name that would represent real power. They shuffled the names of persons Jerónimo didn't know, as they weighed their political and family affiliations. Don Clemente's high-pitched voice had warmed to the debate, while a judge who abstained from participation in a discussion that had been rehashed so many times nodded in a corner, his napkin, covered with crumbs, spread over his belly. The members of the party's two irreconcilable factions exchanged strong words across the remains of the lunch. One deputy left the dining room in a rage without taking leave of anyone. And later, when the sopor began to scatter the table companions to their respective siestas, the minister laid his hand on Jerónimo's shoulder as he gave his right hand a long squeeze:

"Your place is here with us."

Why couldn't the pigeons decide to take their dialogue to other roofs and repeat it for other ears? Rising to his feet, Jerónimo paced up and down the shady part of the corridor, only to have the pillars assure him, one after the other, that his place was indeed here. But he couldn't work up an interest in the place, the incentive was so slim. In his five years abroad, he'd come to accept his natural claim to persons of the highest quality and to objects of the greatest beauty. After identifying himself with all this, it was difficult to reduce himself to the coarse pleasures of his uncle's house. *On dit que Boy est le propriétaire d'un pays exotique quelque part, je ne me rappelle plus le nom. Je crois qu'il l'a inventé* . . . that's what the ladies in Paris used to say. And it was true, up to a certain point. He'd come away because of the war. True. But, more than anything, because toward the end he'd been going around with the center of his pride wounded. And, in order for the symmetry in his life to withstand the test of his own high standards, his existence would have to be different, to spring from its own roots, which were inescapable and stronger than his will. Only a lack of freedom determines one's obligations. And, as he went past thirty, Jerónimo began to feel sure that, in the end, those obligations are the only thing that endow one with nobility. When the war broke out he saw that he had no rightful place in it. His participation would have resembled an elegant sporting gesture. And, because he was growing tired of confirming the truth that elegant gestures were nothing but subterfuges, Jerónimo returned to his crude, primitive, native New World land, in search of obligations that would give nobility to his freedom.

But how could one decide to become part of a world whose loftiest truths are determined by a dish of marinated eels? The aroma of the fish María Benítez was preparing reached him there and mingled with the fragrance of the honeysuckle. When he heard footsteps, he drained another glass of brandy. At the bottom of his small glass, the priest appeared, bent over his walking stick. Before Jerónimo had time to stand up, the old man explained:

"I was held up by some business I was attending to for you."

"For me?"

"Yes, for you. How's the brandy?"

He sniffed the liquor before his nephew helped him sit down in a wicker armchair, on the threadbare shawl, molded by Don Clemente's thin buttocks, that served him as a cushion. The perspiration on the priest's face was like dew on a rosebud, still pink but wilted from so much abstinence. His cleft chin, his stature and his eyes that were blue but devoid of electricity and covered by exceedingly light lashes constituted a fragile but recognizable likeness of the sturdy material of which Jerónimo was made.

"How have you been, uncle?"

"So-so, son. Too many things on my mind. But I don't matter anymore, what we need is to have you in good health. I have something very important to propose to you."

Don Clemente sniffed longingly at his nephew's glass; his self-imposed abstinence, in addition to his poor health, allowed him to enjoy, only at a distance, the exquisite things he offered his visitors. Don Clemente went on:

"I've just come from party headquarters. The Assembly agreed that you're the man we need to put up as a candidate for deputy from the provin—"

Jerónimo couldn't suppress a horse laugh. Was this the great temptation he'd expected his country to offer him? He pictured himself dealing with backwoods apothecaries and country schoolteachers anxious to stir his interest in rebuilding some bridge swept away by the latest floods. How could he explain to his uncle that his spirit needed not that, but something much more subtle to keep him on native soil? The solution his uncle was offering him was something primary. So primary that it drew only a horse laugh from him, which nevertheless didn't dishearten Don Clemente, whose mind was on the instructions he was issuing for uncorking a bottle of very special wine.

"Because today we're going to celebrate."

"What?"

"Your deputyship."

"I'm not interested in politics."

"I knew I was going to have trouble with you. After your father died, your mother did nothing but pamper you. Nothing's worse than traveling. It stuffs young people's heads with nonsense, and they end up marrying foreigners. *Boy!* How ridiculous! Don't let anybody find out that your fancy French lady friends called you by that pansy nickname, if it ever gets around you won't stand a chance in the elections."

"But I don't . . ."

"I sent word to my regular luncheon group that I wasn't feeling fit and wasn't having anyone in today. I don't want your boyish silliness to disgrace me in the eyes of persons who expect so much of you. Your country's politics don't interest you! What a lot of nonsense! Shall we go into the dining room, son?"

Jerónimo followed Don Clemente silently. Vague sentimental memories entangled in the shadows of stationary objects in the rooms they were passing through weren't enough to make him forget that in the eyes of the owners of this ugly furniture and these topheavy drapes covering up the disorder of the *inner* patio, only the useful, the immediate, was of any consequence. And yet . . . and yet . . . as the facile logic that defeated all this welled up within him, a part of him clung to the mahogany side tables and the plush armchairs. He was finding it difficult to maintain his clarity when the disappearing light, or rather the cool shadows on the adobe walls in the dining room, for example, protected everything, except the watermelon that lay already hewn apart on the silver tray, from the assaults of intelligence.

"Uncle."

"Yes."

"I came here to tell you that I'm going back to Europe."

"You can't go, Jerónimo. Listen to me, son, be reasonable. You're the only one left . . . and I had to take it into my head to become a priest, may God forgive me for saying it. You're the last one who can hand down the family name. You don't know how I've dreamed about an Azcoitía playing an important part once more in the country's public life! I waited for you so anxiously, assuming your obligations while you were enjoying an immoral life in Paris. But you're here now, and I'm not going to let you go. This spinach soup María made for me today is terrible! Let's see, what did she serve you with the fish?"

"Capers. It's delicious."

"It smells so tempting!"

"I don't know the first thing about politics, uncle."

"I won't have you saying that your country's politics don't interest you. It's blasphemy. It means that upstarts and opportunists, all kinds of unbelieving radicals, will upset the foundations of society such as God created it, when He vested authority in us. He divided fortunes as He saw fit, giving the poor their simple pleasures, placing on our shoulders the obligations that make us His representatives on earth. His Commandments forbid violence against His divine order, and that's exactly what this bunch of unknowns, this rabble, is up to. Are you a Christian?"

"You baptized me yourself."

"That doesn't mean a thing. Anything's possible after five years in Europe, skepticism is so fashionable. But skepticism is far too complex in these crusading times. We have to defend ourselves and defend God, whose order and authority are in peril. To defend your property with the help of politics is to defend God. I'm sure you haven't even bothered to visit what belongs to you. Have you been to the Casa?"

"To La Rinconada . . ."

"No, the Casa de Ejercicios Espirituales, the retreat house at La Chimba . . ."

"I don't know, I get them mixed up, they're all the same."

"I don't see how you can say that you get them mixed up. How do you expect me to believe that you're a Christian when you never even took the trouble to answer me about the chances of beatification for our relative, Inés de Azcoitía?"

"I didn't go to Rome at the time, and afterward I forgot about it."

"You should have made a special trip, since you took so many frivolous trips everywhere else. If we were armed with her beatification written up in all the newspapers, if you'd come back brandishing it as the symbol of the power invested in us by God, winning these elections wouldn't be such a problem."

"Whose idea was it that I run for election?"

"Mine."

"I don't belong to the party."

"I enrolled you today. All you have to do is drop by and sign, nothing more, it won't put you out, it's on your way . . ."

Jerónimo rose to his feet and threw the napkin down on the table. Don Clemente gagged on his strained vegetables. Coughing until his eyes filled with tears, he managed to ask his nephew:

"Where are you going?"

Jerónimo was all set to answer: to catch the first boat that will take me far away from you people and from this world, I belong in one with more light, and even the absurd sporting gesture of sacrificing my life for a cause nothing links me to but my volition is preferable to this confinement in these inexorable patios where all one can do is reproduce, but my poor uncle goes on coughing, splattering spinach all over his napkin, racked by the cough that may be the death of him. Instead of leaving, Jerónimo went over to his uncle, made him drink a glass of water slowly and slapped him on the back gently, as if he were a baby, assuring him that, yes, he was immortal and would bury them all, that María Benítez would be coming in a minute to help him stop coughing like that, that he could be sure he wasn't going to die in his own dining room, choked by some insipid vegetables.

11

THE CAMPAIGN TRIPS Jerónimo de Azcoitía took in order to leave the imprint, on the minds of the voters, of his strength as a candidate left him little time for other things. And yet, between trips, he attended the parties his innumerable female relatives had him invited to in order to show him off as one more family asset. And things happened as they had to, as ritual among powerful people decreed that they happen: Jerónimo fell in love with the prettiest, most innocent girl who frequented the social salons at the time, a distant cousin with many female Azcoitía ancestors behind her.

Inés Santillana, heir like himself to vast lands and distinguished lineage, possessed above all a supple beauty that was as elusive as a bird's and skin as soft as if it had been washed in honey. Jerónimo was a giant next to her. Inés's lively eyes were golden, sometimes hazel, sometimes green, green especially at night when the flock of pimply adolescents, stiff in tails, surrounded her to ask the favor of a dance and she chose among them, accepting or putting them off with a smile. Jerónimo's appearance on the scene immediately dispersed the flock of suitors; no awkward young Creole was competition for a man of his perfection, wealthy and handsome, still adorned with the prestige of the superior continent from which he'd come.

Inés didn't resist her impulsive suitor's campaign. She had no reason to, since it was love at first sight in her case and, furthermore, their relationship was never established on any basis but the holy matrimony that pleased everyone. During the quiet after-dinner gatherings on the Santillana estate, Jerónimo gave worldly advice to the oldest one of his future brothers-in-law and told wonderful stories to the younger ones while, following the pattern of courtship, he held the skein of wool so that Ines's mother could wind it up. And at night, on the dance floors where the whirling of the young couples described fantastic circles under the lights, the ladies seated on the sidelines, who'd already learned to delegate their emotions to other creatures, sighed contentedly at the meeting of these two privileged beings and felt relieved that Jerónimo, who was certainly old enough, seemed about to settle down.

On the Sunday before the one set for the wedding, the country lunch with which the two assembled clans celebrated the new couple's happy future ended with the women sitting around Inés and asking her everything about her trousseau, while some distance away the group of men, flushed with the heat and the wine, fanned themselves with their straw hats as they settled the last-minute details of Jerónimo's political campaign, which would enter its final phase when he returned from his honeymoon. The future bride looked at Jerónimo from the other side of the table set up under the grape arbor.

During the last months before the wedding, the rules laid down by age-old custom didn't allow the couple much time for intimacy. Inés's hours were wisely complicated with visits, seamstresses, invitations, presents, and in the shadows of the gallery that the family, with discreet signs to one another, left to them for a few moments at dusk, there was little time for her lips to find Jerónimo's lips.

Under the arbor, Inés waited for Jerónimo to finish the glass of port he was drinking with Don Clemente, who looked years younger with the turn his life, embodied in his nephew's, was taking. And, over the protests of the older people who wanted to keep on treating her as a child, she dragged Jerónimo off to stroll with her in the shade of the peach trees.

Inés couldn't understand the involvements that attracted Jerónimo in all this. The rules and the formulas of their courtship, its ritual as fixed and stylized as the symbols of heraldry, inscribed his own figure and that of Inés, the two of them entwined under fruit-laden trees, as in a stone medallion, a medallion that was just one section of the eternal frieze composed of many such medallions, among which they, the betrothed, were but momentary incarnations of designs much vaster than the details of their individual psychologies. Inés's body and soul, both untouched, waited for him to animate her, to get her out of the first medallion and into the sumptuousness of the next.

There were many things Jerónimo had to forget in order to resolve to enter that world. His love for Inés placed him at the very center of this game that was played by rules, stages and formulas. But the certainty that he'd have been able to participate in other, higher forms of life if he'd chosen to placed Jerónimo outside the game as well, at an ironic distance from it all. He merely took pains to see that the magnificent legend of the perfect couple was fulfilled in both himself and his bride-to-be. Why explain to Inés that a person's only as great as that which he sacrifices of his own free will, only as powerful as that which he's capable of keeping immured within him?

"Will you? I promised to take you to her. She sees you when you and I are left alone in the gallery. She hides among the plants outside and watches us kissing. She told me that you look like a prince, she finds you so handsome . . ."

Jerónimo kissed her into silence. The womb heaving against his body would open to procure immortality for him: through their sons and grandsons, the frieze of medallions would extend forever. In the girl's fair skin, in her voice, he detected a sexuality whose force she didn't suspect, and he'd set the seal of his own form on it. Jerónimo murmured: "There's so little time left . . ."

"There's so much . . ."

Jerónimo drew away from her, and they went on strolling arm in arm.

"My name will be exactly like hers. Strange, having the same name as a saint's, isn't it?"

"What are you talking about?"

"Well, about our common ancestor whose name was Inés de Azcoitía . . . the one in the Casa at La Chimba, they say she's a saint."

"I've never heard that before."

"Because your mother died when you were still very small,

and you're a man and those are things only women talk about."

"I've never heard it from your mother either . . ."

"I know she's a saint and that she performed miracles."

"How do you know it?"

"Peta told me the whole story. That there were nine brothers, and that the girl-saint's nursemaid gave her a little cross, made of branches tied together with strips of leather, which she always preserved. They say it was this cross made for her by her nursemaid that saved the Casa from the earthquake. Let Peta tell you about it."

"What Peta?"

"What do you mean, what Peta? Peta Ponce. I've been talking to you about her for hours, but you're not listening to me, because you think I'm an ignorant little girl who talks only about silly things. You'll find out when we get married. She has a present for you . . ."

"Who?"

"Really, Jerónimo! Peta Ponce, who else? I've told you a thousand times that she was so good to me when I took sick. She'd been brought from my grandfather Fermín's farm to embroider my mother's wedding sheets and then she stayed on to help with the sewing. She has a present that she says is worthy of you. Let's go see her."

"Let's go."

They looked for Peta's quarters past the warehouses and the poultry yards, where the mansion broke down into a disorder of utilitarian structures without pretension to beauty: the neglected reverse of the façade. Inés stopped before a door. Something had come over her; suddenly, only that heavy door was important. She turned around abruptly.

"I'm going to take her with me. Mother gave her to me. She told me I may take her with me if I want, because she's of no use here."

"But I haven't told you that you couldn't."

"Well, you're so strange sometimes."

"Will she want to go?"

"Peta Ponce wants anything I want. You don't mind, do you, darling? She's old. She won't be in the way. You'll see."

Inés pushed the door open. Inside, Jerónimo was assaulted by the harsh odor of the storeroom, an odor of sacks of beans and potatoes and chickpeas and lentils, of bales of alfalfa and straw and sweet clover, of onions, chili peppers and pimentos, and of strings of garlic hanging from the beams. After the opulent light and heat of the day left behind outside, it was difficult to get one's bearings and judge distances in that vault. Jerónimo called out to Inés very softly. He thought she'd answer him from a distance, like an echo, but he felt her take his hand and whisper beside him: "This way."

As Inés helped him step around crates, sacks, bales, Jerónimo's eyes gradually made out, in the darkness, the height of the beamed ceiling from which harnesses and reins were hanging. But as they approached a thick wall of bales, a peculiar odor dislodged the harmonious natural ones: the smell of old clothes, of a brazier, of warmed-over food, of things blackened by smoke and alien to the noble proportions of the storeroom. A ray of light revealed a line minutely bristling with tiny straws. In the corner shielded by the wall of bales, a candle's quivering light rescued several objects from the darkness. The soft shadows of the bedstead's iron bars danced lazily on the wall where faded pictures of saints blessed the expired time of old calendars and the clock's single hand. A being seated on a footstool put the kettle back on the burning brazier.

"Peta."

"You've come!"

The heap of rags gathered itself together in order to give human reply to Inés's call. The old woman and the girl embarked on a conversation Jerónimo wasn't prepared to tolerate. The scene didn't fit into any medallion of eternal stone. And, if it did fit into any, it was into the other series, into the hostile legend that contradicted his own: the legend of the stained and the damned, who writhe on the left hand of God the Father Almighty. He had to pull Inés out of there immediately. To prevent her from taking part in this other series of medallions, the ones linked to servitude, to oblivion, to death. Inés was only a child who could be contaminated by the least little thing.

". . . and I've brought you Jerónimo, Peta."

The crone approached Jerónimo and surveyed him.

". . . and he wants you to come and live with us."

"Won't I be in the way, sir?"

Before Jerónimo could answer, Inés intervened.

"No. The new house is big."

"Whatever you say, dear child."

"Didn't you have a present for Jerónimo?"

The old woman dug into the bundles hidden under the bed. She placed a small white package in Jerónimo's hands.

"Open it, sir."

Jerónimo obeyed, more than anything in order to give himself time to decide how to go about breaking Inés's ties with the underside of life, the world of the left hand, of the reverse, of those things destined to perish in obscurity without ever knowing the light. Inside the package, he found three white handkerchiefs of the finest batiste, with hand-stitched borders and initials so exquisitely embroidered that they sent a shudder through him. How could they possibly have emerged from under that bed, from the warty hands of the old woman? They were the three most beautiful, most perfect handkerchiefs he'd seen in his life . . . if he'd ever dreamed about handkerchiefs, it was these, their fragility, their perfect proportions, their fineness, yes, he'd dreamed about these very handkerchiefs, these handkerchiefs he held in his hands . . . that old woman introduced herself into his dreams and stole them. Otherwise, from where in the misery of her world, from what hidden source of power, could Peta have acquired the subtle sense of taste and the skill to make those three masterpieces? A searing pang of wonderment upset the neat order of his world as he recognized a powerful enemy in Peta Ponce.

"Thanks. We have to go now."

"But Jerónimo . . . Didn't you want Peta to tell you the story of the Blessed Inés? And of the Casa? She's so old she knows things no one remembers anymore."

"I don't want to know anything. Let's go."

He took her arm.

"Goodbye."

Before leading Inés away, Jerónimo left a coin in the old

woman's hands, hands that were full of warts, misshapen, tremulous, hands with chipped yellow nails, hands capable of anything, even of creating beauty they had no right to create, for, by creating it, they relegated him to the inferior plane of admirer of the diminutive beauty of those three handkerchiefs. Outside, Inés confronted him:

"Why did you do it?"

Inés was crying as she was dragged along by Jerónimo, who finally released her as they crossed the laundry by way of the narrow passage of two very long white tablecloths, with matching napkins, that hung from parallel wires.

"Why did I do what?"

"Everything. Give her money."

"I don't want you ever to have anything to do with her."

"Peta saved my life."

It was cold in the laundry. A slippery cold, indifferent to the reflections of the sun in the blue water outside in the stone troughs and on the pavement where the wash dripped. Jerónimo wanted to get away once and for all, even if Inés was crying. The childish hands of his bride-to-be clung to him, trying to hold him back and tell him the story:

"I was very young. When my mother was going to have Fermín, she fell seriously ill and I was sent to the nuns in the Casa de la Encarnación at La Chimba so that I'd be out of the way. Peta went with me. And, in the Casa, I started to have violent stomach pains, something here, it was awful, it felt as if I were being torn apart inside. Even now I sometimes think those pains are going to come back and I'm terrified. They sent doctors to the Casa, Father went too, they came there every day because they regretted having taken me to a place that was so far away but from which I could no longer be moved, I was so sick. The doctors couldn't understand it. They shook their heads, that's all, and, although I was just a little girl, I saw I was going to die there. I was dying, Jerónimo, I was dying of something nobody could understand or cure. Each stitch of pain would be the last. One night, when I felt the most terrifying pains, Peta got up. I can see her bent over in the dark, comforting me. I quieted down in spite of the pains and I heard that immense silence you can sometimes hear in the Casa. I let Peta undress me. And, drawing her lips to my stomach, she put them here, Jerónimo, right on the focus of the pain, and started sucking and sucking and sucking, till the pains disappeared completely with Peta's last draft of my stomach. I was left with something like a vacuum, here. She made me swear I'd never tell anyone. You're the first. Not even Mother knows about it. Then something very strange happened: poor Peta Ponce started to get sick with the same pains I'd been having. Peta's gone on feeling those pains of mine all her life."

"Witch! Neither of you should ever again have left that damned Casa. She's sullied your mind and I'm saddled with the job of cleaning it out. First of all, I'm going to tell your mother that you're never to see Peta Ponce again, I'm going to see that the Casa's torn down immediately . . ."

"You wouldn't dare . . ."

Inés took a step toward Jerónimo. She dug her nails into his face. He backed up at the onslaught of those five fingernails, unknown to him until now. He got tangled up in one of the tablecloths and cut the line, and the viscous, wet material fell on top of him, knocking him to the ground with its weight. When Jerónimo succeeded in freeing himself from the sticky shroud, Inés had disappeared. He rubbed his cheek, and his hand came away covered with red: deep scratches, right on the mark, claws that know how to wound and inflict pain. He used Peta Ponce's handkerchiefs to stanch his blood. He sneaked out of the house without being seen. What good would an explanation do him now? It was too late to back out. The wedding was to take place in seven days.

On the morning of the ceremony, Jerónimo entered the Basilica of La Merced wearing the red scars on his left cheek. He made his way down the narrow aisle of white flowers and pleased faces, looking arrogant, sure of himself, dominating the congregation to keep anyone from wondering what those scars on the bridegroom's face were.

The thrill of wearing her white gown, so heavily embroidered it was stiff as armor, stilled Inés's terror as she swore false obedience to her husband before the confident eyes of Don Clemente. In his golden vestments like those on an idol and surrounded by clouds of smoke from the censers, he demanded of her, before God, the most powerful member of the family present at the ceremony, not to harbor impure designs. Before the gold altar, in an atmosphere of canticles and ancient sacred words, Inés swore falsely, knowing very well what she intended to do. A week before, when her mother had taken her to Don Clemente to prepare her for matrimony, the priest, in warning her that it was a mortal sin to deny her husband her body, hadn't known that he was placing a weapon in Inés's hands.

She was aware of how much Jerónimo desired her. And so, on her wedding night, with a clear head, coldly, she committed the mortal sin of denying her body to her husband, whom she also desired. And she'd have gone on denying it to him for the rest of her life if, toward dawn, her body, implacably naked beside him, hadn't set fire to her husband's lucidity. She won; he promised her everything, anything she wanted, anything she asked for, until she finally made him promise, when she sensed that he no longer knew what he was promising, so long as she gave in, that he'd never, for any reason whatever, separate her from Peta Ponce. From that night on, Jerónimo and Inés have never been alone in their marriage bed. Some shadow or other —mine, Boy's, the Blessed Inés's—always keeps them company. On their wedding night, it was Don Clemente and Peta Ponce, fighting to see which would prevail, who urged them on, like puppet masters with their papier-mâché dolls.

12

JERÓNIMO'S FOUR BLACK dogs snarl, fighting over the chunk of warm meat that's almost still alive. They tear it to shreds, barking at it down in the dirt and tossing it around, their red mouths foaming, their palates pimpled, their fangs bared, their eyes flashing from their narrow faces. Once the scraps have been devoured, they dance around him again, wanting to be petted . . . my four dogs as black as the shadows of wolves have the bloody instinct, the ferocious heavy paws, of thoroughbreds. They're docile only with me, owner of the meat they gobble down and the park they guard.

"Throw them some more offal."

The farmhand lets the viscera fly over the leaps of my brutes, who are fighting one another and snarling so much that they don't snare it . . . bite, you stupid animals, don't take your eyes off it, don't fight, can't you see the yellow bitch dog stealing the offal, bite her, kill her . . . the scrawny bitch hovering around the meal intended for my noble dogs made the most of the confusion of paws and snouts in order to steal the dogs' scraps, there she goes, tearing off, hunched up, trembling, her tail between her legs, as she drags the meat across the clearing and vanishes behind the chapel. Before my four black dogs notice the affront, the peon throws them another scrap of meat. Could he have done it to distract them and cover the culprit's escape? I'm sure he'll have to be bought tomorrow at the elections; he'll eat my meat and drink my wine, and afterwards he'll vote against me because he hates me.

"Do you own that yellow bitch?"

"No, boss. Nobody owns her."

"What do you mean, nobody?"

"Sometimes she comes in to steal garbage from the kitchen areas. And she also comes into the park when you go hunting with the black dogs."

"Why don't you people throw her out of the park?"

"Madam won't let us throw her out."

Glutted, my dogs lie down in the cool underbrush beside the ditch. They've spent all morning haunting the corrals where the young steers were slaughtered to celebrate my victory at the polls. The yellow bitch turned up there again, licking the bloodied hides hanging in the cattle pens out in the sun, near the sties on the other side of the clearing where the pigs scratch their backs against the stakes, and getting her snout smeared with blood, on which the sticky flies, stupefied by the heat, feast. The yellow bitch is a mere scrawl there, skin and bones, eager, voracious, capable of eating anything whatever, even the most disgusting things. She haunts the legs of the horses hitched to the post, hunched up in her eagerness to snap at their shins. She's content, as if in anticipation of greater pleasures, to sniff the puddles of their urine and poke her nose in the fresh dung. I have to speak to Inés about her, this can't go on, *the bitch* can't go on, it's not like Inés to accept a filthy animal like this, she who never goes out into the sun without a veiled hat and won't touch a branch without putting on her gloves.

It was late when I stretched out next to her on the balcony. I covered her feet with a vicuña poncho and mine with the other. And we saw the strange constellations appear from out of the shadows dangling from the trees in the park at La Rinconada. The singing of the frogs circumscribes our privacy, protecting us from intrusions.

"What are you thinking of?"

Inés stretched a little.

"I? Of nothing . . ."

Why is she thinking of nothing? She must be thinking of something, she has to tell me what, even if it's only a "my God, the color of Laura's dress is horrid" or a "what a pity Carlos's and Blanquita's marriage is on the rocks." Maybe it's true that you're not thinking of anything, although not thinking of anything at precisely the closest moments is a means of defense, Inés, an escape to keep your mind blank, blocked out by the absence of your being, so that fear and doubt won't leave their impress on you . . . think of anything, so long as you think and can tell me what you're thinking, even if you're thinking about the yellow bitch I'll have to talk to you about, if I can remember something so trivial, when you're no longer somewhere else instead of here, now, with me, someplace where you're thinking of something terribly definite that's the very thing I can't stop thinking about even at moments when this very real passion I feel for you should wipe out all thought, yours and mine, but it can't wipe out an absence, a void you show me and I demand you show me because you mustn't show me the other thing, because it isn't true. I could repudiate you. And hate you. And seek in another what your obstinate menstrual blood has been denying me during five years of marriage. But I can't. Anything except complete happiness would start a reign of terror.

A blue diamond lights up amid the shrubbery in the park, goes off and on again farther away, gold now, twinkles closer by and goes off again, and in the dark bushes more tiny flashes appear that look at you and me and disappear, jewels, stars, eyes, a flash the leaves try to hide and that reappears, multiplying, fading out, moving in and out of the dark bushes, not stalking us but watching over us, because they're the eyes of my dogs roaming about the hydrangeas, slowly now, red, pink, watchful; the steely eyes that stopped flashing yonder light up again, closer now, here in the shrubbery right at the foot of the balcony where you and I are stretched out, like fixed lightning flashes against the line of clearness as fine as the blade edge your perfect profile suggests. I let my hand drop, brushing your hand almost casually. You conceal your profile because, as you look at me, you're broken up into different planes that offer me another version of your face that's not thinking of anything because it isn't here, but the golden eyes, the eyes of steel, the green or blue sparks among the black leaves of the park, confirm Inés's presence and, appeased, shift, flash, are extinguished, fixing us in an instantaneous reflection that dissolves and leaves everything in darkness . . . don't you see, I have to erase everything in her now but complete faith in our happiness, to demolish the anxiety of that word murmured in passing, *nothing* . . . I'm thinking of *nothing* . . . I have time to destroy it because there's a drop trembling on a leaf and there's an eye pupil in the drop, and the lighted pupil gazes at us, the eyes of witnesses who demand our happiness, are watching us to see if the darkness gives some hint of a breach in that happiness, we can't let down those witnesses so anxious to watch our perfect love. I brush your hand lightly again. Do you see how Inés shudders, even if just barely? You can only gaze at that shudder, not feel it, because you're nothing but eyes eager to have us show you our happiness now, right here, you, the witnesses, leave us no choice, if I don't give in immediately to your demand that we expose our full capacity for pleasure, you'll disappear and everything will vanish if there are no eyes to watch us, leaving me reduced to the offal I feed my black dogs, who won't recognize their master's blood, they'll devour me if I don't let them see here, now, that our happiness is complete. I press her hand. It's perfect. Cold. It responds to mine as I barely press it, and I press harder and pull her over to the hydrangea bushes, where we can hide like adolescents.

"Jerónimo . . . no . . ."

"Yes."

"We have the entire house and all night . . ."

"It makes no difference, here."

"I'm afraid."

"Of what?"

"Somebody might see us."

"Who?"

"I don't know . . ."

"Don't be silly."

The ring of glittering eyes has stationed itself in the thicket that surrounds us. Don't be afraid of the witnesses, Inés. Look at how beautiful those eyes are with their blue glint. They all belong to me. Let me undress you before the luster of those eyes. Lie down on this bed of leaves . . . Gaze at her, that's what I have you for, and on me too as I strip off my clothes, gaze at me too: rejoice in my powerful erection, envy it, that's why I feed you, see how I lie down beside Inés in the lanceolate cold of the leaves, how I force her to open her hazel eyes and look at those other refulgent eyes whose pain increases our stature by gazing upon us, how my hands caress your body, how my lips travel over your coolness, making it warm, hot, setting it on fire, how my organ makes you sigh, moan, forget that you're thinking of *nothing*, as I fill up the entire void you won't give over to me and have refused to give over to me during five years of happiness, listen to her moan, how Inés's modesty surrenders and falls and leaves her more naked and more tightly pressed against my body as she murmurs my prodigious name and moans even more as I invade her, and finally screams without caring if they see and hear her when I at last triumph inside her and collapse completely before that multitude of steely, yellow, green, glacial, burnished eyes that light up and flicker, and hide and reappear, eager to watch again, restoring my potency.

The vegetation also hid me, Mother Benita, because I too was watching them; two of those eyes burning in the darkness of the park at La Rinconada, two of the pupils in that chorus that was needed to give that pleasure its uniqueness, two of those eyes, the most avid, the most tortured, the most deeply wounded, were my own, Mother Benita, these same eyes you see before you that are dimmed by fever now, and whose lids you try to lower with your hand to help me rest and sleep . . . sleep, Mudito, sleep, rest, sleep, close your eyes, you tell me, snuff out those eyes that have already served their purpose, lower your eyelids and sleep . . . but I can't shut them because they burn in their sockets as they watch them enjoy themselves among the leaves, my ears cocked for their intermittent words and the sound of their bodies, my nose on the alert for the perfume of love, and, unknown to them, in the heat of their emotions, my hand, this hand you're holding in yours, this hand, touched those bodies while they created happiness over and over again, until finally those eyes in the vegetation gradually flickered out and Don Jerónimo kept looking for them in order to restore himself with the shining eyes grown dim . . . where are they, where are they, they've gone, Inés, they've gone, we've been left in total darkness, maybe there were never any eyes staring at us and everything's always been dark, no, there are the golden eyes, I'm myself again, I desire you more than ever now because I know that you're tired and I'm tired, those gummy golden eyes see how I penetrate you, how you draw new life, those gummy eyes so close to ours, more, more, until Inés let out the final cry, Mother Benita, not only a cry of pleasure but also a cry of terror, for as she opened her eyes to look at the constellation of glittering eyes around Jerónimo's face, she saw the yellow bitch come over to sniff at them or lap up the juices their bodies left on the leaves: the yellow bitch, panting, drooling, covered with sores and warts, hunger written all over her eyes, she, the only one who has the power to draw out that cry.

WHEN THE NEWS arrived that in a town up in the mountains, in the area where the radicals had poisoned the miners with promises of claiming their rights, someone stole the ballot boxes right in the middle of the voting, the conservative leaders grouped around Don Jerónimo de Azcoitía decided it would be safer to bolt the doors and windows of the Social Club. The party had never expected to carry the mining region. It was taken for granted that this area would go to the radicals. But some unidentified idiot, probably a fool-headed drunkard, rode his horse into the schoolhouse where the miners were voting and escaped with the ballot boxes, hoping this supposed act of heroism would earn him Don Jerónimo's favor. The grave outcome of all this: the ignorant crowd in the square in front of the Social Club, probably egged on by the radicals, who made the most of the opportunity dropped in their lap without their having to lift a finger, blamed them, the political bosses, the caciques, for something any fool could see was a wrong move from a political standpoint.

Now, the slightest provocation would be enough for the workers, who'd ridden in from the small towns to the capital of the province, dressed in their Sunday best, to break out in violence and even make blood run. But, fired up by the wine, the crowd milled around aimlessly in the square. They smoked, they split up into muttering groups, but they had no immediate cause for excitement.

Don Jerónimo de Azcoitía spent the whole afternoon shut up in the Social Club, consuming bottle after bottle of red wine with his political confreres, waiting for the crowd to disperse. But the crowd didn't break up. A dark night fell. A gray, muttering mass was gathering under the double row of palm trees that fringed the square on all four sides. And the street lamps weren't going on.

Don Jerónimo wanted to go out, to get into his carriage and leave for La Rinconada as if nothing had happened, which, as far as he was concerned, was true. But his colleagues, who kept peering through cracks in the windows, begged him not to do it. He must stay there for the sake of the country, for the sake of the party, he had to remain, to wait, going out would be defiance, the match that would light the fuse. He argues that they should make the most of this last moment of the mob's bewilderment and leave the Social Club. Furthermore, they should leave one or two at a time, each going his own way as if nothing were wrong, since, as he never tired of insisting, they weren't guilty. On the contrary, it would be very useful to impress the multitude with their complete innocence of the theft. Knowing the mentality of the workers better, the other leaders thought that if they were to leave the Club now they'd better do it secretly, before the inevitable agitator incited the people. It was absurd to go out with the insulting arrogance Jerónimo proposed; it would be wiser to climb up on the rooftops and make their getaway by heading for other houses from which they could reach the back streets, where no one would notice them, because all attention was fixed on the square, on the door of the Social Club. In this way, when the mob decided to attack the Club as the seat of the corrupt oligarchy, they'd find it empty.

But Don Jerónimo insisted that, if they did this, they'd be admitting a nonexistent guilt, which was the easiest way to play right into their hands and upset the election results. Imbeciles, ignoramuses, riffraff, traitors, they can't be trusted; what scum had a finger in this? Dressed in their ponchos and spurs, the landowners drinking with Don Jerónimo at the bar or pacing back and forth among the plants in the gallery weren't convinced. Another bottle of wine, that good one you've got stashed away somewhere, Pancho, and if there's none left, any wine will do as long as it's not vinegar, and some hot dressed-pork sandwiches . . . there's nothing left, we're even running out of bread and we'll surely have to spend the night here if the police don't break up the mob, I don't know what the hell those damn cops are waiting for. The poor hate us. Look at them grumbling out there without the guts to do a thing if someone doesn't lead them. They're jealous of us. They want to take everything away from us. They talk of demands, but they're nothing but a bunch of hooligans, criminals who shouldn't be running around loose. Look at them, they're having a regular picnic. Of course, theoretically and judicially at least, they're in the right in this case. Don Jerónimo jumped to his feet.

"Let's go, Humberto."

"Yes, Don Jerónimo, whenever you're ready."

"What the hell's wrong with the lights in this town?"

"They're going to blame you for that too."

The crush of people was moving in from the side avenues of palms to concentrate on the avenue in front of the Social Club. Some of the gentlemen peered out, trying to spot individuals so as to know whom to wreak vengeance on later. Above the palm leaves the sky still contained some light, which was pierced by the spire of the church directly across the way from the Social Club, on the other side of the square, and that's where Don Jerónimo's carriage was waiting. But to reach it he'd have to pass through hundreds and hundreds of silent men watching the door of the Club they couldn't enter . . . what's it like inside, they say their binges and banquets are fabulous, they win and lose whole estates at monte, the jack of spades came up at the wrong time for the owner of Los Pedregales and he committed suicide, but all we can bet are a few pesos, a round of drinks at the most, and we have to light out when we can't pay for the wine we bet . . . the hundreds of silent men in the square hate us, they're up to something, they're waiting, milling around out there, muttering, with their hands in their pockets. We can't hear the hum of their voices now, but we will later on all right . . . One man gets up on a bench in the square and launches into a harangue: abuses, injustice, corruption, treason; these special elections to replace the dead senator who was one of us just go to show the abuses they'll inflict on us in the coming presidential elections, it gives us a shocking glimpse of the kind of elections we'll get if we let the likes of that Azcoitía dude . . .

"Do you have the pistols, Humberto?"

"Yes I have them."

"Give me the big one."

"What are we going to do?"

"Follow me."

"But what are we going to do, Don Jerónimo?"

"Do exactly as I do."

"What are these nuts up to?"

"Take the bar off the door."

"They're out of their minds."

"Jerónimo, don't . . ."

"What's the matter, I'm telling you to take the bar off . . ."

They'll kill you, Jerónimo, they'll lynch you, can't you see that the mob's hatred for us is concentrated on your person, don't go out, wait awhile and see what happens . . . As no one followed his order to remove the bar, he did it himself: without any help, he lifted the antique iron bar, which was so heavy it took two employees to lift it every day. His arm swelled under the white fabric of his roundabout, for a moment his face turned so red that his blue eyes sparkled. Outside, the shouts died down when someone remarked: "They're opening up."

"Look . . ."

They opened the door and he went out. He put his hat on, after looking at the sky as if he were afraid it might rain. He threw away his cigar. He stared at them from the top of the steps. A buzz rose from the multitude. Beyond the thick of the crowd, men called to one another, come on, come on, the dude just came out, here he comes, don't miss this, it's worth seeing, as the whole town gathered excitedly in the square, running from every side, pouring out of the bars, leaving the doors of the houses wide open, to get a look at Don Jerónimo de Azcoitía. It was a moment of stupefaction, of hands sunk into pockets, of small talk and of cigarettes that were allowed to go out because the important thing was to get a look. Only the water went on falling indifferently from the spouts of the nymphs in the fountain that graced the center of the square. Someone urged:

"Let him talk!"

"Yes, we want an explanation!"

"I have nothing to explain."

He walked down the steps.

"All right, let me through, I'm going to my farm, there's nothing more to be done here . . ."

This wasn't his public voice. It was calm, private, as if he were telling me, as he had so often, that we should go back to La Rinconada because it was late and he didn't want Inés to be worried because he hadn't returned. He stopped to light another cigar, taking his time. He stepped forward, and the crowd curved backward to give him room. He didn't cross over, as I thought he would, toward the fountain with the gamboling nymphs in the middle of the square, to reach the side where it would be easy to get to his carriage. He walked very calmly, as if nothing out of the way were happening, along the avenues of palms around the square, through the mob he cowed into opening a lane of faces sullen under straw hats, of bodies reeking of wine, of vengeance that showed in the men's eyes, of fists clenched but not yet raised. On the outer fringes of the crowd, those who got up on the benches or shinned up the lamp posts to look and shout began to be aroused . . . beat him up, kill him, cut off the bastard's balls . . .

"Why haven't the lights gone on?"

"It's high time, it's the mayor's fault."

"Don't forget to do as I do, Humberto."

"No."

As Don Jerónimo approached the parish church the violence on the fringes of the mob spread to the people farther in. Hats were waving in the air. Shouts that pronounced the villain's name as if to stab him, obscene yells, insults, all the hatred of the masses, traveled toward the center of the multitude around Don Jerónimo, who puffed on his cigar as he walked down the middle of the clearing, surrounded by faces, all identical, that were closing in on him.

"Let me through."

A poorly shaven giant asked:

"Where d'ya think you're goin'?"

"To my carriage."

The giant didn't get out of his way.

"Let me through."

The crowd shrank some more. There was bloodshed in the air. Don Jerónimo could see it. Backing up toward the church door, he braced himself against it and drew his pistol:

"What do you want?"

There was a hush.

"What's going on? Speak up. What the hell do you want?"

The first row of the semicircle fell back, cowed by his pistol. And, like a man possessed, as if suddenly drunk on the success of his own daring, he began to shout at them, threatening the semicircle with his pistol:

"What's wrong, you scum bastards, speak up, tell me what it is I've done to get you all stirred up like this, what the hell do you want, you're such a bunch of imbeciles that you can't even say what it is you want, why are you so fired up, you don't even know why, goddamn sons of bitches, lily-livered bastards . . ."

I saw a blade flash. A hand reaching for a pistol under a poncho. A horsewhip held ready, a stick, a fist clenched hard, someone bending down to pick up a rock, a look that was translated into pinning him against the church door, which opened and allowed Don Jerónimo to vanish as if swallowed up by a trapdoor.

Once inside, I helped the parish priest lock the door. The fists of those wild animals beat against it, and the shouts of the mob grew louder.

"Follow me, Don Jerónimo, this way, come on in, I have a ladder ready for you to go up to the roof and cross over to the houses in back. A carriage is waiting for you. No, not yours, we don't want them to get suspicious."

Tricked, unprepared for the sudden disappearance of the guilty figure, frustrated with no one to vent their fury on, the crowd went on shouting for a while but started to become disorganized, purposeless, not knowing which way to turn, since they couldn't knock down the church door. You could be an extreme radical, but the Church was always the Church. The priest was helping us get up to the roof. From above, I could see the crowd still besieging the church. Someone suddenly shouted:

"There he is . . . there he is . . ."

I remember that raised hand, Mother Benita, I remember the face of the first man who pointed to the roof, I remember each and every one of those raised stares.

"Where?"

"There he goes."

The mass had once more found a purpose. There he goes, tearing across the roof of the parish priest's house, look at him, it's him, Don Jerónimo de Azcoitía skipping out, it's not true that the dude is skipping out but look at him, thousands of witnesses saw Don Jerónimo on the roof, looking enormous, heroic, a shadow standing out against what little light remained in the sky.

"Kill him."

A shot rang out.

Thousands of eyes saw what happened: Don Jerónimo de Azcoitía's heroic form doubled up with pain, lost its balance, and hurtled into the priest's courtyard after sliding down the sloping roof that, instead of delivering the culprit to the mob to be torn to pieces, whisked him out of sight.

When the crowd in the square realized what the unthinking animal that was all of them had done, they started asking who it was, who did it, who was the imbecile, who the criminal . . . it was you, Lucho . . . no, it was Anacleto . . . no, I don't have a pistol . . . it must have been that guy with the handlebar mustache none of us knows . . . there goes the guy with the handlebars hightailing it . . . no, he's not hightailing it, I know him, he wouldn't kill a flea, nobody's hightailing it anywhere, nobody knows who the goddamn criminal is, who killed him when there's nothing in it for anybody because these dudes always come out on top . . . hell, this Don Jerónimo guy has a lot of guts, he may be a dude but he's got guts, he insulted us, thinks we're dirt, makes slaves of us, exploits us, is going to trick us and get on our good side in the presidential elections and buy votes for his candidate, he's going to get us all drunk on wine from his own cellars, and load us on carts like animals and ship us off to vote for the candidate he tells us to, yes, the dude had to be killed.

The police charged in on horses to arrest someone, but the question was whom, and why . . . all right, somebody speak up and tell what happened here . . . anyhow we've got to break up this crowd, you can't pull in a thousand men . . . where's the senator, there's no question he was elected senator, although they're capable of having killed him . . . get a move on, go home, on your way, all of you, and no squawking, we'll investigate later . . . run somebody in, it doesn't matter who, we'll never get to the bottom of this . . . break it up . . . finally there was no one left in the square. The police captain knocked on the church door. The priest was slow in opening it.

"Come in, captain, come in, all of you. It was time you turned up."

That's how they tell it in the history books, Mother Benita, the way it came out in the papers and the way I've put it down on these pages you're reading. But it wasn't Don Jerónimo who fell wounded, Mother Benita, it was I.

WHEN HE SHOUTED, "What's wrong, you scum, speak up, tell me what it is I've done to get you all stirred up like this," as he looked into the thousand eyes looking at him from the square in which the street lights weren't going on, I was present, almost hidden behind the folds of his poncho. No one even saw me. It was he, alone before the quarrelsome mob that was all set to, but did not, attack. And yet, Mother Benita—this is something I can confess to you because I'm down with fever and sick people are entitled to certain privileges—although I was with him, I was against him too, I was with them, full of vengeance, hating him because my voice would never have the authority to shout "you scum, what do you want, all right now, beat it if you don't want anything," and I wanted to go over to their side because he was insulting me too, even if his poncho shielded me, to go over to the side of the anonymous masses again, to multiply my hatred in those hundreds who were hating him, to lose myself among those who were about to lynch him, to side with the victims who were about to turn into killers, yes, Mother Benita, why not confess the truth to you: at that moment my wild longing *to be* Don Jerónimo and possess a voice that wouldn't sound absurd shouting "you scum" was tearing me so to pieces that I'd have thrown him to them with pleasure so that we could all tear him apart limb from limb, take his innards, feast on his groans, his ruin, the end of his happiness, his blood. I could have done it, Mother. People knew me as his trusted man, especially when it came to things he didn't like to do himself. I could have shouted to them: he's guilty, I, Humberto Peñaloza, his secretary, swear to you that I'm certain he planned everything. That would have been enough to make them attack him with sticks and knives, and I could have seen the spectacle of Don Jerónimo's blood shed at our feet.

But what would become of me, then? What would become of the features, still so precarious, that my face was gradually acquiring? If I did this, wouldn't I be ending all my chances to participate in Don Jerónimo de Azcoitía's being? Now at least I was a part of him, a part so insignificant that I was practically invisible beside his stature, but still a part. That's why I let them go on looking at him menacingly but inert, because this way at least some of the hatred that showed how powerful he was belonged to me too.

The priest opened the door for us. We locked it from the inside. He had everything ready in the courtyard: a stepladder to go up to the roof and from there into the house behind, where the carriage was waiting for us to escape while the people concentrated their attention on the church. Being lighter, I went up first, testing the resistance of the moldy tiles. It was very simple: a matter of climbing up the pitched roof from the side overlooking the priest's courtyard and going down the other side, where there was a ladder prepared for us to get down to the courtyard of the house behind. I told Don Jerónimo to wait a minute while I checked to see if everything on the other side was in readiness. But, once I was up the ladder, I couldn't control myself. When I heard the shouts of the mob that was jammed against the church door, I couldn't hold myself back, Mother Benita, I had to stand up on the peak of the roof facing the square.

"Humberto . . ."

Don Jerónimo was calling out to me.

"Have you lost your mind? What are you doing?"

I couldn't answer him. I stood still for one or two minutes, and then I shouted:

"Go ahead and kill me, you scum bastards, here I am . . ."

There's no historical record of my shout, because my voice made no sound. My words didn't pass into history. But someone pointed me out. A thousand eyes saw Don Jerónimo de Azcoitía on the roof. The shot rang out. A thousand witnesses watched me double up with pain from the bullet that grazed my arm right here, Mother Benita, on the spot Don Jerónimo's perfect glove had grazed years before. The scar's getting hard like a knot, bloody like a stigma. How could I still not bear the brand that reminds me that a thousand eyes as anonymous as mine were witnesses that I'm Jerónimo de Azcoitía? I didn't steal his identity. They conferred it on me. History picked out that moment as the apex of the power of an oligarchy that, from then on, declined. But people who read history, whether they're for or against the traditional party, can't help showing admiration for Don Jerónimo de Azcoitía's daring that evening in the town square. People still don't know it's Humberto Peñaloza they're admiring, the heroic bloodstained figure who, outlined against the remaining twilight, insulted them.

"Careful, Humberto . . ."

"Did they kill him?"

No, they didn't kill me. When I doubled up with pain, I lost my balance and fell into the courtyard. I managed to grab the roof tiles and hang on to the gutter, while the priest rushed the ladder over to me and Don Jerónimo climbed up to carry me down unaided. I passed out. They stretched me out on the priest's balcony, among his pots of begonias and his touching cages with their hopping larks and finches.

The great sorrow of my life, Mother Benita, is that my only starring moment, the only one in which I was the lead and not an extra—that brief moment when Don Jerónimo and the parish priest ripped my sleeve and treated my wound—occurred while I was unconscious. I have no record of that moment in my memory. Because, when I came to at the end of a few minutes, I found Don Jerónimo with his own arm naked and stained with blood, yes, Mother Benita, with my blood, with Humberto Peñaloza's blood, his arm being bandaged exactly where mine hurt. When they were done with the bandaging, they put my wounded arm next to his and squeezed my wound so as to draw as much blood as possible with which to stain those false hero's bandages in a spectacular way. Everything had to be very quick, he said, otherwise they might realize it was you and not I who fell wounded, and it's vital that we make the most of this opportunity, because with this attempt on my life—yes, it had been an attempt on *his* life, I'd been nothing, nor could I pretend to be anything, but an accidental stand-in for his valor—I have a weapon to wield in public against those who may charge me with irregularities; I can show my bloodstained arm to the police and the journalists who try to accuse me of breaking the law, they're already beginning to knock at the church door. They whisked me away from the scene in five minutes, sending me up the ladder to the roof . . . hide your pain, Humberto, after all it can't be so great, don't let anyone find out that you're hurt, go on up alone, climb down the other side and disappear, no one's going to ask for you, get away fast to La Rinconada in the carriage . . . I went off to the country, Mother Benita, I vanished.

Disguised in Humberto Peñaloza's blood, Don Jerónimo de Azcoitía went to the church door to receive the authorities and show them his bandaged arm, protesting that it was the last straw, that the country offered no protection to those who sacrificed themselves in its service, that there was no authority anymore, that no one showed respect for the most basic laws and, in spite of it all, they dared accuse him of abuses that he, a man who represented order, was incapable of committing . . . no, why look for the culprit when the person who fired the shot wasn't important, just as the wound wasn't important in itself either, what was important was the attitude of the rival political party that used some poor ignorant peon, egged on by instigators adept at disappearing when the time came to face the music, to eliminate him, Jerónimo de Azcoitía, because he'd won the electoral contest fairly. He was generous with his statements to the reporters, who immediately transmitted them to the papers in the capital. That same night, there was an extra with pictures of Don Jerónimo—Inés has some yellowed copies in one of the suitcases in her cells—of the priest among his finches, of the crowd in the town square, and a long, emotional account of the attempt on his life.

Don Jerónimo crossed the square again, looking triumphant with his bandaged arm, showing off my blood to the thousand witnesses stripped of their violence now, followed by an escort of mounted police. He was Don Jerónimo de Azcoitía, Senator of the Republic. The circles under his eyes, his face haggard in spite of his smile, reflected the painfulness of the wound, although he kept insisting it was nothing . . . don't worry about my wound, there are more important things at stake. In the square and in the bars the rumor began to spread that they hadn't been able to extract the bullet yet, that it was lodged in the bone, that he'd lose the use of his arm, that maybe they'd have to amputate it, well maybe not amputate all of it but . . . look at the dude, he doesn't bat an eye, as good-looking as ever, this dude has guts . . . maybe he's not even as snobbish as they say, maybe he'll even turn out to be a great senator.

13

INÉS OFTEN WENT to spend her afternoons with Peta Ponce when Jerónimo left her free at La Rinconada. To be together was to revive, in the case of the two women, the familiar things of childhood: to recall forgotten persons, games that perhaps weren't games, specters, devotions, and the exciting task of preserving what no longer had a reason to go on existing. All this came back to life in the dimness of the old woman's room at the end of the last gallery and the last courtyard, where Peta Ponce's always waiting, Mother Benita, where the chipped plaster reveals the shape of the adobes and the dampness betrays the monstrous faces of what once could and still can happen, Mother Benita, right there, right here.

While the two women, shut up in the old woman's hiding place, huddled together in the back of La Rinconada's labyrinth of houses, spoke of trivial matters, Jerónimo sallied forth to his masculine duties out of doors: ranging over the countryside at the head of a crew of men who were opening a canal, under his direction, that would water another hundred acres, giving instructions to peons covered with the blood of the vintage, building storehouses, new silos, branding animals for the slaughterhouse. He never brought up Peta's name. The authority in his silence eliminated her. But, whenever the couple went from the country to the city or from the city to the country, Peta Ponce followed them. At the beginning of their marriage, when despair had still not made any breaches in their happiness, Inés whiled away her time with her nursemaid knitting clothes for the future Boy, sewing little jackets and embroidering initials and gay garlands on the luxurious clothes. But eventually, as the heir began to take longer to arrive, the only alternative was to make offerings and say novenas and wait, and go on knitting and embroidering with less and less hope. It was impossible to speak to Jerónimo of the child they lacked. He wouldn't have accepted a subject that deformed the faultless shape of their present medallion.

Peta Ponce was there to talk these things over with her: to receive the sorrow Inés had to keep quiet. They talked and talked, nursing the pain that grew with the years of sterility, as Inés lived out with her nursemaid what she couldn't live out with her husband because it was absolutely necessary for her to be beautiful and elegant and tender and in love and envied by everyone, and no one would envy her if they knew that she went to her nursemaid's shabby room, on those afternoons, to hold endless conversations, to unravel perfection, to pray to St. Rita of Cassia, patroness of impossible things, to moan. Perhaps without knowing it—but I'm not sure, Mother Benita, I wouldn't be surprised if there's been an unspoken decision between them to estimate how long they could cling to their hope, and both women knew exactly what they were doing—as the couple's silent unhappiness increased and the possibility that Boy would be born disappeared into the depths of that passage where only the word *nothing, nothing, nothing* . . . I'm thinking of nothing . . . thundered in their ears; the size of the clothes the two women were sewing for the baby dwindled and dwindled with the perfection of those five years, until they ended up sewing and knitting clothes that could fit only a minuscule doll. Furthermore, they busied themselves making beds and tables and chairs and chests of drawers and wardrobes and cabinets with cardboard and the fragile wood of matchboxes, and diminutive vases made with painted bread crumbs, everything growing smaller and smaller as St. Rita of Cassia, patroness of impossible things, and all the other powers, turned a deaf ear, until finally those objects and those clothes became so minuscule, Mother Benita, that they must be picked up with tweezers and looked at under a magnifying glass to appreciate the fastidious luxury of detail. One of these days, before Inés returns from Rome, I'm going to take you to her cell and let you see Boy's things, yes, don't look so incredulous, if you like we'll go right now and I'll prove that I'm telling the truth; I've gone through all the drawers of that trunk that's a world in itself, because I'm tempted to steal some of those things to furnish the chalet where Iris Mateluna will live after Boy's birth. I know all the linen sheets, the satin bedspreads, the tiny knitted or embroidered baby clothes, everything Inés and Peta Ponce made in that room at the back of the house, where they still clung to their hope that St. Rita or the Blessed Inés would hear them. But in the lowest drawers in that trunk, everything scrupulously classified and dated by the calendar of their despair, there are other things that keep growing smaller from drawer to drawer . . . St. Rita won't listen to us anymore, we have to pray to Inés de Azcoitía . . . but Inés de Azcoitía wasn't a saint, Peta . . . what's the difference if she's not, she may not even be blessed but there are spirits who aren't sainted and yet can perform miracles, greater things than the miracles performed by the saints of the altars, because these spirits that aren't sainted go on wandering through the world, they don't disappear, they live among us, they can give us advice . . . let's pray to Inés de Azcoitía, let's commend ourselves to her, she's your ancestor and will advise us what to do, because this simply can't go on . . . and they knitted even tinier things because the Blessed Inés didn't help or advise them either, diminutive things as the fruitless months went by, till finally, in the last drawer of the trunk, there are boxes that contain clothes and furniture so terrifyingly small that I'm afraid to touch them because they might fall apart. I've spent whole afternoons in that cell of Inés's, seeing how from drawer to drawer, from year to year, from month to month, from week to week, her hopes kept dwindling until they reached the size of the miniatures of the time when she agreed to meet me here in Peta Ponce's room. Things couldn't go on like that anymore. It was impossible to build and knit smaller things because there was no thread fine enough or wood thin enough, just as it was also impossible to break through the circle of perfection Jerónimo drew around himself and his wife. Out of the past, the other Inés didn't answer the pleas of the two crazed women who didn't know what to do next. It was the end. They ran out of hope. None of the powers gave them help.

None? I'm convinced that the girl-saint of the Azcoitía family tradition, who's the same as the girl-witch the father's huge poncho whisked away from the center of the Maule River story to save her from any suspicion of evil, yes, I'm convinced that it was this being who finally whispered a clear plan in Peta's hungry ear. It was at the suggestion of those two that Inés told me to meet her in her nursemaid's room on election night.

While Don Jerónimo triumphed in the town square, disguised as Humberto Peñaloza, the carriage in which I traveled, doubled up with the pain from Don Jerónimo's wound, jogged along the dirt roads that led to La Rinconada at that time. Yes, he'd stolen my wound, Mother Benita, but let me tell you this: nobody steals a wound without paying for it. If he'd wanted to borrow it I would have lent it to him, because I admired Don Jerónimo, but he stole it from me while I was still unconscious, he took it without asking me, convinced that my wound, like everything else of mine, was his property. But by stealing it from me he left me whole, without a wound. Yes, Mother Benita, it was he who made me into Jerónimo de Azcoitía, he and the thousand eyes of the witnesses in the square, he and the journalists who put my bravery on record.

Her way lit by lanterns that flickered in the hands of the peons, Inés came out to meet the carriage at the park entrance, which I never used unless I was with Don Jerónimo. I jumped down from the carriage as if I were neither exhausted nor in pain . . . How are you, are you all right, how's Jerónimo, is he coming back, when? . . . As we walked up and down the balcony facing the park, observed, she and I now, by the dogs' glittering eyes, I gave her the true version of what had happened. My knees went limp, as if I were about to pass out again. Inés took my other arm . . . lie down here on Jerónimo's chaise longue and let me cover your feet with his lap robe, let me stay with you awhile if you don't feel well, you may take a turn for the worse . . . It would have been enough to brush her hand with mine for everything to happen. I felt her admiration burning me up with that solicitude toward the new man I was now. She questioned me eagerly, more and more eagerly, running her questions together, as if she wished, as I wished, the bullet which had grazed my arm had reached her husband's heart. And it wouldn't be strange, Mother Benita, if Inés felt something like that; after all she, like myself, was nothing more than Don Jerónimo's servant, whose job was to give birth to a son who'd be his father's salvation.

As I talk to you about these things, Mother Benita, I see that Inés couldn't have wished Don Jerónimo's death as I wished it, because she loved him. I became sure of that love that night in front of the park, because I was Jerónimo and I felt Inés's love reaching out to me. I shivered. She asked me if I was cold . . . Yes . . . yes . . . a little bit, although the night has turned quite warm . . . She insisted that I go to bed. She was going with me to my bedroom door. She was going to make the substitution complete, to enter my room and give herself to her husband. But she remained outside.

"Good night, Humberto . . ."

"Good night . . ."

"Oh, I wanted to tell you something: if you feel ill or if your arm hurts, you'd better go to Peta Ponce's room—she knows and keeps all my secrets, so it doesn't matter if she knows the wound is yours, not Jerónimo's—she sleeps so little and knows about those things, she's a medicine woman . . ."

Medicine woman, bawd, witch, midwife, wailer, confidante, all the things an old woman is, embroiderer, knitter, storyteller, preserver of traditions and superstitions, keeper of useless things under her bed, of the castoffs of her employers, possessor of ailments, darkness, fear, pain, of shameful secrets, of solitudes and humiliations that others can't bear. I often came to pass the time here in Peta Ponce's room. I used to sit with her next to this brazier where she heated water for maté and toasted lumps of sugar over the coals until the sweetish smell filled the half-light of the room. She boiled water in the kettle. She poured it into the gourd into which she'd thrown a sprig of fennel with the maté, waited a second, stirred the sipper and sucked a little to see how it tasted . . . it's delicious, Don Humberto, go ahead and drink first, Don Humberto . . . and I sucked and she filled it up again and she sucked and filled it up again and I took a little more hot maté without any feeling of revulsion as the sipper passed from those ragged lips directly to mine, because this contact of ours through the maté cemented an awareness that our positions, flanking Jerónimo and Inés, formed a symmetrical pattern. We spoke little. What could I, a university man, a writer, speak about with an old woman like Peta Ponce? We talked about who was sick and with what and what must be done to make him well, and when we were going back to the capital, now that the first frosts were starting. When it came to Inés and Jerónimo, our words skirted them on either side, leaving a hollowness in between. But it was a hollowness that filled all our conversations with its unmistakable meaning, even if we only carried on light conversations about what a lovely day it turned out to be when the day before was so overcast, and what their reason could have been for firing Dionisio, and when Rosalba would get back from vacation, and how with all the rain this fall everyone's going around with a cold. Banal chitchat, but no one makes a maté like Peta Ponce, it can spoil anyone, after one tastes her maté others are tasteless, and I came to Peta's again and again not to take up what we couldn't speak about, because not even our employers dared take up that theme and after all we were only servants . . . I used to enjoy dropping in and sitting down on the footstool next to the brazier, the same one on which Inés sat to transfer her pain to the old woman, and thus, by getting rid of her pain, remain free to carry on her existence with Jerónimo in the medallion of perfect marital harmony. I used to go to Peta's to drink maté. To sit next to this brazier. But also to come in contact, through Peta, with a complete Inés, more complete than Jerónimo's Inés. Sometimes I was aware that indirectly, through some apparently colorless phrase of Peta's, Inés was asking me for help:

"Today she was kind of sad . . ."

"Why?"

"This afternoon I didn't find her looking well at all . . ."

She was in perfect health.

Peta and I knew she wasn't well. I never asked. Things had

to remain unsaid, because I saw a fate already traced out for me behind that silence, and, by breaking it, I'd eliminate that fate. As time went on, this *not well at all,* repeated by the old woman, eventually turned into an urgent cry that not only called for my help but demanded it of me—I was a servant, and she, Inés, whose husband paid me a salary, had a right to my services. She's not well. She's not well at all. She looks kind of low. She's wasting away fast. I'm afraid if something isn't done for her, she'll really be in a bad way. Inesita's not well at all. And I'd just seen her looking radiant in the living room, wearing her puce macramé dress to receive the guests at her birthday dinner party, to which, of course, I wasn't invited. Or else I saw the couple galloping on magnificent sorrels along the endless autumn paths.

It was when her hands could no longer make furniture or sew smaller baby dresses that Peta came out with her plan. Bring him to me. That's what your witch ancestor tells me, she's telling you through me to bring him to me, bring Don Jerónimo to me, Inés, convince him that I exist, convince him to come and see me, she says that if he agrees to make love to you one night here in my room, on the bedding of dirty sheets that reek of my old body, on the mattress that hides countless cabalistic packages, in this darkness with its smell of used-up things, this stillness that's quiet and yet not quiet, with the endless hopping of the thrush in its cage, then, Inesita, then, I swear to you, you'll become pregnant.

Of course. But how could Jerónimo be called to this room, how could he be brought here, to Peta's room, if Peta didn't exist, since his loathing had eliminated her? On the other hand, I, his servant, could come; he stole my wound, and, when Inés said good night to me at my bedroom door, she was telling me without saying it: you are he.

When I woke up later that night with the pain in my wound racking my arm, I was certain that it wasn't a real pain, it was Peta Ponce's power nagging at my wound to drive me on to the tryst Inés gave me in this hovel, to carry out my duty as servant . . . that's what you're paid for, Don Humberto, don't you see that's why they keep you on salary, don't sleep, get up, you can't sleep, you mustn't sleep, Don Humberto, when Inesita needs you, come, we're waiting for you in my room, if you don't come I'll make your arm hurt more, much more, I'll cripple it for life, come, come, we're waiting for you, you have to come now, come . . . right now . . .

I dressed clumsily because the pain in my wound prevented me from moving my arm freely. There were courts and more courts to cross, passageways, meanders of adobe, empty rooms, useless rooms, the anarchy of structures put up centuries back for long-forgotten purposes . . . I might have got lost in these corridors of buckling dilapidated clay, but I couldn't get lost, Mother Benita, because, as I walked on, the pain loosed its hold on my arm, showing me that, yes, this was the right direction, Peta was leading me here, bringing me, dragging me, deep into these passageways and clay courtyards. I knew this was the door because my arm suddenly stopped hurting. I opened it. The hovel was dark, filled with a smoke cloud from a chunk of sugar burning on the coals and with the light hopping of the thrush in its cage. Outside, the house and the countryside conspired with the total stillness. Behind me, the door opened and closed.

"Jerónimo."

Yes, yes, I'm Jerónimo de Azcoitía, I have my bleeding wound to prove it to you. I put my arms around her. I led her to Peta's bed. Inés was crying, repeating Jerónimo's name over and over in order to eliminate what remained of Humberto, and the more she repeated it the more Jerónimo grew, yes, yes, you've eliminated Humberto, who lets himself be eliminated as long as it enables him to touch you, I'm Jerónimo, touch me, you know my body, don't be afraid, I'm Jerónimo and always will be if you let me. I tried to kiss her but her mouth avoided mine, Mother Benita, you see, she kept my lips away from her face as if they were foul. I wasn't Jerónimo after all. Only my enormous organ was Jerónimo. She recognized it. That's why she was letting me lift her dress, and she opened her legs and offered me her vagina, keeping my face and my body away from her so that none of me except my member that was Jerónimo could touch her, so that my hands wouldn't have the pleasure of her beauty, so that the longing of the servant who was serving her would persist, and yet she went on saying Jerónimo, and Jerónimo penetrated her, Mother Benita, leaving Humberto outside, mute from that moment on because she wouldn't listen to my voice demanding recognition. Force her, Peta, let me touch her hand at least, you have the power to force her. But she wouldn't allow me even that because her hands were occupied keeping away all of me except my organ. I, this shell that's Humberto Peñaloza, was of no use to her. That's why I've come to put it away here in this Casa filled with dirt, old women, junk, abjectly degraded things.

THEY TURNED ON all the balcony lights. The four black dogs dance, leap, bark around Jerónimo de Azcoitía while he sends the carriage away with orders to be ready tomorrow morning at seven because he has to go back to the capital at that hour. It's time for bed now. His dogs try to lick him, begging for his attention and his pats.

"Go away now, I'm tired."

Inés is leading him to the bedroom. He doesn't feel like answering questions or talking, he just wants to go to sleep, it's very late . . . tired, tired, so much to worry about, so much to do and all I have is a few hours to sleep . . . the bandages bother me, take them off, Inés, please, yes, all of them . . . no, why should you think my arm hurts when Humberto must have told you that the wound's not mine but his, you have to wash off Humberto's blood with warm water, there's nothing as unpleasant as the feel of dry blood, especially if it's someone else's, a sponge, soap, to remove all this filth that's making me feel so dirty, although it's not someone else's blood, Inés, I bought it, I pay Humberto for services like this, good man, Humberto, useful, you can always rely on him, I'm going to give him a good present, what do you think he needs, I believe he'll like a cape and a slouch hat, since he likes to pass off as a writer among his bar friends, and he's intelligent, he has an exceptional education for a man who hasn't traveled, an extraordinary sensibility, you've noticed how naturally we often talk about things you don't understand. Now wash his blood off my arm. I don't need it anymore, I've already shown it off, it played its part, now it's nothing but a useless crust you're washing off my arm with warm water and perfumed soap so that tomorrow, before leaving, you can put clean bandages on me so I can carry on the deception. Good night, Inés. I have to get some sleep because tomorrow will be a heavy day despite my victory.

They get into their separate beds. They turn off the lights. A few, or maybe many, minutes pass, Jerónimo doesn't know how many because the night waxes and wanes and he closes his eyes and opens them without knowing whether or not he's managed to sleep or even at what hour of the night he's awakened by the screeching of the flock of *queltehues* flying toward the lake. He pricks up his ears: the vastness of his lands looms in the night where the moon counts the indifference of the things he owns, the flock of *queltehues* comes back, the same one, perhaps another, a horse gallops past carrying an unknown rider toward an unknown destination, the barking of the dogs, some nearby, others a long way off, indicates the enormous distances of the countryside at night, that bark comes from the cattle pens, the other one, farther west, must be that of the foreman's dog, and another close by, right here, below the window, among the ivy, so close I can hear the rustle of the body stirring in the leaves, sounds as if it came from inside, from my bedroom, as if Inés were howling . . . it's not howling now, it's only a whining, it doesn't stop whining below my window and now it lets out a sharp cry that cuts through the night, quiet sobs that fill the air again only to culminate in a howl that won't let me sleep, another, and another stretched way out like an arc that reaches to the moon. Why, why precisely today, when it's important that I rest, why? Why this inexplicable compulsion of country dogs to bay at the moon? Why is this bitch dog barking precisely tonight, and right under my window? Jerónimo sits up. He's about to go to the window to drive her away.

"Leave her alone."

It's the first word from Inés in many hours. Does she know why this bitch is howling in the night, what she's trying to tell the moon, what message she carries for it, what things are covered up by the silvery half-light outside where things grow and multiply and act without his authority? The bitch mustn't howl again. He's Don Jerónimo de Azcoitía, who must sleep and go to the capital tomorrow to make important statements. The bitch bays again.

"That dog won't let me sleep."

Inés remains silent.

"Why is that yellow bitch roaming around in the park?"

He sits up and waits for Inés to answer.

". . . I'm going to chase her away . . ."

"No."

Jerónimo falls back in his bed. The yellow bitch runs at large among the cut branches of the park, talks to the moon, whines, scampers off again and then comes near and settles down to bay, unbearably, under his window. A heavy silence falls but it's not a silence because spiders, termites, beetles, weave their lives in those bushes and those trees that belong to him, they drag part of a leaf, cross the cyclopean barrier of a fallen twig, dig holes covered with a whitish spittle, multiply in a matter of minutes into thousands of generations that burrow tunnels in the trunk of a tree or spread the rusty blotch of pestilence on the underside of a leaf. I hear all this out of the silence, I can perceive it all until the yellow dog, the scrawny thief, plants itself under my window again and lets out another howl at the moon. Jerónimo puts on his slippers. Once more Inés says:

"No."

"I have to chase her away."

And, as he savagely ties the belt on his dressing gown, he understands what he has to do.

"I'm going to kill her."

"No."

"Is the yellow bitch yours?"

"No."

"Well then?"

Inés clutches at him, trying to stop him from leaving the bedroom, but Jerónimo shoves her away and goes out. On the balcony, he stops to whistle to his four black dogs . . . naturally, that's why the bitch remained at large, because they, his four noble dogs, were left locked up here in the patio, slumbering under the orange trees. They come to dance around him.

"Easy . . . easy . . . let's go . . ."

The black dogs obey. They walk behind him like shadows, their paws stealthy, their fangs sheathed. This flowerbed of abutilons. The lawn beyond it. The wall of laurels and then the graveled clearing; the bitch is over there howling below the window, unaware that Don Jerónimo's not in his bedroom but among the laurels, all set to punish her.

As she cranes her neck, she aims her pointed snout at the very center of the sky and ends her howl, a part of the autonomy of things that grow and rustle and crawl and reproduce. The chatter of nameless insects is oppressive. And then the enemy of his four black dogs starts another howl, soft and plaintive at first, that will turn into an indecipherable message if he doesn't cut it short. Jerónimo points at the bitch. He snaps his fingers and the dogs fly, it takes them a second, a jumble of slaver and paws and blood and dirt, one minute, no more, in which my four black dogs as the shadows of wolves kill her, stopping her dialogue with the accomplice moon.

DON JERÓNIMO AND I left for the capital on the following day. I didn't have time to go over the park grounds in search of the remains to confirm everything; I must confess that I didn't even think of doing it, so sure was I, at first, of the one thing that could have happened.

Only months later, when Inés de Azcoitía's glorious pregnancy was announced and we returned here to La Rinconada to rest up, was I assailed by the temptation to question the gardeners who must have cleaned the graveled clearing surrounded by laurel bushes. No one remembered any carcasses or signs of fighting and blood, anything, because obviously the body of a masterless bitch, greedy and covered with warts, isn't something even the humblest gardener's helpers bother to remember . . . I don't know, sir, it could be, but I don't remember, how are we going to remember if she was yellow, or if we found her torn to pieces and dead when we don't even remember finding the body of a bitch dog, it must be about three months now that this thing you're talking about happened, sir, you forget things like that, so much dirt collects in this park and it's so big.

And what if the bitch hadn't died? Suppose Inés did *not* really go to the tryst while the yellow bitch acted as a blind for her? Boy's growing in her womb. There was no proof to show that Jerónimo left his bedroom that night, giving Inés the chance to use the bloody diversion of her nursemaid's sacrifice to slip out and join me. Maybe the yellow bitch wasn't killed as Mercedes Barroso claimed in her version of the story, she may have remained at large and alive and lurking around us, it may have been she who followed me here relentlessly without letting me leave this place where I hide in the disguise of just another old woman, to expiate what has to be expiated and hide what has to be hidden. Don't you see, Mother Benita, the frightening probability that Inés and Jerónimo made love in their bedroom as usual that night to soothe each other after the hard day, while the important thing was happening on other planes?

Old women like Peta Ponce have the power to fold time over and confuse it, they multiply and divide it, events are refracted in their gnarled hands as in the most brilliant prism, they cut the consecutive happening of things into fragments they arrange in parallel form, they bend those fragments and twist them into shapes that enable them to carry out their designs. Inés had to give Jerónimo a son. It was urgent that she give him one to prevent everything from disintegrating around them. It was the frantic moment when time runs out, just before the disaster that can be prevented only by immediate action: by sacrificing someone, no matter whom, no matter how it could be done, because things couldn't go on like that—where were they going to find thinner thread, there was no finer wood or paper —by humiliating and wounding, by making substitutions and stealing, vengeance confused with love and happiness, shame with glory, rancor with pleasure. How could one be sure it was Peta Ponce who directed the things that happened that night,

or how, or what it was that she directed? Maybe the yellow
bitch didn't die. Maybe not one cell of my body touched Inés's
body, but . . .

. . . Incredible, incredible, Mother Benita, it was about to
happen, my longing and my father's longing were about to be
appeased because my avidity would obtain the only thing that
could satisfy all the Peñalozas, we were finally going to stop
being mere witnesses of beauty and were going to participate in
it. She came out of the darkness. I grasped her and led her to the
bed and took her, as I've told you. I believe I heard the cries of
the victim and the excitement of the black dogs tearing her to
pieces out there beyond the silence that isolated us. And yet the
silence in the room was so deep that I doubt whether I heard
anything besides my companion panting on the bed. I didn't
hear the bitch's moans because Inés and Jerónimo were in their
bedroom making love, isolated by another silence that differed
from the one isolating us, but whom was it isolating, Mother
Benita, whom, I may not have given my love to Inés in that
darkness but to someone else, to Peta, to Peta Ponce, who took
Inés's place because she's the kind of mate who befits me—
ragged, old, crippled, filthy Peta . . . it was she my enormous
member penetrated and hers the rotting flesh it enjoyed as I
groaned with pleasure over the closeness beclouded with secretions, craving the kiss of her mouth lined with wrinkles, yes, in
the darkness of that night only the eyes of the thrush saw that it
was the old woman's vagina, maggoty with the closeness of
death, that devoured my magnificent new organ, and it was her
deteriorated flesh that received me.

At the moment of orgasm she cried out:

"Jerónimo."

And I cried out:

"Inés."

Peta and I were excluded from pleasure. She and I, the
shadowy pair, conceived the son the luminous couple couldn't
conceive. The old woman plotted everything: the arm wound,
the eyes of the witnesses watching us in the park, the howling
of the bitch dog, the complicity of the moon, the darkness in
this or in some other room, even the loneliness in mine, because

I sometimes nurse the hope that my dream's also Peta's work, and I'd go so far as to suppose that it was all just a dream that, being Peta's work, had the effect of the real thing. Dreaming it was enough for Inés to become pregnant, and it wasn't because Peta and I made love, at the same time they were doing it, on this bedding of dirty sheets, on this moth-eaten mattress, on this cot that creaks as it hides the small incomprehensible little packages we old women hide under our beds. The gardeners didn't find the bitch's carcass, and a nightmarish terror invaded my waking hours. The victim goes on stalking me. Not even as Jerónimo could I mate with Inés. My fate, like Peta's, is to remain outside the mutual acknowledgment of love, but not outside the mechanical act of love; when Inés fell into Jerónimo's tired arms, we revitalized them, because in the darkness of the grotesque couple's room our pained eyes looked for, and saw, their two faces in our faces distorted by longing, as we fulfilled our mission on the soiled sheets.

Terror's one of the easiest things to forget, Mother Benita. There are thousands of subterfuges, well do you know, one can't always live on the verge of terror, that's why you say Our Fathers and Hail Holy Queens and Hail Marys, yes, it was to run away from fear that you sacrificed your life by immuring it here in the futility of the Casa. When Inés's pregnancy was confirmed at last, I forgot my terror for a time; I was dazzled when it struck me that, while Don Jerónimo had stolen my fertility, I stole his potency. His pleasure-seeking member seemed to wear itself out, it turned into a shameful appendage, but my own organ, red as a firebrand, grew. Something similar must have happened to Peta; when the remains of the sacrificed bitch were swept from the park without leaving a trace, not even in the memory of the gardener's helpers, Peta Ponce was reborn. Everyone took it for granted that what gave her renewed energy was the joy of seeing that her pet was finally going to bear a son. But no. It wasn't that. Day after day, the winking of her gummy eyes, her mouth tic, made me surer that the loathsome old hag was pursuing me, that that night, in the darkness of her room, my member brought back to life in her dried-up body the sexuality she was stealing at that very moment from Inés, giving

her in exchange the satisfaction of being the mother of Jerónimo's son. This satisfaction drained Inés of all desire, but it
aroused passion in the old woman who tirelessly lies in wait for
me in order to repeat, with renewed lust, that night's act, and I
don't want to, Mother Benita, I refuse, I keep on refusing, I
ache for a lovely Inés, with soft skin and live breasts, whose
contours my hands go on dreaming; for her thick hair, her arm-
pits and her nape and her delicious pubis . . . No, Peta. Don't
run after me. My member so avid for beauty started to rot from
its contact with your wormy flesh, stop looking for me, die once
and for all, forget your obsession that I'm your mate because
I'm helpless and miserable, the terror over your hunting me
down has made me take cover here . . . I'm not hers, Mother
Benita, although I'd better say I am so that she'll leave me in
peace, at least until Boy's born. Inés promised that you'd be the
midwife at the child's birth, but you won't be, because Don
Jerónimo says, let her think so, Humberto, why contradict her,
how can you believe I'm going to let an ignorant medicine
woman attend Inés and assist at Boy's birth, but, to quiet them,
let them both think that I'll keep my word, meanwhile I'm en-
gaging the best specialists. Later on I'll get rid of her. She's
nothing but a plaything, a puppet made of rags, to keep Inés
happy. Meanwhile, let them sew, stitch, knit; later on we'll
dump that old rag in the trash, don't tell them a word, Humberto, I can talk to you about these things and about everything.
I'm afraid to make love to Inés now that she's carrying my son
in her, and I need to be satisfied, Humberto, I'm a passionate
man, I can't remain abstinent, accompany me, come along with
me; since I can't touch Inés because she doesn't want to be
touched either, I must use my potency with other women, find
me some women, let's go to a whorehouse, because I don't want
to take up with one particular woman, only with faceless
women, find me a discreet brothel, you know all the nooks and
crannies of this town, pay the madam anything she asks for providing me with young women, tell her to close shop and only
let you and me in, fix it up, you've always fixed up everything so
well . . . come on, come along to Doña Flora's where there are
young bodies for me . . . watch me strip this woman called

Rosa, I pull off her slip as if I were peeling off her skin to make her sensitive to my loving . . . this one is Hortensia, I like to play with her enormous breasts, no, don't leave the room, Humberto, watch me take off my clothes too as if I were peeling off my own skin, stay here and watch how I can make love, I want you to gape at the power of my virility, which you don't have, at my experience in arts you know nothing about, see for yourself with your envious eyes, look at my ability to break down Violeta's phony resistance, lend me your envy to make me potent, look at our entwined bodies, try to make out the words smothered by our kisses, the odor of our intercourse, feel us with your hand so that your skin may suffer because I'm perfect, even though I'm not perfect when I'm alone with Inés, you know it, Humberto, I know that the fear of deforming the son she carries in her womb is nothing but an old wives' tale, but it's the excuse I shield myself behind so that no one will see that I've been impotent ever since the night I engendered Boy, you're the owner of my potency, Humberto, you took it just as I took the wound on your arm, you can never leave me, I need your envious eyes beside me if I'm to go on being a man, otherwise, I'll have only this flabby thing between my legs, it's not even warm, look at me . . . and I looked at him, Mother Benita, I looked at him tirelessly, with envy, but with something else too—with contempt, Mother Benita. I want you to know that. Because, when he made love to Violeta or Rosa or Hortensia or Lily, with the approval of my eyes, not only was I spurring him on and possessing, through him, the woman he possessed, but my potency entered him, I entered the virile he-man, I made him my sodomite, forcing him to scream with pleasure over the embrace of my eyes, although he thought his pleasure was something else, I used to punish my employer by turning him into a humiliated creature, my contempt grew and disfigured him, Don Jerónimo couldn't stop being the sodomite of my stare that made him grovel till nothing save my entering him satisfied him . . . anything you want, Humberto, anything you desire, so long as you never leave my side . . . At night, lonely in my witness's bed, because the beds of witnesses are always lonely, I began to hear Peta Ponce wandering around outside my room, coughing or clearing her throat, her footsteps as weak as the footsteps of the old women here at the Casa, I used to see her lying in wait behind a tree or a door or a half-open window, waiting for the moment when I'd give in, but I'm never going to give in, I don't want to repeat the scene, there *was* no such scene, it was a nightmare that produced monsters and it goes on being that because Peta's prowling outside the Casa, I don't understand how she could have guessed that I'm here, maybe Damiana told her but I don't know if she knows Damiana and Damiana doesn't know who I am, of course Damiana was famous for roaming the streets, and they say people know a lot of things in the streets: the gossip of servants as they stand on street corners, with their bags of bread or vegetables, or wait on line in grocery stores, and the rumors they start spread from corner to corner.

But what did all this matter, now that Boy was going to be born? Everything was ready. Jerónimo had finally succeeded in taking Inés out of the static medallion of perfect marital happiness; his gallant hand was leading her toward their preordained positions in the next medallion, in which they'd appear as parents. While Peta and I, fantastic beings, grotesque monsters, carried out our mission of supporting that new medallion, holding it up straight from the outside, like a pair of magnificent heraldic animals.

When Jerónimo finally parted the crib's curtains to look at his long-awaited offspring, he wanted to kill him then and there; the loathsome, gnarled body writhing on its hump, its mouth a gaping bestial hole in which palate and nose bared obscene bones and tissues in an incoherent cluster of reddish traits, was chaos, disorder, a different but worse form of death.

14

DON JERÓNIMO de Azcoitía ordered all the furniture, tapestries, books and paintings that suggested the outside world taken out of the houses at La Rinconada; nothing was to stir a longing in his son for what he was never to know. He also had all the outside doors and windows walled up, except one door, the key to which he kept. The mansion was converted into a hollow, sealed shell consisting of a series of empty rooms, corridors and passageways, into a limbo of walls facing only the inner courts, where he gave orders to uproot the classic orange trees with their golden fruit, the bougainvillaeas, the blue hydrangeas, the rows of lilies, replacing them with bushes trimmed into strict geometric forms that disguised their natural exuberance. He had the annexes that were clustered around the noble part of the residence torn down; he gave orders to destroy the filthy labyrinth of adobe, of galleries and corridors and patios and storerooms, it was necessary to undo the supports that had grown with the years, demarcating and humiliating the neat order of the four courts destined for his son. To accommodate Boy's servitors, pavilions were to be built that were to be scattered around the park the child was never to know. He had all the trees cut down whose tops could be seen from inside the house. Besides, he had the last court closed off with a solid wall, the court with the pond, and at the head of this rectangular pond he put up a Huntress Diana in gray stone carved according to his stipulations: humpbacked with acromegalic jaw and crooked legs, carrying her quiver on her hump and the new moon on her wrinkled forehead. He decorated the rest of the courts with other stone monsters: the nude Apollo was conceived as a likeness of the future adolescent Boy's hunchbacked body and features, with gargoyle nose and jaw, asymmetrical ears, harelip, disproportionate arms and an enormous dangling sex organ that, from the cradle, drew ohs and ahs of admiration from the nurses. As he grew, Boy was to recognize his own perfection in the Apollo's, and his sexual instincts, on awakening, would discover the Huntress Diana's figure, or a Venus pitted by smallpox who had a rear end of fantastic proportions that was ruined by cellulitis, who romped suggestively in a cavern of ivy.

Don Jerónimo saw to all these details, because nothing around Boy must be ugly, mean or ignoble. Ugliness is one thing. But monstrosity is something else again, something of a significance that was equal but antithetical to the significance of beauty and, as such, it merited similar prerogatives. Monstrosity was the only thing Don Jerónimo de Azcoitía would set before his son from his birth on.

He delegated his secretary to visit cities, villages, country districts, ports, mines, in search of inhabitants worthy of populating Boy's world. In the beginning, they were hard to find, because monsters have a tendency to hide away, secluding the shame of their fates in miserable out-of-the-way places. But it didn't take Humberto Peñaloza long to become expert at monsters. In a certain monastery in the provinces, for example, he discovered a Brother whose faith was shaky, an intelligent man deformed by a hump of noteworthy proportions. He went to see him time after time, tempting him with fabulous salaries and a life he'd conduct along any lines he pleased, in a world where deformity wouldn't be an anomaly but the rule. Brother Mateo escaped from the monastery where he'd disguised his terror dressed in the habit of piety all those years. In houses of prostitution, at fairs, in circuses in squalid neighborhoods, Humberto recruited dwarfs of every imaginable variety: with enormous heads, with the wrinkled faces of dolls that have aged, with stunted legs and high-pitched voices, avaricious, proud, intelligent. He discovered Miss Dolly, a very famous *fattest woman in the world*, a huge female of spectacular bulk who wobbled as she walked, who exhibited herself in a sequined bikini, dancing on the sawdust of a circus ring, paired up with her husband

Larry, a clown with uncommonly long arms and legs and a head that looked so tiny, perched way up on top of his scrawny neck, that it resembled that of a pin.

At night, which is when monsters come out of their lairs to roam the parks and the empty lots at the city's edge, Humberto Peñaloza was on the lookout for certain deformed creatures whom, if destitution hadn't vitiated their intelligence, he hired to enter Boy's service. He found Berta, for instance, with the entire lower part of her body disabled, who used the strength in her hypertrophic hands and arms to drag the rest of her over the ground like an alligator's tail; she was a familiar figure in the cheapest section of neighborhood movie houses where, stretched out on the wooden benches, she devoured the wisdom of movie after movie with her lively eyes. And Melchor, reading newspapers and old magazines in his cave by the city dump, was a solid raspberry-colored blob whose clots made his features a scrambled blur. It became a matter of pride with Humberto Peñaloza, as he presented more and more fantastic specimens to Don Jerónimo, unlikely creatures with twisted noses and jaws and a chaotic growth of yellowed teeth jamming their mouths, acromegalic giants, albino females as transparent as wraiths, girls with the extremities of penguins and ears like bat wings, individuals whose defects surpassed ugliness and raised them to the noble category of the monstrous.

Despite their isolated lives, before long the rumor spread among the monsters that a certain gentleman offered fabulous sums for their services. And so, after a time, Humberto Peñaloza didn't have to plunge into the depths of the city night to entice the monsters out of their lairs, for they began to come around, without being called, to the door of Don Jerónimo's house, crowding together noisily in the street to request an audience, asking high prices for what had been an affliction until then, begging for a position, a place, a job, any kind of opening in the humiliation-free world the gentleman offered. Don Jerónimo received letters, telegrams, reports, detailed descriptions, photographs. Monsters from everywhere turned up, they came down from the mountains and out of the forests and up from the cellars, sometimes arriving from remote areas, and even from abroad, to plead for admission to the paradise Don Jerónimo de Azcoitía was creating.

In the office next to Don Jerónimo's library, Humberto Peñaloza interviewed this multitude, pleased with himself at the great variety offered him. He let only the most exceptional specimens pass through to the library; there, after examining and talking to them, Don Jerónimo had them sign a contract or cast them aside. As a matter of fact, only a small number were turned away. After all, it wasn't just a question of surrounding Boy directly with monsters who knew what they were getting into, but also of providing these first-class monsters with a world of submonsters to surround and serve them: bakers, milkmen, carpenters, tinsmiths, truck farmers, peons—in short, with persons capable of answering every need, so that the normal world would be relegated to the faraway and eventually disappear.

Face to face with this elite of first-class monsters who'd look after Boy and educate him, Jerónimo had to perform the delicate task of convincing them that the anomalous being, the freak, doesn't represent an inferior condition of the human species, one that men have the right to look down on and pity; these, Don Jerónimo explained, are primitive reactions that hide the ambiguity of unexpressed feelings like envy, or the shameful eroticism produced in people by extraordinary beings like them, the monsters. Because normal humanity has only the courage to react to the usual gradations that range from the beautiful to the ugly, which in the long run are nothing but nuances of the same thing. The monster, on the other hand, Don Jerónimo contended with feeling, in order to exalt them with his mystique, belongs to a different, privileged species, with its own rights and particular canons that exclude the concepts of beauty and ugliness as tenuous categories, because, in essence, monstrosity is the culmination of both qualities synthesized and exacerbated to the sublime. Terrified by the exceptional being, normal beings locked him up in institutions or in circus cages, boxing him in with their scorn in order to snatch their power. But he, Jerónimo de Azcoitía, was going to give them back their prerogatives, redoubled, centuplicated.

For this—and in recompense for serving his son Boy, also a

monster but who, unlike them, mustn't ever know the humiliation of being one in an uncomprehending world—he was preparing his farm, La Rinconada; in its patios and along its avenues of trees, in happier times, walked a couple so perfect it could produce only a being as exceptional as Boy. The child must grow up confined to those geometric, gray enclosures and never know anyone but his servitors who, from the very first, would teach him that he was the beginning, the end and the middle of that cosmogony created especially for him. He couldn't, he mustn't for any reason whatever, suspect anything else, or know his servants' corrosive longing for the pleasures they'd been denied because they were born and lived in a world not correlative to them.

But, the monsters started to ask, was sacrificing themselves to produce the elimination of a world whose existence, unfortunately, had already made them its victims, worth the trouble? What good, then, would their salaries and this brand-new assurance that they were superior be to them, if they were to be allowed access only to the abstraction of enclosures and bare rooms in which Boy would grow up? No, no, no . . . they must understand, Don Jerónimo exhorted them; besides their emoluments, they'd receive all the rest of La Rinconada in which to organize a world of their own choice, with the restraints and liberties they felt like having, with the pleasures and the sorrows they devised; he was giving them free rein to invent for themselves an order or a disorder of their very own, just as he was inventing an order for his son. There was only one requirement: Boy must never suspect the existence of pain and pleasure, of happiness and misfortune, of what the four walls of his artificial world hid from view, and he must never hear the sound of music, not even from afar.

Not all of them understood Don Jerónimo's complex designs. Some, unnerved by what they considered exorbitant demands, went back into hiding in bristly places, in caves burrowed into bramble patches, in their convents and their circuses. But others listened and understood. Emperatriz, above all, asked many very intelligent questions. She was the first one recruited; she was related to Jerónimo through an impoverished branch of the family, but with an education she supplemented by reading magazines and books, she ran a factory that turned out very fine lingerie, where her authority, despite her Tom Thumb stature, her outsized head, her dribbling bulldog blubber-lip and canine teeth and dewlaps, was feared by all the factory girls. She was to run Boy's hermetic household. She was the only monster who treated Don Jerónimo as an equal, and as a relative, even if only a distant one, she had other ways of access to him and didn't have to pass through the office of the secretary who stood guard next to the library.

"And this fellow Humberto?"

"What do you want to know about Humberto?"

She lit a cigarette and crossed her legs.

"Well, what will his position be with respect to us?"

"I've told you. All authority will come from him. You must think of him not so much as my representative at La Rinconada but as myself, embodied in him, living among you and watching over Boy. After our final meeting this coming week, you people won't be able to communicate with me except through Humberto. The punishment for any attempt at direct communication will be expulsion."

"Not even I, as your relative?"

"Stop the nonsense, Emperatriz; forget blood relationships, after all we have only a great-great-grandmother in common. Humberto will be so much *myself* among you that even he will need to communicate with me only once a year."

Emperatriz stirred around among the sofa's plush gray cushions. Her legs, like those of an obscene doll that reeked of Mitsouko, barely reached the edge of the seat.

"That doesn't answer my question, Jerónimo."

"What, then?"

"Something we've talked about among us because it worries us, Berta, Melchor . . ."

"Oh, really?"

"Look, to put it bluntly, it's this: Humberto isn't a monster. He's a normal being, kind of ugly, and a complete nothing, poor thing. But you must understand that his position among us will be pretty ambiguous."

"But why?"

"Because his presence will always remind us of what we aren't. We'll end up hating him."

"Maybe you're right. But Humberto's role among you is important for at least two reasons. One, because, as the only normal being in a world of monsters, *he* takes on the category of freak, since he's *abnormal,* thus converting all of you into normal people. For Boy, he'll embody the experience of what's monstrous."

"Interesting. And the other reason?"

"Humberto's a very talented writer who hasn't had the peace or the opportunity to develop his creative possibilities. I've entrusted him to write the history of Boy's world, the story of my boldness in placing my son outside the ordinary context of life."

Emperatriz exhaled a puff of smoke.

"Is Humberto a writer? I didn't know. Interesting. This La Rinconada thing may turn out to be quite amusing . . ."

THE FANTASTIC ADVANCE payments Don Jerónimo de Azcoitía granted them against their future salaries permitted them to get rid of all their former belongings, the modest garments that were an attempt to cover up their unusual deformities—their habits and their cassocks, their grimy tatters, their circus, theater or whorehouse regalia—in order to install themselves at La Rinconada with their brand-new wardrobes. Berta brought along four suitcases stuffed with shoes: patent leather, alligator, crocodile, gold with pointed heels for evening wear, flat-heeled dull leather for sportswear, and even a pair—tongues began wagging from the first day—with genuine diamond buckles. Basilio, the acromegalic strong man with the huge head, strutted around in Superman, Marilyn Monroe or Che Guevara polo shirts, and went about in satin swim trunks, soccer shoes with reinforced cleats, towels and bathrobes initialed like a champion's. Half an hour after she arrived in the country, Emperatriz began to try on garnet-colored turbans, astrakhan chechias, straw hats, picture hats of mauve tulle, which collection she'd brought along in a dozen hatboxes. And Dr. Azula, whose Castilian accent commanded respect from the start, with his single eye gleaming with satisfaction almost in the center of his forehead, and with his bird-of-prey hands, hung up ten new suits, made of English cloth, on mahogany hangers, and selected a blue suit, not too dark and very lightweight, in which to strut around the park on the first day, marveling at the imposing mountain range of the New World country to which Don Jerónimo de Azcoitía had brought him, paying him the price of a prince's ransom, to look after his son's health.

Then came the excitement of choosing rooms and apartments, which they began decorating, each according to his or her taste, with objects discarded in favor of the abstract gray of Boy's patios and rooms: fragile Directoire chairs, a pastel drawing by Rosalba Carrera, an immense twilight over decorative ruins that was signed by Claude Lorrain, Venetian chests of drawers, *petits meubles* of inlaid wood, curtains made of sheer silk, of Genoese velvet, of toile de Jouy, items that were auctioned off to those who shouted loudest or elbowed most. Basilio smiled, superior to all those bagatelles; he spread a magnificent sleeping bag from Abercrombie and Fitch on the floor of his room, decorated his walls with photographs of soccer teams and musical groups, and set up a punching bag to stay in training.

15

FROM THE SCIENTIFIC point of view, experts confirmed, Boy's birth was an aberration: the gargoylism that contracted his body and curved his nose and his jaw like hooks, the harelip that opened his face clear through to his palate like the meat of some fruit . . . unbelievable, unacceptable the doctors said, gargoyle babies live only a few days, weeks at the most, this harelip case is unheard of, this hump, these legs, every possible defect seems to be collected in this body, no, Don Jerónimo, you must accept the idea that your son will die, and maybe it's better that way, imagine what the future holds in store for a creature like him.

"Just see to it that he doesn't die. My son's future is up to me."

In Bilbao, his European agents found one of the great specialists in cases of this type, Dr. Crisófora Azula, himself a victim of serious deformities. From the report brought to him, he found the case interesting. And it interested him even more when they named the fantastic salary he'd be paid, even if traveling to America to stay for several years meant giving up his scientific research. But it didn't matter. He'd come back richer in everything, in knowledge, since the Azcoitía case was unique in every way, and with his pockets lined well enough for him to continue his research . . . or perhaps even well enough to let him fulfill his ambition of setting up a specialized clinic.

As soon as he arrived, he got down to the work of supplying Boy with imitation eyelids, patching up his face, composing a mouth he could use, correcting the capricious anatomy that placed the child's life in danger. Don Jerónimo pressed him. He had to do everything immediately, before his son's incipient memory could be stamped with the recollection of physical suffering, with the dread of catheters and serums, injections and transfusions, before his consciousness could record the artificial sleep during which Dr. Azula hacked and sewed him up to organize, in the jumble of his anatomy, the associated organs essential for the functioning of his body.

Yes, Don Jerónimo warned, Dr. Azula must do everything that could be done to make Boy live. But there was one error he mustn't commit: nothing must induce him to make any cowardly attempts to disguise anything that wasn't normal with an imitation of normality or change Boy's condition of monster. Every effort in this direction should be superficial, a matter of skin and fibers that wouldn't erase his insulting abandonment by every power. Any effort to copy beauty would mean imposing on his son a humiliating mask to cover up a defeat that, inverted and viewed in a different perspective, should be a triumph.

At La Rinconada, Humberto Peñaloza occupied the tower Don Jerónimo had had built in the park during Inés's pregnancy. He'd intended it to be Boy's quarters, from whose windows and terraces he was to become familiar with the constellations. Over the fireplace, Humberto hung Claude Lorrain's magnificent twilight. He ordered gray velvet armchairs, he stacked shelves with books he'd always wanted, he covered the floor with carpets in very quiet tones. And, next to a window overlooking the park, he installed a huge desk of solid walnut, with his Olivetti, reams of paper for originals and copies, boxes of carbon paper, erasers, ink, thumbtacks, clips, everything ready for him to begin.

At first, Humberto Peñaloza traveled to the capital frequently to parade his new magnificence, whose source was a mystery, before his old friends and to bask in their admiration for the cape and slouch hat that proclaimed him a well-dressed Bohemian. But the wine was ordinary at the get-togethers of writers and artists in downtown cafés. And, even when it wasn't, he couldn't drink. Always the same thing. His stomach. Damn! It happened every time he got ready to start working on something he loved, as it had in his student days, when he wrote his little book. And, because he couldn't drink, he was left out. Besides, the aspirations of these would-be writers, who believed in the existence of a reality to portray, were so limited, and the small-time painters with their competitive and nationalistic mentalities were such a bore, they had such coarse tastes and they amused one another with the most commonplace gossip. In the old days, he'd been the leading voice in these get-togethers, but he remained more and more silent now, on the sidelines. To the few who were interested enough to ask him why he was so quiet, he answered that his new work was not only taking up all his time but also all of his imagination.

And it was true. Little by little, he reached the point where nothing interested him unless it was related to the world of La Rinconada. His visits to the city grew shorter and shorter. He was always happy to get back to his tower, to the library dominated by the ruins of Claude Lorrain, to the chats on his terrace with Dr. Azula, Emperatriz, and Brother Mateo.

Like a medieval monk in his cell, Brother Mateo made minute anatomical drawings that showed a structure invented by Humberto with Dr. Azula's help. Details of organs and functional diagrams designed for the purpose of ruling out any questions from Boy, when he reached the asking age, by twisting their answers to conform to those charts that illustrated his own perfection. And one afternoon when Brother Mateo, next to the fireplace, displayed the astrolabes and maps of the complete geography of the universe, which was only the sky and the earth of the patios at La Rinconada, they'd already decided, among all of them, that these wouldn't be necessary, for Boy was to grow up believing that things came into being as his eyes discovered them and died when he stopped looking at them, that they were nothing but the outer shell perceived by his eyes, that other forms of birth and death didn't exist, and, so much was this the case, that the most important among the words Boy would ever know were all those signifying *origin* and *end*. No whys, whens, outsides, insides, befores, afters; no arriving or leaving, no systems or generalizations. A bird crossing the sky at a certain hour was not *a* bird crossing the sky at a *certain* hour, it wasn't headed for other places because other places didn't exist; Boy must live in an enchanted present, in the limbo of accident, of the particular circumstance, in the isolation of the object and the moment without a key or a meaning that could subject him to a rule and, in subjecting him to it, cast him into the infinite void it was necessary for him to avoid. All monsters were exceptions. None fitted into any breed or type. Thus Berta's role—she often settled herself into Emperatriz's boudoir to complain about how exhausting her work was—was to drag her lower extremities along Boy's corridors, or to recline on a bench, or to curl up on a step and fondle a cat with a hypertrophic head as she held it against her naked breasts, Berta, Berta, present from the beginning before the child's eyes as an illustration of the inexplicable, the exceptional, the gratuitous.

Despite his privileged life, Humberto waited hungrily for his annual meeting with Don Jerónimo; after all, an experience could be shared only with an equal, with someone who was also not part of the game, because he wasn't a monster. And furthermore, all the memories and the shared feelings and the long years together . . . How was Boy? Was Dr. Azula as skilled and dedicated as his agents had assured him? Had he finished the operations? Was Boy starting to walk, to talk . . . ? No, not that, he was going to take a little longer than an ordinary child, although Dr. Azula had told him, after a series of tests, that Boy's intelligence would develop beautifully in spite of the initial retardation after so many operations.

"That was to be expected."

"Of course."

And he, Humberto? Happy? Don Jerónimo's solicitude made Humberto feel that this was a reunion with the other part of himself, and that he could be a complete man like this only once a year.

"A cigar?"

"No, thank you, Don Jerónimo, no . . ."

"Cognac?"

"I can't . . ."

"Sorry . . ."

Hadn't Dr. Azula been able to cure his gastric acidity, his pains, his stomach cramps, then? Sorry . . . patience. Had he started to write the history of La Rinconada yet? No . . . no, that is, he hadn't started to put it down on paper yet, the cramps, his chronic gastric acidity, every time he started to develop one of his ideas on paper, the pains laid him low for days and days . . . of course the general structure of the work, the characters, the situations, a humorous detail here, an anecdote there . . . that whole world was seething in his head, so much so that it drove everything else out: a good part of the time, he confessed to Don Jerónimo, who couldn't help admiring the artist, he didn't know which of the two was reality, the one inside or the one outside, whether he'd invented what he thought or what he thought had invented what his eyes saw. It was a sealed world, stifling, like living inside a sack and trying to bite through the burlap to get out or let in the air and find out if your destiny lies outside or inside or somewhere else, to drink in some fresh air not confined by your obsessions, to see where you began to be yourself and stopped being others . . . this was responsible for his pain, the bite necessary to get out, or to let the air in.

"I'm sorry to hear that, Humberto."

"Well . . ."

Why not do something radical about it, then? Maybe an operation performed by the hands of Dr. Azula, in whom Humberto seemed to have such confidence. He might be able to eliminate that corrosive spot. No, no, Don Jerónimo, it's not as bad as all that. Maybe it's not even that, not even an ulcer, maybe it's another one of those things I imagine, shut in as I am . . .

"Shut in?"

"Yes."

"At La Rinconada?"

"It's very different now . . ."

"But much prettier."

"I don't know, there are things I feel lost without . . . old patios I liked to stroll in, corridors I miss . . ."

EMPERATRIZ SAT ACROSS from Humberto. She served two cups of tea and, after crossing her chunky little legs, took a long cigarette between fingers as wrinkled as screws, waiting for her companion to light it for her. As she bent over for him to do this, he noticed that Emperatriz's brow, more wrinkled than usual, distended when she exhaled the first puff and smiled at him, suggestively showing her eyeteeth that drooled under the folds of flesh at the corners of her blubber-lips.

"What's wrong, Emperatriz?"

"Nothing. Can't I invite you to a cup of tea without having some problem in mind?"

"But when Basilio went over to fetch me he said it was very urgent indeed."

"Oh, Basilio's always in a rush. That's so he can have time to play soccer with his young boys."

Humberto insisted to himself that she hadn't called him just like that, inopportunely, in the middle of a sweltering afternoon, simply for the pleasure of their being together, that he, gentleman that he was, naturally considered it not only a pleasure but a privilege. Emperatriz smiled at his words, but only when Basilio had left the boudoir after having set up the tea service on the table did she allow herself to wrinkle her forehead again and confess that yes, she did have a problem and, since no one but the two of them ought to know about it, she'd sent innocent Basilio, always trustworthy, to fetch him instead of her calling him on the phone. The telephone operator, the one with enormous ears like bat wings, was an eavesdropper if there ever was one . . .

"Well, what's wrong, Emperatriz?"

"Boy has green diarrhea."

"We'd better see Dr. Azula right away then, Emperatriz, this is very serious, let's send for him, there must be something wrong with the formula, he'll know what to do . . ."

To do away with enjoyment, and lack of enjoyment, in Boy's food, they nourished him, from early infancy, with strained food of homogeneous texture. The formulas, which supplied him with everything that his growing body needed to develop properly—protein, iron, calcium, vitamins—were disguised with the monotonous taste of vanilla. Boy had never had digestive trouble before. And now, suddenly, green diarrhea . . .

"Let's call Dr. Azula, Emperatriz . . . What's his number?"

"No, wait . . ."

Emperatriz's bosom heaved with the details of some portent she had to reveal to him, or maybe it heaved only because he was so close to her in the pink boudoir . . . Wait, let Dr. Azula wait, let everyone wait . . . Her perfume reached him: it was the two of them, only the two, who must be the first to share this secret. A secret which, after all, was no secret, since it had become pretty clear to everyone that during the past year, once the successive operations and the daily checkups stopped being necessary, Dr. Azula had lost much of his interest in Boy. As a matter of fact, his mission was over. Why didn't he go back where he belonged instead of lingering here, lounging about and drinking and getting in everybody's way . . .

". . . useless, Humberto, completely useless . . ."

He felt certain that Emperatriz was working things so that she could gradually push everyone overboard, make everyone useless, exclude everyone. At first there'd been equality among the first-class monsters, who'd throw their parties and masked balls together, and gaily splash together in the pool. Then the elite, created by Emperatriz merely by extending invitations to her teas, invitations which not everyone received, became more and more exclusive, until finally Berta and Melchor, with whom she was barely on speaking terms now, were dropped. The other day, what was it she said about Brother Mateo that wasn't altogether kind and which, to an attentive ear, suggested that it was the beginning of the end . . . and now, Dr. Azula's turn. And after that . . . ?

Emperatriz fell silent to give Basilio time to come in and take the tea service away. Her eyes followed the departure of the acromegalic with his oversized torso, abbreviated legs, orangutan arms, hanging jawbone. He'd once heard someone say that men like him were the world's best lovers, that there was, in fact, nothing at all in them but sex. Emperatriz's lover? Why not? Who else could match the voracious eroticism that Humberto imagined concealed in Emperatriz's tiny body? She smiled maliciously after Basilio closed the door.

"That's another little problem we'll soon have on our hands."

"Do you mean Basilio?"

"Haven't you seen him training in the park with the little adolescent friends he picks up God knows where, from among even the lowest-class monsters? Haven't you seen him in the pool teaching the crawl to the little hunchback who has a face like a china doll?"

"Come on, Emperatriz. Stop it. I'm sure we have more important things to worry about now . . ."

"Things like the green diarrhea, you mean?"

Humberto laughed. As she adjusted the cloth orchid with a hand laden with rings, Emperatriz exposed a fresh, recently depilated armpit.

THE SUMMER SUN beat down so hard that the mauve tulle picture hat couldn't stop Emperatriz's belly, breasts, legs and shoulders from getting burned. And although, in principle, she was interested in what Huxley said about the Beethoven quartet, she found it impossible to keep her mind on the conversation and had to bite her nails to resist the maddening impulse to scratch her pubic hair. What a nuisance, this rule that no one could enter Boy's patios and rooms with clothes on; she wasn't at her best in the nude, while, with her clothes on, she knew how to make them sit up and take notice. The picture hat, so light and so ample, was a concession. She felt like a fungus walking beside Humberto around the pond of the Huntress Diana, not up to contributing anything to the conversation, because the only thing on her mind, the one thing in the world she wanted, was to scratch her pubic hair like a maniac. And of course that was something she couldn't do in front of Humberto, especially when he was speaking of Beethoven's last quartets.

At last, behind Diana and her pack of hounds, next to the ivy-covered wall that sealed off the last patio, there was a cool breeze. Fortunately Larry, the head gardener, had failed to crop the ivy that, in this spot, hung down like a cascade, thus giving her a chance to scratch on the sly if they walked slowly and she got Humberto to whistle the adagio, because, whenever he did this, he closed his eyes and she could take advantage of it to scratch a little.

Suddenly, Humberto stopped talking. Someone, hidden in what must have been like a grotto behind the cascading ivy, was speaking:

"Pa . . . pa . . ."

"Ma . . . mamma . . ."

"Mamma."

A child's babbling and the sound of a kiss. Then silence. Humberto and Emperatriz parted the ivy a little; one of Larry's extraordinarily long arms circled as much as was possible of Miss Dolly's bulk. With his hand, he offered Boy his wife's brimming breast, which he sucked as some of the giantess's milk ran down the face of the gargoyle child, whose scars were already beginning to lose their purple cording. Emperatriz shrieked:

"The green stool!"

"Emperatriz!"

"You're going to kill him, Miss Dolly!"

And Humberto:

"Who taught him this papa and mamma business?"

Miss Dolly pressed the child against the nakedness of her enormous breasts and came out of the hideaway, followed by Larry. Both seemed on the verge of tears when Humberto and Emperatriz faced them at the edge of the pond, saying together:

"Hand over the baby."

And Humberto:

"You're both fired. It's unbelievable that during all these years, with all the trust we've placed in you, especially in you, Miss Dolly, you've been deceiving us. You haven't even understood the first thing about our project. You don't even deserve to be second-class, or even third-class, monsters, playing at having a little monster baby just like you—and with Don Jerónimo de Azcoitía's son, no less. You're getting out this very night."

The giantess wiped her tears. She looked him in the eye and said:

"We've taught him a lot of things."

"What?"

Signaling Humberto with his finger, Larry asked the little boy:

"Let's see, sonny, tell us, what is Don Humberto?"

"Ugly . . . ugly . . ."

And he started to bawl, burying his face in Miss Dolly's breasts, holding out his arms to Larry for protection, while Humberto couldn't resist the impulse to look at his image in the pond . . . ugly, mean, neither monstrous nor handsome, insignificant . . . of course it's all a question of proportions, of harmony, and for Boy I'm creating a world in harmony with him, but *I'm* not in harmony here, I'm not a monster, I'd give my life this minute to be one . . . ugly, ugly, Boy repeated from Miss Dolly's arms, ugly, ugly, ugly, ugly, and Larry and Miss Dolly and Emperatriz were splitting their sides with laughter, all three of them together. Humberto tore the child brutally from his governess's arms. The three monsters stopped laughing. The child started to bellow in Humberto's arms, and he returned him to Miss Dolly.

"Make him shut up."

Emperatriz had taken advantage of the confusion to scratch her pubis to her heart's content, but this brought her no relief. Besides, she was much too furious at Miss Dolly, who sat down on the edge of Diana's pond, rocking the child in her arms. She wiped his runny nose and his drooling mouth, kissing and caressing him to make him hush. Standing like a heron, Larry bent over to help her still his weeping. Miss Dolly began to croon:

> Good Lady Saint Anna,
> Why is the Child crying?
> He's afraid of dragons,
> Unicorns and lions.

And, as he went on crying, Larry sang even more tenderly, from his great height, as he rested one hand on Miss Dolly's shoulder:

> The Virgin did the wash, did she,
> Saint Joseph spread it out to dry.
> It was so cold, yes, verily,
> It made the infant Jesus cry.

From Diana's shadow, in which she'd taken cover so that she could scratch, Emperatriz muttered, as she fanned herself with her picture hat, that she'd had enough foolishness, that they should hand over the baby to her, he wasn't going to be afraid of her, why should he be, after all they were even blood relations . . . and with Emperatriz, naked, sunburned, wearing the mauve tulle picture hat and carrying the child in her arms as she led the procession, followed by Humberto, Miss Dolly and Larry, they went around the pond until they came to the corridors of the next patio. Emperatriz told them:

"Go and get your things ready so you can leave tonight."

Humberto stopped them:

"No, they mustn't leave this enclosure. If they leave here, they'll tell everybody all about our project, and since they're such liars, there's going to be chaos. I'll call up Melchor and tell him to have the car ready in half an hour."

"But Humberto, they can't go away naked. After all, they have their little things they've been buying with the salaries they've earned during the past four years."

"They deserve nothing. Let them leave with one hand in front and one behind, just as they came to us. Go find them a pair of trousers and a dress, Emperatriz, nothing else. They won't leave this enclosure except to go to the station. Don't let them talk with anyone. I'll stay and take care of Boy."

Emperatriz smiled sweetly.

"But he may wake up, Humberto, and he's so terrified of you because you're . . . different."

The bait! The bloodstained hook had pierced him, and he was caught, tied to a monstrous female dwarf who was telling him that the child, witness to Humberto's shame, was afraid of his normal insignificance; witnesses are the ones who have power, she'd laugh at him with the other two monsters beside the pond, she, cradling the child in her stumpy little arms, cradling him perfunctorily, as the rules of the game dictate, the game Don Jerónimo and I . . . yes, I myself invented the rules of this game and that's caught me with a hook that's draining my blood.

16

AS SOON as the car left with Miss Dolly and her husband, Humberto realized that he owed it to Don Jerónimo and to himself to take the situation in hand. He'd call a meeting of all the first-class monsters on his terrace that same afternoon. Questioning them carefully, one by one, he'd get to the bottom of any irregularity that might very well have escaped his notice, since he could keep an eye on things only from the sidelines.

Miss Dolly's and Larry's behavior, which had come to light that same afternoon beside the pond of the Huntress Diana, would be presented to them as an example of criminal irregularity, yes, criminal, because the green diarrhea had placed Boy's life in danger.

The meeting also had another purpose: to stress, to make it clear once and for all, that the very fact that he was normal made him superior to them. They were dependent on him. Not he on them. He was the jailer. Not they, skulking and whispering behind his back. La Rinconada, Boy's quarters, the organization, the diet, Dr. Azula, the layout of the house, the demolition of rooms where it was so easy to lose one's way, everything, everything, had been his idea. They themselves, and their jobs, were his invention. They'd better not turn against him. They'd already seen what could happen to them: like Larry and Miss Dolly, they'd be thrown out of their haven. As he was about to lift the receiver off the hook and ask the operator to get busy and tell them all to be on his terrace within thirty minutes, he heard, as it reached his ears from way over the other end of the park where the pavilions of the monsters stood out, the sound of music and of . . . yes, yes, they were loud peals of laughter. He didn't take the receiver off the hook.

"What the devil! . . ."

He dropped two ice cubes into a glass. He filled it halfway with straight whiskey and walked to the balustrade of his terrace with the glass in his hand. He listened. Yes, music . . . and the hearty laughter of many people, who seemed to be celebrating something special. He sniffed the whiskey. It was so bad for him! But, what the devil, the way things were going today he couldn't worry about his health. He had to calm his nerves somehow. He took a long swallow that, after sending a shudder through his body, cauterized him. He set the glass down on the balustrade and leaned on it with both hands, intent on the winding and rewinding of the undertones of the dusk closing in around him— the crickets, the summer frogs, the voices, the laughter filtering through the elms and the chestnut trees—and straining to make out, amid the hubbub, his name, perhaps, choked off by a horse laugh in the middle of the phrase that would deliver the thrust that would finish him off.

He'd been naïve to let Melchor take Miss Dolly and Larry to the station in the car. It was only a short drive. But those ten minutes had surely been enough for the couple to tell Melchor the other side of the pond incident, in which he, Humberto Peñaloza, a normal, ordinary man nobody in the city gave a glance when he passed by, had been the butt of the three monsters' laughter. That his harmless appearance had caused terror in a child who was a monster too. The laughter, like the singing of the frogs, took on louder tones as evening came on: ophidian mouths, reptile skin, owl eyes, arms like an insect's or a dog's, animal voices, a ravenous bitch dog's voice, all laughing at him. Obviously the news that Miss Dolly, Larry and Emperatriz had made fun of him and that he, terrified by the monsters' derision, had looked at his reflection in the water, was somehow spreading through La Rinconada. The laughter came from everywhere. And it wasn't only laughter but also whispers, murmurs, monsters running with the news from door to door, explosions of smothered laughter, the switchboard busier than ever, the operator making comments and breaking in to correct the versions of those who called one another up so they could get together by rank or the closeness of their friendships and laugh at him, pick apart the fine details of the news, make a game of it, destroy his authority once and for all. Amid the din of the telephone calls mixed with the laughter and with the singing of the frogs, he heard Melchor's stammer clearly, very clearly, as the monster gave an account . . . but no: it wasn't Melchor's stammer, no, it was the ball bouncing back and forth on the tennis court where Melchor and Melisa were finishing a game before the light gave out. No. The monsters weren't talking together about him. He focused his blurry eyes: Melisa, so definitely white in her tennis outfit, had now stretched out in a hammock to crochet. And Berta, next to her, telling her about the tragic fate of her love life for the nth time. José María, the little hunchback with the china doll's face, went through his daily sprint, weaving in and out of sight among the hedgerows. The lights went on in Emperatriz's apartment, directly across from Humberto's tower. The dwarf, wearing God knows what unusual *robe d'intérieur,* was about to sit down and go over the books, as she did every evening.

Before his eyes, reality was displaying the proofs that they weren't laughing at him. Life at La Rinconada was going on peacefully, as usual. Yes, Miss Dolly and Larry had disappeared, but that wasn't important. To begin with, that so-and-so Larry was useless. And, among the monsters who gradually settled at La Rinconada, there was another massive giantess as enormous as Miss Dolly, if not more so.

Humberto sighed. He was going to take another swig of whiskey but, just as he was about to do it, bitter, acid juices bubbled up into his throat from his burning stomach. He tossed the rest of the whiskey on the grass and stepped into his library; work was the best thing in the world to take his mind off his worries. Humberto sat down in front of his typewriter. He adjusted the light. He knew exactly what he was going to write. He had its entire structure planned to the last detail, all the characters developed, all the situations and all the anecdotes composed—even the opening paragraph, down to the last comma, the paragraph that was the springboard from which the cataract of things pent up inside him for so long was singing in his brain, ready to pour out.

When Jerónimo de Azcoitía finally parted the crib's curtains to look at his long-awaited offspring, he wanted to kill him then and there; the loathsome, gnarled body writhing on its hump, its mouth a gaping bestial hole in which palate and nose bared obscene bones and tissues in an incoherent cluster of reddish traits, was chaos, disorder, a different but worse form of death. Jerónimo didn't kill his son. The horror of seeing himself the father of this version of chaos interposed a few seconds of paralyzing shock between his first impulse and its execution, and he didn't kill. It would have meant accepting defeat, letting himself be swept along by chaos, becoming its victim. Very well: this cruel mockery signified, then, that he was being forsaken forever by the traditional powers from whom he and his forebears had received so many blessings in return for maintaining His order in the things of the Earth . . .

No. *Earth* with a small letter. Finally. All of it in his head, all. One sheet, heavy, thick, expensive; it was a pleasure working like that. And this carbon paper that's such a good shade of blue. And the delightful rustle of the copy sheets, so soft, like feminine voices whispering, shushing . . . they were female voices. And male. And they weren't whispering but laughing. Guffawing. Idiot! He'd left his terrace door open and the evening breeze, with its pleasant coolness, was bringing him the murmurs of La Rinconada's upper crust. He got up to close the door.

He went out on the terrace instead of closing the door. It had grown dark. How long had he been in front of the Olivetti without writing anything? If he hadn't had that damn drink of whiskey it would be so much easier to concentrate! He was sure the stomach cramps wouldn't let him sleep that night and he'd get up the next day unable to write a line. Leaning on the balustrade, he saw that they'd parted the curtains in Emperatriz's apartment. Basilio, in white jacket and gloves, was going back and forth, carrying trays to and from the gathering.

But perhaps they'd always laughed at him. And that laughter was only the first circle that shut him in. For, with the years, colonies of giants and hunchbacks and freaks with hypertrophic heads and feet and webbed hands had been growing, forming many concentric circles around the first circle, one circle enclosed the next, and he, Humberto, in the center of all the laughters of all the monsters of all the circles, *he* in the center because he, not Boy, was the prisoner, he, not Boy, was the one Don Jerónimo had wanted to confine, with everyone laughing at him, at the captive-suffocating prison of their laughter, that prison with the windows walled up, the glass panes painted a chocolate brown up to the height of a person so that nobody can look out, the grilles, the iron bars, the boarded-up doors, the passageways one gets lost in, the courtyards one doesn't recognize, the laughter of monsters who pasture flocks in the hills, of acromegalics who sow the wheat, of hunchbacks who fish in the lake and hunt in the forests, of dwarfs who brand the cattle while waiting for the monsters of the inner circles to disappear or die so that, wrapped in the successive layers of less important monsters, they may rise; this is the world, our laughing world, this elite, these chosen prisoners of those who envy we who envy only him, Don Humberto, who envies no one and is suffocated because there's no one for him to envy, but if you only knew that I do envy, I envy the one who invented me and put me here in the center of this envy that's suffocating me. How could Emperatriz be so heartless as to give a party that same evening when her laughter and that of the discharged couple still rang in his ears, shattering them, piercing him? Emperatriz was interested only in parties. Every year she gave a big masked ball, always built around one theme: "The Chinese Pagoda," "Versailles," "In Nero's Time" . . . he recalled last year's: "The Court of Miracles," with all the monsters disguised as beggars and cripples and thieves and nuns and toothless crones and witches, and Emperatriz's own place, adapted for the purpose, converted into a labyrinth of galleries no one could breathe in, of half-demolished walls, of neglected enclosures . . . it was a lot of fun, they say; he inspected the preparations, even contributed ideas for the decorations: how to simulate damp spots on the walls, how to fake perspectives of gloomy passageways with a few strokes on a wall hanging.

What had the discharged monster couple been up to during the half hour he'd been clumsy enough to leave them in the patio with Emperatriz while he went to rummage through the closets for a shirt and trousers? She could do a lot of poisoning in half an hour. No doubt, she'd been spreading a blown-up version of the pond incident, which she'd transformed into a joke, a farce, and by this time it was being passed on from mouth to mouth all over La Rinconada. I can hear it: the frogs are no longer croaking at the light, what I hear is my name, my misfortune, being repeated by jeering lips, all of them in it together, all of them laughing, and I can't slough off the thunderous laughter even if I sit at my typewriter in order to go on writing . . . no, not to go on writing, because I haven't started to write anything yet, but let everybody sit up and take notice: one of these afternoons I'm going to start writing in order to free myself from this circle of asphyxiating laughter in which Don Jerónimo has me imprisoned.

What can I do to relieve the pain in my stomach? There's a knife stuck in my belly. On the left side. No, not a knife, a permanent biting, sharp teeth that won't let go, a hook that's sticking in me; yes, those bloodthirsty fangs I'm familiar with—I know very well whose they are—won't let go until they grab that tiny bit from me that calms me with the pain it brings. The whiskey. Damned whiskey. Why did I drink it? I don't like it . . . deep down I've always preferred red wine . . . with the same results, of course. I lie down on my bed. All my work will explode inside my body, each fragment of my anatomy will acquire a life of its own, outside mine, Humberto won't exist, only these monsters, the despot who imprisoned me at La Rinconada to force me to invent him, Inés's honey complexion, Brígida's death, Iris Mateluna's hysterical pregnancy, the saintly girl who was never beatified, Humberto Peñaloza's father pointing out Don Jerónimo dressed up to go to the Jockey Club, and your benign, kind hand, Mother Benita, that does not and will not let go of mine, and your attention fixed on these words of a mute, and your rosaries, the Casa's La Rinconada as it once was, as it is now, as it was afterwards, the escape, the crime, all of it alive in my brain, Peta Ponce's prism refracting and confusing everything and creating simultaneous and contradictory planes, everything without ever reaching paper, because I always hear voices and laughter enveloping and tying me up; I look at the light in Emperatriz's windows, Basilio carrying trays back and forth— perhaps the monsters are getting ready to dance . . . my pain, here, here, the biting of the bloodthirsty fangs that won't let their tiny prey go, Emperatriz's hook penetrating my flesh. I get up to call Dr. Azula on the phone. Where can I get hold of him? It's urgent. The operator says: at Señorita Emperatriz's place.

But I don't want to see her: I want to tear out this knife, to release myself from the grip of the monster's teeth, to be able to yearn, to remember when I had the capacity to think of other things, to look outside, through the window—light, wind, faces, leaves, books, conversations—but all that's so remote now, from before La Rinconada, from before you yourself existed here by my bedside, Mother Benita, praying, patting my hand, from before Don Jerónimo existed, on that summer afternoon when, looking for a cool place to study my law texts, I browsed at the gallery on the second floor of the Museo Antropológico, while the city's gritty summer covered everything outside with a cowl of tedium. It was difficult for me to study at home. Overly protective, my father flew into a rage if my mother made the slightest noise with the pots and pans in the kitchen. Sitting across the table from me, he set up my books in a way that got me all mixed up, or else he adjusted the light without my asking him, or closed the windows to keep the street noises from disturbing me, when, as a matter of fact, they hadn't been disturbing me at all. I had to get away. The parks; but I've always been frightened of the parks. Churches were cool, but they offered little light. On the other hand, the museum was almost deserted on weekdays. In a corner a sleepy-eyed guard looked, as his head bobbed up and down, like a faulty specimen before, being judged unworthy of embalming, it decomposed and was dumped into the trash. The gallery on the second floor forms a large oval in which I can walk for miles and miles as I memorize sections of laws, without corners to interrupt me; when I let my eyes stray, I look down and see, sticking up from the main room on the first floor, the gigantic skeleton of the reconstructed mylodon nobody visits on weekdays and few people on holidays. That was peace, Mother Benita. Safety. Preparing my examinations in order to go from second-year into third-year law, walking around the oval without interruption, obtaining an LL.B., which was the first step, then the doctorate, and finally, as a judge or notary public, acquiring a face of my own . . . everything was within reach as long as I continued walking around the oval of the gallery on the second floor. Against the gallery's wall, there are showcases containing dry clay objects, crude stone carvings, bowls hollowed out of pieces of wood, bone needles and—piled up in a huge aquariumlike display cabinet—the jumble of crumbling naked Atacameño mummies in a fetal position, upside down, dried up, smile at me from behind the glass. I stop to look at them. I know them. Reflected in the glass of the showcase, my face is a perfect match for the faces of some mummies. Their smiles are my smile that smiles in the presence of death, because I'm going to be such a big lawyer that I won't need the ancient suns of the desert to preserve my features, and their smiles protect me against any danger except the danger of seeing *him*, dressed in very light gray, standing behind me, observing the Atacameño mummies without his face matching any of those smiles. I recognized him. He spoke to me. I answered him. We walked together down the gallery whose oval contains the mylodon on the first floor. I'm studying law. Why?

It was then. I could have been saved from your bite by lunging to the next floor and smashing my head on the pavement. I could have escaped from you by disguising myself as the Araucanian in the black regalia displayed on a dummy whose place I could have taken, but I didn't run away. I don't understand why I answered Don Jerónimo as I did. I told him: I'm a writer. I have an excellent memory, so I got by with little studying. And, on rainy afternoons, I used to go to the Biblioteca Nacional and read, a good deal of Nietzsche, Hölderlin, Shakespeare, Goethe, but also a good deal of Insúa and Vargas Vila and García Sanchiz and Villaespesa and Emilio Carrere, yes, but also the classics, although in my style you'll find more traces of Insúa than of Goethe. They all opened windows for me, sealed up and stifling now, that, after my answer to Don Jerónimo on that cursed summer afternoon, shut me up in this house: I told him I'm a writer. He asked my name. I turned red as I answered.

"Humberto Peñaloza."

"I'll be on the lookout for your next book."

"I'm very glad that you're interested."

"Anything of yours interests me . . ."

My head slumped down on my typewriter. My arms knocked over the desk lamp. My body slowly slid from the chair and fell in a heap on the floor. At the farthest end of the long darkness, my feet felt around for slippers. I covered up as well as I could with the robe . . . Emperatriz, Emperatriz, Emperatriz . . . the thing to do was cut across the lawn to the dwarf's apartment, to at least not die alone, although who knows if it isn't preferable, it may be better to die in the arms of a repulsive dwarf than abandoned in a silent tower destined for the perfect creature.

They opened the door. Thanks, Mother Benita, you're always everywhere, getting them to open the door for me at just the right moment . . . All of them naked in Emperatriz's boudoir, all the monsters who drag me along, Melchor, Basilio, I see their deformities, defiant as if they weren't ashamed of them . . . stop playacting at not being ashamed, you're hidden away here at La Rinconada where you know that no one will turn to look at you and laugh, you're refugees, the circle of terror holds you prisoner, you never leave La Rinconada, you could go out if you liked—you're allowed to—but you don't go out, just as I'm allowed to go out but can't, and I'm normal, you can see I'm normal, how can you help seeing it when you're stretching me out on Emperatriz's pink moiré chaise longue . . . you monsters are afraid to go out . . . we're afraid to go out, we're afraid that they'll see us, that's why we take refuge here . . . Dr. Azula can't help being terrified lest he be seen with his whole body covered by scales and his hands like a bird of prey's touching me, probing, examining me, while Emperatriz slips off my robe, leaves me in pajamas, feels my brow and is going to keep on feeling me, and, at the dwarf's touch, I can't hold myself back anymore, I let go completely and soil myself, and my watery, fetid, black stool stains the moiré, the Aubusson, the *petits meubles*, the veil-like curtains; the naked monsters cover their faces with white handkerchiefs, protect their noses, flee, they can't stand me, because I'm too nauseating, and Dr. Azula thinks I've been bleeding for days . . . this is very serious, we have to operate . . . I'm much too weak for an operation, I've lost too much blood . . . he raises my eyelid . . . white, a blood test's necessary, his blood pressure's going down and down and down and down . . . the monsters hold their noses, nauseated by me but rooted to the spot by curiosity, and shield their faces with handkerchiefs because I go on soiling myself. Blood transfusions, Azula says . . . Who wants to donate blood for Don Humberto . . . I, I, I, I . . . they all want to give me their monstrous blood as if they were anxious to get rid of it . . . they've dressed up in white to cover up the fact that I surprised them in an orgy, naked under their white hospital clothes, disguised as nurses with aprons and masks that can't hide their monstrosities . . . you're Melisa, I recognize you because of your dark glasses . . . you, Basilio, how can I mistake you . . . and you, Emperatriz . . . and you, Azula . . . and you, Mateo . . . and even the telephone operator with ears like the wings of a bat has deserted her switchboard to dress in white too. A red bag fills the vein in my arm with monster blood, and I feel how Basilio's powerful blood slips into me and my arms grow and my jaw enlarges; they're monstrifying me, Berta's blood is crippling my legs, I've lost my form, I have no definite contours, I'm in flux, changing, as if I were seen through moving water, I'm no longer me, I'm this vague twilight of consciousness that's peopled by white figures that come and stick needles into my veins . . . how many red corpuscles . . . he has almost none left. Someone whispers: "He'll never get out of here." . . . Let me out, I don't want to die of suffocation within these adobe walls with their peeling crust, you're only damp spots on mud wall, all of you, let me out of here! . . . If I could only cross the imperceptible line that separates the half-light from the darkness. I'm on the brink. But no, they won't let me cross into the darkness where there's no anguish, they want to hold me on this side, in the half-light, where things have no outline and barely shift about. No, Dr. Azula, I can't stand the tube you put through my nose down into my stomach, the syringe with which they take out quarts and quarts of my blood, Humberto Peñaloza's blood when he was Humberto Peñaloza, my blood before they put monster blood into my veins. They have me shackled to this bed while the monsters wait outside the door of my room, clamoring for my blood, which may be old but is at least the blood of a normal being, and they drink or inject it into their veins, they shout for my blood . . . more of Humberto Peñaloza's blood, more of Humberto Peñaloza's blood . . . I hear the clamor of the bloodthirsty mob crowded together against my door, I can't move, because they've got me immobilized with these catheters that hurt, they ask me how I feel, looking very troubled, they tell me not to worry, that everything will turn out well, that this is all routine . . . no, no one's asked after my health . . . the doctors and nurses say they don't know my name, they ask me questions, they bring file cards to fill with information they know perfectly well but say they don't, they say they found me lying in a puddle of bloody feces and how can they know my name, they're taking away my identity, they're even stealing that from me, from Humberto Peñaloza, Humberto Peñaloza, Humberto Peñaloza, I shout my name at them but my voice can't be heard . . . poor, poor thing . . . and they put away the file cards on which they've refused to write down my name. Mother Benita, they're making fun of me because they know I'm so weak I've even forgotten my name, I can't identify myself, help me, you're merciful and kind. But I don't want to know who I am, besides I'm not the one I was if I ever was anyone, don't go away, Mother Benita, don't let go my hand, don't let me die alone, I don't know how they let you in here. No. Go away. You're not Mother Benita. You're only someone disguised as her. Go away. I'm a stranger here, I can call Emperatriz any time I want, she's not only fond of me like Mother Benita, she also desires and loves me and wants to marry me, and I promised to marry her because I love her too, I can ask her to come and sit at my bedside and wipe away the perspiration on my forehead with cotton soaked in toilet water and take my hand and caress it gently, telling me not to worry, not to be afraid, that she's watching over me.

17

AM I DEAF besides being dumb? Besides being almost blind, because I can barely manage to distinguish shapes and white reverberations that may vaguely be chairs, wardrobes, washstands, persons, curtains, and that appear and disappear and shift and grow hazy and dim and move aimlessly and afterwards, in the midst of their movement, are extinguished, erased? I can't hear their footfalls. Not a sound. Everything's made of cotton and gauze, and cotton has no contours, it's soft, you can pull it to shreds, I can sink my fingers into that cotton shape that's a person, doctor, nurse, whatever it is, or else, with my arms, I can squeeze this bale of blurry cotton hanging on the wall, that simulates dissolving light. I too am made of cotton. I run my hands over my body. I can't feel its form or its consistency, because it's made of cotton and my fingers are cotton and cotton can't explore or feel or recognize, it can only go on being soft, white; sometimes there's the suggestion of a kindly face bending over me with a mask over it that opens its mouth to say something I can't hear, and the soft, white matter again swallows up the mere outlines of a person approaching my bed, because I'm in a bed, the one thing that isn't cotton are the four white iron bars at the foot of my bed, where the chart with my name on it hangs, the chart that the doctor picks up to study and discuss with the white nurse. I sink my head in the cotton of the pillow.

"He's going to fall asleep."

"Good."

"That way he won't feel a thing."

What is it I mustn't feel? Other nurses come over, their faces hidden by gauze masks, now I can't see their grotesque masks underneath, they whisper, smooth the sheets, shake the bottle of blood that's so far away, near the white ceiling, consult the chart, put the thermometer in my mouth, whisper, smile—they always smile, they smile too much when there's nothing to smile about —and one of them gives me gentle little pats on the hand, as you would a very good little boy:

"Go to sleep."

That's what they want. But I'm not going to fall asleep. The blood trickling through the tube down into my vein allows me to hang on to something black, red, so I can endure this white dream that sheathes me and thus listen to snatches of the conversation of those muffled beings whispering that Don Jerónimo sent orders that no expense or effort was to be spared on my operation and care, that they've cut out eighty percent and left me twenty and that it's been very serious, with death threatening.

The hands that lift my bedclothes, that force me to roll over on my side, that pull down my coarse pajama bottom, are suddenly coarse, and coarse the unfriendly needle that pierces me, and coarse the liquid it leaves in my rump, and coarse and hard my wakefulness that borders on sleep. I can't bear the noise she's making as she sits beside my bed arranging syringes and needles in the white enameled iron kidney basin with its thin blue edge. Why isn't she careful to do it more silently if Don Jerónimo ordered them to pamper me? I look at her, intending to repeat this to her, but say nothing because I recognize her. It's she. In spite of her white mask, of standing taller in high boots, of being disguised by her nurse's cap, it's she keeping an eye on me, she moving the bottle of blood around and opening the valve a little, more, more, a lot, and I ignite, turn red, burn up, can't bear the heat and the fire and the pain of all my wounds because I have wounds that hurt I don't know where but that are going to kill me with pain, because the blood coming out of the bottle all at once sets me on fire—my whole body, all of it, cut into slices by claws, torn apart by fangs, dismembered on an operating table: the knife that cuts out three-quarters of me, the burning that cauterizes me, the blood that flows and that I absorb, my body red and multiplied a hundred times, the pain also red and multiplied a hundred times, my body rent by claws and knives and teeth . . . the blood's dripping too fast, it has to be cut down some more, more . . . and I start to grow cool, cold, icy, I'm this chunk of ice that drips and drips, my nose drips and my hands and my feet, I'm a chunk of ice that's melting, and there's nothing left. And nurses come to take my covers off, they're not afraid of disturbing me with their loud talk, they undress me with a look of loathing on their faces, because I've dirtied myself and as the hours pass I get smellier and dirtier, it disgusts them to wash me even if they're used to these things, it's I who fill them with repugnance, the clean pajama they put on me is coarse, hard, I'm sure they picked the oldest and most patched-up one they could find, four nurses together move me over to change the bottom sheet while they talk in shouts about Pedro Pérez, who bought a car and went for a drive with Fernando Fernández, who was fired for getting to work late but told Gonzalo González that they had no right to do it, and they yell out to another nurse, who's laughing outside my door, to order another bottle of serum from the drugstore, they're not quiet anymore, they show no respect for me, they don't treat me as the patient protected by Don Jerónimo but as if I were his prisoner, I believe they're laughing at me because they know he's had eighty percent cut out of me and you can't respect anybody who has eighty percent cut out of him . . . water, water, I think I'm saying water, water, but I must have said something else because they shake their heads in refusal, and no one's refused a glass of water even if they've ripped out eighty percent of him. Something has definitely turned the nurses against me, they're going to make me suffer, that's why they're here, the four bars at the foot of the bed aren't the bars at the foot of the bed but the iron bars of the window, because they're holding me prisoner in this room where all the nurses and all the doctors hate me, they deny me food and water, which can't be denied anyone, and that proves it, and under their gauze masks they screw up their noses at the fetid odor I emit. Even when I don't emit a fetid odor, I disgust them because I'm me and I finally fell into Don Jerónimo's clutches, I committed myself to you, Don Jerónimo. I bound myself to La Rinconada, to Inés, to Peta, to you, to the Casa, to Mother Benita, to these white figures from the ball Emperatriz gave years ago: "In the Hospital." His commanding presence replaced my father's weak demands . . . a Doctor of Laws, son, that's something worthwhile, if you become that you'll be somebody . . . and I told my father nothing and hardly admitted to myself that I wrote poems at night, by candlelight so that no one would suspect anything in our homes that were always changing, always the same, always cramped, with a balcony for my sister to sit at and weave her dream of owning a piano covered with a Manila shawl. Sometimes I used to tell my father at night: "I have to go to a party meeting."

He tied the knot in my tie. When I got to the corner, I undid the knot. I went to the Hercules Bar and sat at a corner table to finish my book. Rosita served me a sandwich, a glass of red wine: "If you don't have it on you, you can pay me later."

I waited until closing time. I took her home: my name's Zoila Blanca Rosa López Arriagada, she told me, blushing as she realized how tacky it sounded to me, but my laughter was quickly defeated by her tenderness when she confessed to me that when she was born, after four brothers, she looked so beautiful to her father, so white, so rosy, that, at the baptismal font, he'd given her the name Zoila Blanca Rosa. I am the White Rose. My fingers stroked the inside of her arms and, just a little bit, her rosy rose, and I lent her a muffler because it was autumn and the plane trees were shedding their leaves, and suddenly everything took a serious turn, acquiring a touching solemnity, although I realized how ridiculous the name Zoila Blanca Rosa was. Yes, ridiculous but serious: that tackiness was my kind of thing, I didn't need any prompting to know that my new university buddies were my kind of people. Those consumptive poets who got together at the Hercules, their wet shoes speckled with sawdust from the floor, and played dominoes with some redcap from the station close by, some of them anarchists, others decadents, all of them poor; goodbye to textbooks, I'd already sold mine to buy cigarettes; to hell with the traditional party and neckties and decorative family names; my ill-shaven friends hardly ever attended classes, they got together at the Hercules to make fun of the professors more than anything else, to open a box sent by some peasant mother, lonely for her boy, from the southern part of the country, because they'd killed the hog so that the boy could eat blood sausages and cracklings and pork hocks with his friends, they had so little money to send him for his studies that at least the box aromatic with hot pepper and coriander and garlic would help him get by the cold winter spells, and she sent him some coffee to help him stay awake, with raw nerve ends, friends, buddies, reeking of wine, their scarves tied aound their necks because it was cold at the Hercules and in the rooming houses where they lived and in the streets they traversed on foot, drenched by the rain, the soles of their shoes worn through, a hole covered on the inside with cardboard—on foot because it was necessary to save the pennies of the streetcar fare so as to treat some friend to a glass of red wine, by selling one's textbooks, hocking one's watch . . . but what do you get out of writing, Humberto, when you don't have a cent to get things published and you need pull if you want a publisher to print you, a name, and you don't have a name, just a loss of interest in your studies and in Nietzsche, whom we don't even discuss anymore because those things are for middle-class kids in first and second year and dudes with suede spats. Luis coughs, until he coughs too much and they carry him off and he's never heard from again.

"He must have died."

"Lucky, dying young like that."

"Treat me to another glass, Rosita. I'll pay you on Monday."

"How are you going to publish your book, then, Humberto?"

By subscriptions, of course. I talked to the printer. A deposit would do. Then, as more copies sold, the balance would be paid, but there had to be a deposit. Then I wrote to you, reminding you of our meeting at the Museo Antropológica, offering you a copy of my book that was written but still unpublished for lack of funds to make the deposit. Several days later, at general delivery, I picked up your friendly letter with a check subscribing not for one but for a hundred copies of the edition of five hundred. I took my manuscript to the printer's.

And when my name—which *I* no longer remember but know is written on the chart the white hooded figures consult at the foot of my bed as they shake their heads, and which *you* don't know, Mother Benita, because to you I'm only Mudito who sweeps and cleans and gets tips and takes care of the plumbing and boards up windows—appeared for the first time, my father was so proud of it he cried. "A budding talent, just feeling his way out of his chrysalis but already showing promise of creations of high artistic sensibility, of refined sentiment bordering on the sickly, who takes delight in the luxury of images that are sometimes decadent, but is a name not to be forgotten because, although new, it's already left its mark, owing to the delicacy of the author's artistic sensibility, on our literature: Humberto Peñaloza." That's my name, Mother: Humberto Peñaloza. I knew I wasn't going to forget my name forever, no one was going to steal it from me, why would these nurses in white, these cotton figures, want such an ugly name? My father didn't know . . . how could he have guessed I had this bent, why had I kept it from him when he'd have understood, because the literary profession too can get you to the top. My name in print like that, in large letters at the head of the article on the Sunday literary page of the most important newspaper, gave our family a name; he wanted me to read it, there in that article in the paper it stood out very clearly, Humberto Peñaloza, which was his name too, and, asking my mother for the scissors, he savagely plunged them into the paper to cut out the article. I told him it was you, Don Jerónimo, who so generously subscribed for a hundred copies of the first printing in order to make possible the existence of my little book of one hundred and eighty pages, with its ugly greenish spine.

"Don Jerónimo de Azcoitía! How the devil did you ever meet him?"

"That's my business."

He stared at me, confused, before asking me: "Have you paid him a visit in order to thank him?"

"No."

"That's the limit. Get dressed immediately . . . your dark

suit, your best shirt . . . if it's not ready, tell your mother to press it. You're going to go and see him. How can you show such a lack of breeding? A son of mine, who bears my name . . ."

The first time that he dared speak of his name.

". . . who bears my name and behaves like an ungrateful hooligan . . ."

I shouted at him: I've been dying of stomach pains ever since you drove the scissors into me in order to steal my triumph. Let my stupid sister stop filling her album with clippings of articles that mention my name, and placing wreaths of flowers and doves around each . . . give me back that album so I can burn it, if you want to know the truth I don't belong to the party anymore, I get drunk at bars almost every night with my friends who are truly happy about my triumph that's not a triumph but merely a slight success, and they know it and appreciate it for what it is, neither more nor less, I don't go to classes anymore, I don't intend to be a lawyer or a notary, I don't want to be anyone, leave me alone, don't rob me of the little I have of my own, my book . . . you won't have a dowry, daughter, he used to tell my sister, who'd already been made pregnant by the owner of the corner bookstore and had to get married before the month was up in order to cover up her shame, you won't have a dowry, but your husband will be proud of this thing you can give him: the scrapbook that repeats over and over that your brother exists, that he's somebody, that he has a name.

"You can't tarnish my name."

"Since when have you had a name!"

I slammed the door as I went out, and I never returned. The night you appeared at the Hercules to look for me, Don Jerónimo, I'd been living with Rosita for two months over a laundry in a wretched little room that reeked of cleanliness. With her fresh body, slight but always warmth-giving, intertwined with mine at night, my father and his demands lost coherence, to the point where my stomach cramps eventually disappeared. She never asked me what I was writing. Neither did the redcaps with whom I played dominoes. My university buddies gradually scattered, joining other cliques in other cafés, but I stuck to this one, I was at home here because Rosita smiled at me from behind the coffee machine . . . I didn't miss them, the consumptive poet died as he should have died, in a seedy room, Manolo obtained a position in the Social Security Department, a wage slave, an old man . . . what can I do, I'm sick of starving and having my mother tell me we've got nothing, nothing, nothing . . . Nicanor went back to his rainy province to marry his childhood sweetheart with the blessing of his parents, because the two families had adjoining properties, small patches of land that, together, perhaps might . . . but Nicanor had never spoken of this secret sweetheart, and I played dominoes unperturbed, until I saw you appear at the door. You went up to the counter to ask Rosita if I was there. You pointed me out with your innocent finger, there in the back of the room next to the heater that gave little warmth, and you looked at me over the cluster of smelly patrons under the yellow light; you, Rosita, pointed me out, turning me over to Don Jerónimo, bound hand and foot, powerless to put up any resistance. I felt the pain here, in a spot that's now covered by layers of cotton and gauze and adhesive tape, and it gradually increased and became sharper and sharper as you approached me among the full tables. With my elbows resting on the marble and flanking my dominoes, I tried to concentrate on my next play, but the sudden stab of pain cut off my breath as you stood behind me, wordless . . . how could you have learned where to find me, perhaps you'd gone to my father's house, perhaps, scraping and bowing, he'd asked you into our touching little parlor with the crippled table and its cover embroidered by my sister, perhaps she'd shown you the scrapbook and introduced my discreet, incredulous, cunningly ironical mother . . .

"Double three."

Don Jerónimo's hand set the domino in place. I jumped up to face him.

"Who asked you to come butting in, you damn dude?"

You laughed. No, you only smiled at first.

"Don't you recognize me?"

The talk at the other tables subsided. The owner and Rosita looked at us through the hanging sausages and the smoke. Somebody muttered:

"There's gonna be a fight."
You really laughed then, saying:
"No, there won't be any fight."

And, making an about-face, you went out between the tables. My opponent, who kept an eye on what was happening behind me, told me that, before leaving, the dude had stopped a moment to write something and hand it to Rosita. I won the game.

"I'm taking off."
"This early, tonight?"
"You can get even tomorrow."

I already knew there'd be no tomorrow. I put my scarf around my neck. I went over to the counter to tell Rosita:

"I'm going."
"Where . . . ?"
"I don't feel well, my stomach . . ."

I was going out when she called to me:

"Listen."
"What?"
"The dude expects you at his house tomorrow at ten."

His calling card with his address on it. I tore it up.

"Let him go to hell."

Of course, I didn't need his address, I knew the yellow façade across from the trees in the park, so that tearing up the card was nothing but a decorative gesture to keep Rosita from knowing that after that night I was never going to sleep pressed against her skin.

18

EVERYTHING, FROM THE very beginning, from the time his glove grazed my arm in the street, everything's been carefully laid out, step by step, with infinite care, making me a prisoner of his confidence when I entered his service, making me a witness of his love in order to hold me prisoner, Inés the bait to get me to swallow the hook, supremacy in the world of monsters where my mean body would take the place of his and be the father of his son, the final temptation, the most powerful hook. I bit, the hook pierced me, and I can't shake free, tied down as I am to a bed that burns suddenly and freezes just as suddenly, injection after injection, bottle after bottle of blood to keep me from dying, not turn me into an *imbunche,* that's what the kindly old witches I live with want me for, and that would be complete peace, with all of me sewed up instead of opened with the precise cuts of Dr. Azula's knife, as I listen to their halting footsteps outside, no, they've come to sew me because they're good, I see them through the window, idling in the street while waiting for me at the corner service station. Why don't they let them come in to see me? They want nothing of me, they're patient. They wait patiently because the old women's time is interminable, they replace one another and live on forever, no, we're in no hurry, we can wait till the bottle empties into poor Mudito's vein.

It's cold outside. There's a cold wind blowing I know I'll never feel again, just as I'll never feel water in my mouth again because they refuse to give me any. They'll keep me here forever in this overheated incubator. I close my eyes to drive away this hopeless longing for the street, for cold air. And suddenly, behind my eyelids, the answer's flashed across a kind of screen: *They want to keep you alive here without ever letting you get out, in order to rob you of all your organs, you see, they're taking out eighty percent . . .* Of course! They started by interchanging my blood: with my own eyes I saw Dr. Azula take syringe after syringe of blood from my stomach and turn it over to the screaming multitude. They're getting ready to go on with the rest. Last night I felt the saw cutting off my feet, the way they traced a red circle around my right ankle and then around the left. And this morning I woke up with enormous feet, with yellow membranes between my toes: webbed feet. I suspect they did the same with my hands. I don't want to look at them. That's why I hide them under the sheet, in order not to see the repulsive membranes that join my fingers, that are enmeshed in thick cobwebs of monster's flesh. There must be a list of priorities controlled by Emperatriz. She must be very busy at her receptionist's desk, dressed in her perfectly starched white cap, mollifying the monsters' greediness for my organs . . . we must do this in the right order, the first-class monsters first, then the second-class, give me your name, what do you want . . . an entire new face to supplant one with deformed features presents the biggest problem of all because there's so much demand for that part of the anatomy, they all want new faces and only a few are available, the process takes more time, it's slower and more delicate, a face is more important than, say, a foot.

And then my skin, they'll flay me and cover Melisa's albino body with my skin, and who knows how many days from now I'll wake out of this forced sleep transformed into a white wraith with a pair of dark glasses . . . and my nose, and my kidneys, and my arms, and my stomach, no, they've already taken that out, at least eighty percent I think they said, liver, lungs, all my healthy parts to go to the screaming monsters who form a line in front of Emperatriz's desk, ready to load me down with their defective organs, which are gradually shaping a new me that will never finish taking shape, and yet, I'll be condemned to go on recognizing myself, looking through the square of that sealed window, waiting for them to put me to sleep again to rob me of another kidney, an ear, my nails to replace them with claws, all the monsters in La Rinconada will be healthy, all of them normal, insignificant, free.

But it can't be. It has to be different. Something else. After all, I'm a limited being. I have only two lungs, one nose, two ears, thirty-two teeth, two hands, two feet . . . when I woke up —I don't know what time of day or night it was because nothing, neither the light nor the shadows, had changed in my window— something strange dawned on me: my feet and my hands weren't webbed anymore. When they're grafted onto me, the monsters' defective members and organs take on normal forms once more. That's why they put me to sleep. In my sleep I feel Dr. Azula's scalpel cutting me up, I feel them sawing my bones, slicing, sewing, slashing, separating, ripping out pieces of my body that weren't my body's but are restored to normalcy by my body when they're grafted onto it, I sleep, but I feel it all, that's why they keep me locked up in here and I'm never going to get out because I'm a nursery of organs and a factory of healthy parts. And to prevent me from becoming aware of this abuse you keep me in a state of twilight consciousness, deflated but with a little air left in me, very little, just enough to stop me from dying altogether, and, with this interchanging of organs, my time will be extended more and more so that, since I'll never be a person again, only a place to grow parts for others, I'll never die, nothing happens, everything's the same, the difference between sleep and wakefulness is negligible, no, Don Jerónimo won't let me die, he wants all the monsters in the world to nurse off me and disappear from the face of the earth, leaving me weighed down with their monstrosities.

I'm a stranger in time now, nothing moves in the street my window frames, it's never day or night, never hot or cold, only this long replacement of organs that renew me, time is static but elastic and bounces me off it, everything is like everything else, neither water nor lack of water, everything of the same color which may be white, dim voices, soft, a clock without hands, a heart without its beat, not being hungry when it's time to be hungry not only because the clock has no hands but because I have no stomach now, I was robbed of it, eighty percent or more it was that they took, I think I heard them whisper, and time will never pass, or take me beyond this half-darkness half-light that denies me my right to the final orgasm of death.

THEY BELIEVE I'm asleep. They all talk in whispers. Dr. Azula's examining the chart, showing it to Don Jerónimo. They ask the nurses for details, yes, they answer, yes doctor, no doctor, why no, doctor, and he hangs the chart up again. I don't open my eyes, but as they've given me transparent ophidian eyelids, I see everything. Let them go ahead and think I'm asleep.

"Is he in condition for the big operation?"

"There'll be two simultaneous operations, Don Jerónimo. I'll have to place you both on two adjoining tables . . ."

"Spare me the details, as long as you bring me out all right. By the way, you can do whatever you want with my genitals, even dump them in the garbage. They were useless to me after this bastard fooled me into making love to a filthy old hag with a rotting sex organ that crippled mine permanently. While he was making love to Inés . . . no, no, don't say that, Dr. Azula, don't you dare, she didn't cheat on me, she thought it was me all along. I can't forgive this filthy scum for touching my wife, for daring to touch what he was born without the right to touch. He must be punished. He must never use his organ again: graft it on me and don't give him mine."

When they left my room I opened my eyes. I looked at the window, the interminable street that was as stationary as the photograph of an everyday scene, without interest or beauty, this dull perspective of a street where nothing ever changes. An immense peace flooded through me as I looked at the blowup pasted on the wall. Before it, in this room, my everlasting life of substitutions would go on. Peace and happiness. Why not? Don Jerónimo said it: that night in Peta Ponce's room I touched Inés. What does it matter, then, if death's forbidden to me? And water? And complete sleep, and total wakefulness? I've found peace. Familiar figures begin to stir in the street. I hear footsteps. They smile at me, furtively at first, from the sidewalk, as they wait for me on the corner; now they make signs to me . . .

come down, come down . . . Rita says she'll open the door for me, Dora tells me they'll protect me, Brígida waves for me to come over, I hear the bells of the church tower of Fray Andresito, four in the afternoon, sunny, it's wintertime but the sun's out, the air must be cool out there, let them wait for me, I signal them to wait for me a little while, I won't be able to go down and join them today, maybe not even tomorrow, but day after tomorrow or the day after, I'm sure I will because by then my operation will be all over . . . Come down, Mudito, *Mudito* because they forgot to replace your throat with another and you're dumb now, or your ears with other ears and you're deaf, come down, we're waiting to take you in, we don't demand anything of you, we just want to look after you, to be good to you, to wrap you, look at the sacks we've brought along to take you with us without anyone noticing that we're taking you, it makes no difference to us if you have no sex organ, we have other pastimes, we'll show you how to indulge in them because, like us, you've been stripped of everything and have the power of wretched and old and forgotten creatures, come and play with us . . . no . . . why they're only innocent little games, but you'll soon see the things that can happen when we manipulate them, and you'll be free to come and live with us, to sweep a little, to clean up, to get people ready for death, to pray . . . shshshsh-shsh, for God's sake, don't talk so much, don't shout, don't call me like that, be quiet, hush, they'll hear you shouting up to me:

"Come down, Mudito."

"Come on down."

"We're waiting for you."

"We miss you."

ARE YOU TOO knitting something for Boy? Who got you into the conspiracy of the seven witches? It must have been during my absence in the hospital. You seem unfamiliar in repose like this, Mother Benita, as if you had all eternity before you, like me, twilighted tenuous, without feeling the relief of extinction, without feeling the windowpane, which must be so cool. Have they got me tied down? You see, Mother Benita, I can't move. The peace of this interminable twilight, which you know as well as I do will never end, attracts you with the gloom of the dull street framed by my window, where nothing will ever change for me. You take my hand because you know I'm terrified that I'll never die, but I'm not always afraid, Mother Benita, sometimes I feel elated, knowing that my time will go on without beginning or end along this street which is another version of paradise—façades, sidewalks, street lamps, pavement, windows, doors, dried-up tree, antennas, cables—because from here, protected by you, I don't think all this is another version of hell, like the shelterless outdoors of the miserable streets I had to endure when I escaped from La Rinconada on finding out that everything had been planned not to revolve around Boy but to hunt me down, to catch me, and I escaped, alone, into the cold, without any features by then, because Dr. Azula left me only twenty percent, disguised as a beggar because I was afraid someone would recognize the look in my eyes, and the inevitable cold and hunger and destitution and misery were then the hostile faces in the streets; the boardinghouse keepers kicked me out when I didn't pay because I had no money, wandering over this flat time stretching out before me, night and day, night and day the faces always the same, some more inclement than others but all equal in their hostility when I wandered through the parks at night, not parks with equestrian monuments and pergolas and lakes but the others, those on the city's fringe that are something between a park and a pasture, no man's lands without guards to watch over them, and that's why we swarm into them at night, kindling small fires to warm our hands or make tea, smothering the tiny bonfire of dry leaves so that we won't be discovered or discover one another, because we might kill one another. Now that I'm down to my twenty percent, I roam the streets unafraid that Peta will find me out, I go into the forsaken parks not to hide from her but to let her see for herself that I'm not the one she's looking for. Let the poor old thing find out that it's no longer worth going to all that trouble, because it's not me but him she has to track down. He has everything, Peta. The one who penetrated you was he. It was he who made you scream with pleasure in that only orgasm your life had been searching for down through the centuries, starting with the original nightmare out of which we appeared. It was his weight that rested on your body that night, not mine, I penetrated Inés, that's why he's stripped me of the organs that touched her, that's why they threw me out into the street, into this street I see in the window, where nothing happens, the empty gas station, the street stretches and recedes, and again stretches and bends in time that's stationary, the rickety beggar dressed in rags, who's frequently seen at church doors because he's deaf and dumb, ambles down the street, drops out of sight as if the wind had swept him away, he's gone into the park where others like him hide out, but he doesn't hide, Mother Benita, I swear it, he builds his fire of dry leaves in a ditch and goes to sleep next to it, hoping that Peta will come around at night and go through his pockets pretending she wants to rob him, Mother Benita, but Peta doesn't want to steal, she's come looking for what she's always wanted from me. I won't wake up because Peta won't find anything. The night will swallow up her roar of rage, but I won't hear it, she'll fasten my trousers and go off to look somewhere else . . . and yet I don't know, Mother Benita, I'm not really sure, sometimes I'm afraid because I don't really know at what stage Dr. Azula has me now, it's possible that he hasn't made any changes yet, that all this constitutes the mere preliminaries and there's no beggar in the street I see through the window, no old women, they left, they returned to the Casa, how I'd like to go back to the Casa and wander through my passageways at night and see Dora and Rita, but they're not in the street that fills the window I see from my bed, the bed cold, the window cold, the street cold, without cars or service stations, sidewalks without people, the wind without leaves on the trees and without clothes to dry, everything static, standing still in an instant that stretches on and on, and you at my side, looking after me, taking care of me silently, watching over me. But you're not looking after me. You're keeping an eye on me, Emperatriz. I recognize you under the white satin domino in which you're trying to pass as a nun, you've made this stop at my bed before going back to the fancy dress ball where your monstrosity, which they'll think is make-believe, will take first prize. You won't budge from my side, hours pass and you remain next to me, holding me here so that I won't get away and will keep my promise to marry you. You're not wearing a nurse's uniform. It's the terrifying bridal gown you've been preparing from the beginning of time, embroidered and studded with rhinestones, its train trails along the floor magnificently, the white veil's stirred by your breath, you never take off your bridal gown day or night in case the right moment comes, as you wait for me to wake up so you can hook me then, your hair swept up into buns and curls and platinum braids, the mask in which your watchful eyes speckled with gold dust and the tiara of glittering gems holding up the white tulle of your purity are all prepared for the final ceremony.

But then . . . you must know it and that's the reason you're waiting, all ready: they haven't operated on me, I'm whole, they haven't grafted on him the organs that possessed Inés, nor have they thrown Humberto Peñaloza's into the trash, I'm whole and that's why you're lying in wait for me here. Emperatriz paces the hallways like a wild animal till I wake up, the wrinkles on her forehead and the folds in her cheeks quivering with fear that Don Jerónimo will snatch me from her hands, my hand in her hand, the veil's drawn back, uncovering her horrible face, the furrowed mask of pain. Nurses! She's the one at my bedside, the lascivious dwarf who never gives up, please, nurses, drive away this mask, give me another shot to keep me from feeling more and more pains, they get worse and worse, I swear I'll marry you, Emperatriz, if you make them give me more shots to kill this pain that's killing me, I swear I'll marry you right here, lying in bed, and you in your embroidered train and your tiara, if you make them give me more shots to blot out your horrible face. You pace, I hear the sumptuous broom of your train sweeping the hallway as you swing around again. You sit down beside me. You take my hand. Everything covered with a white veil, yes, Emperatriz, I can do it, believe me, Humberto Peñaloza can make you happy even if he's Peta's mate, that's why I lift your bridal gown to rape you, that's what you want, Emperatriz, don't deny it, don't try to stop me from getting up, with your fake struggle, don't pretend to weep and wail as you try to pull away my hands that get at your horrifying freckly bosom of an old dwarf and my fingers that look for your sex organ to excite it, although it's always slippery and excited, don't go away, don't go, don't leave me alone, don't run off screaming because I try to rape you, don't run, tripping over the train of your bridal gown, don't desert me in this basement without a way out, pipettes and tubes bubbling, intubations of serum and transfusions beside many other tube lines I can't figure out holding me down, I want to escape, yes, I have to get away so that they won't stifle me to death, to open the window and breathe some air that's not close, but the window's not a window, now I see through the whole trick, it's the blowup of a window they've pasted on the adobe to simulate light and space so that I'll want to open it, to touch its glass that's not cool, because it's not glass but very thin paper stretched over the clay, a photograph, a fake, there's no window, there's no door, no exit, no place to get out to, I scratch, rip, tear away strips of the photograph that fakes an exterior that's never existed anywhere, I pull it off in strips, I tear pieces from the picture of the window in the hope that there's a real opening, my nails hurt, I rip, scratch, nothing, there's nothing, not even light in this room as small as a tomb, I peel off the entire picture, there's nothing, adobe wall, mud wall papered with old newspapers, with hair-raising news that doesn't matter anymore—Flood in the Yangtze-Kiang, Earthquake in Skopje, Famine in Northeastern Brazil—this jigsaw puzzle of horrors, layer after layer of news that isn't news anymore. I've pulled off the window and its false light and its air and its wind and its dull street down which I could have escaped by following the route pointed out by the old women who were calling me, nothing, a tomb of first fruits long gone out of date, dead topics, discussions settled once and for all, it's not even a room, it's dirt, there's no more paper now, there's mud, a dungeon where I was locked up in the center of the earth and sealed off, screaming for help doesn't do me any good. Emperatriz, Emperatriz, save me, my voice can't be heard, Dr. Azula cut my throat out, I don't want to speak, I don't want to scream, because no one will hear me, I'm alone in the center of the earth, boxed in by blind walls in this cellar that closes in on me, bricks, earth, bones, I dig, digging and tearing out with my nails and teeth the memory of that false window they hung there so that I'd believe there was an outside, by digging with my bloodied hands I'll have to get through to something, above, below, there's no direction because there's no outside but there must be because I recall something more, but not much more than this locked cell in which I stir, in which there's hardly room for my body, I'm using up the air, to dig tunnels and galleries and passages in the earth so I'll be able to get out, to create patios and rooms to move about in, any kind of space, not this confinement like a tomb that I bite, scratch, break, without getting anywhere, my space is shrinking, I'm suffocating, there never was a window because there's nothing to see through windows, the fresh air was a hallucination, the water that runs down the ditch an invention they won't let me touch, they won't let me feel on my face the playful breeze that stirs the orange trees and also calls for a shawl, and the feeble sun through the branches of the orange trees faking light under water in which we swim unhurriedly, we must sweep up the rubble from this wall and leave everything clean, ripped old newspapers . . . sweep everything, Mudito, pile it into a neat little heap so there won't be any filth around . . . yes, Dora, don't rush me, because I'm a bit tired, don't you see I'm sweeping while you cover your mouth with your shawl to giggle at something Rita says . . . and then you show that toothless hole, there's nobody here with her face covered, there are no face masks or dominoes or half-masks or hospital masks, no, here everyone has his own face, deteriorating in the natural order of time, as it should, and, with his broom, Mudito makes another small heap of still more newspapers and the pieces of plaster that came down, so many newspapers, there are roomfuls of old newspapers in the Casa, all the useless paper the Archbishop sends us. For hours and hours, Mother Benita and Misiá Raquel have been strolling in the corridor without a stop, they argue, they've talked about everything but mostly about Misiá Inés . . . yes, they say the poor thing's so crushed you should see her, and now all the leftist newspapers do is attack her and make her look ridiculous because the beatification fell through. How foolish, all the millions she has and she takes the vow of poverty! I'm sure it's to get even with Jerónimo because he signed the Casa away without consulting her, taking advantage of her absence in Europe, but I'm sure Jerónimo's never consulted Inés about anything, and when she gets here she'll find that the Casa's been sold at auction, the old women in other homes, the adobe walls pulled down . . . that's what they've been talking about while going around and around the patio, while Mudito sweeps and Rita and Dora are busy pulling up radishes, throwing them into a newspaper cone to put them away and eat them when they have a chance . . . these little radishes are so tender . . . Come on, Rita, Mother Benita calls to her, Misiá Raquel has to leave, come and open the door for us, I'm going to see her off . . . I'll be right back, that's what her eyes tell me, wait for me, Mudito, I'll be right back, go on sweeping, let everything stay the same till I come back to the court that has the orange trees after seeing Misiá Raquel to the door . . . they say they're going to pull this place down, but they've been saying that since I was a little girl, Mother Benita, and used to come here on retreat, you see, they never pull down a thing, everything goes on the same, with Mudito sweeping, Dora bending over her radishes, carefully examining the stump-like blood-red tubers the old women are going to devour.

THREE

19

WHY DO YOU look so worried, Mother Benita? I put down my broom and come to you when you call me without calling me. You said goodbye to Misiá Raquel at the door, you return to the court with the orange trees, and you glance from side to side like someone looking for support, but you don't want to ask for anything, it doesn't matter, I understand that you're asking it of me, come on, Mudito, you're telling me, I don't want to have to ask you to please come with me, follow me down the galleries to the chapel. Only prayer can drive out the anguish I see framed by her grimy coif, come along, Mudito, what I want most is to be alone, and you know how to keep me company and yet leave me alone in the chapel where Mass is no longer said: it's nothing but an adobe storeroom, with benches, an altar, plaster saints, prie-dieus, confessionals—the props of a cult that doesn't exist anymore, but the old women keep on coming there in the afternoon, wandering down the passageways, hanging on to each other's clothes, to say their beads in this chapel that's no longer a chapel. Luckily this afternoon there are no old women around to interrupt my meditation with whispers and litanies, my longing to pray to You, my Lord, in this condemned place where I've tried to reach You for, how many, twenty-two, no, twenty-three years. In the beginning, the Mother Superior used to say to me, yes, I'm looking for a more active job for you, an intelligent nun like you can't be wasting her time at the Casa, and I think that next year I'll be able to send you to . . . I don't remember where anymore. So do have patience, daughter. Go on working with the humility you've always shown . . . but Mother, a little help, no, not only money, send me other nuns, active, young, the two I have now, Mother Anselma and Mother

Julia, have gone the way of the tattered old women around me, the old women have swallowed up the sisters who were assigned to help me, but now share the old women's rags, manias, superstitions, I can't distinguish Mother Julia and Mother Anselma from the other old women anymore. Only Mudito. Are you there in the shadow of the confessional, Mudito, are you with me? Are you back there, Mother Benita, sitting in the last pew, trying to pray, without being able to? The Mother Superior used to say, wait awhile. I waited. With Mudito, I threw myself into the useless work of trying to maintain some semblance of dignity and order in the Casa, without Mudito it would be impossible to fight the filth and the crumbling walls, we're less able to fight each year, yes, and almost not at all now, I don't know what you were sweeping up in the court today . . . another collapsing wall . . . well, something has to be done . . . yes, Mother, something must be done . . . and the Mother Superior used to tell Mother Benita, wait, daughter, wait, I promise to put you in charge of a school next year, with your education and your class you're going to waste at the Casa, but that Mother Superior was sent off to Rome or died and the new Superior wasn't familiar with Mother Benita's capabilities, and so she too used to tell her, wait, daughter, wait, I must get to know you better to see what you can do, there are no written reports on your work, of which there's no trace, they say . . . they say . . . *they say* is not enough, so I have to judge for myself . . . please, Mother, I'm dying of boredom at the Casa, of not having anybody to talk with, I'm dying of fear that this legion of old women will devour me as they've devoured the other nuns, I'm dying of the imbecility and the decrepitude that surround me, I'm already forty-eight years old, fifty, fifty-four, fifty-eight . . . wait, daughter . . . and after a while they no longer said, wait, but you must resign yourself, offer God your sacrifice and it will open the gates of heaven for you because by staying at the Casa you're making such a great sacrifice, if we didn't have you the Casa would collapse, and I'm still here, but now the Casa's going to collapse anyhow, Misiá Raquel said she was sure of it, the auction people are coming to take an inventory of all this junk—wooden benches, plaster saints, a mawkish lithograph of the Virgin and Child—there's no chapel now, a paper signed by the Archbishop deconsecrated it. But Your red presence still burns in the Eucharist. And, after the auctioneers, the power shovels will come and the stone hammers and the trucks and the workmen with their picks . . . where are we going to go, Mudito . . . what will become of us, Mother Benita, where are we going to look for a place to stay, Misiá Raquel's project is another conspiracy to make us the old women's slaves, that's why I saw you arguing with her, going round and round the walks in the court with the orange trees, I watched you from the shadows, nothing was happening, Carmela passing by singing Come Let's Go One and All, there was I with my broom, Dora and Rita were pulling up blood-red stumps . . . yes, Misiá Raquel, Father Azócar promised me that the position of chief housemother at his Children's Village will be mine, but you have a fit every time I mention Father Azócar to you . . . ay, Mother Benita, it's unbelievable how naïve you are despite your age, a lying priest, a politician; yes, they're going to pull this down, but there isn't going to be a Children's Village, because he's going to pocket the money and this property will be broken up into lots and sold so the money can be spent on political campaigning on behalf of the candidate he backs, I can see it right now, it's crystal clear, that's the reason for the rush to bring in the wreckers, now that the elections are just around the corner, let Father Azócar—who on earth knows where he's from—come to me with his stories, there won't be any Children's Village, and you're all going to be left out in the cold, I can't imagine where they're going to put you . . . of course, Mother Benita, I can offer you something else . . . something better . . . something marvelous . . . the tiny flame of the Eucharist flickers and trembles while her shadow lingers in the presbytery, convincing me, tearing down my belief that I'll be able to free myself from the old women someday and work with young people, at clean, large windows; she talks, gesticulates, as if she were preaching to me, I listen to her from the bench at the back of the chapel as she tells me she can offer me something much more interesting.

"What?"

"If I offered you the chance to put a home for old women

into running order and take complete charge of it, would you be willing to do it?"

"But there's no chance of that, Misiá Raquel. It would take a fortune. I made a list of all the inmates with their personal histories, at least as much of them as they remember or want to tell me. Many should be hospitalized. Several have to be sent to the insane asylum . . . poor Amalia, for example, you remember her, the little old woman with one eye gone who used to work for Brígida, she goes around crying, all upset because she says she can't find the finger, and neither she nor anybody else knows what finger she's talking about, but she looks for it everywhere, without even knowing what the finger's like, since she's never seen it, and she talks of nothing else . . . and then there are those nuisances, the little orphans . . ."

"And how about Brígida?"

"But Misiá Raquel! You're acting a bit strange . . . you yourself buried her a year ago, how could you not remember . . ."

"Of course I remember."

"Then?"

"I'm settling Brígida's will."

"I don't see what it has to do with . . . it can't be you shouting at me from the presbytery, Misiá Raquel, you don't shout at anyone except your grandchildren when they steal candy, it's Brígida who's in the presbytery poking around the altar, she must be cleaning as she always used to clean, darning, mending, but no, it's not Brígida, because she's dressed in black and Brígida never liked black so it must be you telling me that Brígida saved up every penny she earned as your servant for fifty years. She was never known to spend a penny on anything. She never went out, she had no relatives, she married my mother's gardener, who soon died, leaving her a very young widow, and I used to give her everything—sheets, bed, radio, shoes, anything she wanted—and all my clothes fitted her perfectly because we wore the same size. She kept her money in a hole in her mattress. And, before going off for the summer at the end of the year, she used to take her savings in a little package to my husband for him to invest for her in stocks that brought a good return, because I don't know whether you know it, Mudito, but Misiá Raquel's husband was one of the richest and most famous stockbrokers . . . yes, yes, I knew, he was Don Jerónimo's friend, they played whist together at the Club de la Unión, and they used to doze together in identical armchairs in the library, with the day's newspapers over their faces. As time went on, Brígida's money grew a hundredfold in my husband's hands. My husband was very fond of Brígida. Sometimes he liked to go in person to the servants' quarters to pay her a visit and bring her up to date on her investments. He used to stay and talk to her for a good while and afterwards he'd say to me:

" 'Isn't it strange how this little woman, who never leaves the house and knows nothing outside of novenas and rosaries, has better ideas for playing the stock market than I do. You don't know how much Brígida has enabled me to make with her suggestions.' Can you believe it, Mudito? . . . It can't be . . . Yes, I believe her, Mother Benita, because I know that Brígida was capable of that and much more . . . In fact, there was a time when Brígida went around very nervous, till suddenly one morning she called my husband's office and, despite all his objections, she instructed him to sell her stocks and buy gold for her. My husband thought Brígida'd gone out of her mind. But, since gold's never been a bad investment, and she didn't stand to lose anything, he followed her instructions. Strangely enough, after this incident, my husband seemed depressed, I noticed he was nervous . . . till suddenly one day he got up early and, although the rest of the brokers thought he'd gone completely crazy, he took all the stocks and bonds we owned and sold them and then bought gold, like Brígida. He was never able to explain what he did. I alone know it wasn't his genius as a stockbroker that saved him, contrary to what everybody said a few days later when the international stock market crash came and people lost all they had, many of them committing suicide . . . we pulled through, and later on, when people were selling very valuable things for nothing, we got a lot of bargains.

"Misiá Raquel, if you wish to make a donation with Brígida's money, why not give it to the Children's Village . . ."

"You're much more simple-minded than you look, Mother

Benita. Let me go on with my story: when I was widowed fifteen years ago, Brígida wouldn't let anyone touch her money, which was invested by my husband in suburban property when it was going so cheap after the stock market crash. His office managed it. She trusted nobody except him. And me. That's why, when my husband died, Brígida took all her money away from his office and put everything in my name, all her houses and her apartments, because, she said:

"'But I don't know how to read or write, Misiá Raquel, I don't even know how to sign my name, so everything has to be in your name.' You see, Mother Benita? The tyranny of the weak: young boys laughing with their intestines all cut up aren't carted off to jail and tortured, the deaf-mute defeats the fists of the cops, and Dr. Azula's operation made me safe from harm, because now nobody can want anything of mine . . . let's listen to the person speaking from the presbytery, the silhouette lit up by the red light of the Eucharist . . . from then on I bought her more houses and more apartments. Since she didn't like to go out and waste her time gadding about in the streets like other servants she looked down on for doing this, I had to do everything for her: I used to go see what houses were up for sale, I'd describe them to her—the neighborhood, the quality of the buildings—and then Brígida would ask me to let her think about it, and the next morning, when she brought breakfast and the paper to my bed, she'd tell me:

"'Buy.'

"And instead of staying in bed and leafing through the latest fashion magazine or talking on the phone to my daughters-in-law, I'd have to get up early to put through this or that deal for Brígida, a house, a piece of land. She gave me a power of attorney, Mother Benita. It's terrible to be burdened with someone else's power of attorney. And since she couldn't stand arguments, she used to mutter: they say nowadays people have such gall and are so argumentative, and she used to delegate me to collect her rents. I'd sign the receipts instead of her, the sale and purchase contracts in my name, I'd go trotting out to the notary publics, go looking for a dependable plumber to fix the bathroom wrecked by the tenants we had to throw out because they weren't married; in fact, I had to do everything for her. And I enjoyed doing things for Brígida, Mother Benita, why should I deny that it kept me going, and that her useless money, whose only purpose was to grow, without doing anybody any good, was much more my own than all I'd inherited. You realize that the life of a woman like me, with grown-up children and administrators to take care of everything, is very boring. And, just as my friends whiled away their time playing bridge, I whiled away mine piling up that useless, hypothetical fortune, I was helping it grow like a cancer, unrelated to anything, of no use to anybody. It was a game. But I wasn't playing it, the game was playing me, because I couldn't get out of it, it became a vice, running from apartment to apartment, flying into a rage because of a broken window, catching bronchitis in the halls of Brígida's rented houses, in her tenements, losing touch with my friends, neglecting my grandchildren who interested me less than the game, losing my voice from screaming at a tenant who wouldn't or couldn't pay, while she, Brígida, waited for me in my heated home, always calm and well groomed, with her gray bun that was so soigné. She used to kneel at my feet to take off my shoes covered with mud because I'd had to slog through a whole new suburb to find out if it was true that some tenants were subletting rooms, they said, and I didn't like them to sublet rooms in my houses. At night I'd fall into bed exhausted by this game Brígida had imprisoned me in, and she'd bring me a cup of tea and some very thin slices of toast, just the way I liked them, and, standing next to my bed with her arms crossed respectfully, she'd question me: 'Do you think you may have paid too much for the wallpaper for the Riquelme apartment, they say there's a factory in San Isidro where they sell wallpaper that's very nice and very cheap' . . . they say . . . I don't know where those voices came from that *say* . . . and, pressed hard by those *they say,* I'd go out compulsively to play the game of Brígida's useless money. When I thoughtlessly suggested that she ought to draw up her will, she cried her eyes out because, of course, now, after all these years of service, I didn't want to go on helping her with her few pennies . . . and things got even worse when I told her no, when what I wanted to explain to her was that there was no reason why she should go on being my servant, she was a rich woman, she could go live in one of her apartments with a young servant to take care of her . . . someone like Iris Mateluna, for instance, to serve her, with the money coming in from her apartments she could live like a queen . . . oof! You should have seen her crying . . . you just want to get rid of me, now that I'm old, to throw me out into the street like dirt . . . And then, because Brígida was spiteful and never forgave me for suggesting that she go live in one of her apartments, she spoke to Inés about coming to live there at the Casa because, she said, why should she stay on with me when she was only in my way. And, as it turned out, she liked living here at the Casa, I suppose it was because I had to come all the way from the other side of town, every other day, to keep her posted on her affairs. But she died without leaving a will. Her entire fortune's in my name. I'm almost finished liquidating it . . . I don't know what to do with all that money, I'm still taking in rent, I'm still working out real estate deals as if Brígida were alive . . . they say that over in the Matadero district . . . they say that liquefied gases . . . but I can't go on being a prisoner of Brígida's money, I can't go on hearing those *they say*'s, I want to break away from her, I'm tired out, I want to get Brígida off my back so that I can live out what little is left of my own life . . . of course, maybe there won't be any left . . ."

She's dressed in black, there in the presbytery. If there were a little more light I'd be able to see the expression on her face and make out her movements and gestures. She's put on a lot of weight . . . Mudito, go light some candles so she can see what she's doing . . . go help her move that little gilt chair, I think she's moving it . . . wait, wait, Mudito . . . she looks more like Mercedes Barroso, so big and fat, dressed all in black . . . she stops to tell me things she can't know about:

"That's why I came to discuss it with you. Now that all this is coming to an end, it's a matter of weeks, you know it, Father Azócar has ordered an inventory taken . . . junk, of course, but we can get something for it and you people will have to go somewhere else and you have nowhere to go . . . I was thinking, Mother Benita, I was thinking that with Brígida's money

. . . a modern institution, something reasonable, with medical specialists, and you in charge of everything. The 'Brígida something Institution . . .' Would you believe that I can't even recall her last name? . . ."

I remain in the shadows, peering at the person Mother Benita hears proposing the plan for us all to go and live in the aseptic hospital, with white masks and nurses taking care of us. But I know you so well, Mother Benita, I know you're going to say no, it's out of the question, even when she insists that she'd buy a pleasant, modern house, with a garden, maybe a little park, she tries to convince you even when you explain, to the being barely illuminated by the Presence in this chapel which isn't a chapel anymore, that there are so many old women, too many . . .

"But they'll gradually dwindle. People nowadays don't have servants like the ones we used to have, the ones you have to worry about all your life. Actually, I wanted to suggest to you not to take in any more old women. To keep those we have now, who'll die off little by little, until there are none left. With your experience, you could take over the administration of the new Casa, a white Casa, a nice one . . . Let the old women who are still left live royally in Brígida's name, with summer vacations, central heating, good doctors, buses to take them on outings to the beach and the country, and in this way all this useless money of Brígida's will be spent, otherwise it will be a burden to me . . ."

"No . . . no . . . I don't want to have anything more to do with old women . . . they always manage to have braziers, even with central heating, and cages with thrushes, or finches, and small bundles under their beds . . . no . . ."

That overblown figure dressed in black has dragged the little gilt chair over to the Eucharist lamp . . . no, don't get up there, Menche, you're too fat, too old, too clumsy, it's a cheap little chair, made of wood and plaster, it's not going to hold you, don't get up there . . .

"No, Misiá Raquel, get rid of your Brígida as best you can. Don't pass her on to me. I've been living with decrepitude all around me for twenty years now. Father Azócar may be all you say, but he knows what he's doing."

". . . I'm going to burn the paper money. It's only paper. Just paper, cut-up newspaper that's only good for burning, I don't think Brígida will mind if I burn it . . ."

Poor Mercedes Barroso! trying to get up on the chair to steal the Eucharist lamp! It's the only thing that's any good in this house, Mother Benita, the rest is junk, I need it for the Monsignor's oratory, which we'll be inaugurating soon, and this lamp, which is a very interesting piece of colonial art, will look very good there, it's a shame to have it buried in this place. They came for Menche in a truck that wasn't even a respectful black, and we had to put a handful of dusty geraniums on her that were picked in the vestibule court, so that poor Menche, who was so funny but so poor, wouldn't depart without flowers . . . not like Brígida's funeral service, yes, that really was some service, and you paid for it, Misiá Raquel, you're so good and so generous . . . don't you believe it, Mother Benita, Brígida had more hidden recesses in her than the Casa does: Brígida's funeral wasn't a gift from me. Despite her horror of death, when it came to making a will Brígida was never frightened by the fantasy of her own sumptuous exequies surrounded by pomp and ritual. Her lifelong obsession was to pay for a magnificent funeral for herself, to plan it to the last detail, and not owe it to anybody. Before she came to live here, she spent a lot of time calling all the funeral parlors to find out prices, the quality of coffins—of course, I was the one who had to go and examine them and fill in the details for her—the kind of metal lining they had, the quality of the velvet or satin, the number of horses, of black draperies with gold tassels, of candelabra with real candles, wax ones, not electric like the ones they use now. But she didn't want the other old women here at the Casa ever to know, under any circumstances, that she was standing the cost of her own funeral. The great ambition of her life was to put all the other servants to shame with this showy funeral, not with her own enormous wealth. What she wanted was to impress them with the fact that she had an employer who loved her so much that she'd given her this funeral; to convert me into the monster of love I'm not, that was the luxury she bought herself with her fortune. Of course I'd have paid for her funeral in any case,

Brígida and I were always very close, but I'm not going to throw money away on funerals as ridiculously pompous as Brígida's, neither for myself nor for my children. Imagine, she'd given me money in small separate envelopes to buy wreaths for her in the names of everyone in my family. They'd have sent flowers anyway, but not ones as expensive as those she told me to buy . . .

Call her, call her, Mudito, you're telling me, but my voice isn't going to be heard in the darkness, Mother . . . That silhouette on the presbytery stage, call her, let's pray together so that her spirit will return to purgatory . . . Menche, go away, what are you doing in the presbytery, let us pray, Hail Holy Queen, Mother of Mercy, Our Hope, Our Sweetness and Our Life, to Thee we call from this Vale of Tears . . . The figure seems to be an invention of the wavering little light from the altar lamp . . . no, it can't be Misiá Raquel, it's Menche, who's so poor she's edging up to the tabernacle to steal . . . don't open it, Menche, it's a sacrilege, only a priest can open it when the Lord's in it . . . but Menche opens it and bends over the white cloth and prays . . . I know the way he bends over, Mudito, I know the way he opens the tabernacle's tiny door, the way he puts his hand in and takes out the little round box holding the Sacred Host and sticks it in between the buttons of his cassock, because it's a cassock, it's not Menche, it's a pompous priest as fat as Menche, who genuflects and stands up . . . it's him. I recognize him when he turns around to watch the little red flame hanging up above, with his hair plastered down as if they painted it on his head with India ink every morning, his bushy eyebrows I can't make out but imagine to be there, his enormous satiny dark eyes with lashes that are too curly and lids that are too fleshy . . . Why don't you obey me, Mudito, and call out to him so he'll know we're here on the last bench, watching him from the darkness, and won't do anything we shouldn't see? . . . It must be a horrible dream of mine in which Father Azócar looks at the Eucharist lamp, gets under it, reaches up, doesn't quite make it, sticks his finger in his mouth like Iris Mateluna and stands there thinking. Then he reaches up again as he gives a little jump, but he still doesn't reach the lamp. It's Father Azócar come to steal the Eucharist lamp! What a horrible nightmare it is, dear Lord, to dream that Father Azócar comes to snuff out the Eucharist light, and to stop the Casa's heartbeat! The Archbishop signed the deconsecration, but the act is only now being put into effect . . . to extinguish the Presence . . . to carry off the lamp . . . the Host . . . Now he's rubbing together his fat white hands covered with black hair. He studies the lamp. It's a mortal sin to dream that a good prelate—yes, he's good, he has to be good if he's the Archbishop's secretary—that a distinguished but very fat prelate snorts as he pushes the little damask chair till it's right under the lamp. He wants to take it down, he's going to take it away. He told me that he would, but not this way, it's theft this way, Father Azócar . . . let him take it, Mudito . . . you there, behind the confessional, help him to put out the Eucharist light and to leave us without the Presence . . . Wait . . . look . . . he's climbing up, he's going to get on the little gilt plaster chair that's so fragile . . . don't get up on it, Father, don't, because you're awkward and fat and Mudito's agile, and I'll have him go and bring a ladder so that you can take down the little lamp that you want to take with you, don't force me to see you making a fool of yourself, please. The chair's cheaply made like my terrazzo tables and my imitation marble pedestals that are really wood and the worn-out linoleum and the wooden benches, it's weak, it's going to break if you climb on it, because you're too heavy. Please listen to me. And you too, Mudito, don't stand there looking at my nightmare and listening to my voice without answering me. Go on, stop him, don't let him climb on the little chair . . . he gathers up his cassock, struggles, groans, he's going to have a lot of trouble getting up there. With his cassock gathered up, he lifts one fat leg, holds it in the air for a second with his foot on point as though he were a ballerina and then brings it down because he can't get up on the little chair. He raises the other leg, snorts, brings it down, he can't make it. He doesn't know what to do. He sits on the chair. He stares at the lamp. He gets on his feet and takes little leaps in an effort to reach the lamp, but of course he can't, he only manages to graze it and make it swing, and the little flame flickers and all the shadows in the chapel, he and I and Mudito and the plaster saints, all of us, go into a wild dance. Now he's kneeling on the garnet damask seat and, holding on to the back of the chair, he tries to lift himself . . . no, Father Azócar, the back's loose, I know the chair . . . his obscene legs . . . his garters . . . Lord, Lord, don't let me try to get even with Father Azócar, who knows that the Casa's nothing but filth, that we're all nothing but filth, don't let me try to get even with him in this dream, I hate him because he promised to free me of the old women but isn't going to, and I hate him, I want to control my dream and I can't. He snorts. He's lifted himself and is climbing up from the chair, which creaks under his weight . . . don't move, Father, you'll fall, keep still . . . but you lift your arms, you touch the lamp, and the chair sways . . . it's quivering, and he realizes this and puts out his arms to maintain his balance like a tightrope dancer at the circus . . . everything's swaying, we're all swaying, and he can't take down the lamp he craves so much. The chair wobbles. He's frightened now. Regrets what he's done. He wants to get off. He gathers up his cassock again and puts one foot down tentatively, like a child dipping his foot into the water and draw-ing it back because the water's cold . . . dancing on the little gilt chair, the roly-poly body with its arms outstretched . . . you're going to fall, Father, Mudito's coming to help you now . . . but he lifts his other foot, sets it down on point, flexes his other knee . . . I hear you puffing because you're fat and afraid . . . help him, Mudito, think of my sin in dreaming this scan-dalous dream, get me out of this nightmare, Mudito, I don't want to go on sinning with this dream, but what can I do to stop a dream that keeps dragging me along . . . and Mother Benita clenches her fist against her mouth to keep from crying with fear . . . Brígida must save me, she'll save us all, that's what Misiá Raquel promised me . . . she covers her mouth to choke back her tears, the thing that's rising in my chest, hurting me, I feel my tears coming, my chest flutters and something keeps rising in me, dear God, I can't control this rising tide, don't let me do it, Lord, don't let me, and when Father Azócar stands with his foot pointing in the air, ready to get down, Mother Benita's guffaw rings out scandalously in the chapel that will never again be a chapel because my guffaw deconsecrated it forever . . . the prelate stumbled and pitched forward.

"Shit . . ."

Mother Benita rises from the shadows, trying to suppress her laughter, and she and I run to the presbytery together to help the priest who's huffing and puffing and swearing as he attempts to get back on his feet.

"Oh, oooohhh . . ."

Mother Benita and Mudito help him to his feet. He falls again, we tug and he puffs till he comes to a standing position, brushing the dust from his cassock, running his hand over his hair in an attempt to restore the perfect falsehood of its blackness. Suddenly, the rhythm of his breathing changes.

"Why didn't you let me know you were here, Mother Benita?"

You can't say: because I was asleep. Better not say anything, better not say: because I was talking to Misiá Raquel, who told me something it would be better for her to tell you herself . . . you'll be able to get Misiá Raquel to help us, or the Archbishop, or I don't know who, we need somewhere to go, now that all this is coming to an end . . . but I can't. Be silent, obey, as I've always been silent and obeyed.

"Why didn't you tell Mudito to help me?"

Be silent. Be silent.

"I don't know if you remember that I called you some time back and asked you to have this lamp ready for me to take with me . . . before the auctioneers come to make up the lots for the sale . . ."

"Yes, yes . . ."

"To save this extraordinary piece . . ."

"Yes, yes I know, Father Azócar, all the rest is junk, I realize it, I accept it, the power shovels will raze us, they'll leave us flat like the ground on which the Casa was built. And we? Mudito and I and the old women? Are we to be pulled down too? His eyes, like satin that's suddenly petrified, tell me that I won't be the chief housemother of his Children's Village. My guffaw doomed me. No. We were all doomed before that, because you'd forgotten us, Father Azócar, not the tiniest bit of alms, not the tiniest show of pity, because we're not important and we're almost nonhuman, just castoffs, yes, yes, don't say no, you look down on us as you do on the rest of the junk at the Casa, and our fate's unimportant . . . what right have you to ask me not to think that, when you and the Archbishop have left us to shift for ourselves, starving, without clothing, in poor health for years and years . . . no, Father . . ."

"Be calm, daughter!"

"You ask me to be calm and you give me nothing to calm me."

Father Azócar draws himself up to his full height: he's enormous, black, shiny, all one piece of brand-new satin, his power erect, his voice sure; his white finger threatening me is cruel, and it's a threat that will be carried out because he'll make sure it's carried out.

"This is a lack of discipline I won't tolerate, Mother Benita. I'll have to talk to your Superior, because we can't let it go at that."

"I've heard nothing from her in six months. She doesn't even bother to come to the telephone when I call, she's so busy . . ."

"All right, all right, that's enough . . . and I'm sending for the lamp tomorrow, leave it with Rita in her office. I'm taking the sacramentals with me now, and after they've taken down the lamp, have Mudito seal all the chapel doors. They're to be opened only when the auctioneers come to take inventory."

He's ready to leave the chapel that's no longer a chapel. He turns to the altar. He starts to genuflect and cross himself, when he remembers that the Host isn't in the tabernacle that's not a tabernacle, that he, Father Azócar, a distinguished prelate, is carrying it against his breast, under his cassock, next to his heart. He turns to the nun again:

"I'll be seeing you, Mother."

"I'll be seeing you, Father."

"Oh, and . . ."

Father Azócar's face softens. For a moment he recovers his satiny eyes. The nun holds his look.

"Yes, Father?"

". . . I hope you won't let word get around . . ."

Now it's you who are in command, Mother Benita, now it's

you who don't lower your eyes because you know that it wasn't your poor laughter but the priest's dirty word as he fell off the chair that deconsecrated the chapel.

"What is it you don't want me to let get around?"

You ask him this cruelly, as you should, because you know: not to let word get around about his ridiculous figure dancing with greed on the little creaking chair, about the bad word he let out as he fell. But you want this priest, this man who humiliates you, to plead, to confess his own humiliation, by saying it out loud. Yes. Let his satiny eyes and his pompous word be at your mercy, as he requests your discretion. But the prelate's eyes harden once more.

"Nothing, Mother Benita . . . don't worry . . ."

Only the little red light, still alive and bleeding like a little amputated stump, is left there, hanging to one side of the altar. Now all there is to do is put it out and take down that piece of silverwork, what it contains no longer means anything because Father Azócar carried off the Host, only the container's important, because it's very valuable, it's a unique piece, Mother. Although the little flame still burns, the chapel's turned into another empty room in the Casa. We feel the wind filtering through the cracks just as it does in any other room. A broken glass, maybe two or three, we must be careful with the stained glass windows. In one corner, mice gnaw and gnaw and gnaw their way into who knows what hidden depths in the adobe walls. I can still pray in this empty shell. The red flame becomes my plea . . . what will become of us, dear God, when these mud walls come down? I don't want to think about it. She closes her eyes.

"My Lord Jesus Christ, God and True Man . . ."

Opening her eyes, she realizes that she's been asleep a second time. A second time, Mudito? Isn't it only another part of the same time? Mudo, Mudito, don't leave me alone, where are you, I feel defeated . . . my threat doesn't frighten anybody, my supplications never end, because I tire and fall asleep . . . I'm going to bed because I'm old and I can't tell when I'm asleep and when I'm awake . . . light a candle, Mudito, light the passageway for me so I can go to my cell and take refuge in my bed.

20

THE AUCTIONEERS OPENED the chapel and took everything out, arranging it by lots in the corridors, each lot with its numbered tag: worm-eaten confessionals, more and more wobbly little gilt chairs with their crimson damask threadbare and torn and stained, wooden benches, imitation marble pedestals, dusty velvet prie-dieus with springs that had given up long ago. The auctioneers warned Mother Benita:

"This'll fetch about as much as firewood."

"You can tell that to Father Azócar."

"Okay. Just so he won't build up his hopes."

"I don't think he will. He took the little that was worth anything, a long time ago."

The auction people also took out the only thing that served the chapel as an ornament, its one luxury: the four stained glass windows, made in the early part of the century, in which four groups of the benefactresses of the Casa, draped in black shawls, kneeling, bowed over hands joined in prayer, with their distinguished names glittering at the foot of each window, were grouped around the stained glass figures, in this order: the first group, around St. Gabriel Archangel with his finger raised and the Virgin with her modest eyes; the second group, around the Immaculate Conception crushing, with her feet so pure, the head of the monster holding the sphere of the world in his claws; the third group, around St. Ann, who conceived the Virgin without original sin; and the fourth group, around the Virgin visiting St. Elizabeth with her womb swollen with an invisible St. John the Baptist who rejoices, inside her womb, that this embrace cleanses him too of original sin. The windows were of Catalonian workmanship, true works of art according to several experts and interesting as examples of taste in that era. After being removed from their frames, they were leaned against the pilasters of the cloister so that, on the day of the auction, a tempting sun would shine through them—everything about them was really lovely, their colors, their almost Chinese borders and decorations, their lotus flowers and herons and things that looked like rushes—and prospective buyers would give at least something for them, although what the devil would those stained glass windows be used for; the presence of those handsome ladies dressed in black, whose identities no longer meant anything to anyone, made useless a piece of work that might otherwise have some value.

Four huge gaps were left in the walls of the chapel, whose doors were sealed with cross-boards. As the auction continued to be put off, birds started nesting in the gaps, and spiders hung up structures like ephemeral stained glass windows that were swept away by gusts of air that made the candles lit by the inmates at night flicker . . . not too much light now, they might see it from outside. Enthroned in the gold and crimson damask chair they placed in the middle of the presbytery that was nothing but a wooden platform now, Iris Mateluna sneezed. Dora blessed her:

"Hail, O Most Holy Virgin."

In Iris's lap, the child sneezed too.

"And Immaculate Conception."

"Wrap yourself well, Iris, and bundle up the child, look, it's very easy to catch bronchitis at this time of year, and they say there's a lot of flu going around in the neighborhood."

Iris turned up the collar of her brown overcoat, whose roominess hid her pregnancy, the obstinate, disquieting, irresolute pregnancy that had stretched on for months and months, and, with it, our fear, while we repeated it's a miracle, it's a miracle, Brígida said so, she knows all about those things, when it's a miracle the pregnancy may be short but it can also be much longer, until the child, in his wisdom, considers that the precise moment has come for all of us to go with him to heaven as soon as he's born, the sooner the better, because they're going to pull down the Casa and who knows what'll happen to us when they start tearing it down, where they'll send us, it's enough to make anybody worry, you can't help worrying, but we must have faith in the child and not be afraid, things will happen when he wants them to and in the meantime we have to look after Iris, that kid's so spoiled now, and always so nasty, but we have to obey and venerate her, surrounding her with canticles and candles and prayers. The child sneezed again.

"Be careful, Iris . . ."

She yawned:

"That's enough. The party was such a drag tonight. Look at the way the baby's nose is running. If the party isn't a lot more fun tomorrow, I'm going to turn you all in to Mother Benita. I've had enough. I'm sick of sitting here all the time and holding the baby, let's go inside. I'm sleepy. I want to go to bed. The baby's wet, that's why he's sneezing."

"Pee doesn't get cold, it holds the heat."

"But only when the baby has rubber pants on, Amalia, and we didn't put any on the child . . ."

"Oh, really? I didn't know."

"When do you know anything, Amalia?"

A month back, before the auction people came to set up the lots, the Archbishop had had the images of the saints taken out. The empty chapel made the inmates very unhappy, although they knew it had been deconsecrated and wasn't a chapel anymore. But Mudito told them not to be foolish, what were they crying for, to go to his quarters, where they found chunks of plaster draperies, shawls, ermines, jewelry, a dagger driven into a martyr's breast, halos and crowns and faded staring eyes and pieces of heads with rays of light around them, the place is overgrown with grass, they have to clear the tangle of brambles to find diabolical tongueless serpents underneath, faces that have become part of the goat's-rue and the teatina grass, legs that have been wrenched out of shape by the pain of ecstasy, fingers leafing through a plaster book or saying their beads. Mudito suggested that if the Archbishop took away their saints, they could put together others, it was the last straw, leaving the chapel turned into a tumbledown shack. The inmates were proud of their finds and of their creations. This became such a pastime that they almost forgot Iris and her child, because putting beings together, assembling arbitrary identities by gluing together fragments that more or less matched, was like a game, and who knows, these pieces we're sticking together may turn out to be a real saint, but what's the difference, that's what Mudito's for, now that he can't do any heavy work, he knows how, he sketches features on the blank faces and suggests combinations of interesting pieces that maybe we wouldn't have thought of, with Iris putting together saints in the middle of the goat's-rue, Dora behind the brambles; and these fennel roots clutch a saint that looks like St. John the Baptist—we have to dig a hole and get him untangled—and a wing with a woman's face, the Magdalen's long hair with dragon's jaws that don't spew smoke . . . we have to use some paint to cover up the crack in the nape where we stuck on this head that doesn't belong to this body . . . no, don't cover it up, it's the Blessed Inés de Azcoitía, who had the scar on her neck as long as she lived, that was the reason for the coif, that's why the Casa was built to shut her in and hide her . . . Amalia says:

"But we can't venerate her, because the beatification didn't go through. Poor Misiá Inés."

"But it may yet go through. They say she's going to leave all the papers in Rome for the lawyers over there and the ambassador to handle everything, but they say the ambassador to the Holy See is a Communist and that's why the beatification fell through. All we have to do is wait for the government to change and send over an ambassador who's not as bad and she'll be beatified."

Looking thoughtful, Amalia says:

"All the worse, then. Let's not put together a Saint Inés de Azcoitía. They say that when the authorities find out that a saint's been worshipped before being canonized by Rome, then the saint can't become a saint because it's idolatry, and the cardinals shake their heads no, that's one of the main conditions of a beatification."

"And where does this one get all that from?"

"But why do you all pay attention to her when Amalia doesn't know anything?"

"Don't you know those are old wives' tales, Amalia? And don't cry over everything . . ."

"I'm not crying, my bad eye's running, that's all. I haven't been able to find Saint Gabriel Archangel's finger . . ."

"Look, I've made this darling little saint."

"It's kind of strange, with those stubby legs . . ."

"And such a big head . . ."

"Makes no difference, it's a saint, that's what, because I made him up with pieces of saints. Let's see, Mudito, what name shall we give him?"

The old women gather around me, among the bushes, among the chunks of plaster, for me to decide on the names of the saints and paint them with my brush on the pedestals of the creations of their anarchic imaginations: St. Brígida, first, because of her delicate fingers that look so useless, and her sentimental air. And a St. Jerome, tall, graceful, it took me a whole sunny morning, with the squatting old women around me oohing and aahing, to get the blue of his eyes just right. The Blessed Inés de Azcoitía, with her huge gash of the *chonchón* on her neck, and her disproportionate ears, was the most popular of the female saints from the beginning. And a St. Peta Ponce with her libidinous look, and a St. Doctor Azula, who all of us thought looked a lot like Amalia, whose blind eye kept tearing.

"But what's the difference if Saint Gabriel doesn't have a finger, Amalia?"

"It does make a difference."

"You have it almost finished. Why don't you let us load it on Mudito's cart and take it to the chapel, it's going to look lovely."

"I don't want to. Not until I find the finger."

"What's got into this ninny, with this thing about the finger?"

Crying, on all fours among the brambleberries, Amalia continues her search.

"Don't pay attention to her, her mind's wandering."

"She's been kind of strange since poor Brígida's death."

"I've never seen Saint Gabriel's finger."

"Amalia's not going to be with us very long."

"Not very long."

They transport their patchwork saints on Mudito's cart and repopulate the empty chapel again, placing the saints around the enthroned Iris Mateluna, with the child in her arms, surrounding her with a court barely discernible in the flickering light of the candles burning around us as we're protected by a canopy that billows with the wind coming in through the four window openings.

Those in on the plot aren't seven in number now. Without anyone knowing how, the rumor spread through the Casa . . . they say that in the chapel . . . they say that Iris Mateluna . . . they say they light candles to her and surround her with flowers and greens, they say she performs miracles, they say, they say . . . there's whispering in the corners of the most unimportant courts, you can hear footfalls scurrying away, the old women spy, there are sidelong glances in the kitchen, questions to trip you up, truths won or lost in a game of monte when the jack of spades turned up without a king, they say that . . . footfalls, shadows, whispers, ears glued to walls, the rumor has to spread, it's only natural for the news to spread when there's a miracle involved, and eventually we had to let more and more old women into the secret circle because they could be dangerous if we rebuffed them, the one that goes around in the white dress with the blue sash as an offering to Our Lady of Lourdes and lives in the laundry courtyard is such a blabbermouth, they're all green with envy, busybodies, snoopers, gossips, and Iris's pregnancy is lasting such a long time and there's nothing we can do about it, we've got to pray, at night the swarm of old women says rosary after rosary in the chapel, around Iris on her throne with the bundle of her child on her knees, the doll she won't part with for anything in the world, they say rosaries and Hail Holy Queens so that this tiresome brat will give birth soon and without trouble, so that the real child will be born and we can stop using this substitute to keep the girl happy—she's a hellcat—so that the child conceived without the stain of pleasure won't take longer, and they can get to hold and rock him too before they die, if the child doesn't take them to heaven before they die. Despite the maddening wind in the corners of the chapel, and the coughing and sneezing and the fear of catching pneumonia, and the sleep that sometimes topples one or another of us in the middle of a Hail Holy Queen, the old women pray and pray, they bow to Iris, who loves it because she thinks it's funny and also because she loves them to spray her with that sweet-smelling mist, and even for them to dance for her, making thiiiiiissssssawaaaaaay, thiiiiiissssssawaaaaaay with their arms, genuflections, creaky knees; why doesn't the child hurry, they have their bundles ready to go with him to heaven, because that's what Brígida promised them, just a few little things done up in packages to take with them, the alarm clock, a shawl, a Spanish deck to play *brisca* but they don't let you play monte up there, don't you know that monte's the devil's own game, the teapot, and maybe we won't even need to take those things to heaven, because they say they give you everything up there, and brand new at that.

Iris keeps putting on weight under her coat. Her eyes are red. She sneezed eight times today, I counted. Of course, it's exceptionally cold out tonight. I sneezed the same number of times, but since she's half asleep with boredom in her presbytery chair, she doesn't wipe my runny nose. They're bringing my little cart now. It's about time. Iris sits on its platform. They place me in her lap. Being a good mother, she insists that they put on my woolen baby cap, the one with the pompon, so that my cold won't get worse. The old women nail back the boards I sealed the chapel with, so that it will look as if nobody's come in since the auction people took everything out. And, preceded by two old women carrying candles in newspaper cones, they pull my cart, with Iris and me on the platform, followed by the retinue of ragged procuresses and midwives, medicine women smelling of herbs, bonesetters, wailers, nursemaids, and small-time witches who don't even know they're witches, down the passageways, praying, coughing, talking, sniffling.

Since Dr. Azula operated on me, my face isn't the only thing that's changed, leaving me this mask almost devoid of features no one's bothered to paint back on. He also reduced me to what I am, confiscating eighty and leaving twenty percent, shrunken and decrepit, centered on my look. The old women take me down to the cellar and stretch me out on one of the beds.

They've sent away the newest members . . . the cellar isn't big, don't be nosy, ladies, for God's sake, we'll let you come down some other day, Lucy, not all of us who want to watch Iris diaper her doll fit in here . . . we want to help . . . we can't all fit, and you'll be in the way, and there's so much to do, we'll call you when we need you . . . Now, Iris, let us undress you, put on your nightgown, go to bed, it's late, praying in the chapel we lost track of time . . . Iris wants to change the baby herself, but she lets us help her because it's hard for her to diaper a baby by herself that's rather on the big side, like this doll. They take off my diapers.

"This doll doesn't wet as much as Damiana."

Numb with cold, my organ lies exposed to their eyes. They believe it's Mudito's organ, but it's not, it's only passing off as Mudito's submissive organ, although they've shaved it on Iris's orders, to make it look like a baby's, it's yours, Don Jerónimo, the organ that touched her. They take hold of my organ to wash it with the sponge, say what an ugly thing it is—I don't know how some women can be so filthy—and dust it with talcum as if it were a piece of pastry they're getting ready to gobble down and make disappear as Don Jerónimo's contaminated organ disappeared, he hasn't touched Inés for years and years and years and years, because I don't want him to touch her, that's why I disguise my potent organ as a child's . . . dear me, when will the real child be born so that we won't have to do these filthy things to Mudito, it doesn't matter if you do them to a baby, I just don't have the stomach to go on doing these things to this doll, every time it's my turn to wash Mudito I feel like throwing up . . . go ahead and wash him, Iris, it's your doll, you leave the heaviest work for us and stupid us wearing ourselves out while she takes it easy, how long will your baby keep us waiting, I'm telling you the delay's making some of us lose faith, don't you go thinking that all the gossip's in your favor, there are many who have doubts, others are scared because they say it's illegal or something like that, the other day I heard that there's an old woman living in the palm-tree court who says that this is a real crime, that she's going to report it because we're all crazy, almost all the inmates know something's going on, they smell something fishy in our whispered conversations, we ourselves are beginning to lose faith, you notice that Amalia, with that bit about looking for St. Gabriel's finger day and night, doesn't come around here anymore, so hurry up, Iris, what are we going to do dear God if they come and tear down the Casa before the child's born, they'll kick us out into the street to beg and sleep in doorways somewhere and in parks . . . no, don't be stupid, they're not going to pull anything down even if there is an auction, that's one of the main miracles the child's going to perform when he's born, but in the meantime let's play with Mudito, who lets us do anything to him because the poor thing walks around in a daze, half asleep, why he looks like he's neither alive nor dead, Mother Benita, what can be wrong with this poor man. You say you don't know what to do with him anymore. He's no help to you anymore. Sometimes he hides and, as he knows the Casa so well because he's been here since long before Mother Benita herself, he hides on us and we have to go looking for him, spreading out through the galleries and the passageways and the courts and the lofts till we find him, because we have to find him, if we don't, Iris gets furious, she flies into a rage and scratches us or beats us with a switch, they'd better bring her her doll right away otherwise she's going to throw herself down the stairs and kill the miraculous baby, and there won't be any miracle then, and we'll all be left like morons holding the bag . . . let's see what you're all going to do then, there won't be a miracle, no, there won't, and you're all going to die off because you're old and sick, so find me my doll, I'm going to report you to Mother Benita and she'll punish you, and to Father Azócar and he'll throw you out into the street, I know the Archbishop's private phone number by heart, I'm going to call him and tell him everything if you don't find my doll, my doll's been wandering around lost for two days . . . and, the lot of us limping and me almost blind because I've got this sty that's giving me so much trouble—I kiss my scapular medal so that I'll have luck finding him—all of us terrified in the darkness that never clears, we have to scatter through the whole Casa, down passageways we never wandered into before, in courts where there are hares . . . look, Rosario, baby hares in this court, let's catch one, they're so delicious stewed with lots of garlic, now that there's almost nothing to throw in the pot, look girls we found hares in a court back there . . . really Carmela how can they possibly be hares, don't be stupid, woman, they're not even rabbits, they're guinea pigs, I haven't the slightest notion how those guinea pigs got into this court . . . Mudito doesn't appear. Iris is screaming, as she stands on a banister, ready to throw herself down and kill her son if we don't fetch her doll, that she's going to turn us all in, until at last . . . here he is, here he is, I found him, sitting on the floor with his arms locked around his legs and his face buried in his knees . . . Mudito's so good, he lets himself be caught without resisting, and we feed him, only a little bit, because now he eats almost nothing . . . and other times when he gets lost it's different because, when we find him and he knows we're going to catch him, he starts running like a little boy and we lose him in the passageways because we can't run so much, until finally, days later—sometimes we have to lock Iris up so she won't do dangerous things and shout so much and whip us—when we find Mudito in one of the rooms where the old newspapers and magazines and old books have been stored, in hideaways he fixes up for himself in the middle of all that useless paper, bundles of magazines, books chewed up by mice, stacks of newspapers, piles of incomplete sets of encyclopedias, books in rich bindings that have become spotted with red because their covers gradually faded, sometimes we find him reading, because they say Mudito's read all the books and newspapers in the Casa, that's why he's not strong anymore, and yet, when we catch him in those coverts, buried away in those caverns of useless literature, he tears off again, he climbs up on the bundles of newspapers that are sometimes piled right up to the ceiling, but we, terrified by Iris's threats, with our creaky bones and all, groaning, scramble after him up the mountain of bound, moldy copies of *Zig-Zag* and *La Esfera* and *Je Sais Tout* that I know by heart, trapping me like an animal, screaming for more old women to come and help, till at last they catch me . . . Mudito, Mudito, don't be silly, give up, why are you running away, we're fond of you and we'll never be mean to you, we only want to ask you to please help us keep Iris happy till the baby's born.

They begin to wrap me up, swaddling me in bandages made with strips of old rags. My feet are tied up. Then they bind my legs so I won't be able to move them. When they reach my organ they tie it up like a dangerous animal, as if they guessed, despite its childlike disguise, that I control it—I hope no one ever finds out what I'm hiding—and they truss my organ by binding it to my thigh, thus nullifying it. Then they stick me into a kind of sack, with my arms bound to my ribs, and they swaddle me tight, leaving only my head out. They put me in Iris's bed, next to her, that's what she demands to placate her fury, that they bind me well and put her doll to bed next to her, under the sheets, because she likes to sleep with her little baby, the way her daddy and her mummy used to sleep in the same bed with her and, while she slept, played yumyum, till one morning . . . Iris doesn't remember anymore and everything bounces back to the present with her doll, in her bed, next to her, to play with.

"Take your baby, Iris."

"Go to sleep now."

"And let him go to sleep too."

"It's a good thing this baby doesn't make the fuss about going to sleep that that ass Damiana made, he falls asleep right away, without crying . . . But don't you let him do anything filthy to you, Iris, that's why we bind him so much, so that he won't touch you and so that his little dingdong won't stand up, let him sleep with you like an honest-to-goodness doll, how could he possibly do anything, the poor thing's so good, maybe he's a saint too, you should have seen his face yesterday when we found him reading something with a binding that looked like the Bible because those big fat books with all that gold binding are Bibles, and there's some that say they've seen him writing things I think they call *pensées*, and they're the kind of thing saints write down, that's why it's all right for him to sleep with Iris who's pure too, still and all the flesh is weak, so it's best to take precautions, after all he may only be a runt of a man but a man after all, and men are filthy pigs always looking for a chance to feel up little girls, bind him good so he won't touch her with his filthy hands of a man, with his greedy flesh that he'll have to bury, because if he ever gets to touch the poor thing she might have evil thoughts and that's a sin, and then Iris won't be chaste and pure anymore and if she stops being chaste and pure then there won't be a miracle and there won't be any child, we had to tell her she's expecting so she wouldn't give us away, things aren't what they used to be in Brígida's time, they've changed a lot, and if there's no miraculous child then we're going to have to stay in this vale of tears waiting for the grim reaper to come and drag us away some night of terror, and we'll get to glimpse his face yet, in this Casa they say is going to come down even if Misiá Inés is arriving from Rome, what are they going to do with us when they tear down the place if they've already forgotten all about us, even the Monsignor, everybody except the child who's going to be born in order to save us, he's not going to let them stick us into a public welfare truck like poor Mercedes Barroso and throw us into potter's field to rot, because of course we wouldn't complain if it was a funeral like the one Misiá Raquel treated Brígida to, we've never seen an employer like her, that would be a lot different, nobody'd be scared of being put into a good coffin, in a real marble vault, white, with your name and the dates and everything written on it and the Ruiz family there praying so you could see they were really and truly upset that poor Brígida'd gone and died on them, but nobody has Brígida's luck, and so we've got to look after Iris, because there has to be a child to perform the miracle of driving away the bad men who bring those black boxes, and so that with his sacred little finger he can touch the hearses and the horses that will carry us to heaven and change them into white ones, and nobody's going to be afraid then, because we believe that white things are harmless, that's why Brígida never used to wear the black shawl Miss Malú gave her for her birthday and she left it brand new . . . who knows who ended up with it . . . maybe it faded and turned white, because the miracle can start any day now, that's why, so as to be all ready to go, we have to make little packages

with the things we're going to take along, the teapot, the alarm
clock, warm stockings because there may be a wind blowing, a
shawl of any color . . .

THEY PUT OUT the lights. They go out. They leave only one old
woman on duty, who is sleeping in the other bed in the cellar.
I hear her stirring between the sheets. Through the bandages
and rags that imprison me, impeding any movement whatsoever,
I feel myself wrapped in the heat of Iris's body. The old
woman's fallen asleep. She mumbles. She smacks her lips, she
sleeps. Lying together here, you and I have learned to recognize
the moment when the old women's irregular breathing enters
the realm of sleep that puts them too into sacks that cut off their
movement and suspend their vigilance.

Don't you touch me.

And you don't speak to me yet, you have to wait not only
for the moment when sleep gobbles up the old woman on duty
but also the moment when pain breaks down my fortitude and
I dare to moan and implore you. You yourself showed them how
to tie me up and cripple my movements completely, I'm afraid
of the doll, you said and, because they're slaves of your uterus,
you order them to lay me down beside you, unable to move an
inch, so that I'll tire quickly and my stiff back will ache and I'll
want to change my position and find a little relief that you won't
let me have, because you refuse to move me and I can't do it
myself, and you want to make me beg you Iris, Iris, you planned
it all, I'm in your power . . . I know, she murmured . . . I'm
pleading with you to move me around a little because I'm getting stiff all over, I can't stand it anymore, maybe I'll have to
remain in this fixed, painful position forever, here in this cellar,
maybe when the old women strip off my bandages at daybreak
I won't be able to take a step or straighten out a finger.

Your breathing's different from the sleeping old women's. I
can't stand it anymore. I know I'm going to start getting a cramp
in another minute. I nag you:

"Iris."

You don't answer, to make me beg you:

"Shift me a little bit."

"I don't feel like it."

"Please, Iris."

"Sssssssshhhhhhhhh . . ."

And you don't touch me.

Motionless, unbearably static, the cramp always starts in the same spot, in the tendons of my instep, they knot up, and the pain knots up my ankle, fixed in place by the bandages, and the cramp crawls up the tendons of my inanimate legs and through my entire body that's helpless against the pain it could defend itself against with the tiniest movement you've made sure I won't be able to make, the cramp keeps climbing, tightening up, constricting my whole left side up to my arm, up to my collarbone, now I can't even defend myself by moving the tendons in my neck, I'm not allowed the slightest movement that could clear up the cramp, you deprived me of the right to move, turning me into your doll because you know that tied up like this I grow stiff and the pain creeps up my body to my neck, and I'm going to have to scream with pain, but I don't scream, I only whisper again:

"Iris."

You don't answer.

"A little bit."

"No."

"The pain's killing me."

"It's your punishment."

"Iris."

"Does it hurt a lot?"

"Yes."

"Would you like to move around?"

"Yes . . ."

"And what would you do for me if I moved you?"

"Anything you say."

"You damn liar."

"No, Iris . . . I can't stand it anymore . . ."

"That's what you get for being such a dirty liar. How many times have I sent you out to bring me the guy who gave me the

baby? Nothin' doin'. You always come back with stories, news
. . . that somebody said . . . a message, nothin', no sign of the
guy, and I've had it. I'm gonna have the baby any day. In fact,
I think I'm even past my time, of course I can't remember the
dates, the days are all the same in this place, but I think my
time's about up, so the guy has to come and get me, that's all,
and give the baby his name. I don't want him to be a bastard
. . . and if he's born here in the Casa what's Mother Benita
gonna say? If you don't bring me the guy before the baby's born,
I'm gonna accuse you of everything . . ."

I whisper:

"Listen, Iris . . ."

"None of your bullshit."

"I've got an idea."

"I'm gettin' sick of your ideas."

"This one's really good."

"I don't believe a thing you say."

"Move me around a little bit."

"No . . ."

"How can I talk to you, then?"

Iris shifts me around in the bed, she helps me draw up and
stretch my legs and it's as if I put them in cool water, soften-
ing the stiffness and dissolving the pain a little. I know. Iris will
leave me in this position until she gets what she wants out of
me, and then when I start to grow stiff again in this silence, I
know, she'll talk to me again and the new pain will disappear
again or at least ease up. I whisper in her ear so as not to wake
up the old woman who's on now:

"He's not around anymore, Iris. Your son's father hightailed
it when they told him I was looking for him, and I lost his trail.
Every time he hears that I'm looking for him, he moves out and
changes neighborhoods until I lose him again, you ought to see
all the different things I've got to disguise myself as so they
won't suspect I'm on his trail . . . he's scared because they're
after him, and that's what scares people most, to have someone
after you, you invent plots and dream up situations in which you
do things that never happened, in order to justify that fear . . ."

"I don't follow you . . . talk clearer . . ."

"When you undo my bandages at night while the old woman on duty's asleep and you force me to get dressed and you throw me out in the street like a dog and you steal my keys and wait till daybreak behind the door, I walk through the whole city, Iris, the city's terrible, I don't know why you want to get out when they give you everything here, they know me in the bars now, the whorehouses, the amusement párks, the circuses, the balconies in neighborhood theaters where they have wooden benches like the ones there used to be in the chapel, I search everywhere, I swear it, but they always tell me he hasn't been around in ages, they told him somebody was looking for him to settle a grudge and he got scared and hangs out at a different bar now, of course nobody suspects I'm the one after him, so they don't mind telling me everything."

You're all ears because you think it's a story.

"Listen, Iris . . ."

"Yeah, but I'm not gonna stay in this crappy place all my life, with you and these old bags."

"I'll let you out whenever you want."

"What am I gonna get out of it? Don't you say Damiana's wandering around out there? I don't wanna get mixed up with that old dyke again. If I go out alone, she's the one who told me, they're gonna take me to have my baby in a hospital where they give young girls a hard time. Yes, sometimes at night I hear Damiana walking, prowling outside the Casa, whistling for me to look out the balcony, but I won't look out, I don't wanna go with her. I'd as soon wait till he comes for me, I'd rather play with the old women at the miracle thing so they'll help me have the baby and raise it, if you don't find the guy. I'm not about to roam the streets begging with the baby. Money, that's what you've gotta bring me if you don't find him."

"That's what I want to talk to you about."

"What?"

"Loosen me up a bit."

"You've fooled me like that before."

"Loosen me up and I'll tell you . . ."

Under the covers, Iris fiddles around with the cords and the bonds that turn me into a package. I can move. I have arms, I have legs: they exist beyond the pain of the cramping and apart from the discomfort and the terror of the eternal tightness . . . Iris, Iris, loosen me up a little more and I'll tell you any kind of plan to fool you again, some fabulous nonsense like a comic-book story so you'll believe it . . . you loosen me up some more . . . they say he used to tell everyone that you're the only one he ever loved . . . another knot . . . and that he had nothing to offer you because he was poor . . . another one . . . that he didn't deserve you . . . this cord now . . . what good would it do for him to come looking for you if he wouldn't even be able to give your son an education . . . I get closer to your attentive ear, advising you at last, tonight, that it's not worth looking for him, because you can give birth any minute now and besides this guy Romualdo didn't have a red cent, he didn't even own the Giant's head he fooled you with, your Romualdo disappeared, he didn't leave a trace, as if they'd torn him to pieces along with the Giant's head, better forget that moron, Iris, don't be a fool, I want to skip out of the Casa too even if I'm scared to death of the streets, sometimes I'd even rather have the cramping I get from sleeping bound up next to you, unable to move all night long, than go out and roam the streets, but now when you untie me and throw me out of the Casa and lock the door from inside to stop me from coming in if I don't give you some explanation about Romualdo, these nights, when I've been searching here or there, I've seen a lot of houses, I've been peeping in windows and now I do know where to get money. Lots of money.

"You goddamn thief."

"Why?"

"I may be a whore, but I'm not a thief."

"Who told you you were a whore?"

"Damiana."

You're not a whore, Iris, you're chaste and pure, I know, I assure you, I promise you. And in the quiet, sheltered night of the cellar I spin a yarn for your ear, to save myself and make you free me, otherwise the pain will kill me, that's why I make it all up and improvise, depending on your reactions: there's a real big yellow house, they owe me all the money and all the power they have and so I wouldn't be stealing, Iris, I'm poor and rickety because they stole everything I owned, they haven't paid any of the money they have to pay me because they wouldn't exist if I didn't exist, I put everything in their hands, I conferred beauty and power and pride on them, without me they'd disappear, see, their money and their jewels and everything they have belongs to me. In the dark cellar your eyes glitter, fascinated by this new story I make up because I have to deceive you so you won't kill me with pain, and if you want me to I can take out that money, not steal it, the money in that yellow house across from the park is mine, and getting hold of the money is a cinch, I know those people who owe me all their riches so well that I know by heart the combination to the safe the man has in his library, hidden behind some books with greenish spines, as you enter, upstairs, on the left-hand side. Sometimes he opens the safe to count his millions. I can take all the money out of it, Iris, yes, Iris, yes, loosen me, loosen me a little more, more, let's not waste time, believe me this time, just this once, and we'll do anything you want with the money.

"But I don't want to go and live with you."

"All right. We'll go halves, and you can do as you please."

You think it over.

"No. That won't help me. I'm a minor. The best thing is for me to stay here. What are they gonna say if I show up just like that, on my own, without papers, to have a baby in a clinic?"

Then I whisper:

"Let's get married."

"Over my dead body."

"I'm telling you we ought to get married only so that you can do as you please. With all the money I'm going to give you, and the marriage certificate, you can do anything you feel like and nobody's going to go asking you any questions. And you'd do well to marry me so your kid won't be illegitimate and he'll at least have a family name . . ."

"What family name?"

"Mine."

"What is it?"

You can't make me say it.

"Why go into it now, I'll tell you all about it later . . ."

Iris's hands have been untying me as she listens, fascinated, to my story that distorts her daydream and lets me go free: naked, with my privates all shaved, but free beside her, lying like a man next to a woman. I could rape you, Iris, right here, and this old hag wouldn't even know it, almost without you yourself knowing it, but no, I'm not going to do it, because I have no organ and I want all the old women to know that I don't so they'll pass on the news to Peta Ponce so she'll calm down and maybe make up her mind, at last, to die, I'm nothing but another old woman on duty to keep an eye on you and be ready in case tonight, at last, the blessed event takes place. You say:

"I don't even have a single girl's identification papers."

"I don't have any papers either."

"Then how . . . ?"

It doesn't matter how, Iris, don't worry, first we'll get the money, everything's possible with money, that's what people say who know about such things. Later, once we've got our hands on the money, we'll think what to do next, don't be a ninny, it's not stealing, I tell you, I can do anything I want with those people. Hand me the trousers and the shirt I've got hidden under the bed. Let me get dressed while lying here beside you, covered by the sheets and blankets so the old women won't catch on, now, let's get up, put your overcoat on over your night-gown: look, I let you guide me, let you lead me like a dog, with my hands tied and a strap around my neck, down the passage-ways to the vestibule, you hold the keys now, you're in control, you're the boss, you force me to go out in the street and wander around that vast area where there are no good little old women feeble-minded with age, and you turn the key in the lock after pushing me out . . . Bring him to me. Today, without fail. If you don't come back with Romualdo I'll tell Miss Rita that you tried to get into me, that they'll have to tie you up tighter to-morrow, much much tighter than today, so you won't be able to move a single finger, nothing, so you'll die of pain and cramps, and the discomfort will kill you, you lousy little mute, and with me right next to you, refusing to move you even if you scream and beg me, yes I know you can hide in the Casa, *your* Casa, but with all that looking for you and chasing you the whole thing's turned into a kind of game, like playing hide-and-seek or tag, only more fun, in the cellars and attics and galleries and lofts, we know the Casa almost as well as you do now and you're easy to catch, look, Miss Rita, I'll tell her tomorrow, this child's wicked, this doll's a filthy pig, I'll tell her, because he gets a hard-on at night, Miss Rita, so maybe we'd better cut his weenie off so it won't get hard, I don't know what he needs a weenie for, Miss Rita, so we'd better cut it off so it won't keep sticking up, because he bothers me and won't let me sleep, and then, if you don't keep your word tonight, you lousy little mute, I swear I'm gonna make the old women cut off your peter.

"Okay."

"I'll wait for you by the door."

"Okay."

"Bring a lot of money."

"Okay."

You open the door. I remain standing in the doorway. You shove me out and close the door behind me like other times. I'm alone in the street, the rain comes down and I don't know what to do next, what story to make up so that in the morning when I give three light raps on the door and you open it I can begin to ensnare you with a story that will sound true, I'll look for glass beads, round beads, colored sequins, that will tangle you up . . . and I'll be inside by then.

Inside, free. Not suffocating. With the adobe walls around me once more. While Iris stands there, captivated by my story, I'll run away from her cruelty and disappear into the depths of the Casa. You all believe you've come to know the place thoroughly. But you're all wrong. There are always hidden corners left, untouched trunks, solid darknesses that you have to feel with your hands to know and that only I know how to penetrate, places from which no one can ever get back, I swear you won't find me this time, I defy every one of you to do it. Or rather, you'll find me only when I let you, when something starts growing in me once more, like the horns of a snail, and I feel the living moment when I need to have you and the old women discover me, to bind and bandage and wrap me into a package again and so enable me to again fulfill my destiny of being a doll tied up in rags to amuse one of the incarnations of a jailbird's daughter . . . and to wait until it's time for you to hurl me into the void of the street once again.

21

SUITCASES, BOXES, STEPLADDERS, sacks . . . a pile of
sacks among which I hide, and a plow whose presence no one
can explain, and an easy chair and a pedestal . . . come,
Mudito . . . the swarm of women pursue me to this loft . . .
come, come, don't be afraid, we're not playing this time and
you have to be afraid only of our games, come, Mother Benita
sent us to call you, she has something to tell you . . . I stand
up and I'm Mudito again, or what's left of him, less and less
every day, oh dear, what are we going to do with this man, he
looks so poorly, Mother Benita says, more sickly every day, getting smaller every day, but she sent you women to call me to
the vestibule so she could give me the news that a cable arrived
from Switzerland, and she wanted me to read it too. I found her
with her hands dangling at her apron and the paper beside her
on the bench outside the telephone room. The cheerful murmur
of the old women coming in to share the news increased while
I read the cable: VOW OF POVERTY INSPIRES ME TO SPEND LAST
DAYS OF MY LIFE IN CASA WHICH IS MINE STOP PLEASE ASCERTAIN
ORIGINAL COURT OCCUPIED BY BLESSED INÉS AND PREPARE CELL AND
BATH FOR ME THERE STOP LETTER INSTRUCTIONS FOLLOW STOP LOVE
STOP INÉS AZCOITÍA.

You have a long telephone conversation with Misiá Raquel
because you don't dare and you never will dare speak to Don
Jerónimo, how can you speak to him when he ignores you and
the Casa and all of us. Misiá Raquel's telling you that of course,
you have every right in the world not to talk to Jerónimo, I
know Inés like the palm of my hand, a vow of poverty with her
as spoiled as she is, didn't I tell you some time ago, Mother

· 278

Benita, that Inés would be furious at Jerónimo for signing the Casa over to the Archbishopric and that she'd get even with him . . . see, this is her way of doing it, Inés never takes revenge face to face, least of all with Jerónimo, it's impossible to take revenge to his face because he never looks you in the face, it's as if he didn't have a face or were too tall and your voice couldn't reach him, and so Inés is going to get even by coming to live in the Casa, because she knows that if she settles in the Casa the Archbishop won't dare touch it as long as she's living here, even if entail and chaplaincy have been transferred, Inés won't stand for any nonsense, Mother Benita, and she's probably fit to be tied right now because the beatification fell through, as we all knew it would, but she wouldn't listen to us and everybody including Jerónimo has been laughing at her, of course, and she's settling down here to keep the Archbishop from laying hands on a single tile, of course, if he makes a wrong move she'll change her will, in which everything goes to the Archbishopric, and leave her fortune to anybody at all, to the SPCA, or who knows who, and you don't think the Archbishop's going to let the big Azcoitía fortune slip through his fingers, do you, that priest Azócar is going to have a tantrum, and we'd better not phone Jerónimo the news, Mother Benita, let him get the surprise of his life, listen, Mother, better have her cell papered, Inés hates unpapered walls, she says they're damp and bad for rheumatism, if you want me to I'll help choose the wallpaper, I know her taste and there's a firm over on San Isidro, they make some very lovely designs and not expensive at all, and since it's best to keep things sort of in the family, Misiá Raquel herself sent over her granddaughter Malú's husband, a young architect with an elegant mane of hair and flashy corduroy trousers, to play what he himself called the guessing game in this labyrinth of courts, how's it possible that they kept no records to help us establish the dates of the various stages of construction, although this is all tacked-on patchwork without any architectural interest, what on the surface may look like unity is nothing but systematic neglect, Mother Benita, but it does have a certain amount of charm, of course Misiá Raquel doesn't know what she's talking about when she says it's the last straw that the gov-

ernment with so much money to throw away on stupid things doesn't take things in hand and save one of the few historical buildings we still have left, you can't say this is an antique monument, Mother, it's nothing but an old junk heap, of course, since we've established something definite, perhaps we might say that this court you call the palm-tree court is the oldest: look at the total lack of ornamentation on the stone bases supporting the cloister's pilasters, the cells that are so narrow and the adobe that's so thick and the corridors that are so cramped, it looks like a prison and, after all, the fact that it's centered around this palm tree that must be at least a hundred and fifty years old gives us a relatively definite clue . . . what a pity there aren't any palm trees like this one left, although this was apparently a forest of palms, the ladies who read American interior decorating magazines from which they learn that palm trees *are out* have been wiping out the last ones, let's hope Children's Village will at least respect this venerable and lovely palm, it adds a certain charm to this little court with its undulating, moss-covered tile roofs but there's no foolproof sign that this was the original court, Mother Benita, although it's certainly primitive enough, but there's proof, who knows, it could be . . .

Positive proof? Who can claim to offer positive proof in this fluctuating, hazy matter? What, for instance, does Inés mean by saying *Blessed* in her cable when the Vatican settled the matter once and for all months ago? Yes, I'm very sorry, Inés, but it was settled for good, with an emphatic *no*. That cable's a rebellion against the highest ecclesiastical authorities, a domestic heresy like a bean stew that reeks of witchcraft . . . an insignificant heresy for others, Inés, but not for you, because it lays bare your complete ineptitude: you weren't capable of giving your husband a son, and now you've also shown that you're not capable of adorning the family name with a saint to be worshipped by the public who, in venerating her, would venerate the family line your useless womb exterminated. And although the Vatican denied you permission to *initiate* the process of beatification—look, they didn't give you permission to even initiate it —you still talk of the *Blessed* Inés. What monstrous turn are

your efforts taking to keep that cloistered girl, who never took the veil and died in the Casa at the end of the eighteenth century, from dying forever, with you, as if her dying would mean that neither she nor you ever existed?

Inés never had the slightest chance of obtaining the beatification. All the proofs are so debatable, everything's always based on *they say*, just the name of the person who heard the *they say* is ever known, not the name of the person who actually said the *they say* . . . it comes down to someone who told someone something in a room that's gone from a house that's gone on a street that no longer has the same name or the same address and is the same street for reasons that cannot be determined—words Inés's grandmother or her mother repeated, or Peta Ponce, or needy aunts whose pride had only rumors like that to satisfy its hunger, although there's a bundle of letters that tell little: birth certificates, death certificates, now and then a later chronicle recalling events that were rumored to be miraculous. The only solid, uncontested fact, with documents to prove it, is the founding of the chaplaincy: toward the end of the eighteenth century, a wealthy landowner of Basque descent, a widower, father of nine sons and a daughter, came up from his lands south of the Maule River to shut up his sixteen-year-old daughter in the convent of Capuchin cloistered nuns whose Superior was the landowner's oldest sister. For reasons not given in any chronicle, the girl never took the vows of a Capuchin, which would have been the natural thing. And it must have taken endless conversations, the true nature of which was lost in the secrecy of the convent, for the farsighted Superior to convince her brother that, in a case like this, the wisest thing was the founding of a chaplaincy that would link the family directly to God, placing the Almighty under the obligation to protect her. As a matter of fact, hadn't he heard that the nuns of the Incarnation had no Casa of their own? Why not build them a Casa where they could hide Inés for the rest of her life, since it was a question of hiding her? And so it was built. As soon as the Casa was finished the nuns, her jailers, moved in, to serve and take care of Inés. This chaplaincy, endowed with the most enviable lands of La Chimba, was so wealthy that it became a juicy topic of discussion in all the social circles of the time, until the wars of independence brought to an end all interest in holy things and munificences, and people could talk only about the blood and fire of the war, and the enemy that was threatening on all sides. Inés de Azcoitía died at twenty in the Casa, in the odor of sanctity.

All this is history. Still, in books written by ladies who took up the rumor later on or by some European traveler whose curiosity gained her access to what was being said in the intimacy of homes in this country, faint echoes of Inés's unequaled piety reach us, echoes especially of what may be considered her most extraordinary miracle: during the most disastrous of the earthquakes at the end of the eighteenth century, the one that leveled most of the houses in the capital and the surrounding countryside, the Casa de la Encarnación at La Chimba remained intact, standing solidly, although it was made of adobe and tile as were all the other houses in those days. They say . . . they say that, before the first tremors started, Inés de Azcoitía—it's also worth noting something very curious: she wore the habit of the Incarnation but didn't take vows in that order either—fell to her knees in the middle of the court while the awestruck nuns watched her from the cloister. Then, as the underground thunder and the tremors that opened cracks in the countryside suddenly threatened to bring down the walls of the Casa, Inés formed a cross with her arms, extending them with a terrible effort in which she seemed to sacrifice herself to support the walls, and she supported them, and the Casa didn't fall. As the nuns were cloistered, they couldn't flee; the lightning flashes over the mountains enabled them to distinguish those saintly hands that saved the Casa: the effort appeared to have changed them into dry branches or stems, the gnarled hands of an old woman. Inés always ate alone in her cell—she never participated in the communal life—leaving it only to attend services in the chapel, or to stroll through the cloister, alone and silent, her hands folded under the apron of her habit, holding a cross made of dry twigs tied together with strips of leather. A gift from her old nursemaid on her First Communion, it was the only thing she managed or wanted to bring along from her home, south of the Maule, and she must have had to smuggle it in.

After the earthquake, the nuns took to watching Inés's miraculous hands with obsessive attention: yes, yes, it was true, while she knelt, illuminated, rapt, or elevated to some level of being to which the nuns had no access, during prayers in the chapel, in the shadow of her habit's folds, her fingers would seem to merge with those sticks of her nursemaid's cross, which were rubbed and warped and blackened by the years and perhaps the centuries, her hands would turn into dry branches and, as they'd rise higher and higher in ecstasy, and the terrified and reverent nuns would abandon the chapel, the branches of her arms would grow longer and longer, out of her sleeves, till, with only one or two candles lit now, her eyes fixed on the new moon trampled by the Immaculate Conception, and her arms outstretched in prayer, Inés would seem to have become transformed into a tree heavy with years, whose wrinkles and knots seemed to tie to its trunk the time-laden face of pain, eradicating the fresh bloom in the pious girl's face. Much later, at daybreak, the light would rescue the identity of the founder's daughter.

The legend of her piety traveled beyond the cloister's walls, from convent to convent, and then spread through the capital. The Azcoitías were pleased to have a saint, in addition to their many heroes, a saint or at least a saintly girl who was on everybody's lips and whose sanctity added luster to the family tree.

But troubled times came, times hardly propitious to the cultivation of sanctity. Of greater urgency were the immediate victory, the recently kindled hatred, the unquenched thirst for vengeance, the menace that would have to be defeated at the cost of one's life . . . and afterwards, building the tiny, remote republic, devising laws, defining classes, doing away with some privileges to create others . . . several decades had to go by after Inés de Azcoitía's death before the rumor, kept alive in the cloisters but dying outside its walls, reached the Archbishop in the form of an official proposal, signed by the Superior of the Casa, to get the beatification under way. First of all, they had to exhume her remains. According to Inés, in her family they've been saying for generations that, when he opened the coffin, the startled Archbishop found its satin lining fresh, clean, new, as if all those years hadn't elapsed and as if a body'd never lain in it. Of course none of this, which might at least have aroused curiosity in the Vatican, appears in any document. Time must have erased the grave of the girl-saint, who vanished without leaving any trace except this Casa, built as a prison for her, that's been growing and growing, proliferating around the legend of the original prisoner whose memory's about to disappear.

ALMOST NOTHING ABOUT the life and miracles of the girl-saint rises above conjecture or the echo of a rumor. And yet, I don't think the following hypothesis is far-fetched: Inés de Azcoitía died a victim of one of the many plagues so common in the past; the wise Superior of the Capuchins—her conscience was stained with the secret confided by Inés's brother before he pined away and died—must have handled things so that hallowed ground wouldn't be desecrated by the grave of a woman who, however much she was a relative and an Azcoitía, had undoubtedly been a witch; that's why the superior refused, from the beginning, to receive her among her pious souls; and that's why the girl never took vows as a Capuchin or as a nun of the Incarnation. And that's why the Archbishop couldn't find her remains in the family vault; this absence of coffin and remains is the kernel of the reality the Azcoitías and their servants have been transforming, over the past century and a half, into the pretty legend of the clean satin in a coffin no one ever saw.

Inés must have heard the details of the family tradition, told and elaborated in multiple versions by Peta Ponce, on long afternoons in her childhood, next to the brazier, while the old woman taught her how to sew and embroider. But, as soon as Peta has a hand in anything, everything becomes weightless and fluid, time expands, we lose sight of the beginning and the end, and who knows what part of time is filled by the supposed present . . . and Peta must also have told Inés the tale of the girl-witch. It's an elastic, changing tale, and who knows if one of its many variations, one Peta used to tell her, didn't stretch to the point where the story of the girl-witch and the tradition of the girl-saint merged, restoring both to their full force.

For we must admit that, even from a literary point of view, the story of the girl-witch is, oddly enough, unsatisfactory. In the beginning, the line the story follows forces us to fix our attention on the landowner's daughter, because she's beautiful, of illustrious birth. But when her father opened his huge poncho to hide what was happening in his daughter's bedroom, his act bent the course of the story and divided it in two. In one part, the popular and immortal part that old women and tired farmhands and children will go on telling for centuries and centuries, the landowner whisks his daughter away from the center of the story, substituting for her a warty old woman whose identity interests no one, who expiated alone what both women should have expiated if the one who'd been the leading figure until then hadn't disappeared without a trace in the story. The other half is the pious, aristocratic tradition locked away and almost stifled in the bosom of a family that's about to die out: a very pure girl experiences mystic ecstasies that save from disaster a few courts that, if we can believe the architect who was going over them the other day, are absolutely worthless. I've seen Don Jerónimo raise his arm and, in doing so, the folds of his poncho, made of vicuña like the landowner's, to indicate that nothing's happened here, that this is forbidden property, that his gesture's intended to eliminate something, to separate from the whole that part he's ready to put on display. Don Jerónimo must have raised his poncho to cover Inés for the very definite purpose of separating that portion of the family secret he could control, the story of the girl-saint, from the terrifying shadows of the popular legend, leaving both versions truncated, incomplete, with some facets beclouded, without the full ramifications the two, combined, would have had: Jerónimo managed to make Inés forget the tale of the girl-witch. What he hadn't bargained for was that the shielding gesture of his arm would cast another shadow over Inés: the fear of extinction. She'd never before felt this as something that sprang from within, it had been something she experienced from without, as a reflection of her love for a Jerónimo betrayed by her incapacity to give him a son. It was this fear of extinction that made her travel to Rome to do everything she possibly could to open a place in history for the girl-saint in whom she, and the Azcoitías through her, could survive. And now her anarchic mind irrationally clings to this segment of that larger truth covered by the noble drapery of oblivion, in order to give her ancestor the rank of *blessed* and have future generations venerate her. But it turns out that the girl-saint isn't her own direct ancestress but Peta Ponce's: Jerónimo's determination to detach, to censure, a reality with such a powerful configuration is creating another phase of uncertainty.

The uncertainty isn't new. It's always been there. What did the father's arms hide when he spread his discreet poncho across the doorway? Was it the moment when the evil head of the *chonchón* was joining the girl's body by means of a red wound on her neck, below the ears like bat wings that were never completely reabsorbed, making it urgent, very urgent, that all this be hidden under the white coif of the habit of the Incarnation? Is it possible that the father's eyes interrupted the process whereby his daughter's hands were recovering their fresh loveliness and that this made them retain forever their gnarled form, like black twigs, deformed by knots and grooves, on dry, twisted branches that it was urgent, very urgent, to hide under the apron of some religious order? Isn't it possible that, confronted by the figures of these women as confusing as images of smoke, changeable and constantly changing and wavering and oscillating, the landowner feared that his daughter would dissolve before his eyes and so he immediately locked her up anywhere he could, in her room, in the convent of the Capuchins, in the Casa designed like a net to trap any incarnation, whether hybrid or already diffuse, of the daughter he loved so dearly?

Perhaps. Everything's possible when Peta Ponce gets involved. I want to defeat Peta and I can't stop asking myself, in the hope of pinning it down, what the common everyday incident was that gave birth to this monster of so many faces covered with polyps, of infinite variations and labyrinthine accretions that may or may not be true and that contribute nothing useful and yet, somehow or other, belong. What really took place? At the end of the eighteenth century a very wealthy farmer of Basque descent, the father of nine sons and a daughter, left his lands south of the Maule and shut his daughter up in a convent, founding for this purpose the chaplaincy entailed to the Azcoitía family: that much is history. But why should a doting father, a widower well on in years, shut up his only daughter in a convent forever? Why punish her as a witch if witches don't exist, nor *chonchones,* nor *imbunches,* nor witches' grottoes? Did he punish her nursemaid so that the common people would go on believing in those masks of fear? Why build a special retreat house to put away his daughter, if it was true that she was transported by mystical ecstasies and had the makings of a saint, whose miracles could and should be shown off?

Inés de Azcoitía was neither a witch nor a saint. I'm sure something very simple happened: the lonely adolescent girl, shut away in the remote rural world of the eighteenth century, when there were practically no roads, or even trails, in a virgin country populated only by animals and roughnecks, fell in love with some country boy who was perhaps more sensitive and beautiful, or simply cleaner, than her brothers and her father. With the old woman, who couldn't refuse her spoiled baby anything, to cover up for her, she had a love affair with the boy, whom the old woman, in her incarnation as a procuress, procured for her. He may have been a neighbor. Or a head groom, or a stableboy, anyone at all, it doesn't matter. I wonder if the father's poncho, spread across the door of a reality that was superior to him, didn't cover his daughter in the pangs of childbirth. Didn't he steer the fury of the farmhands toward the old woman so that they'd destroy her because she was the only one who knew the secret? Didn't he whisk his daughter away from reality so that, locked up in the Casa, she'd expiate a common sin and give birth to a legend instead of a bastard?

What about the bastard? And the bastard's father?

Naturally, it was necessary to get rid of both. Where the father was concerned, all he had to do was not try to find him. Ignore him. Nothing's happened. My darling daughter, who's chaste and pure, is going to take the veil and, as a token of my gratefulness to the Almighty for the gift of her exemplary virtue, I'm establishing this chaplaincy. There's no stain on her name. There's no child, naturally there can't be a father, nor can there be vengeance on the father who doesn't exist. The total silence of the landowner, who didn't even confide the secret to his own sons, because they wouldn't understand a vengeance as subtle as that of not seeking revenge, eliminated the poor timid father, who fled before those nine brutes could kill him, but they didn't kill him because they didn't pursue anyone who doesn't exist, there's no father, there's no son, my daughter Inés is going to take the veil, she's chaste and pure, nothing's happened here . . .

The landowner got rid of his grandson, abandoning him in some peon's house on one of the estates he owned that they had to pass through on their way to the capital. The love child grew up as a foundling without a name or parents, brought up by whoever happened to be available, snot-nosed and undernourished, indistinguishable from the snot-nosed and undernourished children of the farmhands. No doubt he became a man and he too had snot-nosed and undernourished offspring, who spread the blood of the Azcoitías throughout the region, mixing it with that of the peasants south of the Maule. When a gentleman has illegitimate sons by the women on his lands, the sons cling with a certain pride to the brand of the *patrón*'s bastard son, and this furtive pride even seems to bring out in the son the features of the father that everyone, except the father and the official mother, points out as his. But when it's a gentleman's daughter who gives birth to a bastard, her son immediately loses all vestiges of identity, every trace of his lofty origin disappears: in this case, it's not the black bar that crosses the blazon without erasing the arms, it's the stain that darkens and confuses them so that no one can recognize them, because there's no son here, nothing's happened here . . .

Peta Ponce was born on one of the Azcoitía properties south of the Maule, of obscure and anonymous stock attached to the illustrious family of people who spent their lives working its lands and looking after its houses, cutting its corn, herding its sheep and pressing its grapes for wine. They say . . . they say that Peta's mother had an enormous posterior and that every night, during the mosquito season, they made her lie down, stark naked, at the foot of the bed in which Inés's grandmother slept, so that the insects would prefer to glut themselves on her fat bottom, thus leaving the lady's flesh clear and smooth, while she slept the sleep of the blessed.

I'm sure that in Peta's room at La Rinconada, the night they killed the yellow bitch whose remains were never found, the reason I believed so wholeheartedly that it was Inés who was moaning with pleasure under my weight was that Peta has the blood of the other Inés de Azcoitía in her veins and is her descendant, although generations and generations of humiliated forebears have buried all trace of noble blood in the depths of her half-breed witch's face . . . perhaps the girl-saint herself, the girl-witch herself, became flesh under my weight that night in order to receive the seed that produced the monster. Yes, I see the face of the ancestress in the depths of that night. And afterwards, riveting my attention on those pocked features in an effort to see through Peta, I've sometimes managed to perceive, like an echo that comes bouncing, from an infinite distance, through the defile of miserable generations, faint traces of the luminous features of the noble family, of Inés the witch or the Blessed Inés transformed into Peta, forever pursuing me to get me into her power and show me that she belongs to a noble line, that she has a background, that she had mother and father and grandparents and great-great-great-grandmothers, one of them the saint and witch.

She wants to show me this and to laugh at me because she knows that I lost my origin or, rather, she knows the truth, that Dr. Azula cut out the eighty percent of me that included Humberto Peñaloza the writer, Humberto Peñaloza the great man's secretary, the Humberto Peñaloza in cape and slouch hat who recites poems in bars, Humberto Peñaloza the son of the grade-school teacher who was the grandson of the engineer on a toy train that belched so much smoke that it's impossible to see beyond him. Yes, Dr. Azula even robbed me of that modest background, leaving me converted into this pitiful twenty percent. The old women say many things here at the Casa. Now that the auction people are piling up objects in the corridors, it's true they gossip less, fascinated as they are by being able to sit on a pile of eight mattresses and bounce up and down on them like toothless babies . . . look, Zunilda, heaven must be like this . . . but they always have time to gossip . . . they say Misiá Inés is coming next week . . . they say she's arrived and won't be coming yet and maybe she'll never come . . . no, they say it's not true, she hasn't arrived, she made a pilgrimage to Fatima and another to Lourdes . . . they say that when Misiá Raquel gave away the key to her cell to Mother Benita, Mother Benita put on a martyr's look and told her what do you want us to do with all this stuff, as if Misiá Raquel didn't have anything worth saving, and Misiá Raquel's such a good person, but Mother said that now that Mudito's like this I won't have anyone to help me take the things out of your cell and sort them out, ever since Mudito's been going around like that, he's like just another old woman, Misiá Raquel, like Mother Anselma and Mother Julia, I just can't take any more of this, even Mudito's taken sick, why he can barely stay on his feet and when he was nailing up the doors he fell off the stepladder and the orphans had to help me finish the job, poor Mudito, where could he have come from . . . they murmur, they whisper, the old women have been whispering for years and years and their whispers cling to the walls, but the old women don't last long, because of their years, and they die off soon and others arrive and hear the rumors, the gossip they themselves distort and pass on to newer old women who'll die shortly after those before them, having passed on to their successors the horde of shadows and the multitudes of rumors picked up here in the Casa . . . they say . . . they say . . . they say that Mudito was born here in the Casa . . . of course, Clementina . . . poor Mudito, why he's never gone out into the street in his whole life, because he's afraid of the automobile . . . how's it possible, Mercedes—another one, not Mercedes Barroso, she was taken away by the public welfare truck, which comes for almost all of us—how can he be afraid of the horns when he's deaf and dumb . . . that may be, but he's always been here, since before Mother Benita, they say, when there were many many nuns, not like now, and they say that at that time a young girl was found in the doorway of the Casa early one morning and the nuns, who were very good, not short-tempered and bossy like Mother Benita—I just can't imagine why she's getting that way—brought the girl inside the court and there, they say, the girl gave birth to a seven-month baby the inmates at the time nursed and saved from certain death but they couldn't save his hearing or his voice, and they say that's why, being a seven-month baby, Mudito's so puny, of course he's getting smaller and they say he's not quite right in the head either, of course you can't ever tell if people aren't right in the head when they can't talk, look at the way he's been going around lately, poor Mudito's been acting strange, he can hardly move, the poor man looks like he's paralyzed. His body itches from all that filth and his head from the lice he has . . . but I can't scratch myself, with my hands and my arms gone limp, as I sit in the sun all day, when it's sunny, in the Gothic choir chair belonging to a lady who came to her cell to sort out the things she wants to take with her, now that they're going to tear down the Casa, and decided that, no, it's too big, where am I going to put it, and gave it to Mother Benita, and when Mother Benita said thanks but what can I do with such a big piece of furniture now that there's going to be an auction, and what am I going to do when it doesn't fit in my modern apartment, and besides no one uses Gothic pieces now according to *House and Garden* which has such smart things in it . . . but that would be the least of my worries because as all my friends say I have a lot of originality when it comes to decorating my house so I don't understand you and I'm a bit offended that you should say you can't use this choir chair anywhere, how can that be, it's good, made of walnut, it was in the vestibule of my mother's house over on Dieciocho besides they say it's not true that they're going to do any tearing down, because Inés is coming to live here . . . they say she took the vow of poverty . . . with her millions . . . some-one who saw her in Rome, or in Switzerland, I don't know which, in one of those places, told me she's changed a lot . . . they say she stopped dyeing her hair . . . they say her hair's a very ugly gray . . . they say Mudito was brought up by the inmates and the nuns here at the Casa to be a sacristan, that's why he's so good, but he's on his last legs, the poor little thing's so tired that he looks as if he can't even see now . . . that's not true, I can see, my longing look's the only thing I still have left alive in me to connect me with my original self, because they say . . . they say that a woman who used to live here before in the laundry area heard, from a woman who died a long time ago and had heard it from another woman who knew me then, that I was a very lovely baby, with one of those small waxy faces sickly babies have, but with great big sad eyes as if I were always about to cry, and that a beggar woman in a shanty town found me one day at her door, naked, exposed to the rigors of the same night air Iris drives me out into so that I'll go and bring you to her, but all I can do is remain at the front window looking inside, and from out in the rain I see you in your library with its gray armchairs, as you open a panel that's not one hundred volumes of a greenish book with my name on its spine but simulates them, it's only a door to cover up the safe whose contents don't interest me, I'm only interested in getting back to the Casa with one percent less, now that I know that my name exists only on the spine of those hundred fake books, perhaps even my name is faked there, and wait for Iris to let me in like the beggar woman who found me one night at her door, out in the cold. No one in the shanty town knew who my mother was, much less my father, that's something no one ever knows, almost no one has a father, at most a nearsighted grade-school teacher with his dark suit covered with blackboard chalk. But my eyes were so heartrendingly sad—only sad then, an inferior form of the longing that later gave me so much power—that the beggar who found me realized my possibilities and didn't get rid of me, which would have been the natural thing to do because I was another mouth to feed and those were no times for cute faces . . . they say the old woman used to take me out bundled in rags, very few so that the cold would turn my skin blue, and beg in the streets or at church doors, when people came out after the evening novena. When she knew that the faithful were about to start coming out of church she'd pinch me to make me cry. There was so much pain in my face, my moans were so heartrending that kind people gathered around the old woman to see me cry and fill her hands with coins . . . they say the woman never gave me much to eat, so that I wouldn't grow fat and would always be on the verge of tears, starved, with skin you could see through, I was more touching like that, I brought in more money . . . they say, imagine Lucy, wicked tongues say that the old woman took sick and wasn't strong enough to go begging in the streets with me in her arms anymore because, although I was kept on a starvation diet, I was still growing and wasn't light anymore, and since she didn't go out but my fame had spread through the city, she used to rent me to other old women who carried me around in their arms, starving, weepy, to induce people to give alms, and the old women she rented me to also pinched me to make me cry, but when people came out of Mass the old women also petted me, especially when the faithful milled around us to give a little alms for the love of God . . . don't cry my darling, my poor little baby's such a darling, look at the way he cries, he can't help it, he has a spot on his lung, poor little thing, my only grandson, and my daughter's in the hospital and nobody knows where his father is, he's a sharp one all right, he played dumb and turned tail, and me, you can see for yourselves, a poor old invalid, I can't even work to buy a little milk, a piece of bread to put in his mouth so the child won't cry so much and when he doesn't cry it's worse because the look in his eyes . . . and back to the village dragging her slippers along the sidewalk so as not to pay busfare, the coins jingling in her pocket, weighed down, hidden in the folds of her rags, to turn me back in to the old woman who was neither my mother nor my grandmother, only my owner, and who died later on, and I was inherited by another old woman who died and left me to another old woman, and that old woman to another . . . they even say—can you believe it, Melania—that the very first inmate brought him here to the Casa, a very quiet and very good woman they say she was, her name was Peta Ponce, and she was the owner of Mudito, who was too big by then to take out begging, but that woman was very old, and they say one afternoon she went for a stroll alone through the passageways of the Casa, they're so long and get dark very early and there are so many courts and so many cellars and so many corridors, I don't know if you've seen the pile of cushions the auction people collected in the corridor of the next court, cushions and comforters and pillows, well, Melania, they're worth seeing, there are some good things, and as I was telling you, they say this woman went for a walk one fine day through the passageways and she got lost here in the Casa and was never found again, as if the depths had swallowed her up, they looked for her in the cellars and on all the floors but in vain, she never turned up and she doesn't appear in any records as being dead either, so I don't know where she can be . . .

"And now they've cut the electricity."

"Terrible, isn't it?"

"Why would they want to go and cut it?"

"Because they're going to start tearing the Casa down."

"But they're not going to tear it down."

"How come they're not going to tear it down?"

"How can they tear it down if Misiá Inés is coming?"

"Who told you, Amalia?"

"They say . . ."

"She can't come without electricity . . ."

"They only cut it for the time being . . ."

"What for?"

"They're repairing the wiring in Misiá Inés's cell."

"But let's not go wandering through the passages and get lost like the woman they say got lost here, what was her name, no, her name wasn't Peta Ponce, it was Peta Arce, no Peta Pérez Arce, why yes, and she wasn't the one who brought Mudito, because it was another woman who brought Mudito . . . in fact, they say it wasn't even a woman who brought him, they say Mudito arrived here one day when it was raining and . . ."

22

THE PAPER MISIÁ Raquel chose for Inés's cell turned out to be a very light, almost transparent, ocher with a design of lyres, like those the angels play in heaven, some white, others a darker ocher. Very sober, very elegant and not the least bit pretentious, fit for the room of someone who's taken the vow of poverty.

"How pretty."

She opened the suitcase on her bed.

"Yes isn't it?"

She got out of her topcoat and her black dress and put on slippers and a crimson dressing gown.

"It's so elegant, Misiá Inés! I'd always heard that Italian things nowadays are lovely . . ."

"It's Swiss. It's the only thing I bought in Europe, other than half a dozen or so black dresses, all alike, to last me till I die."

Mother Benita helps her hang the disappointing black dresses in the wardrobe and tells her that she thought the beatification was very far advanced and that that was the reason she'd lingered on in Europe. And the row of black shoes with their shoe trees at the bottom of the wardrobe.

"No, I was in a Swiss rest home after the breakdown I had when the cardinals said no . . ."

And she shakes her head, definitively, as the cardinals must have shaken their heads as they said that no, the Blessed Inés wasn't blessed, that you weren't capable of prolonging the family line with a boy and neither could you do it by pulling the beatification out of a chestful of old things and hanging its luster on the family tree . . . you shake your head; you look at yourself in the wardrobe mirror, you touch your hair and continue . . .

". . . and besides, I wanted to let my hair grow out so that I could come back gray, you'll remember that before I left I used to touch it up, a little like when I was young. I wanted to come back with this washerwoman's bun, without trying to impress, just like the old women who live here. And so, how are you, Mother Benita?"

"Very busy, at the moment, with the inventory for the auction."

"There won't be an auction."

"Have you spoken to the Archbishop?"

"Didn't I tell you I hadn't spoken with anyone? I took a taxi straight from the airport, I brought along one bag and sent the others home in another taxi. Let's see those auctioneers show their faces around here tomorrow . . . call me . . . I'm going to give them a good piece of my mind and send them packing, and let them go tell Jerónimo."

Mother Benita closes the shutters of the room. She bends down to put Inés's suitcase under the bed. As she straightens up again, she sees Inés observing the lyres with such intensity that she seems to want to go right through them, to bore right through the depth of the adobe walls and pull out something that's beyond all this and that not even you, Mother Benita, know about. Without changing the expression in her eyes, which remain fixed on the wall, without looking at her, she asks Mother Benita:

"And the doorkeeper? What was her name?"

"Rita."

"How is she?"

"Very well."

"Doesn't she have a message for me?"

"She hasn't said anything to me."

"Of course, Jerónimo hasn't called. He doesn't know I've arrived. The taxi with my things must have arrived while he was at the Club, and he won't know I'm here until later. If he calls, let Rita tell him I'm praying in the chapel and can't be interrupted. I came to pray and do penance here."

"But Misiá Inés!"

"What?"

"Don't you know?"

"No . . ."

"Didn't anyone tell you that the first thing they did was deconsecrate the chapel and that its doors have been boarded up for months, and they've taken out the stained glass windows and everything?"

Inés covers her face with her hands.

"How could they do such a terrible thing?"

"Father Azócar was in a big hurry about the auction so they could start tearing down . . . but things have been dragging on. There's no Mass or anything . . ."

Inés uncovered her face:

"Does Jerónimo even want to deprive me of Mass too?"

"Don't say that . . ."

"You don't know him . . ."

"No . . ."

"You don't know what he's like . . ."

"No . . ."

"I haven't come to the Casa to be deprived of Mass. I'm going to tell them to move my oratory at home in here. We can install it in the next room. And if the Father knows at all what's good for him, let him send me a priest to say Mass and bring me Communion every day . . . anyway, I'm going to see to all that tomorrow. I'm sleepy now . . . I'm going to bed . . ."

"That's too bad! The inmates are all in the kitchen, waiting for you to go and say hello to them . . ."

"Not tonight . . . I'm tired . . . tomorrow. Oh, Mother Benita, remember, and Rita too, that if Jerónimo calls me I can't talk to him . . . there's no chance of his coming here . . . he won't let me live in peace if he keeps calling me up. Always tell him I'm busy."

"Yes, of course."

"Thank you."

"Do you need anything else tonight, Misiá Inés?"

She wanders around the cell touching the lyres with her fingertips. She withdraws them suddenly, as if something had wounded them, and puts her hands in the pockets of her crimson dressing gown. She throws the nun a glance.

"I don't know, Mother Benita . . ."

"Well, I'm going then . . ."

"Where do you sleep?"

"In a court over there."

"The Casa's so huge!"

"Enormous."

"It's as if it had grown while I was away."

"We never get to know all of it."

"They say Mudito's the only one who knows it inside out. Is that true?"

"They say. But they say so many things . . . it's possible . . . everything's possible here in the Casa . . ."

"Good heavens, Mother, don't say such things."

She sits on the bed.

"Here's the buzzer to call when you need me."

"Thank you."

"Don't mention it."

"Mother . . ."

"Yes . . . ?"

"Will you people hear me if I scream?"

"But why should you scream?"

"I'm afraid of spiders."

"We cleaned this thoroughly."

". . . it's just that . . ."

Mother Benita put her benign hands on your shoulders. Standing in front of you, she sought your eyes to ease them with hers, but you turned yours away.

"What's wrong, Misiá Inés? Tell me . . ."

You won't look at her.

"You see, Mother, I've been having terrible bouts of insomnia ever since the beatification fell through. They couldn't do anything about them even in Switzerland, that's why I went into a rest home there. And the few times I do sleep, I have such nightmares, like prisons, as if I were never going to free myself from them and were condemned to live inside a nightmare forever, I often don't even know if I'm inside or out . . ."

"You don't know if you're asleep or awake . . . it's terrible . . ."

"How do you know?"

"I've had them too . . ."

"But not like mine, and I become so frightened. I think the best thing would be to put a phone here in my room in case . . ."

"In case what, Misiá Inés?"

"There's an odor of cement here."

"I don't seem to . . ."

"Haven't they been doing some building?"

"No, they're going to tear things down."

"The Casa wasn't this big."

"It can't have grown any bigger."

"But it wasn't this big."

"How can that be, Misiá Inés!"

You noticed, without knowing it, when you came into the Casa: the doorways I've walled up with bricks and cement, because rooms and galleries have to be walled up so that no one will get lost, I take care of this, the windows I've been sealing so that they won't be destroyed; unknown to Mother Benita or anyone else, I put plaster over them and paint in spots that look like dampness and old age so nobody will suspect that those rooms and galleries and courts and passageways are there behind them. No one notes the change. Only you, who know that when you wall up and close off, the space in the Casa gets bigger, not smaller, because no one, not even the demolition crew or the auction people, will ever be able to enter those places I've closed off.

"Is the bathroom making all that noise?"

"No, it's the drain in the court."

"It's not going to let me sleep."

"I'll have it fixed tomorrow."

"No, tonight. I have to rest."

"I'll go see."

"Wait, don't go yet."

"Do you need anything else?"

"I don't think so."

"Well, then . . ."

"Mother Benita . . ."

"Yes?"

"You believe, don't you?"

"In what?"

"In the Blessed Inés."

"Well, I . . ."

". . . it's just that I've been left so alone . . ."

"What about your husband?"

"You don't know him!"

Mother Benita doesn't understand. When she sits next to you on the bed, you get up and start walking around the room, looking at yourself in the oval wardrobe mirror as you pass it, pacing up and down, up and down your cell.

"But will you tell me, Mother Benita, what more proof that she was a saint can they want besides the existence of this Casa?"

"You'd better lie down . . ."

"Tell me, you, a woman of faith."

"Misiá Inés . . ."

"Tell me . . ."

"You mean about the famous earthquake . . . ?"

"And about her being buried here, in the Casa, and I'm going to find her remains even if I have to dig with my own nails . . . see what they're like now? Do you remember how well groomed my hands used to be? They were my pride. Look at them now . . ."

You take them out of your pockets and show them, trembling, their nails ruined, chipped. Mother Benita takes them, joins them together to stop them from shaking so and then puts them back in your crimson lap.

"It's a shame."

"Do you know what's happened?"

"Neglect . . . you're no longer interested in vanities . . ."

"No, when I'm asleep at night, the few times when I do sleep, it seems that I try to fasten onto something, anything, that I scratch the sheet, the bed, anything at all . . . you should have seen what I did to the head of my bed at the Grand Hotel in Rome because I was dreaming something I can't recall and was trying to hold onto anything at all, and later, in the daytime, I chew on my nails to stop them from hurting so much and they hurt even more . . . that's why I entered the rest home in Switzerland. I went through a very bad time in Rome."

"Don't you want to lie down?"

"No."

"A little cup of tea?"

". . . to burn everything, that's what I came for, to burn absolutely everything I keep stored away in my cells. I'm going to start off with that. But I want to let you know one thing, Mother Benita: I'm not burning anything without first going over it inside out and front and back. I'm going to read all the letters and clippings and contracts and the backs of the photographs. I'm going to go through all the drawers, all the boxes, the pockets of all the suits and dresses and overcoats and even costumes that have been put away and are being eaten by the moths, although Mudito takes such good care of everything . . . in linings and in portfolios, and, as I go over each thing, don't think I'm going to make gifts of them or give them to charities, I'm going to burn them all, all, and Mudito's going to help me . . ."

"But what do you want to find?"

"Anything, some clue that can put me on the right track. There was something. So that I won't scratch when I fall asleep, if I fall asleep, but I don't think I'll be able to get much sleep."

"Would you like a cushion too, besides your pillow?"

"No. I want to do penance."

"Since you've taken off your dressing gown, get into bed, don't walk around half naked, this cell's just been papered and it's still a bit damp. It'll dry up in a couple of days."

"What was I telling you, Mother Benita?"

"That you wanted to find something, I don't know what."

"That's what depresses me most."

"What?"

"That no one remembers, not even I."

"Sleep now. Get some rest. There's so much time ahead for

us to talk. Don't let things get you down. We're all going to spoil you like a baby here, you'll see. And you can stay as long as you want . . ."

Your unkempt gray hair's hanging loosely over your shoulders, your feet are bare, Mother Benita's trying to make you put on your slippers, begging you to lie down, to be calm, to drink a glass of water.

"How dare you be so impertinent, inviting me to live as long as I like in the Casa, when this Casa's mine and only mine? Yes, Jerónimo may have signed all the papers in the world but the Casa's mine, I don't want them to tear it down, I'm not going to let a single wrecker touch one of these walls, the Casa has a secret, something I can't put my finger on that neither you nor I nor anyone understands, but it's mine because I know it has a secret, it's mine, even if I never tear the secret out of it and the secret kills me, of course legally the property comes down through the male line, but it's the women who've preserved the Casa. I'm sure the reason the Casa's never left Azcoitía hands is that a succession of pious women whom no one can remember, each in her own way, with her wiles, her weaknesses, her little tricks and secrets that aren't in history books, has stopped her husband from getting rid of the place, always for irrational, completely subjective motives, it's impossible to understand those motives that made generations of Azcoitía women scheme and weave a protective net around the Casa . . . I don't know what we expect from the Casa . . . imagine us someday as we dig a hole in the linden-tree court, for example, and come up with the remains of the Blessed Inés . . . I'm going to keep them for myself alone, the saint's mine because no one else believes in her, not even you . . . I'm going to keep her because things must be kept, very carefully, even if at first glance they look like junk, they must be hidden, wrapped up, because as soon as you bring something worthwhile out into the light men confiscate it . . . it's mine, give it to me, you don't understand anything, go and do your sewing, go play bridge, call your cousin on the phone . . . they keep what you find, they understand what it means and know how to explain it and explain things away till they lose their meaning . . . I don't want to know what anything means, I want to find something so as not to dig with my nails at night when I fall asleep, if I sleep, at the foot of the bed, put it on me please, like that . . ."

"Do you want me to put out the overhead light and leave the one on the night table on?"

"Don't put out any of the lights, I'm going to sleep with all the lights on, and also leave the one out in the hall on, I don't know why they've spent money adding sections to the Casa lately if they're going to tear it down . . . I find it so huge tonight . . . I'll have to get used to it . . ."

"You'll see, in a few days you'll be happier than in your clinic, and you're not even going to dream."

Of course, Mother Benita, why should she dream, when I'm going to make sure I govern her sleep and lead her along until she gets lost in the passageways and runs into anyone I want, when I want.

"What a pity they didn't think of fixing me a cell next to yours, Mother."

"But you sent a cable asking us to find the oldest court . . ."

"That's true."

"You shouldn't be afraid."

"No."

"She's protecting you."

"If she ever existed . . ."

"Pray to God."

"God has more important things to worry about."

"Drink some water, and your Veronal."

"I don't intend to drink it just yet. How do I know what I'm going to dream tonight, the first night I sleep here in the Casa, maybe I'll dream and find out later on that, while I slept, someone, I don't know who or why, walled up the door of my dream with bricks and cement . . . I wonder why I smell such a strange odor . . ."

You look on every side.

"Someone's walking around . . ."

Your very fine ear, or your need of my presence, heard me scurrying away down the passageway. You signal to Mother Benita to come over and you whisper in her ear:

"The document certifying it . . ."

"Certifying what?"

"It vanished."

"That's impossible."

"Yes. I had it stored away in my cell. I'm sure of it. Jerónimo made it disappear so that the beatification would fall through."

"But Misiá Inés . . ."

"Everything necessary disappears. Only the useless things remain. Maybe it wasn't on Jerónimo's orders . . . I don't know, it disappeared because things sometimes disappear, that's all, but men need them and use them and they use them so much that they wear them out until they disappear . . . unless we ignorant women who understand nothing and know nothing about anything and get tired of everything and cry because we have nothing else to keep us busy, sometimes put things away, hiding them to stop them from using them and then throwing them away and going on to something else . . . not us, we put them away because we call one another up and talk about things and chatter and gossip, but in the nonsense and the gossip we tell one another on the phone, in bed, mornings, with crumbs from the breakfast toast on the bedspread, in that idiotic chatter, sometimes we preserve something that looks trivial, and another woman, a cousin we owe a visit, for example, and call up because going to see her is a bore, takes it into her keeping, wraps, preserves and passes it on. But I have no one to tell the story of the Blessed Inés, no one wants to believe that she even existed, and less still that she was a saint . . . poor little thing . . . she died so young . . . after I die no one will care that she died young. If I sleep well tonight and wake up with energy I'm going to start burning all the things in my cells. Tell Mudito to be ready early to help me, yes, even if he's not as strong as he used to be, even if he's only a shadow now, whatever he is now, he knows what's in my cell, we'll get on with it as soon as it starts to get light because I can see now that, with the noise coming from that drain I thought was the toilet tank, I won't be able to sleep a wink . . . now, after the trip, when I need my rest most. Here, give me the Veronal, Mother . . . who knows what I'm going to run into in my dream, the worst part's not being able to recall the horrors I dreamed. But wait, Mother, wait until I take the cream off my face . . . hand me the little mirror in the red pouch inside my black purse that's in the plastic bag, in a zippered compartment in the suitcase under my bed. Thanks, Mother Benita."

DURING THE DAY, I hardly budge from the choir chair except once in a while, to sit at the edge of the corridor, with my face in my hands, before going to the kitchen when it's cold, steadying myself against the walls of the passageways, you see me as you go by and talk with Zunilda Toro, shaking your head with a sigh, hoping I'll get my health back . . . poor Mudito, he has to get over this thing that's ailing him . . . well, Antonieta, how can it take so long, I'm waiting for him to get well before starting to go through the junk in my cell because I can't do it alone, he knows where everything is, I've forgotten where I put it all, I'd rather wait a few more days until Mudito's himself again so I can rest up before getting down to work . . . but you walk about with nothing to keep you busy, Inés, your piety can't find a center because Father Azócar still hasn't received the dispensation to set up your oratory next to your room, it isn't easy to pray with piety when you have to kneel on the floor. They follow you around . . . Misiá Inés is so good, what a pity she doesn't take care of herself like she used to . . . it would have been much more fun to see her arrive from Europe dressed to the hilt . . . of course . . . but how could she, when she's taken the vow of poverty . . . they say she's so rich she bought the Casa to come and live here and that's why they don't hold the auction, she's going to bring her oratory that has a gold altar, and they say that after that she'll gradually bring all her furniture and things from her house to furnish the Casa and make it look beautiful, that's why those intruders who used to come sticking their noses in everywhere and arranging numbered lots for the auction don't come around anymore now, why, they even wanted to pull down our shacks, where are we supposed to live if they pull down our huts, we're not going to start moving into the rooms at this point, especially when they're going to tear the place down, isn't that right, Misiá Inés . . .

"They're not going to tear it down."

"They're not, Misiá Inés?"

"Not while I'm alive."

"And you're in good health."

"Not like us, we're always coughing."

"Yes, but you don't have insomnia like me."

"Insomnia, Misiá Inés?"

"I sleep so little."

"Poor thing!"

Poor thing, it's terrible not to be able to sleep, but we sleep so much that we don't even know when we're asleep or when we're awake, everybody knows that Antonieta, the lanky old woman we saw you talking with the other day, falls asleep on her feet, and she goes on talking, asleep on her feet. Of course you can't keep busy sweeping, like us, or peeling potatoes, it's too bad you don't like to sew or embroider, the cross-stitch is very pretty.

"I used to like it once."

"But not anymore."

"I don't have peace of mind."

"It kills time."

"Later on . . ."

You often visit Rita in the vestibule. The afternoon Dora came back from her yearly day out at the home of her employers —a couple of days before the feast of St. Teresa, to prepare sweets for her employer's saint's day, because Dora's an angel at making pies and cakes—the three of them were in Rita's little parlor, next to the street door, where the wall telephone is and there's barely room enough for the table for jotting down messages, two chairs and the brazier. They fetched another chair for Inés, one of the little gilt chairs you find everywhere, with crimson damask seats, so that madam could sit there a little while. Dora showed up with two packages. She opened the bigger one: petits fours, slices of cake, meringues, cream puffs, chocolate éclairs, Dora's an angel at making sweetmeats, Misiá

Inés, Rita was telling her as she took the teapot from the coals to make the maté.

"Try some . . ."

And you did.

"This cream puff's delicious!"

"But I must say, Dora, I don't think this mocha cake turned out as well as last year's, I wonder why."

"My hand slipped when I put in the coffee."

"I'd forgotten to tell you, Misiá Inés . . ."

"What?"

"Father Azócar called."

"What did he want?"

"He'll be here tomorrow at eleven sharp."

"Oh, I guess it's to have me sign the papers for my oratory."

"That's right."

"And have there been any calls from my home?"

"Don Jerónimo."

"What did he say?"

"He asked when you were coming home."

You burst out laughing. Surprised, the old women opened their eyes wide, how is it possible that living in a palace where they say the two of them live alone with a dozen servants she should come here and she even laughs because her husband tells her to go back there . . . but Misiá Inés, my God, we'd all like to have someone worrying like that about us, we have no one, nobody misses us or worries about how we are or if there's anything wrong with us, outside of Mother Benita, that is, of course we don't want you to leave the Casa because then they'll tear it down and throw us out in the street to go around begging for charity, but you have to have a baby if you want to go begging and get people to give you money, because if you don't have a baby they don't give anything and where are we going to find a baby . . . Rita gives Dora a kick under the table to stop her from talking about things she shouldn't in front of persons like Misiá Inés, she may get mad, she's not going to understand, nobody understands us except ourselves, you have to be one of us to understand and believe in Iris's baby who suffers, sleeping with her, because Iris tortures him, she goes on throwing me out of the Casa every night and won't let me back in till daybreak, when I'm dead tired, limp in a passageway, in the choir chair that belonged in the hall of my mother's house over on Dieciocho . . . what do you mean you can't use it, Mother, and if you can't use it then auction it off and whatever you get for it will be my donation to Children's Village, but I won't have them coming around to ask me for more money afterwards, I haven't had so much as a glimpse of Inés, they say she arrived looking a mess, I'm dying to see her, but as soon as the doorbell rings she hides like a mouse, I've been here once this week and twice last week, but I haven't even caught a glimpse of her, my friends can't believe it when I tell them over the phone that it's true that Inés scurries off and hides as if she had leprosy; they say, of course, that she may have it, and that's why Jerónimo shut her away with the excuse that she took the vow of poverty, tell that to the marines, as if we didn't know Inés used to be so fond of clothes, although I heard someone say that she goes around with gray hair now and a tight bun and black dresses that make her look like a country priest's poor cousin, what will Jerónimo say, he must be fit to be tied, next week I have to go back to the Casa because I'm going to measure a hammock so I can have cushions made for it, of course Inés's letting herself go like that is the last straw, it's only a matter of taking a little care of yourself, look at me and I'm three, no, two years older than she . . . They haven't been able to see you because you hide when they ring the bell. When they don't ring it you spend the afternoon with Rita, beside the telephone.

"And this other package, what is it, Dora?"

"A Dog Track the youngest boy gave me."

"Let's see."

"I know how to play horse races, but not dog races. Maybe it's played the same way."

"The boy gave me the Dog Track because he lost three dogs and only these three are left, they're plastic, this one's red, this one blue, this one yellow."

"Bitch."

"What's that, Misiá Inés?"

"It's a bitch."

"How can you tell?"

"They're better for racing."

"Do you want to play, Misiá Inés?"

"All right."

"But how? The boy gave me the Dog Track because he also lost the die and you can't play dog or horse races without any dice."

"They say María Benítez has one."

"Why don't you go ask her to lend it to you, Dora? I really feel like seeing my yellow bitch run so I can see what she can do."

When Dora left, you opened your legs, rested your elbows on your knees and held your hands out over the coals. Then you told Rita, almost indifferently, to call up your home and ask for Jerónimo, without saying that you were next to the telephone, and tell him that you wanted him to send over a set each of Parcheesi, checkers and dominoes tomorrow . . . in fact, all the games he could find or think of. Rita dialed the number. You waited beside her.

"Doesn't anyone answer?"

"No."

"That's strange!"

"Why?"

"Because he's always home at this time, lying down, listening to the political news on the radio, with the telephone at his elbow. And, besides, all the servants . . ."

"Now . . . Hello!"

All smiles and bowing as if Don Jerónimo could see her over the phone, Rita tells him she's sorry if she woke him up . . . no, no, she didn't wake him up . . . this is Rita speaking, the doorkeeper at the Casa . . . and Don Jerónimo greets her, saying that he recognizes her voice because they've had to speak together so often lately, asking how Inés is, he's upset because if they call him at this hour from the Casa it means something's happened to Inés . . . no, sir, how could you even think of such a thing, madam couldn't be in better health, very calm and happy . . . Inés grabs the phone away from Rita to hear her husband's voice and returns it so that Rita can answer, she lets them talk some more and takes it away again to hear his voice, then they say goodbye and hang up. Dora comes in with María Benítez. The four women barely fit in the doorkeeper's cubicle. Rita knits her brow.

"What's this one come for?"

"She latched on to me. She wouldn't lend me the die unless I let her come along. She was in bed. I had to wait for her to get dressed."

"What an old pain-in-the-neck!"

"My God, Misiá Inés!"

"What?"

"You talked exactly like Rita."

"Let's see, do it again."

"What an old pain-in-the-neck! The busybody, I don't know why she comes barging into my little parlor when nobody asked her. The smell of the pastry must have brought her, wouldn't you know, you can't have a little peace and quiet anyplace . . ."

They listen open-mouthed to your old voice and phrases of an old woman. They break out laughing, and so do you. You tell them you can imitate any voice. Dora's. Rita's. María Benítez's. You can even imitate that of Brígida, who's been dead going on one year. You play a guessing game. Rita leaves the room and they shut the door. The other two remain inside with Inés and she talks like María Benítez: María Benítez, Rita guesses correctly. María Benítez goes out next. Inés talks like Dora: Dora, María guesses correctly, what an entertaining game, just like in a circus, we'll have to play it with more old women someday, with all the old women when we're all together in the kitchen after Mass some Sunday and with the orphans too, they'll get a big kick out of this new game, and also the games Don Jerónimo said he's going to send over with his chauffeur tomorrow. It was Dora who suggested:

"I'll bet that on the telephone Don Jerónimo would know you're not Rita."

"I bet he wouldn't."

"I bet he would."

"What do you bet, Dora?"

"The Dog Track."

"All right. And if *I* win? I'll give you this black dress."

"But that's too much, Misiá Inés."

"And you only have six."

"I'll bet you this woolen dress against the Dog Track the boy gave you, it's a good one, Swiss, very warm, it'll fit you perfectly."

"All right."

You dial your home. You wait a little. It's he . . . What do you want, Rita, what's wrong this time, you've got me worried because I'm sure something's happened to Inés and you don't want to tell me anything . . . no, no, how can you think such a thing, Don Jerónimo, it's only that she's cold and wants her fur coats sent to her, the mink, it wears so well, she says, and the astrakhan, and also the little box with all her jewels, they're not many and they're not very important, but Misiá Inés says—she's so pious—that she made an offering she has to pay for with all her jewels now that she's taken the vow of poverty, Don Jerónimo. What do you want me to tell her, Don Jerónimo? . . . Tomorrow at twelve? . . . You're coming over? She can't see you because she wants to rest, maybe later, next week or the week after, not now because she wants to pray a lot and repent of all her sins although I don't know what sins a lady as Catholic as Misiá Inés can be talking about, well, you're to send everything, the games and the coats and the little jewel box, with the chauffeur tomorrow at twelve . . . Of course, Don Jerónimo, and you take care of yourself too, sir. I'm sorry to bother you like this, sir, I'm only obeying Misiá Inés's orders . . . You hung up: you four old women burst out laughing and, while you laughed till tears rolled down your faces, you, Inés, were getting ready to wrap up Dora's Dog Track.

"The die belongs to María Benítez."

"Take it, María."

"Thank you, madam."

"What do you use it for?"

"I had it put away."

"I'll play you for it."

"At what?"

"At dog races."

"Against what?"

"Whatever you want."

"Will that dress fit me?"

"I'll bet it against your die. All right, María, you're the red bitch, I'm the yellow bitch. Too bad these animals are so ordinary, plastic, knowing him, I'm sure tomorrow Jerónimo's going to send me a Chinese chess set and an ivory and ebony checkerboard, that's the kind of spendthrift and show-off he is. But look, Dora, this Dog Track board's really old, it's junky, don't you see how it's splitting here in the middle where it folds, it's where Dog Track boards always split, tomorrow, when I have a little spare time, I'm going to sew it together so it won't tear all the way."

"How scary, madam, don't talk like Brígida!"

"It may be a sin, she's been dead a year! Why, she even puts on an old woman's voice . . ."

"I *am* old."

"But you're not María, or Dora, or Rita, or Brígida, you're your own self."

"But I can be Brígida."

"How?"

"Put out the lights."

"I'd sooner die . . . !"

"Amalia, woman, hand me the cookie tin and go tell Mother Benita to stop by here for a little while when she has the time, I have something to tell her, but she's not to put herself out on my account, only when she has a bit of spare time . . ."

Then you laugh like Brígida, and the three old women, serious, huddled in a corner, staring at your stammering, toothless jaw, while your hands move like Brígida's with her little finger sticking up a bit, beg you not to, it scares them, and then you laugh again and tell them, ready, girls, pull your chairs up for a game, no, I'm only going to play with María; all right, the highest number starts . . . Me, six. You, four, I start . . . six again, bravo, it's my turn again . . . four, into the water, back I go. You María, don't shake the die so much with your hands, they're like sticks . . . you throw, your dog moves, runs, gallops, sprints ahead . . . mine can't make it, she falls into the water again and again and again, what rotten luck, I can't pass ahead, she left me behind, my yellow bitch is old, she's useless, she's lame, shriveled up, she doesn't run, she barely drags herself along and almost can't get out of the water while María's bitch reaches the finish line without any trouble.

"María won!"

"You won . . ."

"It's a male, that's why!"

You throw the little plastic animal into the brazier, it chars, you watch it burn as your angry eyes wait for it to be consumed in the wave of fetid smoke, it melts as it hisses on the coals, your eyes burn with the smoke from the plastic . . . what a nasty smell, it's like sulfur, what thick smoke . . . while the old women undress you in the cloud of smoke, stripping off your black woolen dress for María . . . I'm going to have to take in the dart a little . . . I saw you through the smoke, Inés, your naked body shivering, yes, I saw it, I saw it, you can't deny that I saw your body this time and I recognize it, now that the old crones, laughing at your failure, have undressed you and you've come out of the smoke, stooped with defeat, your head hanging down, while, from the doorway that spewed out fetid smoke, the three crones tell you to watch out for the drafts . . . look how the wind carries off the smoke from the yellow bitch . . . sleep well, Misiá Inés.

"I wish I could."

"Good night."

"Good night."

23

I DON'T WANT you to burn anything yet. We'll burn everything when the right time comes. That's why I spend the day being sick, huddled up in my Gothic choir chair in the sun, keeping an eye on you while you wait for me to get well and help you: sitting in the kitchen corridor, you peel potatoes into a pot, with a tattered old woman who may have been Mother Anselma once and with two others who are telling you all about Brígida's funeral. You get up. You say that you have to go and sweep your room . . . no, no, Misiá Inesita, don't you bother, I'll sweep it for you, I'll wash your undies, your stockings, white clothes shouldn't be hung out in the sun because they turn yellowish but you can do it if you hang them wrong side out . . . it makes no difference, because I don't have white undergarments anymore and I want to do it all myself, no one must work for me. It's not something I intended to do but one day I found myself sweeping my room, making my bed, washing my clothes as if it were the most natural thing in the world. I peel potatoes. They mustn't send me my oratory. I pray by kneeling on the floor like the others, and if they can spend their lives without the Sacraments so can I . . . Ladies come, friends or acquaintances of mine, to look for things in their cells and they ask Mother Benita: Don't they say Inés Azcoitía lives here now? I haven't seen her since before she left for Europe! How is she? Why don't you tell her I'd like to say hello to her? . . . They don't realize I'm across the court, they go past me without recognizing me and they leave again, annoyed because they came to snoop and didn't see me . . . they say Inés goes around like a real sad mess, imagine, with her millions, and has gotten so old it breaks your heart, she used to be one of the most elegant women, it's unbelievable . . . but on their way back from their cells the ladies—before they were simply Picha and Olga and Rosa and Tere, but now they're *the ladies*—don't recognize me as they go past, they had to be satisfied with a rolled-up hall rug that Iris Mateluna pulls along on the cart that used to be Mudito's but that he can't pull anymore because Mudito hasn't been well at all, he spends the whole day in the choir chair that's decorated with wooden gargoyles . . . and you come over and put your benign hand on my arm and ask me: How are you this morning?

I barely move my head. My eyes are clouded. You go on your way after taking your hand off my arm that's been paralyzed by the bandages, off my body that's been exhausted by my nightly excursions, if you knew, Inés, if you knew what I know and don't want to tell you, I can't tell you because it has me paralyzed and exhausted, that's what's been wasting me away more and more, I'm already so puny that an old woman could carry me in her arms, but I slip out at night and go to the yellow house across from the park and peer in the window and I hear voices, Don Jerónimo and Misiá Raquel speaking, Misiá Raquel will be coming today, she's respected your wishes but Don Jerónimo begs her and she agrees, she'll be coming to tell you that you're too hard on him, Inés.

"What do you want me to do?"

"I don't know."

"Go get in bed with him?"

"How can you think of a filthy thing like that?"

"You see?"

"What?"

"That it's a filthy thing."

"It's only a manner of speaking . . ."

"Let them leave me alone, especially Jerónimo. Workers have a right to retire and I don't see why I shouldn't have the same right, sixty-three years old, my God, if I'd had children, if I were a grandmother now, Jerónimo would leave me alone . . . He's not going to leave you alone, you know it, he has to get even with you because you didn't give him the son he needed and he won't let me rest . . . the thought of Jerónimo touching me again sexually drives me out of my mind, I can't bear it . . . you put your arms around her and you cry together and you tell her not to cry, that she can't believe that Jerónimo, a gentleman . . . that's what you think, Raquel, he's lying in wait for me out there and as long as he stalks me and waits for me I'll have no peace, all I can have is fear, and the only thing that protects me are these walls he wants to pull down, that's why I have to lose myself among the old women."

"Did you know that Brígida had died?"

"I'm going to have some Masses said for her."

"Thanks. She was fond of you."

"I was fond of her too."

"It's strange, Inés . . . I've felt for a long time that you're withdrawn, aggressive, as if you didn't like me anymore, but when I think that you really loved Brígida, I feel touched by your affection. Because there's no love in you, Inés, it's as if they'd cut it out in an operation, of course the clinic in Switzerland, it's common knowledge . . . they say Inés was in Switzerland, imagine . . . why should she go there when she's always had an iron constitution . . . in a sanatorium . . . for her nerves . . . yes, it could be for her nerves, but there are other things you don't know about: Inés didn't travel to Europe to see about the beatification, that was her excuse, she could have taken care of that matter in a couple of weeks but she stayed a whole year. She could have continued the process by correspondence, Don Jerónimo tells Misiá Raquel in his library with the gray armchairs, he shows her Inés's dossier, he tells her that he even understands your checking into the clinic in Switzerland and staying all the time you needed to recover from the blow—this beatification business of Inés's is nonsense, but after all why should I interfere—but Don Jerónimo's telling Misiá Raquel something else but I can't make it out; the noise the passing cars make, my terror that they'll see me peeping into a rich man's house and may drag me off to jail, cause me to dodge out of sight every time anybody goes past, I can't make out all the words I have to hear in order to follow what's being said, I can't hear because the blowing of the wind deprives me of my hearing; you two talking behind that glass window in the library, the flames in the fireplace, a friendship of many years, more than a half-century, slight blood ties, an intimacy I've never been able to approach, you tell each other things and confess secrets no one on this side of the glass window can hear because the noise is unbearable and I catch only snips of the dialogue that ought to make everything clear to me before you talk with Inés:

"Didn't you make a pilgrimage to Fatima and Lourdes?"

"Yes. But I didn't go to Europe for that, Raquel."

"Yes I know, for the beatification."

"No, for something much more difficult. I went there to become old. To do the one thing that would make him leave me alone."

"I don't understand . . ."

"The Swiss clinic . . ."

Dr. Azula with his single eye gleaming rapaciously. Scaly hands, fingers like claws nobody can break loose from, stretched you out in a bed like the one I know, opened your body, played with your insides, examined them, rearranged them, picked out some that interested him and, while his assistants, also monstrous behind their immaculate masks, sewed you up, he slipped off his rubber gloves. In her head nurse's cap, Emperatriz came to ask how the operation had turned out.

"A rich woman's whim, that's all."

"What good is a hysterectomy at sixty-three? I don't get it."

"That's the secret all the ladies who go to the Casa at La Chimba to poke around would like to know, my dear."

"And what is that secret, Cris?"

"She came to have me take out her uterus."

"Well, our clinic's the most famous in all Europe, so there's nothing extraordinary in her coming here . . ."

Dr. Azula looked at her, his single eye misty with tenderness, love, recognition, satisfaction, fulfillment. He placed his claw on Emperatriz's stubby hand.

"What would have become of me if it weren't for your energy and your drive? I owe you everything . . ."

"Not everything . . ."

"I'd have gone on getting drunk at La Rinconada, as Boy's

slave, if we hadn't escaped in time that night in the downtown café . . ."

Emperatriz is impatient. With the years, Cris is becoming sentimental. He's always harking back to other times.

"Yes, Cris. Look. Are we going to keep her uterus?"

"What for? No."

Of course not, it's no good. You sit on the edge of your bed and cover your face with your hands while Misiá Raquel listens, worried that you're inventing all this, Inés, you've always liked to tell stories, you have an old woman's gift for it, it's simply a matter of letting the old woman blossom forth and take over, that's why Misiá Raquel listens to you, seated in her chair, very rigid, with her handbag gripped tightly with both her hands, because neither she nor anyone else can believe that you bled every month at the age of sixty-three . . . filthy, regular blood that enslaved me like a young girl, at my age, as if it were God's punishment for some horrible thing I did and can't remember, every month, without fail, you don't know how I've prayed, especially when I was younger and had hopes of giving Jerónimo a child, Peta Ponce and I prayed and prayed, Hail Holy Queen after Hail Holy Queen, Our Fathers without letup and Our Fathers said backwards, prayers we ourselves made up to implore mercy of whoever wanted to grant it, scapulars with I don't know what relics that Peta would sew into my corset covers, you can't imagine how Peta and I prayed that this month, at last, my blood wouldn't defile me, thus announcing my purity and Boy's coming, I was the filthy slave of my blood up to my sixty-third year . . . don't cry anymore, Inés, let Misiá Raquel console you without being able to, because you go on crying and crying, you hoped each month that that month your femaleness had at last been exhausted, that you were to have peace so that you could begin growing old like everybody else, but no, blood every month without letup . . . a monster, Raquel, a monster. The worst part of it is that Jerónimo's always been fascinated by monsters.

"Of course. Remember that secretary he had years ago, almost but not quite a dwarf, with a badly sewn harelip and kind of hunchbacked . . . a calamity, you remember him, don't you?"

"I think so."

"What was his name?"

"Yes, I know the one you're talking about . . ."

"His name was . . . wait . . ."

"How should I remember!"

"He was odd."

"But not such a monster as I, Raquel, yes, you admit you're the real monster, Inés, and you go on being one in spite of your operation, because you're going to tell Misiá Raquel that Jerónimo wouldn't leave you alone up until the time you left, that at your age, at sixty-three, your husband, also a monster, forced you to make love with him every night as if you were youngsters, no one can believe you, Inés, and that night Misiá Raquel will go and pay Jerónimo a visit and question him . . . I can't hear very well because a broken-down streetcar goes by, and a truck at the same time, cars, the fire engine sirens, and couples whisper in doorways and the bells of the church of La Merced, I can't make out what you're explaining to Misiá Raquel and I have to go running back to the Casa so as not to miss what Inés is confessing to her between sobs, to at least know the lie even if I don't know the truth . . . very gently, with great tenderness, Jerónimo would start getting affectionate, and I'd end up letting him—why not—even though I had little patience left and frankly I'd have preferred to say my beads or read the evening paper, except that he wouldn't let me. He'd fondle me more and more, gradually, you know very well that at my age no one's a bargain in bed anymore . . . not walking in the corridors of the Casa either, Inés, when you stop by the choir chair to chat with the gargoyles . . . how are you, Mudito, how are you this morning . . . why it looks as if this man starts each day more shrunken than the day before, poor little thing . . . and you go on walking toward your room and, sitting on the edge of your bed, you assure Misiá Raquel that at your age it makes you feel a little ashamed . . . I don't know, with everything drooping, a complete cave-in, so that you even feel some repugnance for yourself, but it doesn't bother Jerónimo, it's as if he didn't see it and wouldn't allow me to be as old as I am, as if the frigidity of my old woman's body didn't have a right to exist, and little by little, every night, he'd awaken, from deep inside my body of a tired old woman, the young woman I neither was nor am. I could have surrendered to him coldly, being able to do this was my only hope, but no, impossible, Jerónimo wasn't satisfied with that pretense that was usual in so many women, he succeeded in exciting me and making me respond despite my sixty-three years, it was as if he had to assign me the horrible job of bringing back to life the remains of a young, enthusiastic Inés and becoming incarnate in her. It's exhausting to come back to life every night."

"Such a lack of respect in Jerónimo! And why didn't he find himself another woman?"

"Don't you see what it was he wanted?"

"What every man wants, I suppose."

"No."

"What?"

"Haven't I told you I was still the same every month?"

Of course, it's what made him interested in you, Inés, don't think it was anything else, he never loved you and you always knew it and you know it now and in order to get even you let Dr. Azula mutilate you, it was the only thing that bound him to you and to no other woman. Jerónimo could have had all the mistresses he pleased, that's what you're telling Misiá Raquel as you try to convince her that all this isn't a lie, that he wasn't impotent from that night on, you'd die of shame if your friends knew Jerónimo never touched you again because I didn't let him, I robbed him of the possibility of doing it and I've come to store it away here where the old women strap me down every night to eliminate me and I let myself be eliminated because I eliminate Jerónimo by letting myself be eliminated, that's what you should tell Misiá Raquel instead of these tall stories, I'll tell her how we used to frequent Doña Flora's place, with Hortensia, Rosa, Amapola tumbling with him before my eyes that restored everything to him, no, you don't want anyone to know, you're ashamed because after that night at La Rinconada he gave you up forever and you're telling Misiá Raquel that you implored God to let Jerónimo fall in love with someone else and leave you alone. He's always left you alone. You tell her he brought you back to life every night, when the truth is that you've always been a castoff.

Sheltered under the lintel of the window, because it's started to drizzle, I can almost hear him; through the glass curtains, I feel as if I'm almost being singed by the blue electric flash of his eyes . . . she used to lie to me, Jerónimo's telling her, Inés used to lie to me a great deal, she'd tell me she was one or two weeks late on a given month, and I'd leave her alone so as not to deform my son. I'd give her jewels, and the mink and everything . . . until I couldn't stand it anymore, Raquel, I couldn't go on deceiving him, I couldn't bear to see his hope growing, and then I'd confess to him, as I'd weep, that yes, it was no, no again, blood again. I couldn't bear to see him suffering in hope . . . you can't imagine how this woman made me suffer, Raquel . . . but you too are lying, Don Jerónimo, because you stopped suffering a long time ago, when you killed the yellow bitch at La Rinconada and sank forever into your armchair at the Club and into your oratorical displays in the Senate . . . that's why, Raquel, so as not to see the poor man suffer, I let it go on night after night, I swear it, without letup, my husband conjured up in this old woman that I am, who only wants to rest and have peace for her devotions and not have to do anything, a passionate body that responded to his, but it wasn't my body and, because it wasn't me, it responded, though I'd have given anything in the world not to respond . . . I had the right not to be a monster, and he killed that right in me.

It's a dialogue you keep up with the gargoyles of the choir chair, incarnations of fear, deaf, mute, perhaps blind, agents of the Void, panic that prefers to writhe and transform itself into monsters rather than be nothing . . . look at this court filled with sunlight; the old women have rolled up the sleeves of their blouses because it's hot. Gargoyle arms. Gargoyle hands carrying a sooty teapot. One of them, sitting at the edge of the corridor, yawns and it seems that everything, we, the court, the sun, are all about to disappear down the interminable dark passageway that starts in her mouth. Another woman ties a string around a bundle of magazines. Mother Benita walks by, they smile at her, greet her, ask her for things, and she leaves, because she has so much work to do, closing the door behind her. I'm aware of the nauseating stench of the food in the kitchen, of faces held together by the threads of their wrinkles, and you confess that your failure as Jerónimo's wife makes you persist in giving him an ancestress who'll relate him to God.

"Those are old wives' tales, Inés."

"That may be, Raquel, but old women have powers and prerogatives that young women don't know about, an anarchy in which everything's allowed, no obligations to fulfill because nobody cares whether they fulfill them or not. And by keeping me young, Jerónimo, forever after me, robbed me of my old woman's prerogatives and powers. Do you remember how often I used to come to the Casa?"

"That mania of yours for collecting junk . . . it never seemed normal to me."

"You're very wrong. It was the most normal thing in the world, old women collect things, I used to come here just as naturally as these old women grow feeble, become decrepit, more useless every day without its having any effect on anyone, getting ready to disappear, the enviable simplicity with which they gradually die off . . . I used to envy them, it's a form of freedom I couldn't buy, I went on being the slave of an order, of cycles that revived hope till finally I couldn't go on and left for Europe with the beatification as an excuse."

I listen to you and I can't believe you. You reduce it to an excuse. Then why do you go into your cells every day to rummage through your things? Looking for something? Or simply to rummage like the old women among their odds and ends? Dr. Azula stripped you of the possibility of being a woman . . . I can't go on, Raquel, he can't go on, no one can, I'm free, I *wouldn't be able* to feel anymore, I belong to that different sex, the sex of old women.

"And does Jerónimo know?"

"Certainly."

"How?"

"I wrote to him, right after the operation. I'd thought it would be best to tell him when I got back, but during my convalescence I realized I didn't dare face him, it would be absolutely impossible to face him with what I'd done to free myself . . . no, I couldn't and I decided to write instead of giving him an explanation to his face . . ."

"Was that when he got rid of the Casa? We all blamed it on one of his famous fits of rage because you hadn't returned or something like that . . . yes, Misiá Raquel, you can't tell by looking at him, but he felt rage and terror and the need to get rid of everything, why should he hang on to the Casa, it was as if this place were the embodiment of his hope . . . it wasn't good for anything now . . . but it's never been good for anything, Inés, you've never understood that, it's the most terrifying and important thing about the Casa, that's why we're shut up in it and why I'm walling up rooms and windows and corridors and courts, so nobody will use them, so they'll disappear from memory, to erase the place Jerónimo knew you were fond of . . . now the filth, the lots of junk, with their labels written in blue pencil, that have been piled up by the auction people in the passageways—the auction's a thing of the past—will remain there forever, with me in my choir chair, with the mounds of moth-eaten cushions bearing lot number 2013; who's going to give anything for it all, only junk dealers will come, there won't be an auction, but neither will there be a Children's Village, there will only be an ever growing number of old women here, we'll invent rites and very carefully cultivated manias, we'll hate one another, we'll listen to what two old women are whispering on the other side of the partition . . . I wonder who has some maté . . . Lucy has a sty . . . the best thing for it is to rub it with a fly's rear end, that's the way to cure it . . . let this be your world, don't let him come to see you, I'm now closing off doors to keep him from ever entering the Casa, I don't want to see him here, I want to become blind besides deaf and dumb, so as not to see him. I want to protect you, Inés, that's never interested him. Doesn't it frighten you more when you think it's *you* he wants? You've done right to seek refuge in the myth of the son, leaving Don Jerónimo outside to clamor without shelter. You're afraid he'll come and touch you now . . . and go on wanting to touch me, even without hope, that would be worse than anything else, unbearable, I can't stand it . . . you say so many strange things, Inés, you're not the same person anymore . . . my lifelong friend, almost a cousin . . . Inés and Raquel are inseparable . . . I don't recognize you and I won't deny that you disgust and frighten me a little.

"How are you going to recognize me when I don't even recognize myself? It's as if someone else were saying the things I'm saying and feeling what I'm feeling."

Of course, Misiá Raquel looks at you and realizes you're not you. For once, although you don't know it, you're not lying. Dr. Azula left you very little: your hair, gray now, but still the same, your fingernails, chipped from digging them into the same nightmares the old women scratch at night in the Casa to save themselves, to keep from falling, so that they won't be dragged off, and of course your skin, your surface, neglected and blemished now, but still yours. What you don't know is that Dr. Azula and Emperatriz changed everything inside the sack of your skin. Dr. Azula's sure eye and his claws that know how to select, Emperatriz's white coif, her concentration as she goes over the accounts and assigns duty hours, behind a white desk in a white room I know, surrounded by white nurses with masks who move about silently in white gum-soled pumps so as not to disturb Cris, who was snoring in their double bed. He slept a great deal. Almost all the time, in fact, till very late in the morning, interminable siestas, drowsy lolling in hammocks during the day, yawns at dusk or between courses at meals. Boredom, Cris claimed. But the truth was that he spent his time like that because he drank too much: his breath ready to go up in flames if anyone held a match to it, his single eye glazed, twitching, bloodshot, and the glass of whiskey always at his elbow. Of course he was bored. But it was his own fault: work, what you call real work, well, he'd had none for years, what with Boy healthy and grown now and developing like any adolescent . . . some acne, tonsillitis in winter, a dislocation of one of the ankles of legs that had always been very weak, things like that.

Emperatriz had to tell him more than once not to be stupid and to stop pestering her about the clinic he was so homesick for, to cut the nonsense about being sorry he'd come to shrivel up here at La Rinconada, a desert without incentives to goad him into recovering his former ambition to remain in the vanguard of his specialty. Shut up, Emperatriz screamed at him, spineless, that's what you are, you say you miss your scientific activities but you prefer your siestas, your whiskey. When she married him she thought she was marrying someone who was *someone,* a genuine scientist . . . only to end up with this: a drunkard who snored. At first, when her spouse's lamentations touched her, she used to tell him all right, don't worry, we've saved the fortune we have in the Banque de Genève, if you want we'll get out of here and set up the clinic in Switzerland, I'll help you turn it into a center that will spread knowledge to all parts of the world. Those plans, kept so alive during the first years, gradually faltered, until time reduced them to nothing. Once Cris had left behind him what he called *the heroic campaign* to save the life of the monster who'd have died without his own expert, but also monstrous, hands, he wanted to publish a study of the case. Don Jerónimo stopped him.

"Dr. Azula, I hired you to attend my son, not to use him as a means of acquiring prestige."

And that ended it. He had three whiskeys instead of one that night. And from then on, everything, projects, ambitions, everything, ended in nothing. Cris used to tell his wife:

"Don Jerónimo made me give up."

"Cut the nonsense. You're just like Humberto Peñaloza, who used to insist that Jerónimo robbed him of the will to write his famous book and that he had to get rid of Jerónimo to regain his strength."

After Humberto's disappearance, Jerónimo delegated the pair, as two intelligent, united persons, to continue the experiment at La Rinconada and carry it through to the end. Now the entire weight fell on her poor feminine shoulders! But the real torture was the annual trip to see Jerónimo and give him a broad description of things at La Rinconada during the year just ended: all the lies she had to think up to keep Jerónimo happy without tempting him to pay a visit as he proposed to do on one occasion when she got carried away and painted him a picture that was far too rosy . . . well, it wasn't easy. She, a poor, weak, and helpless woman, was the only one with the shrewdness to defend their paradise with this annual excursion to make up the lies to keep him away from La Rinconada.

What would happen to him, Cris, and to all of them, if that same evening, in the library with the deep gray velvet chairs, she decided to tell him the truth about everything that had been happening in La Rinconada all those years? She, Emperatriz, could say one sentence to her cousin, and exterminate them all with it. What would Jerónimo say . . . or rather, what would he do, if she told him what was going on . . . for how many years now? Since Humberto left. Naturally. What would Jerónimo say if he saw the rich food Boy gobbles down? The cakes as spectacular as castles made of meringue, ice cream and the multicolored crystal of candied fruit? And the plum velvet cloak Boy liked to wear, and the elaborate clothes he donned at banquets to which everyone was invited, the tables loaded with bowls of fruit like skyscrapers, candelabra with countless branches, turkeys, partridges, the expression of the pork with the apple in its mouth and the parsley look in its eyes? Let them go ahead and drink, eat, get inebriated. A babble of shouts drowned out by the music of intricate instruments that Brother Mateo copied from antique models and he himself played. People in each other's arms on the rugs and on the cushions, clusters of dwarfs climbing up to the naked breasts of *the fattest woman in the world,* sucking on them two and three at a time and sliding down the giantess's braids, hunchbacks biting the cheeks of Berta's rump. Boy whipping her, whipping Emperatriz, with bunches of grapes and spraying the body of Melchor, who was in a drunken stupor, with powdered sugar and that of Melisa with red wine, and making Rosario dance on her crutches. What would he say if he knew that, ever since he was very small, Boy chased after all the women, waving his huge organ at them, and that, following strict orders from Emperatriz, they—whoever they happened to be: Berta, she herself, Melisa, the operator with ears like bat wings, anyone—let themselves be chased a little only to give in to anything Boy wanted, after their mandatory screams, behind the bushes? What would Jerónimo say?

Year after year she gave Jerónimo a report on Boy's fictitious progress, keeping to the general lines of the initial project, which was followed so closely until Humberto disappeared. When Jerónimo found out about his secretary's flight, he almost threw the whole thing over. He came to La Rinconada on an inspection visit. But he was so delighted with the limbo that held sway over Boy's five-year-old mind that he decided to leave everything in Emperatriz's hands, Emperatriz being the cousin so dear to him, and in those of Dr. Crisóforo Azula, a truly remarkable man, judging by the results he obtained. But as the child passed from infancy into puberty and then from puberty into adolescence, it became very clear that it would be impossible to keep him in limbo. How could one avoid toothaches and the divine relief of aspirin? Why do they ache, why does the pain stop, what's happening and then not happening to me? How could one hide the cold of winter and the warmth of spring? Emperatriz never tired of repeating that she was sure Humberto had fled through cowardice when he began to realize that the fictitious limbo would collapse because Boy had an uncontrollable nature, that everything, in fact, was uncontrollable. Or uncontrollable for him because, if the truth were told, in her own way she, Emperatriz, was controlling and had controlled everything for more than ten years: with lies. Those lies once a year were enough. And Boy's weak legs, an ailment they'd never tried to cure. Emperatriz made all means of locomotion disappear—cars, carriages, calashes, mules, horses, donkeys, bicycles, hand trucks, anything that aided human movement—leaving him reduced to the radius covered by the capacity of his feeble legs, so that she could let Boy go out into the park and anywhere he liked and feel sure that the world he could know would automatically be limited by his weak legs. Everyone believed Emperatriz:

"They can't put anything over on me. This wasn't Jerónimo's idea. It had to be thought up by Humberto. He wanted to have his own private circus, to laugh at us, and, with this deceit, he was even including Jerónimo, who didn't know it, among the characters in his circus because, in his own way, Jerónimo's the most monstrous of all. Oh well. The main thing still holds: Boy

doesn't know that a world of cruel, different beings exists outside. The rest, fiddlesticks. Stuff made up by Humberto who's a
liar."

Once, years before, at one of the sessions preceding Emperatriz's annual departure for the city, Crisóforo Azula, who
was in his cups, remarked in front of all the first-class monsters:

"Humberto a liar?"

"Humberto."

"The trouble is you're still seeing red."

"Who? Me? Why should I see red?"

"Because he gave you the slip."

"Me?"

The monsters held their tongues.

"Sure. You said he was going to marry you. If what I'm saying is a lie, why did you have your trousseau, including your
bridal gown with the embroidered train and your headdress,
ready when we decided to get married, overnight, after Don
Jerónimo's famous visit?"

Year after year Emperatriz came back from the capital with
the news that Jerónimo's interest in Boy, in them, in La Rinconada, was falling off. If she could steer things so that Jerónimo
would draw up a will in favor of Boy, leaving her as executrix,
well, let him go ahead and go gaga, above all if he named her
Boy's guardian this year, right now, increasing her salary and
depositing in the bank a large sum she'd administer to keep up
La Rinconada.

Her keys. Her billfold. Her portfolio. Basilio was already
waiting to carry her on his shoulders to the car, hidden away to
keep Boy from asking questions . . . lately Boy was becoming a
pain in the neck with all his questions. It was so hard to keep
him amused with games, and even with parties and women and
the sports events Basilio organized in such a way that Boy'd
never lose!

24

EARLY SUNDAY MORNING, Iris opened the door for him, the caramel-colored mink coat draped over his arm, and the jewel box, a miniature leather chest, in his hand. He passed her the things. She spread newspapers on my little cart and placed everything on top of them that the chauffeur brought, to keep it from getting soiled.

"Wait."

He returned from the car with packages of every size—wrapped board games, boxes of chips that rattled—I have a hunch this is a checker set, Rita remarked, shaking the contents of a box next to Iris Mateluna's ear, and this, what can it be, so many games, dear, what are we going to do with all the things they invent, we certainly won't have time to get bored now.

"How's Misiá Inés these days?"

Iris smiled at the chauffeur, very well, I'm sure she's never been better, not even in her own house, but the Casa's hers too.

"Give her my regards. Tell her we miss her very much."

The vestibule door closes. Rita's stuck her red hands in the folds of the mink . . . what a fine fur, I wonder what kind it is, how soft, it must be very warm, that must be the reason madam asked for her furs, poor thing, there's no heat here in the Casa and she can't be used to it like us . . . let's see, Iris, try on the coat, no, just throw it over your shoulder . . . but I snatch the fabulous wrap from you because it's not yours, you mustn't know that that much splendor exists, you mustn't even brush up against it . . . that's enough, stop it now, these are Misiá Inés's things, I'm going to report you both to Mother Benita, have Iris take everything inside.

Following Iris, who pulls my cart along, now that I have no strength, I cross the vestibule court, the corridor of the kitchen enclosure, where we have to drive off the old women who come over to see what you've got there . . . look, Antonieta, furs . . . they feel and paw them . . . stop it now, they belong to madam, and she'll get mad at you people if you touch the packages . . . what a lovely little box with gold inlay, I wonder what's in all those packages that are so nicely wrapped that you can see they come from shops . . . the linden-tree court, I pass in front of the chapel and, turning off toward the cloister of the palm-tree court, I reach your door. I rap. You open the door for me. Your crimson robe's soiled, its hem's filthy, and it has a button missing. You were about to comb your hair because it's a mess, and when you see me you insert your comb in the gray locks at your nape, but your eyes, bleary with sleep, become sharp when they light on the things I'm bringing you . . . have Iris lay the mink, the astrakhan and the little jewel chest here on the rumpled sheets, don't waste your time taking the packages into my cell, Mudito, help me put the mink on over the robe, and let's take these packages to the kitchen, the old women must be having breakfast . . . We follow you, with my cart loaded with games, down the passageways you sweep with the hem of your crimson robe, as the comb clings to your tangled hair, the sumptuous folds of your mink hang down your back that's beginning to become bent and you hold the blue leather chest decorated with golden fleurs-de-lis in your hands.

The old women are together in the kitchen for breakfast: bread, the huge pot in which the coffee's boiling, sneezes, whispers, smoke from the sticks of wood burning in the black stove's belly, faces that barely have features and are a mere outline of a shape, heads and jaws that tremble only a little but uncontrollably so, the foreshortening of an arm the light reveals among rags, forgetting to reveal the hand, gray enamel cups, an elbow next to bread crumbs that have fallen on the washed and scrubbed and worn-out wooden tabletop, fragments of beings that are reconstituted rise to their feet; the owner's come in, the lady dressed in scarlet, snuggled in a fur wrap, carrying a coffer with fleurs-de-lis, followed by her jester who passes out gift packages, shaky hands receive them, chipped nails tear the wrappings apart, shivering fingers open box lids . . . look, a Parcheesi set, it's been so long since I last played it, and these are checkers, and this is a jigsaw puzzle, and this a chess set but chess is so difficult to play it's a man's game as far as I'm concerned . . . race tracks for horses, for cars and dogs, boards with black and white squares, with pegs, with holes . . . look what I got, Clementina, I wonder what it is, how strange it looks, like dominoes but it's called mah-jongg and nobody knows how to play it but the chips are so pretty . . . cards, lots of cards, dozens of decks . . . we really won't have time to get bored from now on because we have enough different kinds of games to play for the rest of our lives, Misiá Inés, God bless you for all this, you're truly a charitable soul, a saint . . . One crone kisses her hand, another kneels to kiss the hem of her fur, groups begin clustering around the playing boards and the decks of cards, Inés strolls around the tables watching this gambling den, outside in the feeble sunlight of the court pigeons peck but inside, in the middle of the smoke, figures hunch over the boards and hands shuffle cards in the dimness . . . a game of *brisca* with brand-new cards isn't the same as a game of *brisca* with my worn-out ones that I'm going to put away because there's a jack of clubs missing . . . your deal, Zunilda, your turn to steal . . . I don't want to play with Ema because she's a cheat . . . come over to this table, Iris, if you want to play dominoes I'll teach you . . . no, let Iris play horse races over here with us, which is more of a game for little girls, let Eliana play with you people if you want, or Mirella . . . they forget the coffee that's smoking and the bread and the staring eyes of the coals and the Mass they were going to hear on the radio that belonged to Brígida and now presides over the hostelry . . . Father Azócar says it's proper for us because we're old, we're sick, and walking's hard work for us, but we're not hearing Mass today because our benefactress brought us games and keeps an eye on us as she circulates among us while we play, smiling at the happiness she sees in our watery eyes, listening to the dice rattling in their boxes; hands that are almost stiff with cold stack green chips and black chips for a game they know nothing about, little glass marbles fall down and roll on the floor, an old woman squats down, another crawls under the table to look for the milky glass ball among feet that are bursting out of their slippers, swollen feet, varicose veins covered with filthy stockings, but the old women with bunions and grimy skirts don't even realize there's an old woman crawling around because she's, I'm, missing a marble . . . my marble was a milky color . . . Clemencia, get your hoof out of the way . . . what's the difference if there's only one marble missing . . . come on, let's start playing cards, *brisca*, donkey, hearts, but not poker or monte . . . no, my God no, don't start playing monte, it's the devil's own game and it's against the law . . . I don't know what this game can possibly be with so many different-colored chips and such a pretty board, better put it away so Rita can read me the instructions on the cover, I can't read them and don't you go thinking it's because I don't know how to read, it's because the letters are so tiny and my sight is going . . . that's not a domino rule, María, you're making up rules to suit yourself . . . what do you mean I'm just an ignorant old thing . . . time for Mass is over but it makes no difference because they have Masses on the radio all day long and there's a High Mass later that's very beautiful, but we don't remember to hear that Mass either, because our cracked hands are busy shaking the dice boxes, our clay fingers steal an ace of diamonds and move the little blue horse forward six spaces and mix up the chips on the board because Rosa Pérez cheated . . . I'm not playing with Rosa Pérez anymore, let her move to another table, our sunken mouths protest, emitting puffs of indignation while the fire smokes and the coffee gets cold and Misiá Inés paces; she paces about, places her hand on Zunilda's shoulder for a second as Zunilda smiles up at her, she paces about without saying a word, looking, listening, she walks around wrapped in her caramel mink, dragging her crimson robe in between tables where dice roll, horses race, kings battle with bishops, black chips pile up and white ones give out . . . Misiá Inés, you decide whether that's not cheating, you must really know all about auto races . . . no, I know nothing about auto races, but I do know about dog races.

"Let me see, move over."

You sit on the stool. You set down the blue coffer with fleurs-de-lis next to the board. You say you're the yellow bitch. The other five players pick their animals and line them up for the start. You shake the dice box. You place it upside down on the table, covering the die, before saying:

"Well, the game's no fun unless you bet something, because if you don't win or lose there's no sense playing. If the yellow bitch wins, each one of you has to give me something. What are you betting, Rita?"

"My checker shawl."

"Okay. And you, Antonieta?"

"This flowered apron."

"It's a cotton print. What about Rosa Pérez?"

"I don't know . . . my slippers . . ."

"Let's see."

"Look."

"They're pretty broken down. Lucy?"

"This hairpin made of real tortoiseshell."

"It's not much."

"My four tortoise hairpins, then."

When Lucy takes them out of her bun, her hair falls down over her shoulders like a rain of ashes. You put the hairpins on top of the little blue coffer.

"And you, Auristela?"

"My scapular medal."

"It's only cloth."

"But it's big, and embroidered . . . it was my mother's."

"All right."

You're about to uncover the die but before doing it you look at the five old women, one at a time. You don't uncover the die.

"Aren't you going to ask me what I'm betting?"

"Oh, Misiá Inesita, my God, you don't have to bother!"

"You've already given us so many things."

"How can you even think of it, Misiá Inés!"

"No, ma'am, really . . ."

Your hand's clenched over the dice box. The animals at the gate are restless to begin the race. There's a frown on your face, these old women don't know what it's about.

"No, there's no sense in it this way, I have to risk losing something too. Do you know what I want to bet you? If I lose, I'll give you this fur coat, it's good fur, mink, very pretty, look, feel, when have you ever felt anything as soft, as exquisite, everyone envied me for it. I don't need it anymore. Why do I want things like this when I've taken the vow of poverty? And the astrakhan goes to the one who comes in second. And the diamond brooch I have here in the jewel box to the one who comes in third, and my pearl earclips to the one who's fourth, and my sapphire cabochon to number five. I have my jewels here. Would you like to see them? He used to give them to me . . . but I don't need them. No. I'm not going to show them to anyone until someone wins. I'm going to open the jewel box then. Not before."

While you list your bets, amazement hushes the voices at all the tables and then confusion breaks out, chairs are pushed back and tip over, chips and marbles spill, old women cluster around your table, attracted by the sumptuous things you bet, by the luxury of the words *furs, pearls, diamonds, sapphires,* they're a wall of old faces like peeling adobe, of blinking eyes and tremulous mouths, of old women filled with greed by these unbelievable things as the onlookers form a ring of fetid gray rags, brown at best, around the six players while you smile affably, all eyes glued to your hand on the dice box that still hasn't started the game in the presence of the inmates and the orphans, who hold their breaths, awed by the enormity of what their eyes will witness. You lift the box:

"Four. One, two, three, four . . ."

The yellow bitch takes off, chased by the others, pursued by the vengeful riders who leave behind only the memory of a cloud of dust on a silvery night, she hides in the brambles that tear at her mangy skin, she fords puddles and lakes and centuries and ditches but she can never sate the hunger that gives her stomach cramps because the garbage she eats isn't enough, the bones she gnaws on, the spoils she steals and runs away with before they punish her as they've always punished her, she runs in the direction the accomplice moon points out, climbs up hills and down gullies and keeps running to fulfill what has to be fulfilled and never will be fulfilled, she hides to keep fierce beasts from tearing her to pieces, beasts that hate her because she's ugly and scrawny and hungry, but the yellow bitch runs and runs through fields and over deserts and the bareness of rocky places and through forests of hawthorns that grow for the sake of pricking her, and through the streets and the parks, approaching the houses, at night, to maraud in the hope of finding something, the bitch is rickety, infested with lice, cowering, she's not fierce, she never attacks, she never bites even when she'd like to, but when the four black dogs are distracted, playing, she doesn't miss the chance to sneak between their legs and steal the offal, and at night, in the park, her burning eyes watch as they've always watched, she bays at the moon, asking it for advice, clues, telling the moon things it doesn't know and asking it for help and the moon gives it to her, that's why the gardeners didn't find her torn body, the yellow bitch runs and runs and runs, she's weak but she runs and the other bitches can't catch up with her, she's always in front despite her exhaustion, despite the need to rest, she sleeps for generations in forests where no one finds her and when she wakes up she goes out to sniff for food in the garbage dumps, the boys kick her . . . go on, beat it, leave us alone so we can fuck in peace, you goddamn dog, what are you doing there looking at us, don't rip my trousers if you don't want me to kick your snout in . . . look at her, she looks like she's enjoying the whole thing, and I laugh and you laugh and my organ gets soft and you pull up your panties and neither of us has fun but maybe the bitch does . . . and she flies off again and runs and runs, panting, her tongue hanging out, she leaves behind a cloud of dust and the barking of the other furious bitches who can't catch her, always hungry but always alive, more alive and alert than the other bitches, the yellow bitch is about to reach the finish line, and the old women laugh and scream and lay bets and pick their teeth and insult one another and shriek because they all want Misiá Inés to win . . . she's so good to us, don't let the red or the green or the black or the blue or the white dog win, let the yellow bitch win because she had to win, because she always wins . . . finally, the bitch jumps over the puddle with a six, you play again—four, one, two, three, four—and the bitch falls exhausted across the finish line.

"Bravo!"

"Hurrah for the yellow bitch!"

"I won!"

"Misiá Inesita won!"

"Bravo!"

"Hurrah for Misiá Inesita!"

While the old women go over the details of your victory, you stand up. You take out the comb you'd inserted at your nape, run it through your hair, put your hair up in a bun at the back and pin it with the tortoiseshell hairpins Lucy left on top of your coffer: one, two, three, four. Your hairpins made of genuine tortoiseshell, the best, the kind they used to have in the old days, not like tortoiseshell nowadays. The old women observe you silently. You take off your mink and hand it to me to put on my little cart. I can barely manage it. You snatch Rita's frayed checked shawl from her shoulders and put it on. They look at you, frightened, but they understand that this is how it has to be. Antonieta removes her apron without a word and you try it on, and you bend your head for Auristela to slip on the scapular like a relic, to adorn your breast.

"What about Rose Pérez's slippers?"

"They won't fit right, Misiá Inés."

"Let's have a look. Hand them to me."

The old woman's left barefoot while you try on the broken-down slippers.

"They're a bit big on me but it doesn't matter. I'm going to wear several pairs of stockings that are good and thick, for the cold, and then they'll fit right."

"Did you bring along thick stockings, Misiá Inés?"

"No. But you people must have some. Let's see if we can play another game of dog races tomorrow in which you bet thick stockings that I'll be needing badly."

"All right."

"Fine. I'm leaving."

Iris and I follow you with my cart. As we move off down the corridor the voices of the old women in the kitchen fade out. You walk slowly, round-shouldered under your shawl, a tortoise-shell hairpin falls out, you bend down, pick it up and put it into your disordered bun with its straggly hair. You open the door to your room, signaling me to send Iris away . . . Iris, leave . . . I'll tell you later, but you're not interested in seeing or being told anything because you've been fading away, you're only the brute force that pulls my little cart since I can't do it because I'm what you see me reduced to, Misiá Inés, but I get back my strength when Iris disappears and you open the splendor of your coffer: you take out your sapphire, your diamond brooch, your pearls. You put the jewels in the pocket of Antonieta's apron and close your jewel case again. You hand me the astra-khan, which I lay out next to the mink on my cart and follow you down the passageway to your cells. You open the first. You signal me to hand you the two overcoats, you open a wardrobe and, after distributing the jewels among the pockets of your astrakhan and your mink, you hang them among many old coats.

"Does this wardrobe have enough mothballs, Mudito?"

I answer yes.

You seem satisfied. You lock the wardrobe with one key and the door to your cell with another. I follow you down the pas-sageways, across the silent courts, through the galleries, between the lots of pedestals with label number 388, of flowerpot stands with number 883, the interminable little gilt chairs line the corri-dors, I follow you across to the shrine of Lourdes, you cross yourself, I cross myself, and we come to the vestibule. Rita's shivering in a corner, with her arms crossed.

"You look blue!"

"With cold."

But she's not blue, she's pale, tenuous, as if she were fading out. Inés pulls her shawl tight around herself. She dials her home and asks, in Rita's cracked voice:

"Is this Don Jerónimo de Azcoitía's home?"

" . . . "

"May I speak to him?"

". . ."

"Misiá Inesita says to wake him up even if he's sleeping, she
wants me to tell him in person the message she gave me for him
. . . no, nobody else, I'm sorry, it's not my fault, madam says
it's very urgent so I have to do it right away."

You yawn. You don't look at the woman whose voice you've
stolen. Jerónimo always sleeps late on Sunday, you know it, and
he goes to twelve o'clock Mass when he goes. Lately he hasn't
been going much. You wait.

"Don Jerónimo?"

". . ."

"Yes, Don Jerónimo, it's Rita . . . very well, thank you, at
your service, and you, sir, how have you been? . . . Pardon me
for calling you so early today, on a Sunday, but Misiá Inés, who,
I must say, has become very demanding and strange, told me I
had to call you exactly at this hour, even if you were sleeping
. . . You're not sleeping well? I'm so sorry . . . you must miss
her . . . But of course you miss your wife, Don Jerónimo! . . .
Yes, she's well, but she wants me to tell you to send all her
clothes if it's not too much trouble . . . yes, all of it, she says,
everything in the big closet in her bedroom, she's going to need
it . . . yes, the evening gowns too. And also all the jars and
things on the dresser, she says, and the little dressing table too
because she misses it, she wants to feel at home here and why
should it be wasted there in the house, while here . . . yes, sir,
of course, sir . . . and she also says that she doesn't like the bed
they put up for her here in the Casa at all and she can't sleep
nights, she can't get used to it here, she doesn't say so but I'm
sure she can't sleep because she must really miss you . . . oh,
you're such a devil, Don Jerónimo, I'm still single . . . and so
madam says will you also send her her bed with the mattress,
blankets, bedspread, comforter, pillows, sheets, yes, all her monogrammed sheets, she knows how many sets there are so they'll
have to send them all and all her face towels and large bath
towels . . . no, Don Jerónimo, madam will get furious, it has
to be today, she knows it's Sunday and it's hard to find a truck
because people don't like to work on Sunday, but she says you
have to take care of it, it has to be today . . . she said for me to

tell you she'd rather not speak to you because she's a bit hoarse, all of us here have a touch of the grippe, with the fog that keeps coming down at evening service time, it's so strange, at this time of year, I wonder why it is, they say the weather's changing on account of the atom bomb, I'm telling you, those things only bring trouble, Misiá Inesita says that maybe she'll call you next week when she's feeling better because she's got so many things to tell you, she says, but she'd rather rest till she really feels better, yes, poor madam always gets tired, she's either a bit run down or sad . . . it's not that I want to go sticking my nose in what doesn't concern me, but excuse me if I tell you that I think it's because she's been acting a bit odd over the Blessed Inés and all, yes, I think that's why, and because they're going to tear down this place she loves so much . . ."

The servant's ancient voice takes leave of your husband. You hang up. You smile at Rita, go over and pat her hair.

"Are you cold, Rita?"

"Not very."

"But you're shaking."

"Just old age, I guess."

"The weather's bad, as you said to my husband . . ."

"Yes, it's peculiar."

"All right. You won't feel cold tomorrow. You'll see. None of the inmates will feel cold. They'll bring me all my clothes, all my things, and I'm going to give you all a chance to win them from me playing Dog Track, until you win everything and I'm left without anything, because I can't bear to live and own so many things, I want to strip myself of everything, I have beautiful overcoats, Rita, you'll see how you'll win one or two of them, the yellow bitch can't win forever and you're all going to end up with all my lovely things."

Rita smiles happily.

"Good. I'm going to my room. Will you please tell María Benítez to prepare me a cup of hot tea and take it to my bedroom?"

"Strong?"

"No, I like it weak."

"Brígida used to like it strong at night. Amalia used to prepare it for her. Why did they have to take her away in an ambulance, when the poor woman wasn't sick or anything, only because she cried so much over the finger that saint lost, the one she said was an archangel!"

"Poor Amalia."

"Poor woman. We're looking for the finger to send it to Amalia so she'll get better."

"Good night, Rita."

"Good night, ma'am."

25

I'VE NOTICED THAT the very fine lines, like red scars, that
form the contours of your eyes and your forehead, your ears and
your eyelids and your mouth, and even the lines I used to see on
your hands, ringing your nails like leftover incisions and your
wrists like souvenirs of attempted suicides, and the base of each
finger, have been disappearing. Wrinkles . . . yes, why not, they
could pass for wrinkles, and I don't doubt that's what they'll become a few months from now . . . Misiá Inesita's getting so
many wrinkles, the nearsighted old women murmur, she's not
old enough yet to be played out like that, it's because she took
the vow of poverty and now she doesn't keep herself young with
massages, cleansing creams, pomades, masks that stretch the face
muscles, like she used to every week . . . Yes, the old women
are right. You're not what you used to be. The down on your
chin and on your shriveled upper lip has grown out a bit, and
black hairs, thick as bristles, have started sticking out of your
nostrils. But you don't notice these things because there's no
mirror in your bedroom now. You've been betting all your
toilet articles night after night, at the toy dog track—your little
table, your jars and bottles, your silver comb, all your furniture,
your bed, your blankets, your dresses—and the yellow bitch
always wins. And, because you win, your things disappear: we
take your luxurious belongings, all winners, to your cells on my
cart and put them away carefully so that their unused existences
will go on for all eternity and never wear out. Meanwhile, you
sleep on Zunilda Toro's cot, which replaced yours, on a mattress
stained with urine, wearing one of Ema's nightgowns; you drink
tea in one of María Benítez's cups, wrap yourself in Rita's shawl,

drag around God only knows whose dirty sack instead of a handbag, wear stockings you've been winning from Dora and Auristela, and Lucy's drawers, you go around in tatters, comb your hair with a toothless comb and refuse to wear anything but Rosa Pérez's run-down slippers.

And yet, when I look closely at you and you don't notice, I see that those fine scars haven't disappeared altogether. The reabsorption process is slow. You still have to wait several months. I've never doubted that Dr. Azula's the most brilliant surgeon in the world; the wonders he performs in his clinic in Switzerland fill the newspapers. His patients check in with the most varied ailments, but the majority go to him because they want to be rejuvenated, they're hungry for new organs that function better than theirs. But you, so you've told Misiá Raquel, went into Dr. Azula's clinic to get old once and for all. Yes, Inés, I watch you meticulously every day when we carry your monogrammed sheets or a small lacquered chair to your cells; your postoperative scars are fading. Now I'm sure you went to Switzerland to be transformed into Peta Ponce, who always wanted to occupy your body and have you occupy hers soon, when the fine red cords of your scars finally blend in and turn into wrinkles and warts and sacs of flesh and decayed or dried-up skin; Peta and you will achieve what you've been trying to down through the centuries. Life doesn't interest Peta Ponce unless she's part of you. The only solution she saw was the possibility of selling her useless body to Dr. Azula because you were going to fall into his hands. The surgeon took the old woman's body apart, put her organs aside in special containers, placed them in chambers designed by him to supply the necessary oxygen and pump blood, serum and water, he cut the organs with very delicate scalpels so that the incisions wouldn't show later on, he stored everything in aseptic cellars lined with porcelain tiles, without life, without death, but full of waiting, ready for the occasion when the organs would be used. It was there, in Switzerland, that Peta, cut up into sections, waited for you, and you, unaware of it—or perhaps you knew you were traveling across the centuries to make the synthesis of the family tradition of the girl-saint and the folk tale of the girl-witch a reality—went there because you had to go, to the clinic where Dr. Azula and Emperatriz were keeping the old woman's organs reserved for you, to transform you into her, into this filthy beggar with her gray bun, broken fingernails, corns and bunions, warty hands, tremulous head, and she's slowly absorbing and eliminating what remains of the incomplete Inés who went to Europe with dyed hair, a camel's hair overcoat, and alligator accessories.

However, the ancient tradition stipulated that the two of you would have to stop being two different persons and become one. But you're naïve, Inés, you don't know that old age is anarchy in its most dangerous form, it respects no laws or pacts hallowed by the centuries, old women are powerful, especially if they've dragged on for as many years of misery as Peta has. It's too late for you to defend yourself but you'd better know, before you disappear, because you will disappear, that Peta, who respects no pact, is appropriating what's still left of you and each day you're less Inés and each day you're more and more Peta, who's eliminating you completely. I repeat, you're naïve, Inés, sentimental, you didn't realize Peta had another motivation besides becoming one with you; keep in mind the power of miserable creatures, the hatred of witnesses, it may be buried under admiration and love but it's there, don't forget the envy of the insignificant and the ugly and the weak and the lowly, don't forget the talismans they keep stored under their beds or in their mattresses, the vengeance of those who've expiated your guilt, Peta who covered up for you and let you humiliate and use her is now getting back at you by using your body to worm her way into the Casa, because it's what Peta wanted, Inés, and it's the reason for her anger and her greed: to tear me away from the refuge where I lived disguised as Mudito or just another old woman, to appropriate me and claim my love, and, disguising herself, this time with the body of her mistress, to repeat the night at La Rinconada, because you've preserved Inés's passionate desire as I've preserved Don Jerónimo's potency, and you come looking for that potency, to become united with it once more, to claim the pleasure I've denied you for years and years.

You didn't know that Peta's sex drive was what was most alive in her, and you believed that with these grafts you'd turn into a helpless little old woman who doesn't want or need anything, but, as soon as the organs newly joined to your body begin to function, you'll begin to feel the urges of this thing you've been changed into, you'll see how painful it is to hunger for the sexual fulfillment I'll deny you till the end, to feel torn apart inside because you can't forget the night we spent together in your bed at La Rinconada. You'll run after me here in the Casa. When you realize who you are and who it is Crisóforo Azula has transformed you into, you'll give me no peace.

That's how it has to be, that's how it's always been, Inés, Inés-Peta, Peta-Inés, Peta, Peta Ponce, I've never been able to touch beauty because, when I desire it, I turn it into messy boardinghouse keepers, the crones at the Casa, the beggar women who follow me when I venture into the street, decrepit images of beauty my longing creates and my desire destroys, go away, leave me alone, don't come between what's left of me and what's left of her, you, a ragged creature, with hands deformed by warts, approaching from the end of the passageway, enigmatic solemnity hiding your mockery, your touching helplessness a mask that covers the real reason for your coming, to claim me, your prey. What do you want me for? Let me tell you the truth. I wasn't in bed with you that night at La Rinconada, Peta, it was Don Jerónimo, yes, he, and he's looking for your animal heat, Inés spoke to Misiá Raquel about her husband's insatiable potency, it's that that you're dying for, I have nothing, Peta, I swear it, look at my organ, you're looking at it: on Iris's bed, the old women are changing my diapers because I've wet myself to make them happy, see how they grab the chunk of lifeless meat and play with it, with the filthy thing that's good only for the stinking piss it produces, that's filthy, dead—see, I don't even have pubic hair, I'm a baby, I'm impotent, leave me alone, I can't do anything. Leave the Casa. Look for him, he's the one who can satisfy your appetite. Let me have the Casa back, let the old women bind me and swaddle me tight, let them turn me into an *imbunche*. I'm Mudito. Sometimes I'm just another old woman. I'm Iris's doll. Don't you think that if I were potent, when I lie in bed every night with the one who plays at being my mamma but isn't my mamma because I never had a mamma, don't you think her young body would drive me out of my mind when she rubs against my body to make me go through hell, and I tell her no, Iris, that will get you nowhere because I have nothing and therefore I can't suffer? Yes, you made an error coming to the Casa to look for me. You're only one more in the committee of old women that's been harrowing me all my life, Inés-crone, Inés-ugly, making yourself available, but Inés-ugly, Inés-Peta, isn't the one I love, it's Inés alone, luminous, unchangeable, that's the Inés I love, the one you preserve in the photographs in the trunks you keep in your cell, Inés on horseback at La Rinconada, Inés in a russet macramé evening gown, Inés wearing a hat that hugs her head and bares her nape and her high neck, Inés with her hair loose on her shoulders, Inés strolling on Don Jerónimo's arm through the paddock at the Jockey Club, Inés riding in a vis-à-vis with Misiá Raquel who was never pretty, Inés . . . ah, I know you, lovely Inés at the bottom of your locked trunks, in the clothing you've worn and keep stored in the Casa, it's touched Inés's body and so do I, except that Inés saw only my kindled eyes of an onlooker one night in her park and, since Crisóforo Azula operated on her, I don't think she even sees me, here's a few coins' tip for you, Mudito, we're going to put away this crocodile handbag, this porcelain lamp, this Persian rug, this pair of miniatures mounted on velvet mats, this quilted nylon morning robe that's new and very warm, we're going to put away, in cells, all the things I won tonight from the old women at the dog track . . . I can't, Peta, leave me alone, go look for *him* and dig the truth out of him because it's his fault that our fates have taken these monstrous shapes in order to survive . . . I sweeping your bedroom, you on your knees on the floor praying in front of a cross you put together with sticks tied with leather strips the other day, aping your ancestress, not the ancestress of Inés but this woman who prays while I sweep her room and whom I love because Peta's the only woman in the world I've ever loved, but a tip's all I deserve, because my father told me I didn't have a face and was a nobody, that's what he taught me from childhood on, that's why I have nothing left except you; but I can't allow it, before Dr. Azula's grafts grow and their tissues become part of your flesh and the glands begin to secrete their juices, while, though old and slovenly, you're still Inés, I'll possess you and the memory of your beauty will be mine and I'll do as I please with it after I've made use of what's left, I'll flay you and show everyone your hide, the authentic bloodstained hide of the yellow bitch, and then neither you nor you will exist, neither of you two, both will disappear into the deepest passageway, run, Peta, go look for him, why do you want my flabby organ, leave me alone, let me eradicate myself, let the kindly old women bind me, I want to be an *imbunche* stuck into the sack of his own skin, stripped of the capacity to move and desire and hear and read and write, or remember, if I can find anything in me to remember, and hear you praying on your knees in front of the little cross put together with sticks and leather strips, to see myself forced to wonder who this woman is, I know her, who is this woman, poor Misiá Inés has changed so much, she's so good, she's on her last legs, she's a saint, one of the most pious and charitable ladies in the world, and really good, she doesn't paint her nails or smoke like a man the way Misiá Raquel does, she worries about us poor sick old women, she's the only one who worries about us and protects us, it's been almost a year since Misiá Raquel promised a donation in Brígida's memory, and you see, not a thing, no, it's not that she's a bad person, she has other worries on her mind, so many children and grandchildren, while Misiá Inesita doesn't keep up with the fashions or anything, and you say your beads heavy with indulgences because the Holy Father blessed them for you, and your eyes are closed. Without opening them or breaking off your prayers, you give me a signal, only a slight movement of the head, indicating that it's time for me to go out of your room and leave you to yourself.

. . . THEEEEEEEEEEN, the howling of the dogs, the mooing of the cows, the bulls roaring, the horses whinnying, the sheep bleating, were heard in the countryside, and the nuns went into a panic because at that time this was very isolated . . . what's happening, why are the animals terrified of something we don't know is happening out in the night, what are they trying to warn us about, what are we going to do, whom can we ask what this agonizing thing is . . . and thaaaaaaaaaaat's when the terrible thing started: the entire mountain range lit up by lightning flashes, the earth rumbling and shaking violently and cracking open, the nuns screaming and running helter-skelter half-dead with fright because the Casa was shaking as if it were going to cave in . . . and thaaaaaaaaaat's when the nuns saw her in the middle of the court, on her knees, with her arms outstretched like a cross . . .

They've heard you tell this story a thousand times since you came here; you add a little embroidery to the central theme, you make up details and trimmings to electrify the orphans who never tire of hearing you, as if they too were waiting for the final synthesis of the folktale of the girl-witch and the tradition of the girl-saint, all of you like to listen to Misiá Inesita, who's so good, because she imitates the whinnies and the mooing and the barking . . . you do it so well, Misiá Inesita, let's see, again, a cow this time . . . and her baby calf . . . you love to watch her spread her arms out like a cross to hold up the walls that are about to collapse but don't collapse because she holds them up. What they enjoy most is when Misiá Inesita starts trembling like an earthquake: let's play earthquake, ma'am, please, it's so much fun, sitting here on the bench under the palm tree in the vestibule court, Eliana, Frosy, Iris, Verónica and Mirella gather around you and you shake violently and tremble and they tremble too, scared to death by the disaster, dying with laughter, their bodies and their arms and their legs becoming confused with your limbs, till finally Eliana steps on Frosy accidentally . . . hey, you big pain-in-the-neck, get off my back . . . the safety pin Iris uses to close her brown overcoat pricked me, you scratched me on purpose . . . all right, girls, leave me alone now, I'm burning up, oof, it's so hot here, now that we've finished playing earthquake we're all going to say a Hail Holy Queen together for her soul, which the unbelievers want to forget, asking her to please reveal the truth about herself . . .

an apparition . . . a sign . . . any irrefutable sign we can cling to so as not to have to dig our nails into the night. They pray . . . eyes shut . . . hands joined . . . voices contrite . . . they follow your prayers that lead them through the meanderings of your devotion . . . Hail Holy Queen, Mother . . . Amen. And now let's end with an Our Father, that's all, Misiá Inés, let's play something else now, yes, then we'll pray some more, when it gets dark, nobody feels like praying in the daytime. Let's play now.

"What do you want to play?"

"Parcheesi."

"No, checkers . . ."

"No, disguises . . ."

"No, races . . ."

"No, girls, today I'm going to teach you how to play something else."

You rise to your feet . . . Follow me to the vestibule, don't let anybody see us because it's a very dangerous game, Iris, come along with me, dear, stay close to me . . . your old woman's expression is furtive, you look out the corner of your gummy eye, you hunch along, your hands turn into claws, and the orphans laugh, imitating you . . . ooh, how scary, they better not see us or they'll punish us . . . there's nobody in the vestibule, I think Mudito was the only one hanging around . . . the orphans follow you, copying your pretended stealth, advancing, hiding behind the jasmine, behind the stone grotto, and, dodging behind the pilasters in the corridor, everyone arrives at the doorkeeper's safe and sound. The orphans sit on the bench . . . you open the door of Rita's cubicle and you ask from the doorway: "Who wants to start?"

"Me first."

"No, I asked before you did."

"No, we'd better start with Iris."

"All right."

Iris stands in the center of the vestibule while the others make themselves comfortable to watch the show. She's very fat because I'm going to be born soon. She listens to madam's instructions:

"Look, the game goes like this: I'll dial a phone number

and start a conversation. You have to answer as if you were at the other end of the line, but without making a mistake, and guess who's talking with whom."

The white pasty face, without makeup now, displays neither enthusiasm nor aversion, neither yes nor no, it's the little girls on the bench who say:

"What a tough game!"

"It's a lot of fun, you'll see."

"It's a grown-up game."

"And I'm going to give all of you a prize . . ."

"A jewel . . ."

"A dress . . ."

"Money . . ."

"A Dog Track . . ."

Iris isn't interested in prizes, she's waiting in the center of the vestibule for them to cheer her on . . . it'll be hard trying to win, Iris, but I'll be guiding you from the crannies in this Shrine of Lourdes without a Virgin or Little Bernadette . . . I'll lead you from here as I've led you so many times in your excursions into the neighborhood, with the Giant, to the empty lot, to the magazine shop, to buy a Coke, to make love with ambassadors and generals and academicians and journalists and Don Jerónimo and Romualdo. If you obey me you'll win. You alone can win, because you don't exist, neither Mirella, nor Eliana, nor Frosy, nor Verónica would be able to win because they do exist, on the other hand, you're nothing but wrapping, so don't be afraid, smile at Inés, say yes, okay, the prize will be so magnificent and so terrible that only I will dare to receive it through your miserable person. You watch madam smile as she dials the number . . . the phone rings and rings. When Iris hears the click at the other end of the line, she frowns and begins to pace up and down the vestibule, as if she understood all this, and it fills her with a lot of worry. Iris is listening and taking it all in.

"Hello . . . hello . . . yes, yes, I want to speak to him . . . yes, good afternoon, how have you been, sir . . . all of us here are fair to middling . . . why should I lie to you, I can't go on, I don't know what to do . . ."

Iris stops in front of the door and, opening her pudgy hands with a helpless gesture, asks:

"But what's wrong now, for heaven's sake?"

"What's wrong is that you've neglected us so much that this holy place is turning into a sinful gambling den, they don't just play for fun anymore at the games Misiá Inés had them bring here, no, it only started out that way. Imagine, how is it possible, now they bet everything they own: overcoats, blankets, broken-down clocks, calendars, cages with or without thrushes, torn umbrellas, all their clothes, teapots, stockings . . . they're addicted to gambling, they've lost all sense of decency . . ."

"Don't exaggerate . . ."

"I don't know, that's the story going around, the old women are very crafty, I haven't been able to prove anything, they hold things back, sometimes I get the dreadful feeling that I don't know half of what's going on here in the Casa . . ."

Now, Iris, puff out your cheeks, arch your worried eyebrows, pace up and down the vestibule with your hands behind your back, your coat as long as a cassock, your pompous air, and your preoccupation becomes a shade fictitious when you insist that it can't go on . . . we have to put a stop to this business right away . . . while the girls lined up on the bench watch Iris's act. You go on talking on the phone. One elbow rests against the wall. You shift your weight from one leg to the other, you don't look at Iris, because you're completely taken up with this phone that picks up your words, you adjust it, shift the receiver from one hand to the other:

". . . the worst part of all is what they're saying about Misiá Inés. They're things I hear through a partition, whispers that are hushed when I enter a room: they say Misiá Inés always wins because she's protected by the Blessed Inés, there's a lot of talk about the saintly girl here in the Casa now. Too much. I can't put up with it anymore, if they answered me to my face and told me the truth, well, I wouldn't feel so helpless, but their smiles and their hedging, it's as far as I can get with them, they mix me up with their lies, it's like a growing wave that's invisible and that I can't control precisely because it is invisible, imagine what they say . . . they say . . . always *they say.*

They say that Misiá Inés compels the saint to protect her in the game and, to get her protection, she has her worshipped here, she's promised her that this will never be a Children's Village but her Shrine, with basilicas and pilgrimages and all, it frightens me when I hear them saying their beads, and they seemed so innocent to me once. When I see them picking mauve lilies I'm sure it's to decorate some image of the Blessed Inés that they've hidden away somewhere and venerate."

Iris stops abruptly in the center of the vestibule. Her dark overcoat sweeps the ground. He's terrified, furious, he opens his satiny eyes wide, raises his arms as if to halt something and exclaims:

"Heresy. This is heresy! Don't let this sacrilegious story get out of the Casa . . . !"

". . . and she takes everything the poor old women bet . . . not one of them has a blanket left, or a shawl, or a brazier, they shiver as they go through the corridors, there are several with bronchitis because they walk around half naked through these halls, and you know the drafts in the Casa . . ."

"And what does she do with all that trash?"

"She bets her own things against the old women's worthless stuff, her things are so beautiful—furs, furniture, jewels, dresses, fine shoes, all sorts of things—and, since she always wins, she puts away the valuable articles, for the saint, that she bet against the worthless trash, she says, it seems she's waiting for the cardinals to beatify her . . ."

"But doesn't she understand that it definitely fell through over a year ago?"

"I don't know. She sleeps on a straw bed because she's stored her sheets and her good furniture. She goes around dressed like a beggar. She has nothing left that's any good. And she continues putting up the better things she wins from the old women against their poorer stuff and, when she wins, she wraps what she bet—it's for the saint, she says—and stores it, and she puts on the slippers she just won, that are falling apart even more than the ones she had on, and stockings that are more ragged, and more tattered drawers, she takes off the ones she was wearing and makes packages and stores them . . . for the saint . . . she fixed up her bedroom with castoffs and she dresses in rags that get worse and worse because she changes them every day, each time I see her she looks like a different old woman, filthier and more broken down, it's hard for me to recognize her, her cells are getting cluttered with packages filled with her own things and with trash . . . she wins a pair of shoes that are worse than the ones she's wearing, which she takes off to put on the ones she's just won, she's walking around in the most incredible slippers . . ."

"Incredible! Incredible! All that filth . . ."

Iris puts on an act, puffs up like an infuriated turkey cock, she feels personally offended by all the dirt, she gathers up the train of her superb cassock so as not to drag it along the suspicious-looking floor of the vestibule where she's pacing, while the girls applaud her act . . . this man, who's so important, is going to tolerate things only up to a certain point . . . you hang up . . . Iris's airs are gone, she's changed back into the fat girl wrapped in a ratty overcoat that's too big for her, and you look at her and ask her who the two persons just talking were, but you shake your head to indicate you don't know, because the image that illuminated you for a few moments has disappeared. You could go on talking if I told you things from where I am, and you could carry on the dialogue forever, she tells me that they're things the old women have given her and that since she's taken the vow of poverty she has to come down to their level, she goes around slovenly, covered with lice, the other day in the kitchen area, in the sun, Ema was combing the nits out of her hair with a fine-tooth comb . . . why go on . . . Answer Inés, Iris. You know who you are. You know with whom you were talking:

"Well, Iris?"

Obey me, then you'll win the prize I need, answer, don't leave me changed into a shadow among these painted rocks, I need the prize, you've got to win it for me:

"Mother Azócar talking with Father Benítez . . ."

Stupid! You got all mixed up . . . the girls hold their bellies with laughter over Iris's confusion . . . what a big fool

this one is, when's she going to learn . . . she lost, Iris Mateluna
lost, Misiá Inesita, now it's my turn to play the game, it's so
much fun . . . Iris didn't win because she said something silly
. . . You correct yourself:

"Mother Benita talking with Father Azócar."

"Bah, it's not funny now."

You make them shut up: you raise your hands. Despite
your rags and your lice, your blotchy hands preserve your authority as proprietress, as the lady with a mink over her shoulders carrying a box with gold fleurs-de-lis as an offering.
Superior powers can't remain indifferent to magnificent gifts.

"Let's see, Iris. This is your last chance to win the prize.
Tell me the number I dialed. What number was it?"

You don't hesitate as you say 83 72 91, I put the number in
your thick head to make you win the prize I yearn for and must
have, the blood Dr. Azula stole from me will run through my
veins again, I'll stop being a damp spot on a wall, you'll rescue
me, or perhaps not, perhaps by hearing his voice I'll withdraw
more into myself, until I'm totally eliminated.

"Eight three, seven two, nine one . . ."

"Very well, Iris. See, girls? Iris isn't stupid. Now you deserve the prize."

"What are you going to give her, Misiá Inesita?"

"I want to play now, after Iris, so I can win something
beautiful."

They wait for you to produce something dazzling from inside your rags, a precious stone, sequins, a jewel, but you don't,
you throw the door to Rita's cubicle wide open.

"Come in."

Iris obeys.

"Dial six three, seven six, eight four."

Iris dials, the phone rings, and you go sit on the bench,
where the orphans make room for you. Someone answers at the
other end. The miracle's going to take place: I'll hear his voice.
We're going to talk.

"Hello . . . Is Jerónimo in?"

They ask us to wait, they're going to call him.

"Now it's he: hearing him is your prize, Iris."

You answer from the bench, in a gentleman's voice, with the orphans looking on:

"Hello Jerónimo. How are you?"

"Inés."

"Yes, look, Jerónimo, I wanted to tell you something . . ."

"You can at least say how are you. I haven't had the privilege of hearing your voice since you arrived . . ."

"Stop the nonsense. I have very important things to tell you. I've thought this out very carefully during the weeks I've been in the Casa. I don't want the Archbishop or Father Azócar or anyone to touch any part of my inheritance. I've decided to adopt Iris Mateluna. I'm leaving her everything. She's to go on trying to get the beatification, she's to prevent them from tearing down the Casa so they can make money on it . . ."

"Nobody wants to make money, Inés, don't worry."

"This place is terrifying, Jerónimo, I can't rest easy because she's buried in here somewhere and I want to bring her back to life so that she won't be in the ground or inside the adobe walls, you should see, horrible faces come out of the walls at night and crowd into my room. I'm going to tell Mother Benita to have a bed put into my room for Iris Mateluna, so she can keep me company, you don't know how alone I am . . . you should see how upsetting it is to press the buzzer and wait for them to wake up and come to me three or four times every night . . . or the martyred faces they put on when I wake them so they can make me a cup of hot tea, as if it were so difficult, of course in this place they have to start out by lighting the stove with coal, but, after all, the Casa and these old women are mine . . ."

"You must be driving them crazy too . . ."

Iris flies into a rage and screams:

"What do you mean *too?*"

"I mean you've got *me* half crazy."

"Don't lie to me. That's not what you meant. You think they're crazy *too*, like me."

"Now look here, Inés . . . we have so many things to talk about . . . so many personal things, between you and me . . . what's happened . . . Listen to me, Inés . . ."

You get up and move forward with your hands outstretched as if to touch Iris, perhaps caress her. You'd give her anything to make her understand you, your tone's soft, your speech as enveloping as your arms, your inflection as loving as the palm of your hands . . . don't touch me, Jerónimo, you're never going to touch me, understand?

"I'm getting fed up, Inés."

"What's making you fed up?"

"Well, since you dismiss my love like that, I'll tell you: your presence in the Casa is ruining the Children's Village project. Everything was almost ready, and the auction was about to take place, when you showed up . . ."

"Yes, the whole Casa's full of items with labels that are beginning to turn yellow."

"The sale of the land in the back part of the block was about to be closed, and half of the construction was to be financed out of the proceeds, because the property's very expensive, with the Archbishop putting up the rest. Next month, there will be a final meeting with the people interested in the land back there and they'll give their ultimatum: the deal goes through immediately or not at all. It's natural. You can't keep businessmen waiting forever. Either Children's Village is going to be built or it's not going to be built. Nothing can be done with you over there."

"Yes, I know."

"Is that why you're there?"

"That and other things."

"What things?"

Iris drops the phone, leaves it dangling on its cord, and faces Inés:

"Do you think I'm going to let them *sell* holy ground? You're . . . you're out of your mind, Jerónimo, if you think that on top of everything else you've done to me I'm going to let you join the conspiracy to take away this land on which the saint is buried and that you and that priest Azócar want to sell to the highest bidder."

Iris has an insolent look on her face. She waves her arms, her eyes glitter—brown, yellow, green, above all brown because her overcoat's brown—but they flash angrily and she shakes her fists with determination as she excitedly defends your particle of eternity. Inés steps back and demands:

"You have to leave the Casa, Inés."

The two voices meet and become entangled. Iris lets out a guffaw. Inés asks:

"What are you laughing at?"

"If you think I'm going back to live with you . . ."

You let your hands drop. All the hardness in Jerónimo melts: he pleads, the most pathetic tenderness gentles his eyes, he inclines his neck, a sweet note enters his voice:

"Inés . . . if you want me to, I'll come for you myself."

"You're telling me that to soften me up with your lies, you're sure that's not your husband's intention, you know the Casa fills Jerónimo with terror—loathing, he says, but it's terror—you're sure he'll never come here because he sends his enemies to be locked up here, to rot, transformed into little old women who cough and play *brisca*, the Casa's filled with all the people Jerónimo wanted out of the way, those who know too much about his life, his machinations, or his weaknesses, those he wants to eliminate because they stand in his way . . . they say . . . they say that for more than a century the Azcoitías have been sending all the people they've wanted out of the way to the Casa. Who knows whether the famous saint was no more than a headstrong girl whose rebellious spirit had to be broken . . . and whether these adobe walls were put up in order to curb her? That's anyone's guess. To tell you the truth, Jerónimo, I realize I'm just another one of your victims."

"How can you think that, Inés!"

As you say it, your eyes are moist with the tears you hold back. Iris has left Rita's cubicle with all our fear and our hatred and our envy and our shock and our love worked into her doughy features that can be modeled into any face. You feel sure that all three of us are in on this—you, Iris Mateluna and I —and that our only wish is to make that man who looms before you disappear, because the only way to find peace is for Jerónimo to stop existing; the three of us know that, it's written in Iris's enraptured eyes that never leave you. You're both crying, you break into sobs together and we seek refuge in each other's arms, kissing, promising one another that everything will work out, yes, things will take an upward course and from the summit we'll get an overall view . . . don't cry, Iris, don't cry, Misiá Inés, don't cry, Don Jerónimo, don't cry, Inés . . . that's enough. The orphans applaud and chatter about how well Iris played the part . . . she's a born actress, and where does Misiá Inesita get all those stories she tells . . . this is so much fun . . . it's my turn to play now . . . no, mine . . . mine, Señora Inesita. All the orphans surround Iris and you as both of you sob with your arms around each other in the middle of the vestibule, while in Rita's cubicle the fallen phone dangles and I hear a voice saying:

"Hello . . . hello . . . May I speak with Humberto Peñaloza?"

26

NO ONE WAS able to speak with Humberto Peñaloza because
as soon as he heard that name he fled down the corridors into
the depths of the Casa, Humberto Peñaloza doesn't exist, he's
an invention, he's not a person but a character, no one can want
to speak with him, because they must know that he's a mute.
His vulnerable shadow took cover far away in a room cluttered
with bundles of newspapers and magazines the dampness has
made soft . . . Mudo, Mudito, don't go away, don't disappear,
you'll starve to death, no, where are you, Mudo, Mudito, where
are you, looking for you will tire us out because we're old and
feeble and we're terrified of sudden drafts, don't go starving to
death on us, Mudito, look, even if we don't know where you're
hiding we're leaving you plates of food in the passages and corridors so you can eat when you feel like it, like a dog . . . But
shadows don't eat until they dare become somebody, and the
nameless shadow that feels no hunger wants to melt into the
other shadows in the room, to shrink to newspaper size. The
shadow without name or hunger shrinks as it hides the terror
that stops it from mingling with the other shadows and acquiring the flat dimensions of a news item, squeezed into its
hole in the dried-up newspapers; terror's centered in its small-
ness, it fills me till I can't bear myself, without movement, without hunger, without hearing, blind almost . . . almost blind,
but my eyes still hold their power, and because they hold it, this
small bundle that I am won't be able to stand the terror that
provides no way out and compresses it, and I realize that the
undelayable moment has arrived. I must be born.

One morning I woke up in Iris's bed, almost suffocated by

the heat of her body and the covering of her sheets . . . look, look, the baby was finally born last night, look, I'm not swollen anymore, look at him cry, and he's wet, I didn't know it was so easy to have a baby . . . but it's not easy, Iris, it was easy in your case because it's a miraculous baby, that's why you didn't even feel it . . . she got through it so well that she doesn't even seem to have lost much weight . . . of course, but the baby had to be born, it was high time, so long past the nine months and no matter how much of a miracle it is one starts getting a bit jumpy and doesn't know what to make of it or do when the pregnancy goes way past the nine months . . . but what nine months are you blabbing about, Ema, this was a miraculous pregnancy so there's no point from which you can start counting the nine months, all this stuff about the nine months is silly, you're getting just like Amalia with this business of the nine months, she never could get it through her head and that's when she took to searching for the finger, they're going to cart you off to the nuthouse too if you don't shut up about the nine months bit, the child's already born, see? . . . What a skinny, puny baby you had, Iris, a child with such sad-looking eyes! But it's the child. There's no doubt about that. It's the child, it's Boy, look, why he seems to have a tiny little halo but still and all a halo . . . And they dress me in the silks and tulles of the baby wardrobe Inés had been keeping for me in her trunk. In the things in the upper drawers. Yes, because the ones in the lower drawers were still much too tiny for me. As I gradually shrink, Inés will give them to me.

They treat me with care and attention. I didn't deserve this before, when I was only Iris's doll. They let me suck her breasts, I'd like to play with them with my hands, but I can't because they've got me swaddled so tight. Iris pets me and covers me with kisses. With Iris enthroned in her gold and crimson damask presbytery chair, as she holds me in her arms, we receive the reverence of the faithful, their prayers, their canticles, that are barely above a whisper so that the others won't hear, because they're an envious lot; they light candles, they surround us with flowers, and Inés prostrates herself among the other old women who address their requests to us . . . let me get over my rheumatism . . . let them give us beans instead of chickpeas next week . . . let them release Rafaelito from jail for the swindle they say the boy pulled, although how could he possibly have done it he was such a good child when I was raising him and he had maize-colored hair . . . look, I've got it right here, do you believe me now . . . a Hail Holy Queen so Mother Benita won't find us out, an Apostles' Creed so the child will grow up to be a saint . . . an Our Father so he'll never leave the Casa . . . and the old women pray and sew and sing around us, we've brought the bed and the crib in here, we've moved everything into the chapel because there are so many of us old women now that we don't all fit in the cellar, we pray but we also play in this den where Iris and I preside among the plaster saints that have been pieced together and painted over. Yes, Hail Holy Queens and Apostles' Creed, but also leather boxes in which dice rattle, chips on the floor because there are no tables and if we want to play we have to do it here because Mother Benita would never let us play in the kitchen this late because we burn too many candles and the Archbishop doesn't send money to pay the bills, but Misiá Inés is so good and so devoted to Iris that she says her name isn't Iris Mateluna but the Blessed Inés de Azcoitía, she gives us a lot of money to go out muffled up in our shawls, if any of us has a shawl left that Misiá Inesita hasn't won from us at Dog Track, and buy fresh flowers, the most expensive, and candles and more candles and all the things we need for worshipping the Blessed Inés, who survived and now has been discovered by her so we can all be happy . . . this little child the Blessed Inés has in her arms is all skin and bones, I thought baby-saints were chubby and blond like in paintings, but this one's dark . . . it doesn't matter, the important thing is that he's a miraculous baby conceived without stain and without sin, how could this be anything but a miracle, but we're not going to tell anybody, that was Brígida's advice and she was right, we can all look after him among ourselves without teaching him anything and with us doing everything for him . . . I'm his arms, you his mouth, she his feet . . . oh my baby's so beautiful, Iris says . . . the girl-saint's child is so beautiful, they didn't believe in her in Rome but you can see with your own eyes that she's performed this new miracle, and her son will perform the greatest miracle of all by doing away with the experience of death for us: he'll see to it that we don't die; instead, when he decides, every one of us who's served him will climb into a white hearse drawn by three pairs of horses harnessed with mantles and plumes and white reins and we'll ascend to heaven . . . just let the envious old women and those heretical unbelieving priests in Rome wait, one of these days they won't find a single one of us in the Casa, because the saint and her son, who was born without any man defiling her, will take us up to heaven, although I think, Rosa, it would be so much nicer if everybody saw us, don't you think so, Misiá Inesita, if all the others, the envious ones the child won't save, and Father Azócar, and Mother Benita, and all the neighbors, could bid us farewell, singing to us here at the door of the Casa, and it would be nice if they had it on the radio like Masses and soccer games, with the child, grown a little bigger, holding the white reins of the white horses in his hands, and we with our sacks slung over our shoulders in the white hearse that will have to be very roomy because there are so many of us, not just seven like there were at first, as we go higher and higher in a shower of petals, saying goodbye to all the others, feeling very sorry because we can't take them along . . . girls, we really wish we could, but there's no room in the hearse.

You're the most zealous convert; you have everything planned. Once Jerónimo's dead you'll put the fortune you'll come into at the service of the Blessed Inés de Azcoitía to rebuild the Casa, which will perpetuate your own name . . . I knew that by coming to live here I'd find her at last, and this child she carries in her arms will have to convince them in Rome and he'll bring shame upon the ambassador to the Holy See, who's a Communist, yes, I'm ready to set out for Rome again, I'll make any sacrifice for the saint and the child. When I come back in triumph, the Archbishop will have to return the Casa to me, and I'll turn it into a sanctuary, with frescoes of the saint's life painted on a gold background, and many priests and canons and other persons will investigate the miracle and write about it and about the saint so that everyone will know her, and we'll

also build rooms where she and the child and all of you will live
. . . oh, no, we don't want anything, Misiá Inesita, don't let
them tear down anything, don't let anything change until the
child grows up, it will be better if you don't go to Rome until
the child's a little bigger, stay here with us so he can be raised
as he should be, without moving inside his swaddling clothes,
tied up tight till he performs the miracle of taking us all up to
heaven . . . But, of course, we have to wait until Jerónimo dies
for the fortune to come to me. We have to make him disappear
so he'll leave me alone, so he won't call up Raquel to convince
me to speak with him, it would be different if all he wanted was
to speak to me but his existence so close by will always threaten
us with the danger of bringing us back to life . . . go away,
Jerónimo, far away, where your will can't bend ours into sub-
mission . . . He's an unbeliever. I'm telling you this confiden-
tially. His show of piety is all politics, nothing else, and that's
why we have to wait for Jerónimo to disappear so we may en-
throne Iris with her son in her arms, what do I care if the cardinals say no, once I have Jerónimo's fortune in my hands and can
build a sanctuary to perpetuate the name they tried to bury, in
the meantime, you'll all be here with me, without any cares, no,
you're not going to die, the child will perform his miracle before
you die and he'll take you to heaven, to a place exactly like this
one, but we have to wait, to wait while singing and praying, and
also playing at the dog races where I'm gradually stripping you
of everything . . . the old women shiver in the chapel, they
have no shoes, I form a pile beside me with all the things I win
and afterwards put away for the child, nothing's for me, everything will be for the child—diapers now, cotton, toilet water, the
best talcum, candles, flowers—his needs will be different later
on and he may need any one of the things I've been winning
from the old women, I'm always the yellow bitch, I can't shake
her off, I'm forced to make her run through forests and down the
roads and over the countryside and to make her ford ditches and
lakes, she comes to life in my hands, not that I want to win
things from them, poor old women, the only reason I need filthy
things is to go on picking the filthiest and most moth-eaten piece
of clothing to take the place of another I had on that was a little

less filthy and tattered, I don't want to win, it's the bitch dog who forces me to win, by running over the track . . . one, two, three, four, water, back you go, two, three . . . you, Rita . . . you, Rosa . . . my turn now . . . the yellow bitch's shadow is enormous on the wall, and it flickers and runs while the candles burn down and my pile of rags for the child, in case he needs them and because the yellow bitch forces me to make her win time after time, keeps growing, my pile of junk the witches tearfully hand over, their poor talismans that not I but the bitch wants, as it runs along the walls of the deconsecrated chapel presided over by Iris and the child on their throne, and the old women blubber, they have to play, like me, we obey the bitch dog, we're greedy, our hands pull off clothing, grab broken-down clocks, the calendar with its last page seven years old, slippers, an odd stocking, the raspberry bathing cap . . . I won, I won . . . the yellow bitch won again because she can't lose, and I shout and snatch things they beg me not to collect, although I don't want to take advantage of these old women, I don't want to clean them out, but the yellow bitch does, I obey her because then she runs and barks and bays at the moon and fords puddles . . . one, two, three, four, five, six, I get to throw again . . . you're so lucky, Misiá Inesita . . . she's off again, five, one, two, three, four, five . . . her shadow seems enormous on the wall, the old women don't notice how big and how alive the bitch's shadow is because they're aware only of my board and the fear that I'll grab away some umbrella ribs, a faded scarf, that's all they're aware of . . . run, bitch, run . . . come on, Iris, put down your child so they can change him, come and play with me . . . what do you bet . . . well, I like your brown overcoat, and I'll bet these slippers that used to belong to Rosa Pérez, you throw first . . . four, one, two, three, four . . . now the white bitch . . . one, two . . . tough luck . . . and the blue bitch races over the board and the red bitch does too, but the yellow bitch runs and runs, till her feet bleed in order to reach the finish line first, and so I pulled the brown overcoat off Iris's shoulders even though she tried to stop me . . . I'm cold . . . I don't care, although I'm sorry the saint's cold, I fight to take it away because the bitch wants it . . . what do you care if you're cold,

Iris, you've already had your baby and you're not swollen anymore . . . well, if you like, as a special favor, since you're the
saint, tomorrow I'll give you a chance to get the overcoat back
so you won't feel cold, you certainly won't feel cold in bed with
your loving baby, babies keep mamma very warm when they
sleep in the same bed with her, and nothing can keep *me* warm,
my bones are getting colder and colder and colder and colder
and I don't know how to make them get warm.

THAT'S EXACTLY WHAT I'm afraid of: your bones and your flesh
will turn cold forever, a positive sign that the grafts Dr. Azula
did on you in Switzerland are taking hold. It means that this
process that's already so far advanced will erase you completely,
driving out the very last particle of warmth that Inés Santillana
de Azcoitía succeeded in hiding in the hollow of her hand and
that's to be replaced by the dryness Peta Ponce's warty fist encloses. Yes, you have only a few days left, Inés, we have little
time; your feeling this insistent cold creeping up your bones like
weeds that cover ruins until they choke them is the sign that the
end's near, that once you're eradicated, I'll be left in the Casa
with Peta, shut in, boxed in by these walls, with no way out,
cornered by the old women who'll say, look, I finally got here,
here I am, I'm your other half because I'm grotesque, I've come
back to you so we can repeat the night at La Rinconada and I
can collect the love you owe me; to get through these walls
you're locked within, I allowed Dr. Azula to keep me in jars, to
keep me cut into little pieces that were neither alive nor dead,
with my organs inside chromed machines that supplied them
with oxygen, serum, blood, to make them function until she
came looking for me, and you went to look for Peta, Inés . . .
I'm tired, Dr. Azula, I want to get old, give me old organs and
skin, a harpy's features, thinning hair I can sit back and comb
into a bun that won't pretend to be elegant . . . That's one thing
you're already doing. You walk around in tatters, with matted
hair. You're afraid of drafts. You've turned into a liar like them;
did you think I wouldn't know what you told Misiá Raquel's a

lie? Don Jerónimo's virility disappeared after our night at La Rinconada, after I locked my eyes away in this Casa so he wouldn't have the pleasure of my envy, and I have his potency, it's mine, it's mine to keep with my manuscripts in a box under my bed. And yet, Misiá Raquel persuaded you to agree to see Don Jerónimo next Tuesday, today Tuesday, tomorrow Tuesday, but all-week-long Tuesday the witches chant around their burning incense, and that's why, now that you're turning into a witch at last, you chose Tuesday to make him set foot in the Casa for the first time. I don't know what evil you plan for him, if your transformation is complete by then and the dryness and cold in your bones have given you the power of old women to defeat Jerónimo with your absolute ugliness.

The child will stop Don Jerónimo from coming into the Casa. I can't let him come in or allow his pearl-gray or dove-gray glove to brush my elbow, he might reappear from out of the past, dressed for the races in a gray cutaway, or with his arm in a sling and his bandage stained with my blood as in the clipping Inés has preserved as a keepsake, it appeared in an issue of *Mercurio* forty years ago, you can't bring your arrogance of the well-rounded man to this destitute place, your arrogance of the being who lacks nothing, because then, because I've been reduced to twenty percent of myself and even this is constantly dwindling, I'll hear that longing voice urging me from within . . . there he is, Humbertito, humble yourself, ask him a favor or something and he'll surely grant it, since your request will be insignificant, beg him to fix it so you can buy a house on easy terms, to get them to lower the rent on the house we live in, to find you a job, to give you a letter of recommendation, entreat, flatter, envy him because he has everything and is everything and you have nothing and are nobody . . . and I'd pounce on him with the fury of a starved animal to sate myself with his things, to devour him until I had my fill, yes, yes, I know I'd do something frightening that would mean the end of us all, if Don Jerónimo appeared at the Casa, I wouldn't be able to restrain myself if I had to open the door and let him in to find what's left of Inés, I'd have to hide to keep him from seeing my eyes which have been saving my life ever since I was a baby in the shanty where they say an old woman found me, and you too need them now, here in the Casa, because I'm a baby with such a sad spiritual look in my eyes that I must be a saint, the old women say . . . don't deny it, Don Jerónimo, don't reject my eyes but don't come to the Casa, if you try to come I'll have to plunge into the streets again to look for you and make you disappear . . . how can I get allies who'll help me stop you from even crossing the threshold of the Casa . . . Wednesday, Thursday, the days follow one another like the others before them, night appears in the few windows that haven't been walled up, falling as brusquely as a card that's turned over suddenly so that its back won't show, like the backs of all the cards in the deck, while other old women play dog races in the chapel at night, with candles all around them, at my feet, around the gold presbytery throne; those two are declared enemies now: Inés and Iris kneeling on the floor, each on her side of the board, surrounded by the old women who are hypnotized by the contest, frozen there by the excitement they pass on to others. Iris is almost naked because Misiá Inés has been winning everything from her, she feels cold, her eyes are bloodshot, heated only by her fury because she no longer has an overcoat or a dress or shoes or a slip, all her clothes are in a pile beside Misiá Inesita who's so good and is a real expert at games, Iris is trembling, she shakes the die in the box, gusts blow in through the gaps once filled by stained glass windows, her teeth chatter, her face is set in a mask of rage as she throws the die down on the board; she loses her bra, takes it off, Inés puts it on her heap, because the huge shadow of the bitch won and she has a right to the bra, leaving Iris with her breasts swinging from side to side, and the old women scream . . . don't play anymore, Iris, the devil's got into you, don't be stupid, you're a chip off the old block, they say your father who was shot lost his life playing monte and that's why he had to commit murder . . . it's the first time I've heard that story, I don't know if it's true but they say . . . they say so many things . . . you're hooked on the game, Iris, don't play anymore, girl, for God's sake, you're even losing weight, yesterday you bet Misiá Inés your portion of chickpeas, today your portion of lentils and your bread, besides all your clothes and your magazines and your used-up rouge, you can't go on like that, girl, for God's sake, go take care of your baby, his nose is running all over the red damask of the throne, give other people a chance to play dog races, let others offer themselves as victims to the yellow bitch dog that's been stripping off our clothes night after night, but you're the limit, just look at yourself . . . I can't lend you my shawl now although I'd like to because it upsets me to see you squatting there naked, shivering next to the board, but I can't lend it to you because I have to take care of myself, don't you see I'm getting over my sore throat . . . and me my rheumatism . . . and me my stiff neck . . . besides, you're playing because it's become nothing but a vice with you, because you hate Misiá Inesita since you started playing dog races with her, at least commend yourself to some saint, kneel before this image called St. Brígida even if she doesn't look at all like the one they carried off in a black hearse and we'll have to move to the white hearse, pray to her, but Iris doesn't pray. Inés doesn't pray either. Before, Iris was the saint but now she's only her enemy, Inés wants to strip her of everything . . . what more does she want, what's the girl going to bet now if she has nothing left but those filthy panties. The yellow bitch always wins.

"Well. What are you going to bet now, Iris?"

No, no, we old women yell at you, pleading with you to use your brains a little . . . you're thin, Iris, you've got a cold . . . we're surrounded by one another's pained faces in the darkness . . . no, Iris, the devil's got a hand in this, you should show more character . . . don't talk about the devil, it's scary . . . and there's only one candle burning, next to the board, as Iris kneels on one side, showing her enormous breasts I can only suck, without ever being able to play with her like Damiana and like babies who play with their mammas' breasts, her naked breasts with their nipples stiff with cold . . . put your nipples in my mouth and I'll warm them for you by rubbing them with my rough tongue . . . and she, Misiá Inés, the owner of the Casa, her shoulders covered with a checked shawl and her bun loose, kneels on the other side, looking at Iris, throwing her a challenge:

"Well? What's your bet?"

"My baby."

First the brief dead silence of astonishment, then the uproar . . . you can't do that, Iris, you're a degenerate brat, betting the child of your womb, and besides he's a saint, look at the poor little thing crying because you've abandoned him on the damask chair when you should be worried because he's not in his crib, well covered up, look at the way his nose is running, look at the pained look in his eyes, because child-saints understand things and he understands that his mamma's betting him against the yellow bitch dog on Misiá Inesita's board, she's such a good lady and so charitable but she's become such a gambler here in the Casa, why she doesn't even look like the same person anymore.

You, Inés, are weighing me with your eyes, figuring how much I'm worth, to decide what, of all the things you can wager, you can use to match Iris's bet . . . bet something beautiful, Inés, I beg you, please, something sumptuous like your caramel mink, your pearl earclips, the right to touch your flesh before Peta Ponce takes it over completely, bet something that will tell me I'm worth a lot.

"I accept."

"And what's your bet?"

You glance around you, the heap of rags, you feel it, no, not those things, you smile, you bring your hand up to your mouth the way some old women do to hide their missing teeth, and suddenly you go beyond the usual gesture and put your hand into your mouth, take out your prosthesis, lay it beside the board and are left with a sunken, toothless mouth like those who are saying: we had no idea, Misiá Inesita, my God, we all thought you had such beautiful teeth for your age, we used to talk about it, we admired them, it must be the good nourishment she's had since she was little, we used to say, but we were born poor and grew up undernourished, and our teeth started to go to ruin at fifteen like Iris's.

"My teeth."

The faces carved into the darkness quiet down. The women hide their hands in their rags, their watery eyes gleam, they've witnessed so much and are now witnessing this. The ring of si-

lent old women tightens around the two kneeling at the foot of
my gold throne, one on either side of the board; the yellow bitch
dog's Inés, the white one's Iris, the dice rattle in the boxes.

"The highest number starts."

Inés throws a two, Iris a four. Iris begins. Another four for
the white dog, one, two, three, four. The white bitch is made of
plastic and is balanced on a small platform of the same cheap
material, Iris's hands make her advance along the ordinary cardboard track with its clumsily drawn houses and slopes and rivers.
Inés throws a five. Restless, all set, the yellow bitch races off
with a howl across the countryside: one, down the dusty road,
two, she crosses the laurel hedge, three, she pauses to drink a
little water halfway across the pond in which the moon's reflected, and, with the four, she scrambles up a gentle slope until
she comes to a barnyard with the five and goes on running and
running; the white plastic bitch falls behind while the yellow
bitch is almost out of sight, she runs faster than ever because she
wants me, I'm going to be hers, that's why the yellow bitch
pushes herself so hard, to deserve me with a spectacular win
. . . one, two, three, four, five, six . . . Misiá Inesita's so lucky
. . . she plays again . . . four, one, two, three, four . . . I'm
going to belong to Inés because the yellow bitch will enable her
to take me up in her arms just before they turn into Peta's stick-
like ones that would trap me and allow Peta to take possession
of my organ with her rotting one, and mine would rot in hers
that's crawling with voracious worms, the yellow bitch is saving
me from the old woman's arms . . . run, run, yellow bitch baying at the moon and following its beams . . . the plastic bitch
has dropped out of sight, the old women scream, wring their
hands, say their beads, they don't even know whom they're rooting for now but all of them bet on Misiá Inesita although poor
Iris is cold . . . I'm going to belong to you, at last, even if it's
only in memory of an Inés too perfect ever to have existed and
yet so cowed by the yellow bitch who slips in between the
rushes at the edge of the swamp to hide from the ten dangerous
riders, the yellow bitch, whose flickering shadow condemns some
of the old women's faces and momentarily rescues others . . .
one, two, three . . . what does it matter if it's only a three when

you have such a short way to go, Misiá Inesita . . . let's see, Iris, come on, hurry, don't shake the die so much, throw it . . . oof, only a two . . . now you, Misiá Inesita, you're going to win easily . . . one, two, three, four, five, six, back you go . . . but you get to play again because it's a six: three, one, two, three . . . just right, you win, hurrah, the yellow bitch reached the finish line and Iris screams and covers her face with her hands while the happy old women congratulate Misiá Inesita, they dance with joy while Iris turns into a useless shell, she's not the saint now, she's nobody now, Inés stands up, she gives her dentures a kick and they fly out of sight into some corner of the chapel, she takes me in her eager arms whose softness I remember, she's the true saint, she's miraculous, she sits majestically on her throne with me, the old women bow, they light more candles, petals rain down, incense, Misiá Inés performed the miracle, she's the true saint, she's the owner, worshipping her will start here in the chapel tomorrow with Boy in her arms, Boy conceived without masculine intervention, conceived by the Blessed Inés de Azcoitía, in whom the ecclesiastics in Rome don't believe because they're heretics who don't believe in miracles, they're all Communists, they don't have faith like good people in the old days, have the chapel doors opened, run and tell the news to all the old women in the Casa, the saint reigns supreme, even over those who only suspected the miracle, they come from all the courts, barefoot and muffled up in shawls, carrying candles in holders, dragging their flannel nightgowns, they say Misiá Inesita performed a miracle, she had a baby in the chapel tonight, at her age and without being touched by any man, they pad through the Casa as fast as they can so as not to miss the show, forming a veritable legion as they hurry through corridors, courts, and passageways to venerate Misiá Inés and congratulate her on the miracle, she's the Blessed Inés de Azcoitía, who'll take them all to their salvation not in a single white hearse but in a parade of white hearses, maybe one for each old woman because Misiá Inés is a millionaire, they say, and we'll go off to heaven singing, taking all our things, we old women are making merry now because we won't have to die, we used to be terrified at the thought of it and now we don't have to be afraid of the dark passageways and the huge empty rooms where Iris must have got lost; who cares about her, now that there's all that pomp and splendor ahead, she has nothing to do with all this, no matter what Mother Benita and Father Azócar and even the Archbishop himself may say, we'll establish rituals here in this chapel with the Blessed Inés de Azcoitía presiding on her gold throne, the child in her arms, like in the paintings. In the corridors drafts catch at the shawls of those on their way here, those who knew nothing finally hear from the trembling lips of the other old women what they were so hungry to know, and they run to prostrate themselves, they're lit up by their awe over the miracle of the saint brought back to life in this toothless figure dressed in rags who has gray strings of unkempt hair like theirs, they all sing together now, they kneel together, I recognize Mother Julia with her forehead touching the floor, the chorus of voices saying rosaries to us, Eliana in ecstasy as she answers Our Fathers with Hail Marys, until Inés says: All right now, I'm tired, I want to go get some rest, it must be late. While I get ready for bed, get the child ready for me like nursemaids do with the children of rich people, who take their babies to bed after they've been washed and powdered and perfumed, the mother cuddling her child. Not before.

"It looks like the child's sleepy too."

"He must be wet."

"He has to be changed."

"He has to be changed before we take him to Misiá Inés."

"Yes, take him to my bed."

"Are you going to bed, then?"

"Yes, I'm tired."

"All right, as soon as he's ready . . ."

"I'll try to wait up for him in bed."

"We won't take long."

"Just wash his fanny."

"Do you think maybe he messed himself?"

"Let me smell . . . ugh, yes . . ."

"What a filthy baby."

"A little respect for the child, Rosa, please . . ."

"Yes, ma'am, good night."

"Good night."

They're washing me, the forty inmates assist at the ceremony, they shave my pubic hair, my testicles, they handle my organ without scorn because they know it's something useless, let's put the child on a white mattress, on a white sheet, and we'll put him naked like that in bed with Misiá Inés, she's going to like that because children give off more warmth like that, yes, then we'd better shave him all over, his skinny legs, his chin, we have to be careful with the delicate complexion of a lady like Misiá Inesita.

YOUR ROOM'S DARK. *Our* room. Beside me, under the sheets, in our bed, you breathe deeply and rhythmically in the sleep induced by the Veronal you can't stop taking every night to overcome the terrors of fitful slumber. You don't know it but, in the still night of the adobe walls, in this dark room and this warm bed, we're going to act out the magic of a moment whose fulfillment these walls have been plotting from the very beginning. Inés. How you used to walk down the corridors of La Rinconada! Your long neck, your voice that was a little husky perhaps but always warm, your long legs, your small head, the way the book you read while lying on your *lit-de-repos* slipped out of your hands . . . your vaguely outlined face faded away slowly in the twilight of the corridors and I can't recover it now, the honey of your skin, your hazel eyes, now green, now yellow, the way you tilted your head a little as you spoke to me, as you went from a smile to the verge of laughter you never quite broke out into; you're here, in this bed with me, an embodiment of beauty even if you're no longer beautiful, and yet you're still you, you're not Peta, who'll be coming to look for me from within your flesh that's still Inés's flesh, that I'm going to touch now, before Peta surfaces. I smell your fragrance here, although I also smell the odor of old age, of decrepitude, of lecherous desire, that's creeping up on you and will drive out your fragrance, I stroke your coarse hand and pull mine away, offended by the coarseness, but I wait quietly because you're still Inés, I want to be under your sheet, in the halo of your warmth, it will bring out my potency, mine and not your husband's, let my desire cross the loathsome barrier of what you are now, let me lie naked beside you and I'll gradually rid you of your ugliness, your rapacity, your old age, your madness, your stupidity, the successive disguises you have never cast off, let me bear your foulness a little longer to help me discover, in the horrible depths of your stench, the Inés that can never change, that's hidden under this filthy wreck, let me evoke you as you should always have been, so that my potency may recognize you here in your warmth caressed by my naked body. You're asleep. I hear you sleeping. It's a pity you have to snore. Our heads are on the same pillow. If I could only restore some of your youth, if I could only tear down Azula's handiwork, then, I'm sure, I could get through to you, and my body would desire you as intensely as my imagination desires you, if you had Iris's soft skin, her high breasts, her smooth legs, yes, Don Jerónimo, if Inés had these things you'd come to know that my virility's more real than yours, but not like this, I don't want to humiliate myself again, I want to break out of my confinement, I want to touch beauty as it really is, not disguised in flesh that's creased and soiled with filth, disguised in these gray straggly strings of hair, in this body that stinks under her unwashed nightgown. But you're you. Let *you* be the one to touch me first. Ask me.

I take your sleeping hand and brush my body with it. You have to recognize me, Inés, accept me even if only for the moment, as I am, whoever I may be—Humberto, Mudito, old woman, baby, idiot, fluctuating damp spot on the wall—awake now because you're touching me. Without, night sprawls over the countryside. The thrush keeps hopping, looking at us from his cage. I'm awake because your fingers, coarse now but not warty yet, close around my organ, they stroke my belly, you turn toward me in your sleep, still Inés, you draw close to my naked body that will be all ready in a second, as soon as your toothless mouth searches out mine instead of avoiding it. Your sleeping body presses against mine, you turn over on your back in your sleep, pulling me with you to make me mount you, and then I touch you, your breasts are flaccid in my hands, and I cry out:

"Inés!"

You wake up.

"Jerónimo . . ."

You didn't say Humberto. You used the same hateful word Peta Ponce used that night at La Rinconada, and in the darkness she mixed up everything and confused time and reflexes and planes that are confusing me again now. Those syllables addressed to me again! Then I won't admit that it's you either. I don't know who you are, you're not Inés, I touched you and my magic wand turned you into a toothless harpy; the old woman risen from the depths of your body to its surface took possession of you, the witch tied to the tree trunk came back from the golden horizon and became incarnate in the girl, Dr. Azula's and Emperatriz's grafts have won out, you're an old woman, you're Peta reborn under my terrified body, and you stiffen up under it as you scream and push me away, but I don't love you, Peta, you nauseate me, I'm afraid of you, you've replaced Inés completely, you've eliminated her, I don't want to touch your wormy flesh even if you scream and I scurry off in the darkness and disappear into the shadows of the passageways where your screams of terror ring out, hoarser and hoarser, it's no longer your voice, it's Peta's, an old woman's voice, toothless gums crying for help, you're afraid of death, Inés is no longer here, only Peta's here, she finally worked her way in by getting Dr. Azula to disguise her as Inés, and it's Peta shrieking . . . help, help, Mother Benita, for God's sake, help, I can't turn on the light, I'm afraid of the dark . . . but the buzzer, yes, the buzzer, rings, it shrills through the Casa . . . Misiá Inés's buzzer, what can be the matter with madam that she's asking for help and crying . . . and they don't know that you're not Inés anymore but Peta and they come to help madam, who's calling for help and crying . . . Mother Benita, please turn on the light . . . you wake up crying, sitting up on the edge of your bed, almost naked, screaming that a minute ago there was a man pawing you under the sheets . . . I must have been raped, I can't take any more, I can't defend myself because Veronal puts me into such a deep sleep . . . and she can't take any more, she just can't . . . Wasn't it a bad dream? Mother Benita suggests. Wasn't it the same ancient nightmare? . . . No, no, it was real, look, Mother, the finger marks on my breast, which he squeezed hard to hurt me, the pain woke me up . . . no, Misiá Inés, you don't have to show me anything . . . you, old women, go away . . . they'd better not know about these things, Misiá Inés, they're big gossips, you know . . . off to your beds, it was only one of madam's nightmares . . . yes, yes, Mother Benita, please make the old women go away . . . but frankly, Misiá Inés, how am I really going to believe that a man, a degenerate, got into your bed tonight when there isn't a single man in the Casa, please stop screaming, calm yourself, drink a glass of water, drink . . . no, I don't want to take anything else, you never know the things they make you drink and they may be dangerous . . . Of course, Misiá Inés. See how you listen to reason? Those bad dreams are brought on by the medicines you take to make you sleep.

"Dreams?"

"What else?"

"How dare you insinuate, Mother . . . ?"

"A nightmare."

"No, that's not what you're insinuating."

"What, then?"

"That I'm crazy."

"Misiá Inés . . ."

"Naturally. You're just like the others. They all believe I'm crazy because I came to live here. But I'm leaving the Casa this very night, I won't stay here another minute, it terrifies me, how can these scandalous things happen in a holy house like this, it's the last straw and it's all your fault, Mother Benita, don't say it's not, because you don't keep your eyes open, you should see the things I could tell you about, and I'm going to tell them when I get out of here, don't think I won't, just imagine, a strange man in the bed of a woman like me, an old woman who only wants the peace to spend her last days in prayer, keeping the inmates happy and helping them all she can, humbling herself for her sins, and look what happens, now I can recall more things that naked man was doing to me in bed, yes, he was stark naked, don't think I didn't see him run out of the room even if it was dark, don't think I didn't feel his thighs between mine, his

. . . it sends shivers up my spine just to think about him, to think how I'm being subjected again to the slavery I thought I'd shaken off forever, that man tried to rape me as I've been raped every night of my life, because it's never been tenderness or passion or love, Mother Benita, always rape, every single time, from our wedding night on, always a matter of being taken by force, never something shared, always with a stranger in under the sheets with me making me feel things that were different from the things I wanted to feel . . ."

"Misiá Inés . . ."

"What?"

"Don't say things you'll regret later on, things about your private life . . ."

"I don't have a private life. My private life was another person's."

"I think the best thing I can do is call Don Jerónimo to come and get you."

"Yes . . . no. He's at La Rinconada."

"Then what shall I do?"

"I don't know . . . I'm leaving . . ."

"How? Where?"

"Call up Raquel."

"All right, I'll go . . ."

"Don't leave me alone for anything in the world."

"If you like, I'll call one of the inmates."

"Not for anything . . ."

"Mudito then . . ."

"All right, Mudito. You can get started, I'll throw a few things in my bag and Mudito will go with me to the vestibule to wait for Raquel . . ."

You dash out of the room and down the passageways, Mother Benita . . . this is serious, Inés has gone raving mad, it's impossible, this can't be happening, I can't be loaded down with these responsibilities on top of everything else . . . And, of course, you call Misiá Raquel . . . Poor Inés has always had these obsessions, of course, plain madness, she says that if Don Jerónimo comes near her she'll jump out the window and kill herself, I'll call a doctor to go over immediately, Mother Benita, she has to be taken to a sanatorium . . . they say she was in one in Switzerland . . . yes, Mother, but not for her nerves although, from what you've told me about tonight, I suspect it must have been a kind of mental hospital and Jerónimo's tried to keep it quiet, you know how proud he is . . . but how can I believe that a woman like Inés can have such a filthy kind of insanity . . . well, Mother, it will take me a little time, I'm sure the ambulance will get there first . . . and the public health doctors did get there first, all in white, while Inés waited in the vestibule, crying, and when she saw them she started to run away screaming, and between the doctors and the assistants and myself we caught her, they tried to give her a tablet but she spat it out, it's useless to try and give her a shot because the needle may break, and I helped the doctor and the male nurses put a strait jacket on Peta Ponce, who was kicking and spitting and biting, saying that she wasn't crazy, that all the old women in the Casa were crazy, that I was a filthy swine because I'd got into her bed, and we fastened the strait jacket, she screamed that they ought to go look in the chapel if they didn't believe her . . . this poor woman's raving, the doctor said . . . poor lady, the male nurses said . . . I shook my head sadly, Mother Benita was praying, while the tears welled up in her eyes while we fastened the strait jacket among all of us and she kicked and tried to bite . . . poor lady, poor Peta Ponce, both of you locked up in Inés's body, you'll end your eternal persecutions behind bars in a mental hospital, far from me, without ever getting what you wanted me to give you, guarded by male nurses who are strong brutes but uniformed all in white, who'll put you through the mill, yes, when you reach the hospital you'll have become part of Inés's flesh, and later, in there, maybe one of the two will prevail or maybe not, maybe you'll be Peta sometimes and sometimes Inés, or else, confined to the same body, the two of you will experience the most complete love together, Azula's miracle will have been fulfilled, with Peta rendered useless, Peta locked up because she was crazy, because no one will believe the horrible stories you'll tell, obsessed by the hallucination of a naked man in your bed and the thought that it was me, me with the potency I wouldn't surrender to you, Peta, I refused it to you, and I got even with you and Inés, who denied me her mouth as if I were foul, and you, Peta, they'll lock you up disguised in Inés's flesh so you won't come looking for my organ anymore, they'll carry you both off in the same body, I won't have to fear Peta or desire Inés, because you'll both be prisoners in an insane asylum while I, with all the calm in the world, will put my potency away in the box under my bed, where all we old women store away so many things.

They managed to give her an injection. She calmed down gradually. They placed her on the stretcher. Mother, don't let me go away alone, please come with me, I'm so frightened, you implored before falling asleep, and you, Mother, on your mission of mercy, get into the white ambulance that carries them all off to the asylum. When you wake up it will be in a white room with only one window that won't be a window but a huge photograph that you'll think is a real window, because they're even that considerate with the insane, they place a photograph there to make us believe there's an outside as well as an inside. You'll never get out again. No one will believe that I or any other man was in your bed, no man gets into bed with an old woman like you, Peta, not even I, the most despicable of them, trash, trash, here in the Casa there's nothing but trash, Father Azócar says, but I had to go through the difficult motions of starting a rape to get rid of you. Inés doesn't matter. I invented her in order to lay my hands on beauty, but you'd always existed there, deep in the young Inés's beauty, forever and ever, alive like a bonfire, changeable as water, waiting for the moment when I believed I held beauty in my arms so that you could conjure it away from me, as the landowner made the girl-witch disappear and put you in her stead to receive the punishment, and from the depths of the centuries you tried to reverse that change. But I defeated you. If you're a witch, and I doubt it—you may be nothing but an ordinary miserable old woman—I fooled and eliminated you. Inés was merely my decoy. It's you who'll suffer, locked up, because you'll know that I, the thing you desired, am far from your clutches, and you'll be watching a bright window, placed very high so that you won't be rash enough to run away and look for me, nor be tempted to tear the deceptive window out with your fingernails. That's why tomorrow I'll seal all the windows I still have to wall up here in the Casa. None of them can be opened now. I've been walling them up so carefully that nobody can even tell they were there at one time, because at night, on my scaffolding, I devote myself to making breaks in the plaster, pores filled with white slobber where spiders hatch, the peeling scabs of successive coats of old paint, to create an impression of decay. I've been eliminating the windows. As I'll have to eliminate *him* now. You'll worry over the health of your poor sick wife you won't know is Peta Ponce. I have to eliminate you. My imagination is your slave just as Inés's body was your slave, you need my imagination in order to exist, Inés and I being your servants, Inés and I being heraldic beasts invented to support the symmetry of your heroic proportions, one of us on either side of you. I've eliminated her. You're starting to topple. Now I'll eliminate myself and make you come crashing down and break into a thousand fragments they'll load on Mudito's cart, and Mudito will haul them away to his court, where time and wind and the rain and the weeds will rot and erase you. I have many blank pages waiting for me to write your ending, I have lots of time to invent the most abject ending for you, because now I'm safe here in the Casa, tonight it was left without Mother Benita's ordering presence, anything can happen, now that the old women have cleaned out the chapel without leaving a trace of our occupation and have gone off to bed. They'll get up tomorrow with their minds blank for the creation of a new world, I'll make them dance behind my walled windows, the entire Casa eradicated, without openings by which to come in or go out, the *imbunche* Casa, all of us old women being *imbunches* now, we fear nothing now, I'm not afraid of Peta Ponce, because Mother Benita carried her off in a white van, tied up in a strait jacket, screaming but gradually stopping her screams, in order to bury her in a hole in the middle of the earth perhaps . . . Mother Benita took her away in a white van, Misiá Raquel, what a terrible thing to happen to poor Misiá Inesita, and the poor thing's such a good person . . . they left about half an hour ago and Misiá Raquel's also leaving, to see you in the hospital. When Misiá Raquel leaves I know that all the old women and the orphans are sleeping so as to forget everything. I open the vestibule door, the only opening the Casa's being left with. I open the street door and go out, closing it behind me.

27

TWELVE O'CLOCK MIDNIGHT struck in the tower of the church of La Merced a while ago. In the summer streets the heat chases the sweaty shirts and naked shoulders that turn white, for an instant, before disappearing behind the darkness of some corner. The downtown café lights stay on, although they might as well go out, because almost all the tables are empty . . . only a bearded young fellow dying of boredom next to his sleepy straight-haired girl, three men by themselves, the three of them in blue suits and trimmed mustaches . . . man, it's the last straw the low salaries we get and always have got . . . and the usual bottle of wine, people who'll never get to be anybody, wishy-washy, colorless people who can pass for one another, with nothing unusual about them, Emperatriz reflects as she follows Dr. Azula between the tables stained with red wine, the sandwich scraps collecting flies on a plate, the crumpled paper napkins; the fluorescent light blinks as if it wants to go out . . . it's such a sleazy place, Cris . . . that's all right, we don't have time, let's sit at this table and call the waiter with the soiled jacket.

"Two espressos."

The Rolling Stones wail for the audience that's seated on gaudy little chairs, immune to the group's musical urgings, pleas and lamentations. Coffee. It's necessary to keep a clear head at a time like this when one has to decide one's entire future, on the spot, right here, now, in the screaming vulgarity of this place.

"Let's skip off, Emperatriz."

"Where to?"

"Europe."

"Do you think Jerónimo wouldn't find us there if he wanted to get even with us? Remember that Europe isn't as far away as it was in your time."

"Yes, with this 'fly now pay later' business . . ."

"Yes. Anyhow, will you please tell me why you're so scared of Jerónimo? Are we his slaves? Why should he get even with us because Boy escaped? After all, it's not our fault. We can stop working for him the minute we feel like it. If you only knew, I'm up to here after fifteen years of Berta's chitchat."

"Emperatriz."

"What?"

"Let's use this chance to get out. We have our entire fortune in Switzerland. It's been growing with the years, it's considerable."

Squatting in the acanthus patch in the park, across the street from the big yellow mansion, Dr. Azula had waited for the yearly interview to end. He'd watched them talk and laugh in the library, sip cognac in large snifters, smoke, go over the contracts together to readjust the larger salaries, turn out the lights and look at slides of the bucolic life at La Rinconada.

As she left, Emperatriz said to her cousin, no thanks, tonight she'd rather he didn't have her taken to the Crillon in his Mercedes, it was warm out, it had been so long since she last strolled through the city streets . . . she'd like to walk a little, to wander through the places she used to be so familiar with.

"Good night, Jerónimo."

"Good night, Emperatriz."

She went across the road to the park, and Cris appeared from out of the acanthus patch. He told her in two words: Boy disappeared . . . How? When? Impossible. Tell me, tell me. What are we going to do, my God, what are we going to do? Didn't he leave any clues, something to go by? . . . No, nothing, everyone blames everyone else at La Rinconada . . .

The dwarf remains silent a moment and closes her eyes.

"There's something I want you to tell me, Cris."

"What?"

She keeps her eyes, moist under their false lashes, closed and stretches her hand out on the table, pushing aside the sugar bowl. Cris takes her hand in his claws and presses it; the question and the answer are unspoken, but he still has to show contrition.

"Emperatriz, my love, how can you doubt it? Despite my little weaknesses, the silly things inactivity more than anything else has made me do, you are and will go on being the only woman in my life. Let's leave tomorrow, on the first plane!"

With her face lit up, she opens her eyes to look into Cris's single one and realizes that, around them, the other tables in the café have been filling up, the aisles between the tables are packed with people standing there and staring at them . . . they separate their hands, they hide them, but we go on standing there, fascinated but not very amused, because we can barely understand, as we ring Emperatriz and Cris with the curiosity of homogeneous persons, destroying them with our amazement, imprisoning them, rooting them to their chairs with our stupefaction; we're not like Emperatriz and Cris, we're identical with the onlooker beside us, because no deformity singles us out. Our stares shackle them and deprive them of movement . . . lowly bank clerks . . . detectives . . . ministerial flunkies . . . queer-looking long-haired young pip-squeaks who ought to be put in jail for being revolutionaries or fags, what's the difference . . . maybe little whores . . . traveling salesmen between trains . . . a blind man, a beggar woman, a policeman in plain clothes . . . our curiosity immobilizes them. Emperatriz manages to whisper: "Let's go."

"Let's go."

"Yes, let's go."

"Pay the check, Cris . . ."

"Waiter!"

The waiter comes over.

"How much do I owe?"

"The boss says to tell you there's no charge, and to thank you . . ."

"But why?"

"Well, you've attracted so much attention that it got around that you were being lovey-dovey in here and people started coming in from the street to see you . . . take a look at the tables, all filled up and it's bringing in a lot of business at an hour when there's not a soul in all the other cafés around here. It's on the house . . ."

Emperatriz grabs her briefcase and follows her husband as they make their way through the crowd of onlookers, who break into applause when they see them leaving . . . no, Cris, we're not going anywhere, let's return to La Rinconada and hide there, the sooner the better, Jerónimo won't bother us for another year and Boy won't be able to stand a whole year outside . . . excuse me, let us through, let us out, don't crowd the door . . . no, it's not a circus . . . autographs, what kind of autographs do you expect us to sign . . . come on, Emperatriz, I have the car parked a couple of blocks away . . . People still jam the entrance to the café as the pair disappear down the street. A slovenly beggar with flashing eyes and eloquent hands followed them, trying to make himself understood . . . a deaf-mute, Emperatriz said, give him something, Cris, what a sickening way to go around dressed, what an insignificant-looking character, so puny, he's trying to tell us something . . . I put words together that they can't hear, I gesticulate, in an attempt to explain the need to get rid of Jerónimo . . . we all need to destroy him, that's why I came here, I left the Casa to come and find you so we could plot together . . . what does this little man want . . . why don't you go away and leave us alone . . . he's desperate, yes, desperate, because we have so little time before Jerónimo makes his move, this beggar must be hungry, look, he's so ragged, his face is as transparent as a ghost's, look how his legs shake . . . they stop under a street lamp as if to help me, the monsters' pity reaches out to me, they watch my lips move, they learn to read syllables and words, and then concepts, on my dumb lips, they understand, they listen, stunned, I don't have to gesticulate so much now, we talk, you two and I have so much, so very much, to talk about, you must follow my instructions to the last detail, promise me that not a sign that he ever existed will remain.

"BERTA . . ."

Berta didn't answer.

"Where in the world are you going like that?"

Berta continued dragging herself along.

"Have you gone stark raving mad?"

She was heading for Boy's part of the house, naked, her eyes glassy, a vague look in them, without answering Emperatriz, who went on exhorting her . . . how indecent, Berta, in this dreadful weather too, and I'm not trying to nag you but do be reasonable, neither one of us is young enough to go around showing ourselves like that . . . Berta . . . Berta . . . incredible, naked and dragging herself along like in Humberto Peñaloza's time. She was doing it to upset her, Emperatriz, her best friend, her only friend for years and years . . . answer me, Berta, you're out of your mind going around like that, your arms have lost the strength to pull your body along, it's gotten so broad-hipped, I'm telling you this even if you get offended, because you've got to snap out of it . . . Berta wasn't offended. Her enormous hands grasped the grass of the lawn, the gravel . . . Listen to me, Berta . . . the steps leading from the garden to the corridor, as she dragged her tail along, and, as in former days, she knocked three times with her forehead on the door of the lodge that separated Boy's quarters from the rest of La Rinconada. The doctor and his wife glanced at each other as if to say: she's gone out of her head.

The door opened. Huge, naked, still as strong as a gladiator, Basilio opened the door and let them into the vestibule. Without so much as a glance at Basilio, Emperatriz grabbed the handle of the door to Boy's first court, but it didn't open. It was locked.

"Who has the key?"

"I do, Señora Emperatriz."

"Open up."

"You can't come in."

"What do you mean, I can't come in? I can enter any part of this house I want to."

"Come in, Miss Berta . . ."

Basilio opened the door with the huge key, and Berta slid away toward the patio without hearing Emperatriz's exclamations . . . Berta, Berta, tell me what's going on . . . and the giant locked the door again. He placed the big key ring around his forearm, the keys dangling like charms on a bracelet.

"Basilio."

"Ma'am?"

"Will you tell me what this is all about?"

"I don't understand, ma'am."

"You're a lummox."

"Nothing's changed here, ma'am, it's my shift . . ."

Looking up at him from her froglike stature, Emperatriz screamed:

"Give me those keys!"

Basilio didn't give them to her.

"What do you mean, nothing's changed, Basilio?"

The door opened from inside and Boy appeared, stark naked, with the authority of his huge sex organ dangling between his rickety legs, with his short arms, his sunken chest, the weight of his hump throwing his face forward, where the pointed arch of his mouth was trapped between his nose and his chin, with his artificial forehead, his ears and his lips incomplete like those of a fetus, the electric arc of his blue eyes uncovered by lizard eyelids . . . for the first time, Emperatriz felt those electric eyes scorching her, and her will power reduced to ashes. Boy greeted the couple.

"Yes, Emperatriz. Nothing's happened here."

"I don't understand."

"Take your clothes off, both of you, and come in. I want to have a little talk with you. Creeps! You're so repulsive you're not even funny, I feel like crying instead of laughing. And better start getting used to going around naked, Emperatriz, because nothing's happened here. Follow me, you two."

Emperatriz mumbled something.

"I don't understand you, Emperatriz, better speak up. I'm warning you this is the last time you and I are going to discuss certain matters. After that we'll draw a veil over your shameless behavior during the last twelve years . . ."

"Shameless behavior, me . . . !"

"Yes, your shameless behavior and your husband's too,

you've betrayed my father's brilliant idea and have exploited me
. . . yes, Emperatriz, wipe that frightened look off your face, I
know now what it is to have a father, I know who my father is,
I know what his scheme was, and I know very well how much
and what will be mine once my father dies, yes, now I know
what ownership means, and what dying means . . . don't look
frightened, calm down; you learn a lot wandering around out
there for five days. As I've told you, we're going to draw a veil
over things: nothing's happened here. I'll be considerate with
you and I won't report you to my father. I could do it but I'm
not going to, because as a matter of fact that doesn't fit in with
my plans."

Why had they come back to La Rinconada? Switzerland
would have been so easy, so convenient, she could travel on her
husband's Spanish passport. A beggar's soundless words had
forced them to return to this hell.

"I'm waiting for an explanation, Emperatriz."

All those faces watching us in the café . . .

"All those faces watching you in the café?"

"How do you know?"

"I know everything now. I have allies outside who are helping me carry out my designs, because I also know what it is to
have designs; my allies are those who suffered with me during
the five days I wandered around outside, those who identified
with me when I tried to turn into a human being. They told my
father that I ran away, and he'll come, Emperatriz, he promised
to, he wants to see if it's true that you've been fulfilling your
obligation to hold me prisoner, in limbo."

"Today?"

"I don't know, maybe a few days from now, you know that
my father's been slowing down with the years . . ."

"My God, Jerónimo really is running to seed!"

"Of course, and you take advantage of it. I want to warn
you about one thing. My father's going to come here, but he
knows nothing about how your little tricks have made nonsense
of his original idea. He realizes that his presence at La Rinconada is necessary . . . a visit, a visit I—and you, because you're
going to help me—will make sure lasts a long, long time . . ."

"But what's Jerónimo going to do here?"

"We'll see. If you don't want me to throw you and Azula and the other monsters out for people to follow you around and laugh at you as they laughed at you the other night in a café and as they laughed at me in the bars and the streets and in a whorehouse where they wouldn't even let me touch any of the normal women because, they said, monsters are the devil and bring bad luck, and the whores threw me out . . . if you don't want me to kick you out and break up this paradise, you have to play my game and obey me. I've already warned the others. I'm going to erase the outside world. And if you don't obey me I'm going to tell Berta that you're just a poor relative, that you never set foot in the aristocratic school you talk about, that you know who's who in society, but nobody knows who *you* are."

"I'll die if Berta finds out!"

"All right. I agree to keep silent about a lot of things, but you have to play my game because you're my prisoner. We have to eradicate the outside world. You, Azula, will operate on me again; this time you'll cut out the portion of my brain where I must have collected all the experiences of those five days on the outside, and afterwards you'll close me up again, leaving me as ignorant and pure as I was in the old days."

"It's going to be difficult . . ."

"But it can be done."

"Yes, it can."

"What's within my quarters is all that counts. The rest is yours to do with as you please, it doesn't interest me, keep it all, Emperatriz, I'm giving you La Rinconada and the rest, you and Azula can do what you like with my fortune when my father dies if you allow me to turn back into an abstraction. After five days on the outside, I'm not interested in living. A poet said: 'Live? Live? What is that? Why not let our servants do it for us.' You're my servants. You'll experience what I refuse to experience. Now that I know reality, only the artificial interests me."

"What about *him?*"

"Who, my father or the other fellow?"

Emperatriz hesitated before answering:

"Jerónimo."

"If I'd had a monstrous son like me, I'd have done exactly the same thing he did with me. I saw him going down the street one morning, dressed in very light gray, holding a glove in one hand. That's why your scalpel, Azula . . . I offer you and Emperatriz everything I'm going to inherit if you root out those five days. Graft them on someone else and let him live in my nightmare. Then I'll shut myself up in my quarters, where you two will stick to the original order."

"And Jerónimo?"

"He'll come. Very soon. My friends are already whispering in his ear, tempting him with the greatest of all temptations . . ."

"What?"

"That I ought to have a son. And so, after passing through the hell of a monstrous link in the chain, the family stock will be purified. I want the operation to be performed as soon as possible, Azula. Everything goes to you, provided you maintain my limbo. Are you leaving or staying on?"

They regarded each other silently.

"You're free to go."

Emperatriz had closed her eyes, holding her pudgy little hands, one on top of the other, in her lap. She and her husband shook their heads. Boy said:

"All right. We have to start getting things ready. The truth that was invented for me will be *the* truth, and I'll die without anguish because I'll have forgotten *what* dying means. Lots of *fattest woman in the worlds,* start fattening them up for me, Emperatriz, all of them the same, all flesh, and you, Azula, go over your vanilla-flavored recipes so you can again nourish me with them starting today, I'll never eat anything else, and the succession of fat women will be like a succession of well-prepared strained baby foods: nourishing, they'll keep my system functioning well, but I won't desire anything else."

"But Boy!"

"What, Emperatriz?"

"What about *him?*"

"Who?"

The dwarf closed her eyes and screamed, a sharp prolonged cry. She calmed down in a second.

"Do you see, Emperatriz?"

"What?"

"The pain of wanting to touch someone who can't be touched?"

"Was he the one who told you everything?"

"He was."

"Well! When is Jerónimo coming?"

"I don't know, but when he comes I'll be the seventeen-year-old Boy he dreamed of. With one difference: until he disappears and I can undergo Azula's operation to root out those five days, it will all be pure fiction, I'll be putting on an act and so will you. Later, when Azula operates on me and my father disappears, I'll turn over everything to you and you can maintain my truth from the outside."

Dr. Azula got to his feet.

"I'm not going to be part of any crime."

"Who mentioned crime, Cris? Don't be silly, darling."

28

"DID HE DECORATE all this?"

"He . . ."

"He developed very good taste. Humberto was intelligent. This is a very pleasant apartment. One could spend his whole life here . . ."

"This is the bedroom."

"Tell them to bring my suitcases here."

"I thought you were going to stay in my apartment . . ."

"I don't know, seeing all this, I'm tempted to live in Humberto's. You . . . What's your name?"

"Basilio, Sir."

"Bring my luggage and put away my clothes in the dressing room while I attend to other things."

They went out to the terrace, from which they could see the huge luxurious lawn, the swimming pool, the particolored beach umbrellas, the elms, the araucarias, the magnolia and eucalyptus trees in the park, and beyond them the mountain range.

"I'd forgotten how pretty all this was."

"It's extraordinary. Cris always says . . ."

"And this? The library. My Claude Lorrain. It's been so long since I last saw it! It's like running into an old friend you haven't seen in ages and asking yourself how you've been able to go through life without his conversation. It's not just any Claude, it's extraordinary, Claudes as important as this aren't found anymore . . . And this, the walnut desk where Humberto used to write . . ."

"He did very little writing."

"Too bad. He had talent to spare."

"As a matter of fact, he never wrote anything, Jerónimo. He spent his time thinking about what he was going to write, and sometimes, in the evening, when a very nice group of us got together here, he used to tell us his projects."

"Well, maybe it was all for the best. One of Humberto's foibles was his belief that my life would make a good biography."

"Yes, he started out by talking about that, but later on he distorted everything. Humberto had no talent for simplicity. He felt the need to twist normal things around, a kind of compulsion to take revenge and destroy, and he complicated and deformed his original project so much that it's as if he'd lost himself forever in the labyrinth he invented as he went along that was filled with darkness and terrors more real than himself and his other characters, always nebulous, fluctuating, never real human beings, always disguises, actors, dissolving greasepaint . . . yes, his obsessions and his hatreds were more important than the reality he needed to deny . . ."

"Interesting, Emperatriz. You're a good literary critic . . ."

"So many years of living close to him."

"Of course. But, you know, I think the poor man's main problem was his need to give me spiritual stature and a consistency I lack, and so he had to invent a biography for me, in which he got lost . . . ah, Azula, come in, come in, it's good to see you, sit down, you, Basilio, a whiskey for the doctor. Such a pleasant house, isn't it?"

"My place is also lovely, cousin."

"Yes, Emperatriz, but, in you, good taste has no appeal. You were always poor, and I believe your mother worked for the Telephone Company . . ."

Emperatriz blushed; no matter what anybody said, her mother had been a great lady.

". . . but you had something on which to base your good taste. Humberto's, on the other hand, was pure invention. Anyhow, let's not talk about him, you and Azula are here to keep this place going . . ."

Everything was going the way he wanted it, Emperatriz reassured him on that score, nothing was going to let him down;

the results of the project entrusted to her were, frankly, excellent. Would he like to get some rest after his trip or go and see his son right away?

"No . . . I'm a little tired. I'm famished . . ."

"Do you want to see him after lunch, then?"

Hesitating, Jerónimo said maybe not, better not do it today, really he was extremely tired, today he preferred to stroll through the park—it brought back so many memories for him—to meet the people out there or maybe take a good siesta, and have them prepare the terrace so he could spend the rest of the day there. Perhaps tomorrow, yes, probably early tomorrow morning . . .

But the next morning he had them saddle a horse for him. He rode out alone, over the paths on his estate, past the ponds fringed with rushes, to listen to flocks of *queltehues,* to visit the tenant farmers' huts occupied now by third-, fourth-, and fifth-class monsters . . . well done, Emperatriz, congratulations, surrounding the main houses with an isolating belt of monsters seems to me like a marvelous precaution, Jerónimo told her at dinner that night, his face reddened by the sun and wearing a beatific smile that softened it.

"Emperatriz . . ."

"What?"

"I've suddenly felt like having . . . a small boy's hankering . . ."

"I wonder what?"

"I remember the blancmange Peta Ponce used to make here at La Rinconada in a copper pot, a blancmange made with very fresh milk. The old woman spent whole afternoons stirring the pot like mad, and the sweet came out with a slight taste of hawthorn smoke, with the milk a bit curdled . . . well, I suddenly remembered and I felt like having some . . ."

"But Jerónimo! Nothing could be simpler. I'll have them make it tomorrow without fail, and you'll have it for breakfast day after tomorrow . . ."

Day after day, Jerónimo kept putting off his visit to Boy's quarters. The slightest thing—a certain bend in one of the avenues of giant hydrangeas, a corner in the corridors—summoned up memories of his wife. Emperatriz never tired of asking him questions about Inés, her jewels, how she dressed . . .

"All her things are in safekeeping."

"Where?"

"At the Casa de Ejercicios Espirituales de la Encarnación at La Chimba . . ."

"Oh, the family's chaplaincy."

"Yes. There are cells and cells filled with her things. A real feast for the moths, I suppose."

"Too bad all that will come to an end!"

"An end?"

Jerónimo stopped, hovering like a giant over Emperatriz: she felt a twinge of fear, seeing him so handsome, with his still-abundant white hair. To face him, to look at him, was like noticing, suddenly, in a café, that the mocking crowd is shattering your innermost self . . . as she looked up at him, the dwarf felt faint.

"Nothing's coming to an end."

"Well, you're not eternal . . ."

"No?"

"Well, I suppose . . ."

"During these weeks I've spent so pleasantly here at La Rinconada, I've thought it over and decided that this can't end. Let Boy get married, yes, and things won't come to an end. I don't know if it's the taste of the blancmange prepared by Peta Ponce that has made me, suddenly, want so much to have grandchildren."

"And what about us, cousin?"

"Haven't I been paying you good salaries for I don't know how many years? I'm sure you'll be able to get along."

"There are things money doesn't take care of."

"That's a ridiculous cliché."

"Don't you believe it."

"What do you mean?"

"We're your victims too."

That was the word she wanted to come to.

"Yes. Victims. Protected by us . . . by our monstrosity, your son is king. We're the props: the painted backdrop, the flies, the papier-mâché heads, the masks. If they're withdrawn from around the central character who was born a king on stage . . . well, he'll be swallowed up by an abyss. Your plan won't be so easy to carry out . . ."

"You're trying to protect yourself."

"Yes. Remember I go out once a year. And that excursion once a year makes me doubly sure I want to go on forever forming part of a painted papier-mâché set. Are you thinking of taking him with you to find him a bride and disbanding us?"

"I don't know, I don't know anything yet. I want to see him. I'm very curious to see him. Tomorrow."

As soon as Jerónimo retired to Humberto's tower, Emperatriz and Dr. Azula met with the monsters and then went to wake Boy. They told him the details of his father's project: to marry him off to a homely cousin so that they could have sons and grandsons, to have him live in the city, to devote himself to politics, to business, to become a member of the Union Club. He wants La Rinconada to come to an end.

Boy had a long laugh. La Rinconada wasn't going to end. He'd see to that. If they, the first-class monsters, helped him, he'd make sure they kept this hideaway. Once Jerónimo fell into his hands, nothing would break up La Rinconada, the papier-mâché world Emperatriz had referred to would become a reality, she herself would never have to go out into the world again. Yes, yes, faced with the danger of having to return to a world they did not and would rather not remember, they swore to do everything Boy said, because they had to stick together and forget their differences in order to protect their world as it stood. They were to let nothing endanger it. Jerónimo had no right to. They weren't prepared to be his instruments or form part of a world he took it into his head to break up for no reason at all, because he remembered something, because he ate blancmange or was afraid or felt nostalgic . . . because he was now tired of his other games, like a minor god who never got past a frivolous and spoiled childhood in which his old toys always have to be replaced with new toys his boredom will make old and destroy . . . like an arteriosclerotic deity who, in creating the world, was stupid enough not to protect himself against the dangers that might arise in his creation . . . no, no, this was going too far, they weren't ready to sit back and watch him set fire to them as if they were only a lot of costumes and games and boards and chips and old masks, they weren't going to let him force them to go out once more into something called reality; every year, when she'd returned and recovered with a couple of days of bed rest, Emperatriz would tell them hair-raising things, he couldn't leave them to the mercy of the outer world they didn't remember, we don't want to disappear, we don't want La Rinconada to break up: they'd go along with Boy in whatever he wanted. Following his lead. In everything. They'd be his pawns if he promised to defend them against the infernal father who'd destroy them if his son didn't defend them against this lord who believed himself the owner of the world because he only invented it. Yes, Boy could count on them.

DESPITE HIS AGE, the naked Jerónimo preserved the perfection of his build, as if the years, as they passed by him, had found no flaws to become snarled in and accentuate. When she saw him enter Boy's first court, the dwarf let out a genuine cry of pain, she fled to keep from seeing or being seen by him, sobbing, disobeying Jerónimo who warned her not to overdo it, after all it was only a question of feigning terror in front of Boy and Boy wasn't there yet. But the dwarf ran screaming down the corridors, naked, warning the others to run too, to watch out, a horrible creature had appeared, who knows from where or how. Berta was moaning, curled like a dying lizard behind some rectangular shrubbery that offered no holes to crawl into, but she couldn't take her hallucinated eyes off the apparition crossing the court and calling out to them in a friendly way. Melchor tried to drive him off with branches. Basilio threw rocks at him. Melisa hid behind the pedestal of the hunchbacked ephebus, shouting to Boy to run away, to take cover wherever he could, that something she couldn't understand, something horrible, was happening. Seeing Jerónimo at the end of the corridor, Boy advanced until he was ten steps away from him; he stared at him for a minute, steadfast, his eyes devouring every detail of the apparition . . . no, it can't be, he covered his face, spun around and fled to the rear of the house, letting out howls of anguished confusion . . . take him away, don't let him stay here, Emperatriz, what is this apparition that makes me feel something I've never felt before that wasn't scheduled and makes me cry with terror although I don't know what terror is, Melchor, Basilio, explain it to me . . . it's revulsion, sir, it's loathing, sir, it's fear, we feel it too, it's horror in the presence of a creature so outlandish that he may be dangerous . . . what does *dangerous* mean . . . calm down, sir, you'll get used to it, we all have to get used to it and besides he doesn't seem to be evil . . . yes, he must be evil, he's evil because he's so unusual that he's terrifying, because he's inconceivable . . . calm down, sir . . .

That day Boy refused to go near his father again.

While the adolescent slept that night, in Emperatriz's dining room Jerónimo congratulated the dwarf on the convincing way she and the others had acted. For a minute, he said, he was afraid a rock thrown by Basilio would hit him.

"It wasn't all acting on our part, cousin . . ."

"Do you mean I'm really such a sight?"

The guests laughed.

"What a notion, cousin! But maybe yes . . ."

"What?"

"It's just that when we're inside, in the house, the rules of the universe you invented have been in force so long that we don't have to act, at least I don't . . ."

Everyone agreed.

". . . and we don't have to act horrified at your monstrosity, because, as a matter of fact, in there you're the one who's a monster."

Jerónimo drank a glass of wine.

"Wonderful. A bit uncomfortable at first, but then, I'll gradually get used to it. I may also succeed in making him get used to me. I don't know, I'd really like to get to know him, to speak to him."

"Later, little by little, when you learn his language."

"Very well."

"Overcoming his extreme sensitivity, handling your appearance adequately so that, besides being unique in a world where the unusual has never existed, well, all that's going to take a little time . . ."

"What do you people advise me to do?"

". . . to be patient."

Every day, and remaining each day a bit longer than the day before, Jerónimo would undress in the porter's lodge and enter Boy's quarters. Every day, at a certain hour, Berta reclined her inert naked flesh, stricken by the years, on some steps, leaned against a pilaster, or dragged herself along the paths of trimmed square hedges, followed by her cat with its hypertrophic head. Every afternoon a *fattest woman in the world* went in to give the adolescent his dosage of pleasure. Every morning Dr. Azula examined Boy. A ritual, everything was a ritual. Three times a day Emperatriz served him his food disguised in vanilla . . . every day Melchor . . . every day Basilio . . . a prepared schedule, measured doses . . . and now, imperceptibly, several minutes each day so that the boy wouldn't notice that a new element was being introduced, Jerónimo walked through the corridors naked, indifferent to the terror his appearance caused in those beings who fled as he went by. He became accustomed to being grazed by a stone hurled by Basilio, to a blow from Melchor that would leave a mark on his face, or to Berta, made hysterical by his presence, digging her nails into his thighs. Boy observed him from a distance. But he observed him. That was a step forward, they remarked at night in Emperatriz's living room, satisfied at the progress toward a father-son relationship.

"He's curious about me."

"Wonderful; it's the beginning."

"What we have to do now is get him to come closer, to let himself feel attracted by my monstrosity."

The next day, according to plans made that night, the senator pretended to doze on a bench in the sun, realizing that Boy had started to study him from a window. Brother Mateo's arguments overcame the adolescent's repugnance, his reluctance to approach his father and examine him; Brother Mateo had to hold Boy in front of Jerónimo in his monumental repose. Boy closed his eyes. He only pretended to look; his father's image was already engraved behind his eyelids with incisions that were too painful.

"Do you see now, sir? He's not so horrifying."

"Yes, yes he is . . . more horrifying than when I see him from far off."

"If you think about it a little, you may find him funny . . . look at the ridiculous monotony of his proportions, for instance, and his back that's so straight and his complexion that's so smooth, the same all over, without interesting texture or surprising tones . . . don't tell me he's not funny, like a balloon that's been blown up . . ."

Boy let out a horse laugh that broke Jerónimo's sleep. Doubled over, tears welling in his eyes, Boy held his stomach, laughing and pointing at his father with his twisted finger . . . you're right, Mateo, he's not ferocious, look how he lets me whip him with this switch, it's such fun to pull his hair—stand up, walk, look—he obeys and walks, Mateo, so stiff, his steps so even, his head so high, he's so funny, so this is what laughter is, I didn't know what laughing was like and I like to laugh, no, I don't want him to leave, don't let him get away, I want this monster to stay here so I can laugh at him, I want him to hop . . . Hop! Once more! More! Now on one leg! . . . Make him run now, look at the way he runs down the path and comes back panting, it's so much fun, bring me a *fattest woman in the world* so I can put him in bed with her and see what he does, if he knows how or can do anything, look, Emperatriz, look Mateo, look Berta, look, Melisa, how this monster tumbles with the fat lady, he can't do a thing with her, look at that thing that's shriveled and wrinkled like an old glove and that he has where I have my magnificent organ that gets hard at the slightest provocation.

"I must say I was a bit upset . . ."

Emperatriz almost choked laughing. Too bad he wouldn't come to her birthday celebration.

"But why shouldn't I go if you invite me?"

"Humberto never came to the parties we gave."

"Maybe he didn't, but I . . ."

"A masked ball. I give one every year. And I don't know if you'll enjoy it, because, besides the first-class monsters, we invite the second- and third-class, in order to have more people . . . I don't know if you'll like such a mixed crowd."

"There's nothing a good costume won't hide."

"We can count on you, then?"

"I'd love it."

They told him that Emperatriz gave balls that were simply fabulous, always based on a theme, last year, for instance, the theme was "The Swiss Chalet," and everyone wore dirndls and lederhosen, and Emperatriz's place, her boudoir and salons, had been decorated with simulated snow and edelweiss on the windows.

On other occasions, it had been "The Alhambra," they told him, and the never-to-be-forgotten "Hospital." This year Emperatriz had decided that the theme would be "The Court of Miracles." She'd decorate her house and her garden like a ruined convent, and they'd dress up as libidinous old women with frazzled hair, starved beggars, cripples and sacristans and thieves, friars and nuns . . . the object was to rival one another in the sumptuosity of their rags, in the exquisite styling of their misery, she'd have damp spots and peeling plaster painted on the walls so they could stroll around in narrow passageways and simulated cloisters, between toppled walls and deconsecrated chapels, and abandon themselves in an unlimited orgy . . . why shouldn't they go the limit when everyone would be wearing the masks of normal human beings eaten away by sickness and destroyed by poverty . . . nobody would recognize anybody else.

THAT NIGHT, AFTER Jerónimo went off to sleep in Humberto's tower, the monsters went to talk things over with Boy. They found him looking dejected. It was clear that he was holding back something. Emperatriz urged him to confess what it was, because if they didn't confess things to each other now, their plans might fall through. Boy whispered:

"Dr. Azula . . ."

"Yes?"

"I want to discuss something with you. You've promised to wipe out those horrible five days in which I learned everything. Isn't that right?"

"Yes."

"I also need you to cut my father out of me. Can you cut my father out, Dr. Azula?"

The doctor thought about it.

"Perhaps that image is lodged too deep in your brain . . . a tumor that's putting down roots and spreading by metastasis . . . I don't know. If I did it I'd also have to cut out a large part of your brain, and then, of course, you'd have the mere shadow of consciousness left, you'd live in a kind of twilight, in a limbo not very different from death without sinking into it, alive, but . . ."

Boy buried his face in his hands. They heard him moan. The monsters looked at one another. How could they show him their sympathy? No one moved. No one lit a cigarette or said a word until Boy, covering his face, said:

"I want to look like him. Save me, Azula . . . take out as much of my brain as you want, leave me reduced to a vegetable, but cut him out of me . . ."

The following day they told Jerónimo that Boy was obviously impatient to communicate with him, but, to accomplish this, instead of visiting his quarters at certain times, he'd have to move in and live there. Boy asked for him. Sometimes, at night, he woke up screaming for them to bring him his monster. Jerónimo was delighted to accept; the prospect of speaking to his son in a few days, even if only about the most rudimentary things, filled him with happiness, and procreation was, naturally, one of the most rudimentary things about a human being. He'd have to go to Boy naked, of course. Basilio watched him undress in the porter's lodge, opened the door for Jerónimo, who went in, and then the giant put the bolt and chain in place and locked the door with the key. That night the secret meeting took place on Humberto's terrace, with the monsters around Boy. They had to stop everything up.

"Do you have the documents ready, Emperatriz?"

"All of them."

"Hand them to me . . . and ink, so I can sign them. One, two, with copies, power of attorney with six copies . . . signing so many papers is such a bore . . . these others are less important. Oh yes, and my will, all my fortune in usufruct for a cooperative or society with Emperatriz as its president, who'll see to it that La Rinconada's is preserved and grows . . ."

On the following day, when they happened to run into each other near Diana's pond, the adolescent allowed his father to address him, saying, very well, he'd listen to him, but he must crawl like an animal, yes, like that, and he was to speak to him from that position and no other. Jerónimo started telling him that he was his father . . . but I don't know what *father* means . . . and that his mother . . . what's *mother* . . . I have to begin by explaining everything to this child, and from this position, following him through the corridors like a dog, trying to explain to him, while Boy not only failed to understand but laughed at his words. Till he finally turned around, looked down at him and walked away with a yawn.

Jerónimo got to his feet as soon as Boy disappeared. And he went around the courts looking for Emperatriz to tell her that it was still uncomfortable but at least it was a step forward. As he tried to approach her, the dwarf screamed at him:

"Go away, you disgust me, don't touch me, don't come near me, I don't know what's got into Boy, going in for these creepy things that only get in the way."

Emperatriz refused to hear him out. Jerónimo thought the dwarf was really stretching things a bit. But he recalled what his cousin had told him once: that, when they were in the courts, they didn't *act*, they *reacted*, impelled by the rules he and Humberto had set years ago, they were no longer free, being conditioned by rules imposed by Jerónimo. He decided he'd get out that same night . . . what was he doing here, uncomfortable and humiliated, after all, when his gray velvet armchairs were waiting for him in the library of his yellow house across the way from the park . . . he'd send Boy to a clinic or some such place, he'd look for one, and scatter all those disconcerting masks . . . or false faces . . . he was weary, he'd suddenly grown weary of all this, it wasn't comforting to have them laugh at his advanced years, to make him walk on all fours, to order him to wash windows, sweep hallways and empty rooms and galleries and interminable courts, to seal off doors, plaster walls, burn old newspapers, clean the sportive Venus's pitted rear, do pirouettes, run with the pack of lame dogs in hot pursuit of him, without tails, mangy, earless, their eyes flashing in their hypertrophic heads and their fangs dangerously drooling slobber down their snouts, to have to obey any of these monsters who, after all . . . yes, yes, why should I be afraid of them when I can drive them away the minute I feel like it . . . every day he told himself he was going to tell Emperatriz that the farce could go no further and to send them packing, but he never got a chance to speak to her . . . I drop into bed bone-tired, I dream of monsters surrounding me, I see them when I wake up, I can't tell the difference anymore between the monsters of my waking hours and those in my dreams, the hideous faces with the huge noses and hanging jaws and mouths jammed full of teeth, all of them laughing themselves silly because I'm the monster, they shout this at me day and night in the confusing passageways where more unfamiliar monsters keep showing up because all the monsters are strangers now, I'd like to run into just one of my familiar monsters, but no . . . I must be dreaming these passageways covered with cobwebs, and if it's a dream it's natural that my monster friends, those of my waking hours, can't come into the dream to rescue me, please save me from this persecution in which they yell at me that I'm the laughingstock of the whole world, I can't remember anymore where the exit is, I'm not familiar with these passageways and courts, they've just put them here, if I could find the exit I could convince Basilio to let me out, but Basilio's not here, there are people around that look like Basilio but they're not Basilio, they're cousins, brothers, uncles, maybe, exactly like him, but not him, because they don't answer except with taunts when I plead with them . . . Basilio, open the door for me, I'll give you anything you want if you let me out . . . it's not Basilio, because he throws rocks at me that cut my chest, these hunchbacks, these albino faces, bulldog heads, bulky giantesses waddling along hot on my trail, are all gruesome creatures I own, whose names I used to know and whom I used to talk with, but they're deaf and dumb now because all they want to do is chase me around so that I'll get tired and collapse into my bed and sleep without being able to warn Emperatriz in all seriousness that it's gone far enough, to stop these games, to get the law after them all, but they also chase me at night, wearing me out too much to face the day, picking me clean of everything except the desire to beg for mercy, at least a respite, but they won't let me have one, they shout and scream and whip me and laugh all around me, I bring my hands up to my face to touch my features and recognize them even if they're only the monstrous features I've always had, yes, yes, yes, I admit that I've always been deformed, never a man who held important public office or was ever loved by beautiful women . . . no traces of that man's features remain. I stop, sweating, panting, and face the crowd of elegantly dressed monsters, of monsters fresh, ready to go back to their completely normal lives as soon as something . . . I don't know what . . . I don't want to think what . . . occurs or doesn't occur. I'm the only one that's different, I blush with shame when I realize I'm the only naked person at this sophisticated party. Looking so very elegant, my son steps up to me:

"What gives you the right to carry on like this? Are you out of your mind? What's wrong with you?"

"What's wrong with you people? Something strange is going on here . . . Emperatriz, give me the keys . . . but they can't hear, because their earsplitting laughter fills my head and is going to make it explode, because it's sealed in there, one burst of laughter, his, shrill, final, challenges me to see if I ever again dare say that you're the abnormal one and not I, and I say yes, and Boy calls Basilio . . . come, Basilio, let's take him there to look at himself . . . and Basilio and the other robust monsters drag me along as I kick and scream . . . leave me alone . . . but they pull me to the pond of the Huntress Diana and force me to get up on the edge. All the monsters watch the scene from the edge of the pond presided over by Diana with her hump, her acromegalic jaw and the half-moon on her forehead. Basilio holds me down by one arm, Boy pins down the other . . . let go, let me go . . ."

I hear his voice:

"Look at yourself."

I lower my eyes to see what I know I'll see, my classic proportions, my white hair, clean-cut features, blue stare, cleft chin,
but someone hurls an insidious stone into the water's mirror; it
splinters my image, shatters my face, the pain's unbearable, I
scream, I howl, doubled up, wounded, my features in shreds, I
break free of the hands pinning me down and I run, trying to
rip with my nails the mask I can't take off but know is a mask
because Emperatriz's dance is tonight and I've disguised myself
as a monster, I scratch my face and it bleeds and my bleeding
proves to me that it's not a mask, but I scratch more because I
have to remove it despite the pain and even if I'm left without
a face, yes, I recognized myself as a twisted monster in the reflection in the pond; they, the others, are harmonious beings,
tall, normal, it's I who am the buffoon in this court of princely
personages wrapped in the luxury of their costumes, I alone am
naked, I have to find my clothes to cover my deformities and
stop them from laughing at me. I used to have clothes. I look
for the door in the passageways that are suddenly deserted, I
want to find the porter's lodge but there are no doors, they've
sealed them off for Emperatriz's ball, they've put up cobwebs
and peeled the walls and extended the galleries with false
perspectives that make me bang my head when I try to escape
through them, they've walled off everything in order to box in
my monstrous image, yes, it's nothing but an image, I have a
different one, now that they've disappeared I can run over to
Diana's pond before anyone finds out and I can recover the
other image I don't find in the water, only a jumble of features
floats there, those broken-up planes, that exaggeration of traits,
those suppressions, sutures, scars, shoulders that don't fit the
body, the erased neck, the fluctuating length of arms; it's my
blurred image waiting for the afternoon light to melt away so
that it can reassemble in a different form, but the light doesn't
erase anything, because it's a full moon and I can't run away if
I promised Emperatriz to be at her masked ball, and that's why
I put on this face that bleeds because I can't pull it off. Broken
to pieces, the mask doesn't cover anything, if I could find some-

one to help me and lead me out, running after me with cats whose freakish heads can trap me in the darkness that's total now outside their burning eyes, no, no, there's some light at the end of that simulated passage, voices, perhaps my friends, perhaps music; I run . . . it's me, it's me, wait for me, I'm weak . . . but I'll still make it to the light and the music . . . I stumble, I fall, my face is smashed against the brick floor; kneeling, I press together what features I have left, in order to piece them back together, to create something like a face, as if it were clay, it's soft, maybe I can reconstruct my old features, but I can't remember what they were like; when I try to mold a face for myself, pieces stick to my hands, I crawl toward the light, I open the door with my head, like a dog, Emperatriz's ball, they lied to me so that I'd come as a tattered monster. Familiar and unfamiliar faces are dancing in the light, with monumental wigs like tall frosted pastry, with golden turbans and strands of pearls, opalescent masks, brocaded dominoes, pointed satin slippers dancing a minuet, whirling crinolines, three-cornered hats in hand, glittering uniforms, beautiful papier-mâché masks hiding monstrous faces, coquettish dimples; the couples are dancing, fingers touching delicately, they're drinking from chilled glasses when I come crawling in so that they won't see me, I came costumed for a different ball, a ball where everything was walled-up doors and endless passageways and imbecile creatures shielded by merciful adobe walls, not this ball where everything's bright and fine and light, they deceived me, I have to escape before the marquises and the cardinals and the princes and the halberdiers laugh at me, they're going to give me a trouncing because I came disguised as a monster and they didn't, I did, they didn't, the water in the pond will help me change my face, the moon outlines to the last detail my mask floating in the water, if I could only take it off, tear it out of the water where maybe the separation of flesh and flesh would be less painful . . . to kneel at the edge . . . to stretch my arm and tear off the mask of terror.

Much later, when the couples went out to the garden to get some fresh air, they saw him floating in Diana's pond . . . Save him! Call the others to save him if he's alive! . . . They throw down their fans and their purses to help in the rescue with drag hooks and lines: they pulled a twisted, horrifying, monstrous creature out of the water. Rising to his full height, Boy lowered the electric arc of his blue eyes and recognized him:

"It's my father."

Emperatriz agreed.

"Yes, it's Jerónimo."

And, upset by the gravity of the accident suffered by the senator, who perhaps, at his age, shouldn't have had so much to drink at a masked ball, all those perfect creatures took the necessary steps to send the body to the capital in the richest coffin. They also made everything ready so that, as soon as the authorities and lawyers returned to the capital, Dr. Azula could perform the operation needed to excise from Boy's memory those five days he spent outside the house, and the image of his father, down to its most deeply buried roots.

The news of the senator's death caused real consternation in the capital. The entire country remembered, then, the eminent public man's services, and he was paid the country's highest honors: his remains were taken to the cemetery on a gun carriage shrouded in the nation's tricolor. Many considered this improper, for Jerónimo de Azcoitía's role had been political rather than historic, and his name would endure only in specialized texts. Despite the pros and cons of the honors granted·him, or perhaps for the very reason that these existed, everyone attended his funeral. In the family mausoleum, his body occupied a vault with his name and the dates of his birth and death, placing him on equal terms with the Azcoitías who preceded him. Speakers evoked his achievements, the lesson of this exemplary life that marked the end of a race. The changes in the contemporary world notwithstanding, the country acknowledged itself his debtor. A heavy iron chain sealed the grille of the mausoleum where, within a few hours, the flowers would begin to rot. The gentlemen in black turned their backs on him and slowly disappeared among the cypresses, lamenting the end of such a noble line.

29

AS SOON AS I got back that night, with everything taken care of, I went to wake them up one by one in their shacks to tell them that Mother Benita had taken Inés away. Of course, they judged, it must be on account of the cold, how could the poor lady live here with this cold freezing her bones, there's no way to heat any of the rooms in the Casa, she should have built herself a good shack, well made, in one of the corridors; Mudito, if he'd been well and not ailing the way he is now, could have helped poor Misiá Inesita build herself a shack like the ones we live in to keep from feeling so cold this winter, which goes on and on and looks like it's never going to leave the Casa, she must be used to her comforts with central heating and all, Misiá Inesita's really spoiled, well, a lady as rich as her, how else could it be.

"What did she take with her?"

Nothing. An overnight bag. She left everything, our little things we needed so badly and we're going to be able to get back now. The murmuring flock grows with the old women who keep coming out of the shacks, down the passageways, toward the chapel, one or two of them carrying candles stuck in holders, to recover their things. They open the doors and light more candles; the old women pounce on the heaps of filthy objects they lost playing at the cursed Dog Track, they don't shout, they don't fight over the things but recognize them and pass them out . . . this flowered semimourning cotton apron's just like yours but it's mine and the other one in that other pile's yours . . . the soft shapes of the identical, interchangeable old women have been spotting what belongs to them: gaping shoes, odd stockings, shawls . . . look, Rita, I found your checked shawl here, the one you were saying you needed so much the other day . . . blankets, comforters, woolen skirts; each thing returns to its owner's hands after its brief stay in other hands that didn't leave their mark on them . . . this is Auristela's scapular . . . that's Rafaelito's lock of hair for Clemencia who was so upset about losing it . . . there's Lucy's rosary she says the Pope blessed, although nobody believes it . . . whose stockings are these, they're gray wool . . . if they have holes for bunions they're mine . . . all of poor Iris's clothes, even her brown overcoat.

Iris wears it all day long now. Since there are buttons missing, she fastens it at her chest with a safety pin. It still has remnants of beaver trimming on the collar and pockets because the coat Brígida gave Iris is very good and really warm and ever since the poor girl came down with a cold she never takes it off, look at the snot running from her nose and the way she wipes it on her sleeve or with her hands that are cracked with chilblains. Watch her. But nobody looks at Iris anymore, not even the other orphans, who, now that Mother isn't here, spend their afternoons fooling around on the telephone, playing as Misiá Inesita taught them.

I watch Iris. I shadow her from a doorway or crouching behind the Arabian jasmine; she likes to sit in the corridor, under the ornate stained glass windows the auction people leaned against the pilasters. She stays there, listless, letting the hours go by, inundated by the rays of the sun as they penetrate the glass, like passive matter splashed with amber, and when the sun rises a little, a strip of blue sky that crosses her face, a star at her mouth, on her shoulder, vanishes as Iris floats with white water lilies on the aquamarine light, shaded by a pious shawl, disrobed by the rosy reflection from a holy tunic; while for hours on end I observe Iris's slow mutations, evening approaches, the wind shakes the real-life branches that stir the light in which things are dissolving below the stained glass windows as Iris dissolves in shifting iridescent pools, but the reflection of one of her hands has rescued her face, revealing a new sharp profile now that she gathers all her hair at her nape with a rubber band and her features are bared, bringing into view a bony structure that has a certain nobility whose origin's beginning to be evident: it's you, I recognize you, she baptized you before they carried her off to the mental hospital, Inés, Inés naked and roseate in the reflection of the tunic, the pure Inés, the Inés before Jerónimo, the Inés before Peta, the Inés before Inés, the Inés before the saint and the witch, the Inés before me; you've absorbed the color of the tunic and you remain standing in the glow of the windowpanes without knowing where to go or what to do or who you are, naked, just risen from sleep, your hands joined, as you watch the lengthening shadows in the court that keep hiding me as I move along without being seen, the less than twenty percent of me advancing intact, all of me whole, erect, as I approach the remnant of light that undresses you below the stained glass windows, I'd like to eradicate that twenty percent and rest but I can't do it because you exist, Inés, because you're my prisoner within these impregnable walls, Inés, because you're making me descend from my limbo into the hell of an existence where desire's compulsory, and you won't let me forget that I breathe and have breathed but have never breathed enough, that I love and have loved but I've never satisfied any desire, Inés, you stroke the cat purring against your breast stripped by the light in league with the silence of this remote court to urge me on, you're ready, Inés, I'm ready here in the shadows, two paces away from you, waiting for your arms to release the cat before the darkness clothes you again, and I go over to the naked Inés and whisper in your ear:

"Inés."

You answer without surprise:

"What?"

I'm going to sate myself, and Peta won't come between us, and Jerónimo won't spur me on or stop me, because neither Jerónimo nor Peta exists now, their demands have been wiped out of existence, I'm free before this free woman: this is hell. Don't move away, Inés, even if the light's gone and you're covered with clothes again, I hold you tight against my body. You shiver. Not with cold; your eyes say that what you feel isn't cold, nor does it parallel what I feel, it's terror, don't be afraid of me, Inés, let me guide your hand below the stained glass windows as if under a multicolored awning, your tense hand in mine, but it disobeys me, your eyes full of terror, your rumpled hair against the crystal firmament, and your thighs slip away from mine, and your mouth, as always, from the beginning, from the original nightmare, rejects my mouth because my mouth's foul; I want to take revenge because you reject my mouth, which isn't foul, and I force your fingers to feel my organ, you grab it, you squeeze it as only a piece of potent meat can be squeezed and you sink your nails into it and with a mad jerk you pull it out by its roots, nerves, arteries, veins, testicles, tissues, my body being drained of its blood in torrents that splash you; look at your bloodstained hands, look at the way the blood runs down your legs, forming the pool you stand in as you scream, hysterical, pale, upset, your eyes closed, you don't want to see the blood that's drenching you and you moan because you don't understand, you wouldn't reject me now if I drew closer, because you've taken away my dangerous instrument, leaving an unhealable wound between my legs, I don't scream, I'm obliterated by the shadows, you scream, call, summon, spellbound in the pool of blood, asking for help, and the lightless glass overshadows you while the old women arrive on the scene . . . what's wrong, what can be the matter with this girl that she's screaming so much and doesn't recognize us . . . and she collapses in the pool of blood. She mutters:

"It's a lie."

"What's a lie?"

"That I was going to have a child . . ."

What child is she talking about? Mudito's the son we waited for, such a long time, and he was born such a long time ago that there's nobody here in the Casa who can remember when he was born, that's why succeeding generations of old women have been bringing him up, the obedient child does only what we let him do, the child's a saint and he always remains a child, above all at night as when Mother Benita was here, but now that she's not and we've all installed ourselves in the chapel the child's a child all the time, that's the reason we're there with our bags and our packages, all prepared, all of us living together in the chapel like after the war or an earthquake, waiting for the moment when the child will take all us old women from the Casa to heaven in the white hearses drawn by horses with white caparisons and he'll call other children who are holy like him so they can bring garlands and play trumpets and lyres. Iris shakes her head. No, no, no . . . you're denying my sanctity, you're terrified because I acquired the power I wanted.

". . . I was blowing up, and it's been hurting me here for days . . . Miss Rita, it's not true that I used to bleed every month before . . . I only said it so you wouldn't think I was dumb, because all the other kids knew how to read . . . that was one thing I could have . . ."

But what makes you so important, Iris, the old women ask, and what difference does it make whether this is your first period, now that we already have the child and we're all prepared to leave? . . . Iris is raving, she's talking about the time she used to go out at night, and about that Giant, as if there were giants, she hangs on to Rita's skirt, whimpering . . . anybody'd think they were killing her, with all this bawling about something that has to happen to all of us, and all she has to do is take a bit of Eve Salts and an aspirin . . . now, girl, don't cry like that, what's this crazy stuff you're saying, who was it you wouldn't let do any more than feel you . . . and she and this Giant she keeps mentioning . . . because Iris is ranting: they played yumyum but never nooky, playing nooky's bad, but not yumyum, and she started to blow up from fear and hide under the brown overcoat . . . you're lying, bearing false witness against the child, shut your mouth, you say he used to throw you out into the street at night so you'd go meet the Giant and then come back, and you used to tell him everything the both of you did, where he touched you and you him . . . he's a pig, a degenerate, he tried to play nooky with me and I got scared and that's why . . .

"He listened to your filth?"

"How could he, when he's deaf?"

"He's not deaf."

"Liar."

"Aren't you ashamed, Iris?"

"It's things she makes up."

"No . . . he made me touch him . . ."

"Scum!"

"How can such a young kid . . . ?"

"It's true . . . and he used to ask me things: what else . . . what else?"

"He's mute."

"He can't ask anything."

"He's not mute; he's a liar."

"Don't you dare blaspheme against the child!"

"We're going to beat you to death if you keep on talking like that . . ."

"I've got a switch here."

"I'll use my shoe."

"It's true!"

"How can you say that when the child's a saint?"

"What this one wants is to take the baby away from us."

"And carry him off."

"You've got no claim on the child, Iris."

"The child's ours."

"We're going to hide him."

"Yes, better hide him."

"The child was born in the Casa years ago."

"Nobody remembers who his mother was."

"And he never had a father."

"No, because men are filthy."

"And he can't tell who his mother was."

"Of course not, because he's dumb . . ."

Iris stands up, her hands, the brown overcoat, her legs, smeared all over with blood. Through the awning of colorless glass the real stars glitter. Iris is furious:

"He's not dumb."

Dora gives her a slap.

"And he's not a baby."

Lucy whips her with the switch across the legs.

"He's not a saint."

Rita pulls her hair.

"Whore!"

"Yes, whore!"

"When you were ranting, you confessed your sins . . ."

"You used to go out and solicit, without telling us."

". . . and you never repented . . ."

"You little whore!"

"She has to be punished."

"Yes, let's punish her."

"Yes, for being a whore."

They bring you to the chapel. Rosa Pérez and Clemencia have already cured me of the wound you left between my legs, they covered the hollow with wads of gauze and bandaged it, swathing me well so that the child wouldn't wet himself at night and mostly so he wouldn't soak his little sheet, it's so hard for sheets to dry in this kind of weather and there's nothing filthier than sheets that smell of baby's wee-wee. When I see you come in and move toward my crib and stand there looking me over as if you were thinking, as if you could think, I cover my frightened face with my little hands and blubber:

"Wicked!"

"D'you see?"

"Even the child knows it."

"Wicked."

The child's first word. He's learning to talk, and he mustn't learn anything. All on account of that filthy moron, Iris Mateluna, what a whore she must be that even the holy child who's never been out of the Casa and is all innocence knows she's a dirty whore who shouldn't live here in this holy place, surrounded by holiness, misery and old age.

"Take her away!"

They look at me open-mouthed: the child's started to perform miracles, his power's manifesting itself, he commands us because he knows we'll obey him and he wants us to put this trash out of the place he lives in. He's suggesting in the best way he can that he won't perform any miracle or take us to heaven until we clean out this holy place. We have to get this whore out of here . . . let's see . . . let's dress her up like a whore . . . They let out your hair and it falls down to your waist. After taking off your coat, they slip a sweater on you that's tight around your breasts . . . and you, María, you're so short, lend us your green skirt, it'll be short and tight on her and not just her breasts but her behind will stick out too, they make up your eyebrows with soot, your compliant eyelids with dissolved charcoal, making your mouth big and red so you'll be a real eyeful . . . let's see how you make out in your business, Iris . . . no, not the coat, even if you're cold, your figure won't show with the coat on and men like to see the figure of whores like you. Rita and Dora muffle themselves up in their shawls and, as they have to obey the child, they take you out into the street; and so, flanked by those two tattered bodies, Iris leaves the Casa embodied in a big artificial doll all painted up just like the Giant . . . Now go on, don't stand there like a dope, you've got to work and make a living . . . the old women shove her, she obeys my strict order to go away forever, they plunge into deserted back streets, they cross small treeless squares encircled by windows with all the shutters drawn, they wander down narrow lanes without street lamps so that no one will recognize them, as if anyone could recognize a pair of old women exactly like all other miserable old women who roam the streets, they cross an empty lot and reach the avenue where they pretend to examine the posters outside a movie under a poorly lit marquee. People go in and out of the theater, and people walk past in the street without seeing them, Iris is so stunned that she doesn't realize that here's a movie at last, with actresses, dance numbers, starlets who close their eyes when they're kissed . . . a nothing, you're nothing but an empty shell, you walk in emptiness, following the old women who keep a short distance between you and them so that people will think you're alone. A man in a dark suit whistles at you as he goes by. The old women catch on, they grab you and hustle you down a side street toward the back of the poorly lit block . . . look, the man's following us . . . The three hide in a doorway. The man goes by, whistles again, stops at the next corner a moment and, as he returns to the avenue, passing in front of them, the old women tell you, now, go on, and Iris moves forward to ply her trade, so she's sure to go on being a whore, what else can be in store for a papier-mâché doll with an empty head except to be slit open and torn to bits by hungry men like the one who's going off with her, he offers her a cigarette and disappears with her . . . goodbye, Iris, goodbye . . . don't smoke, Iris, you're too young . . . well if you're going to be a whore you might as well smoke, it's decided, it's a future, maybe you'll even have a good time, because they say whores lead a real easy life, getting up late and all, and to think what a fool I was when I was thirteen and my father died and I went to work in some rich people's house and had to get up at the crack of dawn, well, yours truly started bleeding pretty late, but this Iris is a devil, look how she took advantage because she was blowing up and tried to put one over on us and make us believe it was a miraculous pregnancy . . . yes, Rita, don't cry, she'll get along, that gentleman had a kind face and he took her in a taxi so he can't be bad, and I'm sure he'll get her some other kind of work because it can't be too pleasant to spend your time doing that filthy thing with people you don't even know, even if they pay you, but being plump and all, Iris will get along because it's the plump ones men go for . . . yes, they say we go for women who've got something you can grab hold of . . . I wonder what that means, we old women don't even understand that kind of man's talk, they might as well be talking Chinese sometimes, and when you're getting older and older you understand less and less what men talk about. That's why we mustn't teach the child a single word, we've got to make him forget the ones he already knows and we know that he knows because he said them, they begin by saying one or two things and, afterward, he may start saying bad things that we don't understand.

WE'RE LIVING in the chapel. Like refugees from a disaster area, the old women sleep on piles of rags, on pillows or maybe a mattress, huddled together to protect themselves from the cold, each with a sack containing her most prized belongings that she's thinking of taking to heaven, improvising braziers in tin cans. One group remarks that Iris's disappearance means they'll soon be leaving, someone coughs, another group prepares the

washtub they'll put me in to give me a bath; they have a fire
going in an oil drum over which to heat my water, they've been
tearing up baseboards and throwing them into the fire, and
chunks of flooring and door jambs and the presbytery's turned-
wood railing and the small gilt chair, and they go on saying that
this place is never going to be demolished although they themselves have already started its destruction, they're wiping out all
traces of this chapel where they worship me with the primitive
liturgy of looking after me and cleaning and feeding and dressing
me in Boy's clothes, his entire baby wardrobe, because I turned
the keys over to them, they opened Inés's cell and her trunk
and they've brought everything, they dress me up pretty and
pamper me as I always dreamed of being pampered. The days
are short at this time of year. They almost never go out into the
light. They've forbidden the orphans to leave the chapel, there
may be bad men out there who'll carry them off like they carried
off Iris Mateluna, for being disobedient and a liar. The orphans
too pamper me, I can't tell one from another now, they're just
like the old women, with their rough hands, their coughing, their
minds in a daze, their stealthy padding . . . they might hear us,
they might see us, bad men might come along, how scary . . .
It's night most of the time. I'm almost all baby.

At night the old women leave the Casa. I wonder what's
become of Mother Benita, eh? Haven't you heard from her,
Mother Anselma? Oh, you're not Mother Anselma, you're only
Carmela, what's new, Carmela, did you find your archangel's
finger . . . oh, you weren't looking for the finger, it was Amalia
who was looking for it, I wonder what's become of Amalia, she
was one of the first, remember, I wonder what's become of her
and where they've got the poor thing locked up, it's not Carmela
but Eliana who's wearing Carmela's moth-eaten shawl on her
head and I got them mixed up . . . how are you going to know
why Mother Benita hasn't called if you're getting more stupid
than that stupid Iris, too bad you don't have a woman's body yet
because if . . . Isn't that right, Rita, we could . . . ? Doesn't
any of the orphans have tits or an ass? No, none of them, so we
can't take them out into the street like Iris to earn something
and bring in money so we can have something to fill our bellies

with . . . But it's odd that Mother Benita hasn't called, not even once, don't tell me it isn't, and the oddest thing of all is that she went off without even saying goodbye to us when she used to keep telling us that she loved us so much . . . it's the limit. Nor Father Azócar, who used to call all the time about the least little thing. Who cares! Who cares, after all, the child will soon be taking us away and when they come they'll find the Casa empty . . . they deserve it, because they forgot all about us, there's no food left, we may be old and have light appetites but we've got to have something to eat . . . that's why I said dress Frosy up like a woman and take her out into the street and offer her to men, but no, men would know she's nothing but an eleven-year-old kid and they're not going to give us anything . . . if we had something to drink, tea or maté or coffee or some vermicelli soup, something, anything at all, it's the last straw, forgetting us like this, but it doesn't matter, we'll even the score by giving them the shock of their lives when they find out there's nobody left in the Casa. One night, Auristela went out to beg and came back with maté and sugar. Others went out after that—the nerviest ones, Rita and Dora, as a team, Zunilda Toro whose nasal twang's very convincing—and the rest followed suit. They never stray very far from the Casa because they get tired and are afraid to get lost. It's as if, at twilight, a slow wave of filth and supplications invaded the neighborhood, begging voices, tiny footsteps that follow but could very well be giving chase, fetid breaths saying thanks, the knotty hand that snatches the coin and hides it in a tattered skirt, eyes that flash for a second and are extinguished. An old woman follows a young man along a wall, imploring him to give her a little something, insisting in a wailing voice; the boy quickens his step but the old woman keeps up with him and, nervous about running away, he gives her something quickly, to make her go away and leave him alone, he gives her more money than he should have given her. One evening a bunch of them came back with bags full of vegetables and groceries; they told how they'd followed a lady on her way back from shopping and the hungry old women pressed her so much with their sniveling and their whining in the deserted street that the lady suddenly took fright at all the coughing and crying and persistence, and she dropped her shopping bags and ran off, what can you do, they said, the Fates are daughters of necessity, so they say. They started going in groups to the corner grocery, where some kept the owner and the shoppers busy with their old wives' tales while the others shoplifted, useless things sometimes but always in an attempt to steal things like loaves of bread and tea and sugar, how can we feed our forty old bodies even if we only have small appetites, we always ask for something, a little cup of tea, a piece of stale bread to lay on the embers left by the wood they use to heat water to bathe the child. They place the child near the coals so he won't feel chilly, sometimes they practically roast me but I can't cry out because I have no voice, yes, these harpies want to put me on a spit and roast my tender flesh to a crisp over the coals and gobble me down, but no, they lay me on the bed . . . we have to treat the child well, look at him Auristela, look Teresa, look at those saucer eyes of his, look at the way he's looking at us as if to tell us to wait a little longer because he's going to perform the miracle any time now, to have patience, the hearses will be coming soon, they've been ordered, wait, wait . . . but how can we wait if we're starving to death? The liturgy of changing me, washing me, wrapping me in diapers, drawers, swaddling me tight before a nonexistent altar, before the remains of forgotten hybrid deities whose plaster crumbles with the humidity; an arm falls off, a dragon's tail too, they shatter on the floor, the old women trample the pieces when they run to meet those coming from the street . . . let's have a look, what did you bring in today, girls? They tell how they went to a meat shop and, while the butcher was busy cutting some kind of tripe for a nearsighted lady, they were able to lift . . . look, a whole side of lamb, a party, a party . . . they tore up more flooring, they knocked down a door, they started a fire and waited until they had incandescent coals, on which they put the ribs to roast, and the delicious aroma floated toward my nose. That night, while they were still squatting around the fire and gnawing on the lamb bones, they stuck me into a gunnysack, leaving only my head out, like a trussed-up live turkey: they sewed me up good and tight inside the sack so that the child wouldn't move around . . .

one more stitch, there, with that special needle for sewing sacks, better put another sack over him, Zunilda, since you're not eating right now and you're strong, put him inside this other sack and sew it up . . . I too would like to get in a stitch or two, because I know a stitch nobody can cut through. . . . They place me in the crib. While they celebrate the filching of the side of lamb, while I hear the tooth stumps gnawing on bones, while I squint at the shapes moving in the half-light and the faces molded in the shadows, I gulp down the baby mash they feed me, they've given me nothing else for weeks now and it makes me want to throw up, and I refuse it and the old women complain . . . this child has no appetite, what can be wrong with him, it could be the cold, better stick him into still another sack and put in a few more stitches, come on Carmela, you have more sacks. . . . Carmela's sewing. The coarse, stinking jute sacking scrapes my neck until it bleeds, I'd like to plead with them to loosen the opening a little bit, where my head sticks out, but how, I don't know how to talk, I was born dumb in the Casa, they say, and now that I have no hands to make signs with I can't communicate with them. My eyes don't have the power to beg them to relieve me and they don't look at my eyes when they give me my strained food, or when they wash my face with a rag, or when they sew another membrane of sacking around the last one that's scraping my chin now, they don't see me because I don't matter, I'm only passive matter onto which they gradually project their images: the child, Boy, the miracle . . . feeding time, how come you don't have his mash ready, María . . . just a second, it won't take a minute, the child's going to start crying because he's hungry . . . but I don't cry or speak or say *seepy* or *wee-wee*.

Since they go out almost every night now, they leave me all alone in the chapel. Maybe in one dark corner a few creatures remain, too ill or feeble to go out, stirring in their filth or coughing or spreading rumors, it must be some dying old woman that I can't make out and that the others forgot about in their excitement over their newest sally. Because now they come back very late with their spoils. They say there have been muggings in this neighborhood. Old women criminals lie in wait for passers-by at corners, they trail them whimpering and coughing, insisting and harassing, wailing and begging, till they force the person into some poorly lighted alley and five or six crones slip out of the darkness and pounce on the victim, with cords and sticks, and clean him out of everything he may have on him: money, packages, clothing. They say several persons have been found naked and beaten up in this neighborhood. Doorways are dangerous. Something that looks like a tree trunk in the dark may be a toothless, shivering beggar who can lure you with her litany of miseries and ailments to an empty lot where the bloodthirsty gang jumps you . . . better not go around alone at night in this neighborhood, it's not what it used to be, in the good old days, it's been ruined by these crones . . . but how can it be true . . . it must be a lie . . . nobody believes . . . honestly . . . how can we believe that a bunch of ancient beggar women, from God knows where, have taken over this quiet neighborhood, they say some people are thinking of moving to other neighborhoods, they say they went in to beg from that kid with the used-magazine store when he was all by himself and six old women robbed his cashbox, better look for another room in some other boardinghouse far from here, it's dangerous to go out at night because a bundle of darkness suddenly comes to life and pounces on you to rob you of the little you carry in your pockets, they trail people, very slowly, and suddenly something that looked like a shadow rises up and changes form and attacks, that's what happens, maybe those old women there's so much talk about in this neighborhood are only shadows of fear, but there are certainly a lot of old women . . . well, I don't know if there are a lot of them but it does look like there are more than there used to be around here . . . she goes out with her head wrapped in her shawl, dragging her slippers, sliding along the wall, alone, but when you see her moving ahead alone, stooped and lame, you can bet there's an armed gang of them waiting around the corner, so you immediately cross over to the street lamp on the opposite sidewalk, but you make out a couple of old women hidden in the doorway of the house farther up the street, then you go into the middle of the street and run into a group of shadows coming toward you, and you want to turn back but there's only a wall without windows because I walled them all up and made them look old with my brush so that no one would notice they were missing there, only faces, only rags, sometimes they attack and sometimes they don't, it's a question of luck because you can't be scared of little old women who scurry like mice and later come here to the chapel with their booty, to divide the spoils, to pick out things to take with us, I'm taking this extra large lady's overcoat for Mercedes Barroso, and this gold watch chain for Brígida, who'll be pleased, poor thing.

"I saw Iris."

"Where?"

"Near here."

"How?"

"She had a hat on."

"Nobody wears hats now."

"But this girl I'm talking about was wearing a hat and she stared at me."

"In my time hats were . . ."

"Iris had better not think of trying to get in here."

"I think that's what she wants."

"Why?"

"I don't know, now that she's probably rich . . ."

"To steal the child from us?"

"To take the child away from us?"

"Before he performs the miracle?"

"She can't . . ."

"We have to put the child away in a safe place."

"Yes, we'd better hide him."

"Don't let him notice we're going to put him away, because if he does he might get scared."

Each one pretends to go about her usual chores, or actually goes about them: María Benítez is cooking dumplings, somebody said she'd taken some food coloring from the grocery store the other day . . . give me the coloring to put in these dumplings, they're not like real dumplings without coloring but there's nothing like them when you make them with turkey stock . . . they break up the flooring with an ax and liven up the fire with the splinters, they sew by candlelight, they arrange their junk in their burlap sacks. Four of the women come over to me with a huge sack and pick me up, saying to me, little darling, nanananinaca, don't my baby go getting frightened, we're going to look after you so that painted-up hussy won't come and steal you and do filthy things with you, who are a saint. They put me inside the sack. The four of them kneel around me and sew up the sack. I can't see. I'm blind. And others come over with another sack and put me in it too and sew me up again, droning prayers I can barely hear, so that I'll perform the miracle when I will it, but let it be soon, very soon, because Ernestina López is dying there in the corner, she's ill, she's crying because she says she doesn't want to die; they sew, they tie more sacks over my head and other women approach and I feel another wrapping of darkness coming up around me, another layer of silence that muffles the voices I can barely make out, being deaf, blind, dumb, a small sexless package, all sewed up and tied with strips of cloth and strings, sacks and more sacks, I can scarcely breathe through the weave of successive layers of jute, it's nice and warm in here, there's no need to move around, I don't need anything, this package is me and only me, reduced, not dependent on anything or anyone, hearing them address their supplications to me, prostrate, imploring me because they know that I'm powerful now that I'm finally going to perform the miracle.

30

"THE MOMENT'S come, my daughters . . ."

From the step of Rita's cubicle, Father Azócar looked over his group of daughters: thirty-seven old women, the detritus of thirty-seven lives, pale, skinny, feeble, dirty, crushed, thirty-seven according to the list Mother Benita told him he'd find in the top drawer of her desk, he'd already counted them, they were indeed thirty-seven old women, all more or less in poor health. They wouldn't last very long in the new Casa.

". . . the moment's come to depart . . ."

They knew it. All morning, four young priests, their elegant cassocks a black color never seen before in the Casa, where everything turns gray, had gone through the courts, passageways, shacks and rooms, rounding up the inmates like four benevolent black dogs rounding up a flock, and led them to the vestibule, helping them carry their sacks, bundles, baskets, suitcases, small packages and boxes tied with strings or strips of cloth. Seated at Rita's table below the telephone, Father Azócar scratched out the name of each one as she came up. Some peered into the street: there they were, waiting for them, white, enormous, gleaming, reflecting the morning sun, parked in front of the Casa. They weren't hearses, of course, nobody uses hearses anymore, they were beautiful modern buses, their glass windows tinted a light green, and maybe they even had heating, which would be nice because to climb as high as we're going to have to climb to get to heaven we ought to have heating.

"A white house especially prepared to receive you is waiting, in the middle of a garden, up in the high part of town. Bedrooms, a chapel, bathrooms, marvelous kitchens, a dining room, you'll see, and if we were a little slow in coming for you, it's because we wanted everything to be in tiptop shape without a single detail left out. These buses you see at the door of the Casa are also yours, to take you on outings when the weather's nice, and Mother Benita's studying the possibility of taking you to spend the summer at the beach . . ."

"And how's Mother Benita?"

Father Azócar shook his head, worried. At first she wasn't at all well: something like nervous exhaustion, the doctors said, but now, after a week's rest, she's like new, waiting for all of you. Between her and Misiá Raquel Ruiz they've completely settled the estate of Brígida Oyarce, I don't know if you remember her . . ."

"How could we ever forget poor Brígida!"

"Was Brígida an Oyarce?"

"No, she was Reyes Oyarce . . ."

They started arguing about Brígida's surnames: Oyarce on her mother's side and Reyes on her father's, Reyes on her mother's and Oyarce on her father's side . . . no, that's not true, Carmela, you're lying, Oyarce was only her husband's name, not hers, Misiá Raquel ought to know, let them ask her . . . no, Auristela, you weren't Brígida's friend so don't come telling me you know more than me . . . see what a liar Lucy is, Father Azócar, she says that Oyarce was neither her maiden nor her married name, that her name was Brígida Farías Reyes de Castro . . . they're screaming, coughing, and, although a minute ago they'd refused to let go of their bundles or the statues they carried wrapped in sacks, they put everything on the ground to take part in the argument, each is the only one who really knows, all the others are wrong, the versions of who Brígida was multiply and become complicated and contradict each other—an Oyarce family had raised her but she was really a Reyes, a Reyes family had raised her but she was an Oyarce, she'd served in the home of an Oyarce family before going to Misiá Raquel's —but what has all this got to do with her last name being Oyarce, it must be Oyarzún or at least Oyanedel. Father Azócar was struck dumb by their noisy wrangling. Brígida existed only in her fable, climaxed by the legacy Misiá Raquel turned over to the Archbishop at last, now that there was no way of saving the Casa from the wreckers. Depressed and run down, Mother Benita let herself be convinced that she wasn't young enough anymore to take on a new task like that of chief housemother of Children's Village, modern technology required a good deal of preparation and study for something like that and it would be better if she went to end her days with the other old women in the new Casa purchased with Brígida's money. Mother Benita accepted, saying:

"I give up."

"Don't say that, Mother."

"It's old age."

"It catches up with all of us, Mother."

"I didn't think it would catch up with me."

"How's that . . . ?"

". . . or that it would catch up with me some other way . . ."

"I don't understand."

"It doesn't matter, Monsignor. At least grant me the privilege old women are entitled to, of saying things that don't mean anything. When can we start moving into the new Casa?"

From the discussion about Brígida's surnames, they go on to quarrel among themselves over this or that one's right to consider herself Brígida's closest friend, and from there to Brígida's things, over which one had kept what item, the pale blue satin bedspread, the portable radio after Amalia was taken away nobody knows where, the picture of the Annunciation, the small scissors, the *polissoir*, the raspberry bathing cap: the living Brígida, more substantial than any of the tattered creatures with voices sifted by the years. Father Azócar had intended to explain to them where Brígida's fortune and legacy had come from, tacking on a brief account of the history of the Casa, referring to Inés de Azcoitía and the superb projects that would begin to take shape on the same site as soon as they started pulling down the Casa the following week . . . what's the use, what's the use, things become so scrambled in the minds of the old women that nobody could straighten them out. In his pocket, he rolled into a tiny ball the scrap of paper on which he'd jotted some notes for his speech that morning and threw it on the floor. It rolled to the feet of one old woman, who snatched it up, in the middle of an argument with her neighbor, spread it out carefully and folded it without bothering to read it, if she knew how to read, and put it away: just in case. Father Azócar had been watching her. Incredible! No wonder Mother Benita's been dying to get out of this hell. Better not explain anything to them. Let them go on believing whatever they wanted to believe, because reason and unreason, causes and effects, weren't real for these anarchic creatures. Oh well. The best thing he could do was take them out of the Casa and put them aboard the buses. Waving his arms and the papers with the lists, he made them quiet down.

"Father Silva."

"Yes, Father."

"You and Father Larrañaga take that . . . that woman who's so ill to the first bus. She has to be hospitalized. As a matter of fact, the doctors are waiting for us so they can start things off by giving them all a checkup today and they'll decide what to do with this . . . What's her name?"

"Ernestina López."

"No, Lucy, Ernestina Rivas, widow of López."

"Yes, here it is: Ernestina Rivas, widow of López."

Someone opened the vestibule door and asked for a stretcher. They laid the sick woman on it and the old women jostled one another in the doorway to see her lifted onto the fantastic white vehicle. Poor thing, Señora Ernestina was so sick, just about done for! But when Father Larrañaga seated her by the green-tinted glass window, she seemed to regain her strength immediately and, bathed in a shaft of sunshine that spotlighted her through an overhead window, she smiled at her friends and made signs to them with her hands as if to say, hurry up, girls, it's real comfy in here. They closed the vestibule door again. Yes, let's hurry and leave. The old women picked up their packages and bundles. . . . Ladies, please take as little as possible with you, Father Azócar told them, you'll be given everything new, there. . . . Didn't I always tell you, girls, that they give you everything new in heaven? . . . Yes, but I'm not about to leave this saint I love so much, with her dragon tail and all. Nor my bag with my little things. Nor this St. Gabriel Archangel. . . . Isn't it Amalia's? . . . Sure, I'm taking it to give back to her, I'm sure Amalia's up there where they're taking us and she must have found his finger by now . . . As little as possible, daughters, only indispensable things. . . . They spent all morning sorting out their belongings, doing up packages that were a little less bulky, Carmela has a real suitcase and packs all her stuff in it. Baskets, bags made of mattress ticking, or plain sacks they sling over their shoulders, smiling because they're really going to leave now, and the young priests also smile, content to be taking these poor ancients to a home provided for them by compassion, while the brilliant project of the future will go up on this site: gyms, towers, theaters, study halls, libraries to attract the young and keep them out of mischief in the streets; this has to be torn down, it won't cost a thing to wreck, it's only adobe or mud partitions, the future will begin the minute the old women pass out the door, happy but so touched that they're all crying, and we too are touched. Father Azócar calls for silence once more.

"Let's see, Father Silva . . ."

"Yes, Father."

". . . stand by the vestibule door and open it as each inmate I call by name comes out. The orphans first. Let them go on the same bus as the sick woman so that it can drop them off at the Orphanage before going on to the new Casa. The chauffeur already has his orders. There are five orphans. Let's see: Eliana Riquelme."

"Present."

"Verónica González."

"Present."

"Mirella Santander."

"Present."

"Eufrosina Matus."

"Present."

"Iris Mateluna."

No one answered.

"Iris Mateluna?"

The old women shrugged, threw up their hands, thrust out their lower lips as if to say, how should I know, I have no idea, don't go blaming me if you're thinking of blaming somebody, I've got nothing to do with this business, if there is any business, and besides you should have seen what Iris Mateluna was like, somebody ought to tell Father Azócar the truth. Rita volunteered:

"Father."

"Yes?"

"Iris left about a week ago."

"How can you tell me she left?"

"But I'm telling you. She was obstinate, you should see . . ."

"Being obstinate has nothing to do with it."

"No, but you ought to see how bad she was."

"No, Rita, she turned bad, she never used to be . . ."

"Why did she turn bad, Rita?"

"I don't know, Father, she started getting bossy and all . . ."

"How, when?"

"When you left us all by ourselves."

"Yes, Father, she used to take to the streets at night."

"And she disappeared."

"Dear God! A fifteen-year-old girl can't vanish into thin air."

"Almost sixteen."

"But she vanished all the same."

What can we do, Father, it's not our fault, she wouldn't listen to anybody and she used to go crazy over men, some neighbors told us she used to stand in the open window on the second floor and call down to the men who went by and the whole neighborhood knew she carried on and, stupid us, we were the last ones to find out, and afterwards she vanished, it's not our fault, you all left us to fend for ourselves, starving, maybe Iris took off because she was hungry and we used to call the Archbishop on the phone and we even used to call you, Father Azócar, but the secretaries always answered the same thing, that we should wait just a few more days, and when word got around that we'd have to stay and starve to death here in the Casa without you giving us a thought, well then, I say Iris Mateluna must've taken off because she was scared, as soon as we see Mother Benita we're going to let her know that's the last straw, letting something like that happen, I'm really put out and I'm not sure I really want to see her up there . . ."

"Where?"

"Don't they say she's going to be up there too?"

"Yes, she too."

Father Azócar said that because he didn't know what to answer. Better not take up the problem of Iris Mateluna just now. They must leave the Casa immediately. The problem of Iris Mateluna would be settled later on. She would turn up. He'd see what should be done about her disappearance, or flight, or . . . whatever it was, they must go, right now, if they took a minute longer to leave this place the old women would put down roots here, they'd take over the Casa again and they'd not let it be demolished. Later on, he'd see about Iris Mateluna. She was the chubby one, the one with the broken incisor his terror suddenly made him remember, no, no, they had to leave right away and not think about this Iris thing, it might stir up a hornet's nest. If it does, let it be outside, once the Casa's vacated.

"Someone's ringing the doorbell, Father."

Iris! It's Iris Mateluna coming back at exactly the right moment to solve everything, Father Azócar prayed.

"Father Silva, please open the door."

It's not Iris. It's a young barefoot peon, with his pants rolled up above his calves, lugging a huge pumpkin with a hard gray shell, rugged like a prehistoric animal's. The peon asks:

"Is this the Casa de Ejercicios Espirituales de la Encarnación at La Chimba?"

"This is it . . ."

"Where should we leave them?"

Dora answered:

"Right here, in the corridor."

He set it on the tiles and dashed back, but halfway down the path of astounded old women he passed another peon, loaded with another pumpkin that he deposited next to the first one, doubling back as fast as he could and passing another man loaded with still another pumpkin that he left, returning on the double and passing another and another and still others, all of them rushing to fill the court with that settlement of creatures in silvery armor, of grotesque irregularities, and nobody dared utter a single word in the face of this invasion of creatures from another geological age, past or future, whose growing number couldn't be stopped, as if they were reproducing obscenely right there in the corridor because they were lugged in at an uncontrollable speed on the shoulders of the sweating peons, there were two peons, no, three, no, five, no, two, that took down pumpkins and still more pumpkins from the loaded truck parked right in front of the white vehicles: pumpkins, listen, all those pumpkins, how nice, we'll be able to make beans with pumpkin sauce, they're so good now that summer's almost here, and pumpkin doughnuts in winter, and pumpkin bread for St. John's Night, pumpkin sweets are also good and *cazuela* doesn't taste like anything without pumpkin, this kind with the gray shell's the best, María Benítez chipped in, evaluating their quality, until, pulling himself together, Father Azócar looked through the vestibule door and shouted:

"What's all this?"

The peon going past him whispered:

"Pumpkins."

"Yes, I know but . . ."

The driver, who was loading the pumpkins on the shoulders of the carriers, answered him:

"They're from the Trehuenque farm, from Misiá Raquel Ruiz. She left orders over a year ago for us to bring what was left of the crops here to the Casa but the foreman had forgotten all about it, so he's sending this truckload of five hundred pumpkins now."

"Five hundred!"

"Yes, the kind we ship out for export."

"But what am I going to do with five hundred pumpkins?"

"Ah, I don't know, Father. That's up to you."

When Father Azócar went into the vestibule again he found that the order he'd managed to establish had now deteriorated: the orphans got out of the bus and, mingling with the old women, were flitting around the pumpkins, Eliana dancing on top of them, others straddling them . . . giddyup, giddyup,

giddyup, little horsey, 'cause we ain't gotta, ain't gotta furways to go . . . we can't leave these pumpkins behind, we've got to tell Father Azócar that we want to take them to heaven, they're ours; Misiá Raquel, who's such a good lady and always keeps a promise, like with Brígida's funeral, sent us this little contribution of five hundred pumpkins . . . cut it out, you kids, just look at Mirella and Verónica, let go that pumpkin, it's too heavy . . . and the sweaty, puffing men bring in more and more pumpkins, the silver-plated shells multiplying all along the corridor, the old women surrounded by them, stepping around them, trying to pick their way between the monsters . . . come on, stop it, Mirella . . . and the orphans dropped the pumpkin, which split open, exposing the rich orange velvet of its viscera, spilling out seeds joined by slobbery ligaments to the meat that lodged them in its hollow . . . you nasty little brats, you went and broke the pumpkin, you don't know how high a pound of pumpkin sells for right now, and that pumpkin's going to go bad, don't throw the seeds in the court, you know pumpkins spring up anywhere you drop a seed and next year this will be a jungle of suckers and leaves that'll choke everything and creep everywhere, even in the rooms, and yellow flowers, yes, it would be lovely to see all those pumpkins growing . . . well, if it's so lovely why don't we take this one's seeds to heaven and there, they say, there's a garden, don't they, we can plant the seeds and grow a lot of pumpkins for *cazuela* and pumpkin doughnuts with plenty of brown sugar sauce . . . yes, Auristela, get some seeds into your pockets to take up to heaven and plant them there . . . all these pumpkins, oh dear, and they're still unloading more and more, five hundred pumpkins seem to be more than you'd think, they're so big there isn't enough room for them even in the corridor, the kind they ship out for export, I'm going to count them, yes, why don't we count them while Father Azócar argues angrily on the phone with Misiá Raquel . . . sure, what does he care if we go hungry . . . hey, why don't some of us put a couple of pumpkins in the hearses while he's arguing on the phone, let's see if about six of us can do it together . . . the drivers give them a hand and they manage to put a pumpkin in one of the white vehicles; the young priests raise Cain, they try to reorganize the scattered flock, to free them from the spell of those cucurbitaceas wrinkled like rhinoceros fetuses. Father Azócar comes out of the phone room, he lets out a couple of roars and the old women troop back to the vestibule. He orders them to file out immediately, no, don't worry about the lists, let them sit anywhere they like in the buses, they all want to go in the same one because the other one, they say, the one carrying Ernestina López and the orphans, is going somewhere else first and they want to get where they're going as quickly as possible, and finally they manage, with instructions and shouts from the four priests and Father Azócar, to take out some of those who were jammed with all their bundles into the same bus and distribute them more sensibly. Father locks the door of the Casa, at last . . . this doesn't look very secure, but it doesn't matter, who's going to break in, to steal what, when there's nothing but dirt in there, we're not even going to hold an auction, we're going to strip the Casa in two days and start wrecking. Father Azócar gives the workmen a tip and the empty truck returns to Trehuenque. The neighborhood children, the owner of the corner grocery and her husband, the woman who used to comb her hair in the window, all come out to say goodbye to the old women, happily settled in their seats: better open a couple of windows a little, there's such a nice sun and they say heating's not healthy for the bronchial tubes, you have to be careful at our age, especially when you're not used to it. The vehicles start rolling. The old women say goodbye with tear-filled eyes, waving handkerchiefs to those who wave to them but whom they've never seen before, and to cheer themselves they begin to sing:

> Come one, come all,
> With flowers galore
> To Mary's door,
> Come big, come small.
>
> Once more we kneel,
> Here at your feet,
> O maiden sweet,
> O beauty's seal.

THERE'S NO ONE left now. I've recovered my clarity intact. My intellect's orderly once more and plunges to the depths of my transparence, where its light penetrates the last terrors and muffled ambiguities: I'm this package. I'm hidden under layers of burlap sacks, the old women packed me in them and that's why I don't have to make other packages, I don't have to do anything, I don't feel, I don't hear, I don't see anything, because nothing exists except this hole I'm in. The burlap, the awkward knots, the cord stitching, scrape my face. My nostrils are filled with lint, and my throat too. My body's shrunken because they sewed me up so tight. I know this is the only form of existence —the smarting of my scraped skin, the asphyxiating lint, the pain in my wracked body—because if there were some other form of existence there'd also have to be a past and a future, and I don't remember the past and I know nothing about the future, hidden as I am here in the blissful repose of oblivion, because I've forgotten everything and everything's forgotten me. The only thing that can be said about me is that I'm the companion of solitude. I watch over it to keep anything from disturbing the sack that protects me more effectively than the adobe of these walls. Yes, I remember the walls. But I recall nothing else, and the future will extend only to the moment when they collapse. There's little time for all this to end, as it must; a cloud of dust will rise when the hungry jaws of the power shovels disturb the centuries-old repose of the adobe that makes up my world, and afterwards the violence of the stone hammers and the steam rollers will force the boldness of the earth, that thought it could take the form of walls and labyrinths, to yield and will thus return it to its natural state of level ground made up, like all ground, of stones and fragments of wood and leaves and branches that will eventually rot or dry up, of lumps of earth, of occasional pieces of painted plaster, an eye, a dragon's jaw, rags, papers that will gradually disintegrate, sacks where there may be someone screaming, no, save me, I don't want to die, I'm afraid, I'm so weak, stiff, unable to move, without sex, without anything, razed, but I won't scream, because there are no other forms of existence, I'm safe here inside this bundle I've never come out of, owner of this hole that lodges me perfectly because it owns me. They say there are ephemeral passageways, useless courts, hallways with simulated perspectives, objects whose use no one remembers and that are stacked in piles, splotches of decay slowly spreading their landscapes over the walls, the light veil of dust falling from the worm-eaten wood, rooms filled with silence no one's ever broken because there's never been anyone in them, although they say there has been and that there still may be, but I don't believe it; someone's stirring in a corner out there, there *is* someone, there *is* an out-there, there *is* another cough besides mine, but so weak that it may not be a cough, there *is* a movement I'm no longer capable of; it's very slight, like that made by shadows as they take shape and move without footsteps because there are no feet to make them, it's neither cat nor dog nor rat nor fowl nor bat nor rabbit I hear breathing beside me even though I can't hear; how's it possible to cough so weakly, even if it's nothing but a structure of shadows I need to see, I need, I need, and terror sets in with need, the need to see the face of that shadow breathing and coughing so close, to recover my sight and the out-there, I bite, I chew the sack that covers my mouth, gnawing away to discover the features of the shadow that exists out there, I chew cords, knots, patches, ropes, I bite my way through but never enough, another sack, another layer it will take me a century to conquer and a millennium to get past, I'll become old without knowing anything but the taste of jute in my mouth and without ever doing anything else but gnaw this hole damp with slaver; my teeth splinter but I have to go on gnawing because there's someone waiting outside to tell me my name and I want to hear it, and I chew and bite and tear: I chew, I bite, I tear, through the last crust of sacking in order to be born or die, but I won't be born or die because there are hands that seize the rip and, with a huge needle, sew the opening I was going to look and breathe through, air, fresh air, air like the air from a window they wouldn't let me open because it was a fake, but my memory went back through that opening for an instant, toward the air from that window, and I was left shut up in here, longing for that air and that window, and I can't, because my longing and I don't fit in here together, only I, because that longing for imaginary air makes unbearable the itch of the fluff in my nose and my throat and the repulsive taste of jute, another opening, my nails dig through geological layers of sacks to find a way out, my nails break, my fingers bleed, the skin of their tips broken, their knuckles reddening, another sack and another and another and another, yes, now, another hole, but the hands out there turn over the bundle I am, without saying a word, because, if the hands belong to someone, he or she doesn't want to reveal anything to me, they start sewing again, stitch after stitch, sewing the rip so that I'll no longer be able to get out, and I want to see that face, I extend one foot brutally and, with its heel, with all my might, I make another opening, but the warty hands sew again with a skill only those hands have, short stitches, many cross-stitches darn or embroider a scar on the weave of the sack, I can't get out, I can't even breathe the simulated air on the other side of the window. Wait. And for centuries I wait for another geological layer to be formed, with the detritus of millions of lives that they say exist, to bury my longing once more. My space is being cut down more and more by patches the old woman's been sewing so that I won't get out, it's an old woman who's been sewing, I felt the old age of her hands fingering the sacks as she sewed, I bite and tear, once more she keeps sewing to cut down my space, her hands turn the bundle over to see if there's a tear that may have escaped her gummy eyes and she finds one and mends it as carefully as if she were embroidering initials on the finest batiste instead of sewing burlap. There are no more orifices: the package is small and perfect. She puts away her needle. From a corner in the chapel, she drags out another sack and throws the new bundle into it, and with it a package of sugar, several pairs of woolen stockings, lots of paper, maté, rags, trash. She heaves the sack onto her shoulder with a tremendous effort. She leaves the chapel, wandering over the desert of infinite simulated passageways, of everyday courts, gliding slowly along walls of darkness or condemned clay, and, as she goes by so lightly and softly, spiders, mice, bats, noiseless guinea pigs, awkward, soft moths, ancient pigeons no one ever thought of throwing into the stew, all scurry . . . slowly, after years or centuries, she manages to reach the vestibule court and makes her way through the jungle of pumpkin runners and leaves that are devouring the cloister, falling in cascades, huge horizontal leaves, tender green stems filled with juice, erect yellow flowers, and the thick foliage she opens her way through closes again over her tracks, tracks that may or may not have remained among the leaves and the suckers that filter the light of the sun and the moon; the vestibule door, she takes out the usual key and opens it, the heavy outside door, she also opens that and goes into the night with her sack on her back, hunching along in her slippers, hugging the walls as if she didn't want to lose the protection of the shadows, she crosses side streets, walks slowly block after block, stops to beg, whining, she receives the coin, puts it in a fold in her skirt, goes on her way, crosses bright avenues, plunges into the park, the avenue of leafless plane trees, until she comes to the iron bridge. She knows how to do it despite her years; she's done it so many times, ever since she was a child, with other children who grew up by the riverbed: like a girl, she lowers herself by the iron girders and drops with her sack. They're under the bridge, around a fire. She comes over. She sits on the ground, inside the ring of light. There are few, tonight. The flame fragments their faces, then it dies down some and they all draw closer to the remaining embers that are beginning to whiten.

She says: "It's not much of a fire."

She puts her hand in the sack, pulls out papers and kindling wood to revive the fire. She leans on her sack. A scrawny bitch dog covered with scabs comes over to be petted. She sprawls at the woman's side. No one says anything. Overhead, the dry branches of the plane trees are an X-ray held up to the electric lividity of city sky. The old woman drinks maté from a small wire-handled can that's blackened from being on the fire so often. She dips her hand into her bag again, takes out a loaf of bread and offers it around, somebody accepts while the new arrival complains:

"It's a poor fire tonight."

"Rotten."

The old woman puts her hand into her sack again, takes out more papers and kindling wood and feeds them into the flame, and it flares up momentarily. But it lasts only a short while. Someone says he's leaving to take cover elsewhere because it's going to be a wicked night . . . yes, it's sure going to be real wicked . . . and several of them leave. The paper and kindling-wood fire doesn't last long . . . Goodbye, aren't you coming with us, the night's so bad here under the bridge . . . no, I'm staying, I'm tired . . . and they go without further goodbyes, leaving her all alone. She coughs. She snuggles up in her shawl. She moves closer to the embers because the wind's picking up, and the bitch dog also goes away. She calls her:

"Psssttt, psssttt . . ."

But the bitch doesn't come back. The old woman stands up, she grabs the sack and, opening it, shakes it out over the fire, emptying it into the flames: kindling wood, cardboard, stockings, rags, newspapers, writing paper, trash, it doesn't matter what as long as the flame picks up a bit to fight off the cold, who cares about the smell of something being singed, of rags that don't burn easily, of paper. The wind disperses the smoke and the odors, and the old woman curls up on the stones to sleep. The fire burns a little while next to the shape left there like just another package of rags, then it starts to go out, the embers grow dimmer and burn out, turning to very light ashes the wind scatters. In a few minutes, there's nothing left under the bridge. Only the black smudge the fire left on the stones, and a blackish tin can with a wire handle. The wind overturns it and it rolls over the rocks and falls into the river.

A Note About the Author

José Donoso was born on October 5, 1924, in Santiago, Chile, into a family of doctors and lawyers. After three years at the Instituto Pedagógico of the University of Chile, he was awarded the Doherty Foundation Scholarship for two years of study at Princeton, where he received his B.A. in 1951. Mr. Donoso has taught English language and literature at the Instituto Pedagógico of the Catholic University of Santiago, Chile, and held an appointment in the School of Journalism at the University of Chile. In 1956 he was awarded Chile's Municipal Prize for journalism; and in 1962 he was awarded the William Faulkner Foundation Prize for Chile for the novel *Coronation*, which was his first work to be published in the United States. Mr. Donoso was Visiting Lecturer in the Writers Workshop at the University of Iowa, Iowa City, from 1965 to 1967. José Donoso lived in Europe for fifteen years but now makes his home in Chile with his wife and married daughter.

A Note on the Type

The text of this book is set in Caledonia, a Linotype face designed by W. A. Dwiggins. It belongs to the family of printing types called "modern face" by printers—a term used to mark the change in style of type-letters that occurred about 1800. Caledonia borders on the general design of Scotch Modern, but is more freely drawn than that letter.

Nonpareil Books

FICTION:

Hasen
by Reuben Bercovitch
160 pages; $7.95

The Mutual Friend
by Frederick Busch
224 pages; $9.95

The Obscene Bird of Night
by José Donoso
448 pages; $10.95

The Franchiser
by Stanley Elkin
360 pages; $10.95

Searches & Seizures
by Stanley Elkin
320 pages; $10.95

Bear
by Marian Engel
144 pages; $9.95

Desperate Characters
by Paula Fox
176 pages; $8.95

**In the Heart of the Heart of
the Country** & *Other Stories*
by William Gass
240 pages; $9.95

Fairy Tales for Computers
ed. by Leslie George Katz
260 pages; $7.95

The Chateau
by William Maxwell
416 pages; $10.95

The Folded Leaf
by William Maxwell
288 pages; $9.95

Old Man at the Railroad Crossing
by William Maxwell
192 pages; $10.95

Over by the River & *Other Stories*
by William Maxwell
256 pages; $10.95

Time Will Darken It
by William Maxwell
320 pages; $10.95

They Came Like Swallows
by William Maxwell
192 pages; $9.95

Disappearances
by Howard Frank Mosher
272 pages; $10.95

Five Women
by Robert Musil
224 pages; $8.95

Famine
by Liam O'Flaherty
480 pages; $9.95

Days
by Mary Robison
192 pages; $8.95

Oh!
by Mary Robison
224 pages; $9.95

Kindergarten
by Peter Rushforth
208 pages; $9.95

All Sail Set
Armstrong Sperry
192 pages; $8.95

All *Nonpareils* are printed on acid-free paper that will not yellow or deteriorate with age. All are bound in signatures, usually sewn, that will not fall out or disintegrate. They are permanent softcover books, designed for use and intended to last for as long as they are read.

The purpose of Nonpareil Books is to return to print books acknowledged as classics. These books, produced to the highest standards and presenting a wide range of subjects and titles, are at most bookstores. For a complete list, please write to David R. Godine, Publisher.

David R. Godine, Publisher
300 Massachusetts Ave.
Boston, Massachusetts 02115